REVIEWN PRINT

"Sharon Hays I   that will keep you guessing a   right on every page and charac   who to trust, **Mysteerie Manor** is at the to ... the Genre." Carol Givner, Editor and Producer November 2010

"When was the last time you read a book that; had the suspense of an Agatha Christie mystery or the tingling eeriness of a Stephen King story? A wry sense of humor like the old THIRD MAN series, with a house so strange its personality stands out like one of the characters. Personalities as diverse as they are interesting, that you will connect with right away. Action and sub-plots keep your mind interested and moving. That's what you're in for with Hays Mysteerie Series.

Read the MYSTEERIE MANOR series, by Sharon Hays, a newcomer that is taking the writing world by storm! Just when you think you have something figured out, another unexplained character shows up from the shadows. Clergymen, gay psychics, mediums and a litany of highly unusual characters all await your examination-or quandary, while danger awaits your every turn. And just when you think you've come to the end-well, I won't tell you anymore. But that will surprise you, I promise! Trust me on this one. You'll be glad you did!"

Patricia Griffin Ress
Co-host or NIGHTSEARCH radio show and author of 39 books on the paranormal

Mysteerie Manor-Review by Martha A Cheves, Author of Stir, Laugh, Repeat

"Maryanne O'Donnell has just had her first of many more to come experiences with the strange inhabits at the Valencia Manor in Boulder, Colorado. After the death of the late owner, the Manor had been put on the market with her best friend Joan Bishop; the agent with the listing. Maryanne has a degree in anthropology and history, with her specialty being; dealings in antiquities. She is tossing around the idea of investing in this late 1800 Italian mansion. She managed to convince Joan into giving her the keys for an early peek before it was officially placed on the market.

It had been rumored that the Valencia Manor was haunted and a few moans and groans could be heard coming from the house, but after all, it was an old house that still had some settling to do, she thought the activity coming from the upper part of the house couldn't be passed on as age… but spirits? Maryanne or Mario didn't believe in them, even if it meant calling in a Priest or even a medium… Mysteerie Manor is a spell binding story that kept me turning the pages and now has me impatiently waiting to read the sequel. The author left the ending open for another great story that I'm sure will take us all deeper into the world of spirits and phenomenon's of the house and its past history."
http://marthaskitchenkorner.blogspot.com   March, 2011

Mysteerie Manor II – Review by Martha A. Cheves, Author of *Stir, Laugh, Repeat*

'The fateful day she walked into the Valencia Manor, her life had taken many turns. What had started out as a property investment opportunity had become an intriguing nightmare of unexpected events and mysterious, supernatural, confrontations. Murder, strange accidents and tragedy all took their turns in the bizarre adventures at the eerie mansion, known as the Valencia Manor. Constructed in the late 1800s, it had its share of uninvited guests and inhabitants.

The Manor wasn't the only thing that Maryanne inherited. She acquired the ghosts, both good and bad, that called the Manor their home. The physic found more than expected when she returned to the Manor and when Mario informed her of the mysterious deaths that had been occurring around the area she had no choice but to give them her professional opinion that they may be dealing with the "undead."

Reading Mysteerie Manor and Mysteerie Manor II made me remember my very first "horror" book, Salem's Lot. I read it at night, which was a mistake, and had trouble sleeping afterwards. I couldn't even leave a curtain open for fear that an unsuspecting predator would be looking in. These two books bring some of those feelings back. Author Sharon Hays has succeeded in giving me the creeps, even while reading during the day.

Reader Reviews:
"Once I got into Mysteerie Manor, I couldn't put it down! I want you to know that you are a brilliant author, and I really enjoyed the book. It is so cool how you are able to make the characters come alive. I know their personalities as well as if I were watching them on TV. I love how you put names of them that correspond with people we know. It's just so cool how good that book actually is. Interesting how she and Joan had that 'connection'. I can't believe how you made everything so real and put it together so well." - Terri Williams, Utah

"You have written an excellent mystery series, that peaked my curiosity as I read with intensity, while the story develops into highs and lows that completely captivated me. With never-ending suspense, I could not quit reading until half-way through. I finished in two days, juggling between my job and home. I seriously recommend Mysteerie Manor, if you're looking for an edge-of-your-seat series to spice up your paranormal mystery senses." Darla Pepper, Wyoming

Reviews for The Tumbleweed Family children's book:
Sharon Hays' new release THE TUMBLEWEED FAMILY is a must-have book for children of all ages. Set in a gentle story, teachings of personal safety alongside lessons of environmental conservation underscore the beauty of Wyoming and the need to respect parents and the planet. THE TUMBLEWEED FAMILY is entertaining and informative.
—Carol Givner, Literary Editor, Publisher (Studio E), and Producer April, 2011

****

The Tumbleweed Family: A Wyoming Adventure
Sharon Hays; illustrated by Daniele Montella
Xlibris, 24 pages, (paperback)
$15.99, 978-1-4568-6825-3
(Reviewed: April, 2011)

Young Willie and Tillie Tumbleweed should have known better than to ignore their parents' admonitions and play outside on a windy day. But readers will learn from the adventures that result when the two tumbleweeds are blown about Wyoming's prairieland, a place teaming with interesting creatures and plant life.

Author Sharon Hays introduces readers to the wildlife endemic to the state. As Willie and Tillie are bounced around by the wind, they meet Wyoming State Bird Maddy the Meadowlark and Wyoming State Animal Billy Buffalo. They also come across a deer, wolf, bull-moose, elk, owl, and eagle, who watch over the children until their tumbleweed parents can arrive to take them safely home. Each animal is depicted in bright, engaging artwork (including a brief historical bit about tumbleweeds) and its national treasure, Yellowstone National Park, for good measure.

****

The Tumbleweed Family – A Wyoming Adventure – Reviewed by Martha A. Cheves, Author of Stir, Laugh, Repeat

The adventures of the Tumbleweed Twins Willie and Tillie take place in the beautiful fields of Wyoming. As they play around and are tossed amongst the beautiful flowers, a gusty wind comes up sweeping them farther and farther away from their home and family. Even though their little adventure is a bit frightening, it's not in vain as they meet other plants and animals that work together to protect them until their family comes to take them back home. This little story is so cute yet educational. Not only does it give a little history about our beautiful state of Wyoming, it also teaches that through working together we can accomplish just about anything in life. I would love to see this become a series featuring each state. With fun books like this, morals, history and even geography can become more fun for our kids.

http://stirlaughrepeatcookbook.blogspot.com April, 2011

COMING SOON… 'An Opulent Tableau of Essence'
This soon to be published 8x11 book of exquisite compilation of art and poetry by diverse artists from around the globe. This is a high-quality, hardback, that anyone would be proud to display in their home. Photography, digital illustrations, acrylics, oils and poetry spill out onto the pages with emotion and soul. 2011

Mysteerie Manor

Not without humor, this paranormal thriller is an edge-of-your-seat read about a team of sleuths forced to brush up on their supernatural savoir-faire after a crime is committed at an old mansion.

An intense drama with a supernatural bend, Mysteerie Manor by new author Sharon Hays is a smart and spellbinding thriller of the paranormal. With punchy dialogue, this character-driven murder mystery keeps readers on their toes and as the suspense builds along a runaway spiral of surprise consequences, not many will guess what comes next—or who.

Available in print and on Kindle at www.Amazon.com

Mysteerie Manor II

In a continuation of the suspenseful, paranormal thriller, Mysteerie Manor, Maryanne ends up inheriting the eerie mansion that she has always wanted. The Valencia Manor had been cleared of spirit activity with the help of a psychic and a priest, they thought…until more strange activity begins to occur at the Manor and elsewhere. This uncanny tale keeps readers on the edge, while new and diverse characters emerge into the ongoing saga. Once you pick it up, there's no turning back!

Available in print and on Kindle at www.Amazon.com

The Tumbleweed Family: A Wyoming Adventure

Our story takes place in the picturesque State of Wyoming, USA. Willie and Tillie, the Tumbleweed twins, are whisked across prairies by a sudden, powerful, wind-storm. The journey takes them across colorful fields, prairies and hills filled with flowers and trees, where they meet many different species of wildlife, who help them find their parents. They discover a variety of birds, animals and landscape creatively illustrated by talented artist; Daniele Montella. The story is informative, imaginative and fun, with a moral value for children.

Available at www.tumbleweedchildrenstories.com and on Kindle at www.Amazon.com

www.SharonHays.com

MYSTEERIE MANOR

II

The House That Keeps on Giving

SHARON HAYS

iUniverse, Inc.
Bloomington

Mysteerie Manor II

The House That Keeps on Giving

Copyright © 2011 Sharon Hays

All rights reserved. No part of this book may be used or reproduced by any means, graphic, electronic, or mechanical, including photocopying, recording, taping or by any information storage retrieval system without the written permission of the publisher except in the case of brief quotations embodied in critical articles and reviews.

This is a work of fiction. All of the characters, names, incidents, organizations, and dialogue in this novel are either the products of the author's imagination or are used fictitiously.

iUniverse books may be ordered through booksellers or by contacting:

iUniverse
1663 Liberty Drive
Bloomington, IN 47403
www.iuniverse.com
1-800-Authors (1-800-288-4677)

Because of the dynamic nature of the Internet, any Web addresses or links contained in this book may have changed since publication and may no longer be valid. The views expressed in this work are solely those of the author and do not necessarily reflect the views of the publisher, and the publisher hereby disclaims any responsibility for them.

Any people depicted in stock imagery provided by Thinkstock are models, and such images are being used for illustrative purposes only.

Certain stock imagery © Thinkstock.

ISBN: 978-1-4620-1855-0 (sc)
ISBN: 978-1-4620-1856-7 (e)

Printed in the United States of America

iUniverse rev. date: 6/7/2011

This is purely a work of fiction.
Names, characters, places either are the product
of the author's imagination, or are used fictitiously.
Any resemblance to actual persons; living or dead,
events or locales, is entirely coincidental.

Dedication:

Family and Friends
Teresa Hall
Appreciation to Marie A Cheves
Remembrance to my dear friend and 'guide', Vivian

Prologue

Maryanne withdrew files from her briefcase and placed them across the table. She became totally absorbed in research, when she heard a click at the front door in the living room. Smiling coolly, knowing Mario would let himself in, she eagerly awaited his entry. A deafening thump slammed hard against the wall, startling her. An ice-cold breeze swept into the room where she sat, heart in high gear.

"Mario, is that you?" There was no answer. She moved uneasily toward the living room, heart still pounding in her chest while she peered into its anomalous commotion. No one was visible, but the door stood open wide; the room almost at sub-zero temperatures. A bitter-cold wind whisked through, accompanied by a distant, haunting voice like a stranger from beyond was trying to communicate. It became more voluble and intense while various lights began to flicker off and on. She stood paralyzed against the wall. Pictures fell from hangers as if an invisible hand had lifted and tossed them across the room. Furniture slid effortlessly, as if a team of ghosts were rearranging furniture in a satirical frenzy. Maryanne shivered as she stood fast, all of her senses in tune with the supernatural spectacle.

1

Earlier:

Maryanne O'Donnell drove toward the mountains thinking about all that had happened. *'How did I end up here? Was it predestination, written in the stars, or was it a vision that I created in my own minds eye and desired so intensely that it happened?'* These and many other questions played across her mind as she drove toward one of her favorite destinations.

On a crisp Monday morning in the Colorado Rockies, the emerging fall season was beginning to paint a kaleidoscope of red, brown and golden hues. The once green canvas of countless trees that had rendered the ever shifting landscape was changing after it had spent the summer months sharing its effervescent foliage with the mountainous terrain. A flaming sun poked its head over the massive peaks, casting beams of light against the colorful landscape. The mountains were still laden with vibrant foliage and early morning seemed to portray its splendor even more than usual.

Maryanne brushed her thick, long auburn hair back from her face as she made her way toward the mountains, on a getaway where she could reflect on recent undertakings and clear her mind. It had always proved excellent therapy to help settle her anxieties and concerns. She had started her day early, in order to steal time for the relaxing get-away, while bathing in the brilliant array of splendor that emerged as she drove into its quiet seclusion. Her camera was ready to capture an odyssey that she had never before seen quite so impressive. She photographed brilliant splashes of color that emerged as the sun climbed out from behind mountain peaks, radiating its grandeur. After she had spent more than an hour basking in its radiance, thoughts of the last several months began to flash through her mind. Not so long ago, if not for one house that captivated her, things might have turned out very different.

The fateful day she walked into the Valencia Manor, her life had taken many turns. Joan Bishop, a good friend from her college days, and now a real estate broker in Boulder had given Maryanne a heads up on the property before the listing had come out, aware that she had been searching for such a property. What had started out as a property investment opportunity had become an intriguing nightmare of unexpected events and mysterious, supernatural phenomenon. Murder, strange accidents and tragedy all took their turns in the bizarre adventures at the Valencia Manor. Nonetheless, through all of the mystery and misery, it had become a reality; The Valencia Manor would be legally transferred into Maryanne's name today. Several months of legal ramifications had come into play when the owner had suddenly been killed in what had been deemed manslaughter. The details had played out in a court trial held just two months prior.

Harold J. Arnold had pleaded guilty to assaulting Mrs. Irene Dirkshire, who had inherited the Valencia Manor from her brother, John Farthington. John had become ill and passed away, leaving his sister, Irene, as the soul inheritor of the Farthington Estate, which included the Valencia Manor. Soon after Irene Dirkshire was awarded the Estate of John

Farthington, she was killed. A manhunt that lasted well over two weeks for suspect Harold J. Arnold, a distant cousin of Mrs. Dirkshire, had been fruitful. He confessed that he had accidentally killed her when he went to her home to obtain a copy of the title to Valencia Manor, and the will. When he was summoned to the stand to testify, he admitted that he had called and threatened her, demanding that she turn over documents that would name him as part owner of the Farthington Estate and the Valencia Manor. After receiving the threatening phone call, Mrs. Dirkshire went to her attorney and had her will changed, knowing Harold Arnold meant business and that he was a dangerous man. When Mrs. Dirkshire listed the property for sale with Bishop Realty, Joan Bishop, Maryanne's friend and the owner of the realty firm, introduced Mrs. Dirkshire to Maryanne.

Maryanne had been looking at investments and kept her eye on the Valencia Manor for several months before she moved to Boulder. Mrs. Dirkshire, an elderly woman with energy and determination had been impressed by Miss O'Donnell in the short time she had known her. Prior to Irene Dirkshire's death, she had come to love and respect Maryanne. When she received the threat from Harold Arnold, she immediately instructed her attorney to make changes in her will. Irene Dirkshire had no living relatives and had included in her will, that Maryanne should be named as the beneficiary of the property should something happen to her before it was sold. Unfortunately for Mrs. Dirkshire, that is exactly what took place and what eventually led to Maryanne's inheritance of the historical Manor. During the trial, Harold J. Arnold went into detail, describing how he had visited Mrs. Dirkshire's home one evening a few nights after calling her, demanding the documents and warning her that she had better cooperate. She was an elderly woman but he misjudged her tenacity, and was not aware that she had spoken to her attorney after he had called and threatened her. Harold admitted that he had demanded the documents relating to his past ownership in the manor, but when she refused to give them up, they struggled and he pushed her into a table, where she hit her head and subsequently died from the injuries. He assumed he would inherit the Valencia if something happened to Mrs. Dirkshire, which would have been possible had there not been enough evidence to prosecute him. The lawyers were almost certain the death was deliberate, but there was not enough evidence to make a solid case out of the charge, so they went for the aggravated assault and manslaughter theory. It carried a life sentence for him since he was already a three-time loser. At least he would be out of society for life. He had already been in jail and prison prior to the incident.

Maryanne was reluctant at first, to accept the unbelievable gift of the Valencia Manor, because she felt so bad about the death of the lovely Mrs. Dirkshire. Maryanne spent weeks trying to find other relatives who might otherwise be next in line to inherit the property, but after careful searching to no avail, and legal counsel, she felt more at ease in accepting the gracious offer.

After a long, beautiful drive through the mountains, pondering over the events that had taken place, Maryanne arrived at the County Title Office where her attorney, Thomas Deleon, was waiting on a bench by the office entry. He stood up, rearranged his jacket and straightened his tie. His six-foot frame loomed over Maryanne as they shook hands and spoke briefly about the property transfer and engaged in small talk before going inside to complete the transaction.

"Are you ready to own the Valencia Manor with all of its ghostly inhabitants?" He questioned jokingly.

"I'm ready as rain, as they say. The ghosts are harmless, and one must worry more about the living, I think," she smiled widely.

"You look radiant this morning, Maryanne. Your green eyes reflect the excitement of such a bequest."

"If I didn't know you better, I'd think you were trying to flirt with me," Maryanne chuckled. "Thank you for the compliment though, Thomas. I am relieved that this is finally going to be over today. It has been a long time coming. I never actually thought it would become a reality, and yet here we are. It's like a beautiful dream at the end of a long nightmare." She flashed on such an impossibility of any kind of relationship with Thomas. She was not the least bit interested in Tom, even though he had made a pass or two at her since they had known each other a few years back. His looks were not bad but his arrogance and attitude had always turned her off. He was an excellent attorney though, and that had always been her first consideration.

"Well, it has been a long nightmare, and you did earn it, in a manner of speaking. You were a prisoner there for over two weeks. That ought to account for something. You deserve it and then some. Just accept the Manor as a payoff for a stint in hell for two weeks and stop worrying about why and how?"

"I guess it's better me than Harold J. Arnold."

"That's true." His face turned from a smile to that of subtlety. "And that would have been a real disaster. We can only thank your lucky stars it turned out the way it did."

After a few signatures and paperwork, Maryanne strolled out of the office with a clear title to the Manor. She opened the documents, studying them once more in near disbelief. Reading them over, she finally slipped the title papers into the envelope and took in a deep breath as she sat down on the bench outside the office, relieved that this was the final step. Now she could go forward with her plans to renovate the Manor, and begin the journey of a long term commitment toward financial stability. Maryanne's thoughts reflected back to Hanna Michelle Smith, the once mistakenly accused criminal and kidnapper, who turned out to be an innocent and abused young woman that had served a relentless stint in her own hell at the Valencia Manor. The detectives and the psychologists presumed that she could have been inside the manor for several years. She was obviously inside the manor when the property was listed with Joan Bishop, Maryanne's friend and real estate broker, but for an accuracy factor, there was no evidence at this time to determine how long.

Hanna Michelle, the obvious victim of a vicious man's madness, was discovered in an unexpected show of events, when Maryanne had first been associated with the Valencia Manor many months ago. Sheriff Olson and Maryanne were still trying to find out who had kept Hanna hostage there, and why. Subsequently, Maryanne O'Donnel had been held captive in the Manor for more than two weeks, by Hanna Michelle, who at that time was a victim herself. She had become confused and misguided from her tragic captivity. However, Maryanne had formed a bond with Hanna during her confinement. She was determined to help Hanna regain self-reliance and confidence now that she was free from the grip of the horrible Manor. The Boulder Police Department had still not come up with any evidence as to why Hanna Michelle was still living inside the mansion when it was presumed to be vacated after the owner, John Farthington, had passed away. Maryanne had done her share of research; trying to find out the identity of this unknown woman. The actual name, Hanna Michelle Smith had been given to her by the Centennial Peaks Psychiatric Hospital in Louisville, Colorado, because there were literally no documents or knowledge of how she ended up in the Valencia and her true identity. For the time being her name would remain Hanna Michelle Smith.

As Maryanne leaned back against the bench remembering the long journey from the first time she saw the Valencia Manor, until this day, she took the cell phone from her purse and called Mario, the Detective who worked on the case and eventually Maryanne's love interest. His answering machine responded, so she left him a short message informing him of the final outcome. Now it was time to return to her office and finish a project that she had been working on for several weeks.

After the Valencia Manor had been cleansed of the evil that dominated it, and no other spirits seemed to be haunting its dark, empty chambers, Maryanne began to delve into serious work at her business of acquiring and selling artifacts and antiquities. She was financially tapped, and needed to sustain herself once again, since the trust she had inherited from her parents had diminished to a few thousand dollars. It was time to get down to business and create new cash flow. After acquiring a perfect location for her new store on Broadway, in the Pearl Street Mall area, she formed an LLC, and named the business *Valencia Antiquities.* She had been doing quite well after spending several thousand dollars in marketing and advertising. It had paid off with four new clients who were interested in several high-priced artifacts. Various other clients included daily patrons who wandered in window-shopping, or random impulse buyers picking up items here and there. The location was perfect. A new client had stopped in inquiring about artifacts connected with the famous mining town of Cripple Creek, a historical mining town that had been developed into a modern tourist gambling location. A small town that was full of stories connected with hauntings and paranormal activity. She was looking forward to visiting the location, especially now that she had experienced a little taste of the paranormal. Her new found interests had led her on new expeditions in areas where legends of ghost haunting seemed to be a familiar occurrence. She would be investigating other well-known places in the mountains where the gold mining days of Colorado had been so prevalent. Another very interesting location she had not yet visited was the famous Stanley Hotel, where Stephen King had been inspired to create his great mystery, "The Shining." She was considering asking her new friend, Vivian Gilbreth, the psychic, to join her in those ventures. '*What psychic wouldn't want to visit historical locations of that caliber?*'

After Maryanne had labored with love at her store on Broadway, it was time to close. She set the alarm, and locked the doors, returning to her charming bungalow on Mapleton Avenue. Her small house was set back, slightly secluded on the quiet street surrounded by its protective, maturing oaks. She had been working on updating the house since she moved in and it would soon be ready for sale. A bit more renovating and the house would be ready for the market.

A trip to Dublin, Ireland had been in the works with Mario Ramos, her love interest for more than a year. He had sprung the news on her last week that they would be departing in three weeks. Since the news had finally sunk in, Maryanne had been floating on a virtual cloud, keeping reality at close range. Maryanne had first met Mario when her friend Joan had been attacked by an intruder in her office, many months ago. He was one of the detectives who answered the call. She was immediately drawn to his dark, mysterious charm, with eyes that melted her every move. Their affair was still in full bloom and looked like it was going to be a permanent pleasure. She was very content in the love department. Little did she know it wasn't just a vacation, but Mario had purchased an expensive diamond ring, and had a plan to purpose while they were visiting the enchanting city of Dublin. They had talked about marriage for months now and she would soon experience the fruits of her and Mario's plans. Mario had already secured reservations at an upscale hotel; the Shelbourne Dublin Renaissance. It was built in eighteen-twenty-four and had been meticulously restored to retain its historical charm. Though Dublin had been one of her business destinations and her family's heritage, she had never been to that particular area, or the hotel, which had a very captivating history. Its reputation for being a most exquisite place for romance and weddings preceded it. Mario knew just how to please Maryanne. She was looking forward to the trip and quietly hoped he would propose while they were there. Though marriage had been discussed many times, they had never really followed up with the idea, but both knew they would eventually take that final vow. Mario had planned an elaborate vacation, and indeed, she would be in awe when the event took place. He had been very careful not to let her in on certain details of his plans when they visited the enchanting city of Dublin.

When Maryanne approached her house, headlights reflected against the recently upgraded brick exterior. Her thoughts drifted back to when she had first moved in. The house had been significantly updated from its neglected condition when she saw it for the very first time. She pondered over plans to renovate the Valencia Manor and eventually sell her house and move into the grand estate. It would be a huge undertaking, and she didn't want both projects taking place at the same time, so she continued to complete as much as possible on her house before she began the Valencia renovation project. Next week, the new roof would be installed and the interior paint would be completed. The entire project would be nearly finished before leaving on her trip to Ireland.

An hour later Maryanne prepared a light dinner, and enjoyed her proverbial cup of pumpkin spice coffee, while she read the Rocky Mountain News. When she was caught up on the local and national update, she reflected again, on the Valencia Manor, realizing that the dream would soon be a reality. When she and Mario returned from Ireland, her comfortable little house would be listed with Joan's real estate firm, but she would wait until the contractor had completed a portion of the Valencia before moving out of her house.

Maryanne's mind had been reeling with concern about Hanna Michelle, and she had made plans to pay her another visit. It had been a few weeks since they spoke, when Hanna's attitude had changed significantly toward Maryanne, in a way she could not quite comprehend. When she met with Hanna, a cold and callous woman had emerged, unlike Hanna's personality on previous visits. It was perplexing and she had been feeling concerned about why Hanna had suddenly changed her attitude from one of caring to a bitter, cold and resentful person. There was no reason that Maryanne knew of, why the sudden change had taken place and it weighed heavily on her mind. It had been quite some time since that unsettling visit and Maryanne was excited, but anxious as to how Hanna would react to her visit now.

Hanna had recently been released from the Centennial Peaks Psychiatric Hospital in Louisville, Colorado and moved into a facility where she was being supervised, but with more freedom to see how she would handle merging into school and society. She had apparently been doing well, and now the Doctor was planning to move her into a home with two other young women, where they would be supervised by a house mother and she could begin school at a career college in Denver. She would be training for a career in interior design. She was going to be released two days before Maryanne returned from Dublin. The head psychiatrist had informed her about it a week ago, after Mario and Maryanne's flight-schedule and hotel had already been purchased. Maryanne had considered changing the plans, but there were too many complications with the reservations and she was unable to change at such a late notice, for their trip to Ireland.

Dr. Marks said Hanna would be fine, but supervised quite closely at first, since this was a trial period to see how she adapted to society, work, school and new friends. She would be allowed a bit more freedom to come and go on her own.

Maryanne still felt a strange distancing between them since the visit when Hanna Michelle was so cold and indifferent to her. Doctor Marks assured Maryanne it was nothing to worry about and that it was caused from Hanna's anxiety about moving into a different environment. Since her traumatizing experience at the Manor, there would be many things to overcome, Doctor Marks had explained. Maryanne had visited her several times, with not too noticeable a change, and she still felt something was not quite the same. The institution had done wonders with Hanna though, since she had been placed into the facility. Her memory had opened up and she had redeveloped excellent learning skills and speaking abilities. She was very intelligent, and it seemed like she would be able to function quite well on the outside. As it turned out, she was exceptional in math and took to computers quickly, even though no one knew for sure what or where her former educational training had been. Hanna could remember many things, but being in school was quite vague. Her memory was coming back slowly but there was still a lot to remember and discover about her life. Maryanne had put an article in the local newspaper to see if anyone knew of Hanna or where she had come from. A few people came forward, but when they finally met her, they had been mistaken. No one had any information at all of her previous history. Maryanne was still in the research process trying to find out more about Hanna's former life, prior to being discovered at the Valencia Manor in extremely critical condition.

Maryanne's phone blared, startling her while she was deep in thought and she picked it off the cradle where it hung near shiny refinished cabinets.

"It's about time you called, Mario," she kidded as she had glanced briefly at the caller ID. "You must have had a busy day."

"Matter of fact, there was a break-in at Exquisite Jewelers on Larimer St, near Broadway. They got away with a diamond collection worth over a million. Haven't found any significant clues yet. The owner had been holding the collection for a client who was flying in from Salt Lake City. His flight will be arriving this evening around ten-o'clock at DIA. Chief Olson wants me to meet him at the Denver Hilton, later on tonight. He informed me that he hated being the bearer of bad news, but somebody's got'ta do it, and guess who's the lucky man?" he chuckled.

"I'll be heading to Denver in a while, to break the news to John Remigi, the unsuspecting victim, or so it seems at this point. The collection was worth over one and a half million and he was getting a deal for a million cash at that. I have been consumed with the investigation and I finally took a break to call you," Mario went on.

"I figured something had come up. I know you well enough by now, Mario. Do you have time to stop by? I can whip up something to eat before you go."

"I'll stop by for a minute or so just to see you, but don't go to any trouble. Chief Olson just bought me dinner at Dots half an hour ago, while he gave me the details, but I do want to see you for a few. Be there in about an hour. Talk to you later, sweetie."

Maryanne and Mario's relationship had blossomed into a full-blown romance. She could not be happier and was eager for their excursion, where they would finally be alone for ten exciting days. While she reflected on romance, she threw together a crunchy, grilled-cheese sandwich and tomato bisque soup, never eating a full meal unless Mario was coming over. It never seemed quite worth the effort for just one person. Mario came over to spend the night two or three times a week, but she was perfectly fine with a few nights alone; *for now,* she thought.

Maryanne withdrew the files from her briefcase and placed them across the table. She became totally absorbed in research when she heard a click at the front door in the living room.

Smiling coolly, knowing Mario would let himself in, she eagerly awaited his entry. A deafening thump slammed hard against the wall, startling her while an ice-cold breeze swept into the room where she sat, heart in high gear.

"Mario, is that you?" There was no answer. She moved uneasily toward the living room, heart still pounding in her chest and peered into its anomalous commotion. No one was visible, but the door stood open wide; the room almost at sub-zero temperatures. A bitter-cold wind whisked through, accompanied by a distant, haunting voice as if a stranger from beyond were trying to communicate. It became more voluble and intense while various lights began to flicker off and on. She stood paralyzed against the wall. Pictures fell from hangers as if an invisible hand had lifted and tossed them across the room. Furniture slid effortlessly, as if a team of ghosts were rearranging furniture in a satirical frenzy. Maryanne shivered as she stood fast, all of her senses in tune with the supernatural spectacle.

Edging backwards, Maryanne picked up the phone and dialed 911. A complacent voice asked the usual questions, as she pleaded for help. The voice on the phone continued speaking in a collected tone, but she was unable to respond. She stood in terror as the strange grumbling continued to resonate from within the walls. Backing away, she retreated to the kitchen and waited anxiously for help. Shaking with fright and shivering from icy cold temperatures, the deep, unearthly, groaning continued to expound. She could not decipher the low-pitched babbling. The sounds were eerie and profound, as if not from this world. She recollected similarities of earlier experiences at the Manor, several months ago.

She pushed the speaker button and dropped the phone, while an emergency tech continued his routine discourse. Noise in the house became unfathomable until the words were no longer distinguishable and only the grumbling and moaning that had taken over the house was apparent. Another deafening thud crashed as if something had been thrown hard against the wall once more. A powerful, invisible force pushed hard against her forcing her back against the bar. Jabs of sharp pain shot through her and then the unseen force loosened its grip and she fell to the floor. As quickly as it started, the cold breeze quit and the room returned to its usual temperature in an instant. The front door slammed and she heard the familiar click from the front door lock. The house became silent. A voice from the phone on floor in front of her repeated instructions and asked her the usual questions as she lay immobilized on the kitchen floor. She reached over and picked it up.

"Hello." Her voice was meek and subdued.

"There should be someone there shortly. Are you all right?"

"Yes…I need help." The front lock clicked again and she lay in terror, fear flowing through her veins.

"Who's there?" Shaking and terrified, her voice was barely audible. The front door opened and someone else was inside the house.

"Maryanne, where are you?" Mario came rushing into the kitchen and helped her to her feet. He cradled her gently as he pulled her against his chest. I heard the call come in over the radio and came as soon as I could. Another car is on the way. Are you okay? You're white as a sheet." He pushed hair back from her face, bent down and looked into a blank stare, her pale face covered with distress. Mario took the phone from Maryanne and spoke briefly to the emergency operator to inform them that help had arrived.

"What the hell just happened here? The house is a disaster. Are you hurt?"

Maryanne could barely speak. "I wish I could tell you, but I am not really sure. Someone was here. A freezing wind pushed through the house and when I went into the living room, the door was open and no one was there. I thought it was you. She added details, while holding tight to Mario.

"I must have scared them off. I didn't see anyone outside when I drove up. They got away fast. Did they speak to you at all? What did they want?" Mario threw questions one after the other with decipherable concern.

"No. Not that I could really understand. There were loud, inaudible mumblings and unnatural noises, familiar to those at Valencia Manor. It was bizarre. Some words were recognizable, but I could not make any sense of what they were trying to say. I don't want to talk about it right now. Just hold me, Mario. I only hope the uncanny activity doesn't begin again."

"Don't worry about that right now." Mario held her for several minutes while she calmed down and then un-wrapped his arms. He pulled out a chair where he sat her down, placed a chair in front of her and took a seat. He pulled her close and cupped her face in both hands, placing his lips against hers. Then he held her, and they rocked back and forth, while she continued to regain her composure. After a few minutes, the officers arrived and he walked her into the living room. After filling them in, he ordered them to continue a search in and outside of the home. Maryanne was exhausted and in pain. She leaned back on the pillows of the sofa, while Mario placed a quilt over her.

"Do you need a Doctor?" Mario was concerned. Maybe I should take you in to get checked. Let me see your back." He examined her back and a mark was visible where she had pressed hard against the bar.

"Are you in pain? Should I get you a Doctor?"

"No, Mario I'm okay now. It was more frightening than painful. I feel a lot better now that you're here." She wrapped her arms around him and held him close.

"I'm in a tough spot here. I wanna stay, but I have that appointment in Denver in a little while, so I have to leave now, but the officers will remain here. You get some rest and they will keep guard until I return." He kissed her on the forehead and held tight to her hand. She was becoming sleepy and Mario gave instructions to the officers. He jumped into his pickup and headed for Denver via the turnpike. It was unsettling that Maryanne had experienced a re-run similar to Valencia Manor's strange apparitions. He had planned on telling her about the reservation at the Boulderado Hotel and Q's restaurant for tomorrow night, but under the circumstances, he would wait to spring it on her until he returned. She may not even want to go at this point. As bad as he didn't want to leave her, his work for now was top priority and he sped along the interstate toward Denver and the victim of the jewel theft.

*   *   *

Maryanne finally regained some rationality, which she thought was in jeopardy a time or two and had just turned on the TV news when her phone rang. She had been quite relaxed, and awkwardly reached for the phone.

"Hello?"

"Hi Maryanne. It's Joan. You sound sleepy. Did I wake you?"

"No, I'm all good, now. Watching the news. Had a bizarre experience a little while ago." She enlightened Joan about the phantom intruder.

"You have got to be kidding! I'll be right over; keep you company for a bit. I hope this isn't a repeat performance of the Valencia episodes."

"No Joan, it's okay. Don't bother; thank you. I'm fine now. Mario has set up patrol here while he makes the run to Denver. I hope it isn't a re-run again, either. Never again would be too soon for me." She tried to make light of it and explained that the officers would be there until Mario got back into town and assured her that she would be fine. Maryanne seemed to be acquiring a thick skin when it came to unforeseen circumstance.

"So how are you and Steve getting along?" Maryanne questioned, trying to rid her mind of the recent dilemma. "I know you've had some rocky times lately. Are things improving between you two?" Maryanne flashed back on a time several months ago, where Steve had actually became violent with Joan, and since that time she had been very concerned about the recurrence of such actions, and Joan's well-being.

"Yes it is, actually. I wanted to talk to you about that. It's why I called. Since we reconnected, he proposed, and we are in the midst of trying to set up a wedding date. I know it's sudden but after all that has happened, I finally came to the realization that he has genuinely improved since he received counseling, and it seems to be working. I waited for you to call. I know you've been busy, but I wanted to talk to you about it. I really shouldn't bother you until you've had a chance to settle down. Why don't you go to sleep and I'll talk to you tomorrow?"

"You've got my attention now, Joan. I really wanna hear this! You have to tell me now."

"I'll tell you briefly and don't worry about anything tonight. I just wanted you to know that Steve gave me a beautiful diamond last night. We had been talking about it for quite some time, but finally made it official. It was quite comical the way it happened. You sure you wanna hear this now?

"Yes Joan. I'm totally fine! Police are here and all is well, but I'll never sleep now, unless you tell me. I'm dyin' to know, and I have another selfish reason. It'll keep my mind off the weird incidents that have just happened."

"Okay…if you insist," Joan hesitated and then continued to explain her proposal. "It was quite comical. He had ordered a pizza and we were going to spend a quiet night watching TV. I opened the box to find a gorgeous diamond sitting right in the middle of the Pizza, in a little gold box. You know me; I cried of course. I really didn't expect it, especially after the trouble we had gone through those last few months. But since then he has been such a sweetheart and I know things are going to be better. I decided to accept his proposal."

"Congratulations, Joan. I'm happy for you and wish you all the luck."

"Thanks, I am going to need it, right?" she giggled.

"I wanted to ask if you would help me put together a bachelorette party. But, under the circumstances with the unwelcome intruder at your home, I don't think now is the time to discuss it."

"I don't mind keeping my mind focused on something else. In fact, I do know of a few male dancers around town. Some of the girls have talked about it now and then. I'll check it out tomorrow. When do you want to do this?"

"He wants to have a small wedding right away; here at Saint James Church, so it's going to be a fast and furious planning. I don't have the faintest idea where to start, but I think I have to set up the party by the end of the month. We could have it after you and Mario return from Dublin." Joan was obviously very anxious. "Don't worry about it now, just go to bed and get some rest."

"I'll get on it tomorrow morning. I'd be glad to help in any way I can. After all, you are my sister." Even though they were not related, Joan and Maryanne had been very close and Joan was the only person Maryanne knew who would fit the description of family since her relatives had all passed away so long ago.

"So you know; I am glad you two are getting along again. I had a feeling you and Steve would eventually reunite. I only wish the best for you and hope everything works out, Joan."

"You sure you don't want me to come over? I could crash in your extra room and be there in case any more strange visitors show up," Joan asked with concern.

"Please don't worry, Joan. The officers will keep watch and

it's all good. Glad you called. It created a great diversion and I needed that right now."

"Thanks for the encouragement Maryanne and sleep well. If you need me just call," Joan added.

"I will. Oh…and just to let you know…I almost forgot. Some new clients came in recently, looking for some unusual artifacts. Very odd couple; according to my assistant who met them when I was out. I've not had a chance to meet them yet. They are apparently moving to Boulder from Russia, and they are real-estate investors. She gave them your card, as I instructed her to do when a customer was looking for real-estate, and with your expertise, of course I always recommend the best. They were looking for a professional broker and will probably be contacting you. I believe the gentleman's name is Borislav Vasiliev. Have a good evening Joan and don't worry I will let you know more tomorrow about what happened here, and most important…about the male dancers for your party," Maryanne chuckled.

"Thanks for the recommendation, and I appreciate your referrals. Talk to you tomorrow. If you need me, don't hesitate to call."

When Maryanne hung up, she thought about the problems that Joan and Steve had experienced. Even though Joan had played the happy card with her engagement to Steve, In the back of her mind, Maryanne couldn't forget about the violence that Steve had displayed not so long ago. She worried about Joan and the sudden plans she had for a wedding. She tried to erase her worries about Joan, and then returned her attention to current files she had left open-ended, earlier, before the bizarre interruption.

She was not sleepy at this point and work was always her best diversion. Mario would be returning from Denver much later. After completing various work related files, Maryanne retreated into the bedroom, which had recently been redecorated giving it a relaxing atmosphere. Burgundy and browns, with hints of gold and sage-green toned scarves swooped across and down, in a creative design that complimented the tall windows that accented two sides of the room. Muted sage-green and intense gold donned her walls. Beige wooden blinds covered the windows and had been left slightly open to allow sprays of light during the day. On auto pilot, she pulled the blinds closed, and lay-back on the beautiful antique brocade chaise lounge that she had discovered on one of her many quests. It had been placed it front of the windows on the west wall, where she could relax and read from time to time. After reading another chapter of a current mystery novel, she slipped off her shoes and undressed, throwing on a silky light sage-green robe. She moved the accent pillows to the chaise and turned down the covers. The current redo of her room added a relaxing ambiance. Whether it had anything to do with color, she thought could be the reason, after reading a decorating book on the subject of color's importance in mood. It seemed to work for her, none-the-less. Cherry-wood furniture added to the warmth, completing just the right combination of color and design. She knew it would impress any buyer when it became available to show. She crawled into bed, accompanied by the book and missing Mario. The antique table-lamp was perfect for reading. When she was halfway through the seventh chapter, she drifted off; Lamp still burning on the night-stand next to the bed and slipped quickly into a deep, sleep.

2

Mario knocked on the door of room 3104. A short red-faced man with salt and pepper hair opened the door expecting the Detective, and invited him inside. Mario flashed the badge and introduced himself.

"Detective Mario Ramos." Mr. Remigi eyed the badge and gestured for him to enter and offered Mario a seat.

"John Remigi," he quipped. "Something to drink?"

"Thanks Mr.Remigi, water will be fine." Mario sat in an easy chair near a table where the only source of light in the room was a small lamp next to the chair. Mr. Remigi handed Mario a bottle of cold water from the small refrigerator, flipped on a light over the table, and took a seat across the table from Mario.

"So what's this all about Detective Ramos? You said it was important. I have a feeling the news isn't so good."

"Well Mr. Remigi, it's not." Mario hesitated for a moment…"Your Quincieria Diamond Collection has been stolen in a robbery at Exquisite Jewelers." Mario looked him eye to eye. The man drew in a quick, breath and leaned back, his oversized belly protruding above his belt. His pudgy fingers grasped a pen that tapped nervously on the table. "What the hell happened? That collection was worth a small fortune!"

"An armed man with an accomplice robbed the store last night at closing. Got away with over two-million in jewelry and stones. Your collection was one of them. It was actually the major part of the heist. We are doing everything we can at this point to recover them and find the perps. The cameras were on, so we feel very confident that we will solve it quickly. The films are being studied as we speak. We are trying to get ahead of this right away. The sooner the better is the only way to recover goods of that caliber. They were wearing ski masks and it will be difficult to identify them. We are performing an in depth study of the film, though and we have found shoe prints and other possible evidence that will be pertinent to the case. The two clerks were immediately forced to the floor and were not able to give us much, but one or two small clues can often break a case. I promise that you will be the first to know, if and when we find any part of it." He paused. "How many people were aware that you would receive the collection through Exquisite Jewelers?" He was eye to eye with Mr. Remigi and caught a nervous twitch on the left side of his face. Mario honed in on every detail, aware that a possible suspect or victim might change their demeanor at any given moment. Mario had mixed thoughts as he continued to rattle off questions. At this point, it could have well been a setup or an inside job. But in any robbery, one had to be aware of every possibility. He would keep it on the back burner for the time being and wait for more evidence to surface. Mario had a supply of never-ending files in his mental library that he would draw from. He had an amazing ability to recall every detail, down to the fine points of a case. It was that special quality that elevated him to head Detective in the precinct.

The man seemed uneasy as he spoke, "I am shocked. I had been trying to acquire that collection for five years. I finally found and purchased it. Now it's gone? My girlfriend will be devastated. She was about to be the recipient of the gift. I promised it to her when we became engaged last year. I guess

I'll wait till morning to call her. I have to collect my bearings and digest the news before I let her know. Will it be on the news right away?"

"Mr. Remigi, you didn't answer my question. Did you tell anyone the collection was going to be coming in and when? There's always the possibility of someone you know being implicated. Not saying it is; just covering all the bases."

"N-no, I don't think so. I mean, I didn't tell anyone I was picking it up tomorrow." He again, seemed just a little too nervous and Mario was making mental notes of every detail.

"But you just said your girlfriend knew she was going to receive the collection as a gift."

"Yes she knew, but I don't think I told her when. At least I don't remember telling her that." Beads of sweat were beginning to form on Remigi's forehead. Mario's keen sense was analyzing every answer, thinking quite possibly that he was connected to an employee there, and it had been a carefully calculated robbery. On the other hand, he might not even be implicated. Maybe his girlfriend planned the whole thing. At this point, it was a guessing game and Mario always kept an open mind, filing every action, word, deed and any evidence together in a file that he referred to as his personal attic. These were feelings and senses that he picked up from questioning suspects and witnesses. Mario was an expert at interrogation; one of Boulder's best.

"In the morning, the news will reveal some detail, but we haven't leaked much yet. Trying to keep it quiet, if we can, before the news crews mess everything up, as sometimes happens. It could hinder the investigation. Please keep a lid on it for now. It's to your advantage, I assure you. Again, I am sorry about your unfortunate circumstance and we are doing everything we can at this point. We will stay in touch and keep you informed. Meanwhile, if you could come to the Boulder Police Station tomorrow at eleven in the morning, we would like to go over the details with you. Get a statement."

With that, Mario gave him a sullen look, a firm hand shake and left.

"I'll see you tomorrow at eleven." Remigi's eyes quickly escaped Mario's. He expelled a deep sigh and closed the door to his room. Mario wasn't sold on the sorry act, but was always open for more feedback before he banked on it. He headed back to Boulder and mulled over details until he arrived at the station to file his report and sign out for the evening. It would be almost three in the morning before he was ready to leave the station. Mario's cell phone beeped and Officer Tratnik had left a text. 'Call me.' Officer Steve Tratnik was a close friend who worked at the Boulder Police Department with him. Mario dialed and Steve picked up.

"Hey Steve, what's up?"

"It's all good. I knew you were still at the station so I sent a text, hoping you would get back to me before you turned in for the night. You got a sec?"

"Sure. What's on your mind?"

"Wanted to give you a heads-up if you have a minute. Nothing about business…just personal stuff." Steve breathed deep.

"Joan and I are getting married. Kind of sudden, but actually, it's been a long and difficult relationship. We finally have the kinks worked out. I've been going to ask her for a while, but I had some problems to work out and I think I've done that. I proposed."

"Damn, I wasn't expecting that. Congratulations, Steve. I wish you the best. I know you two have had your problems along the way, but the main thing is that you've worked through them. So when's the happy day?"

"We haven't set a date as of yet, but planning on doing it fairly soon. I'm letting Joan handle that part, so I'll go along with whatever she wants. You know women and weddings. They really get into the perfection of setting everything up and stress themselves out more than they should."

"Easier said than done," Mario jeered. "Ask any woman who is planning a wedding! Just don't tell her I said that," he laughed blithely.

"Oh, I'm not complaining. At least I am not the one doing it! I have to set up the bachelor party, though. You're the first one on the list, Mario."

"Yes, I'll be at the bachelor party. Just tell me when and where."

"I'm hiring a limo and taking everybody to 'The Den', on Highway eighty five at the Wyoming state line. The former owner sold it not long ago. It used to be called The Clowns Den Gentlemen's Club and it was changed it to *The Den*. I'm sure you remember the place. I talked to the new owner about the party yesterday. The Holiday Inn is just a few miles up the road from the club. The club offers a service where they would pick us up from the hotel and take us back. Thought that was a nice touch. I have spent a night or two at The Den back in the day and it was a classy club. Beautiful ladies and well run. No fights and wild stuff, you know. A lot of the guys I know have had their bachelor parties there, or at least attended one. The limo can drop us off at the Holiday Inn. That way no one has to drive. I'm only asking the guys in our squad. Nothing too big, you know."

"I like the idea; should be fun. I haven't been to a strip club for years. Used to hang out once in a great while but it never was my thing. I guess I'm just an old fashioned guy. I remember going to that club years ago and it was pretty nice," Mario chuckled. "I'm sure Maryanne won't mind."

"I'm too old for that stuff anymore, too and when you have a hot lady by your side, well…who needs it, right? A bachelor party's alright, I guess. Joan is planning on a bachelorette party, too. I'm sure she'll have Maryanne included in the plans to set it up. I'd like to be a fly on the wall for that one!"

"Wonder if they're going out or hiring a male stripper?" Mario laughed.

"Beats me. She never said one way or the other. But I know I don't want to have a party at home and clean up the mess, so I'm all about goin' out. Talk to you at the station tomorrow, Mario."

"Take care, Steve." Mario was in transit to Maryanne's to stay the night. Maryanne was most likely sleeping by now. When he arrived, the officers were still on duty as instructed. He approached the squad car where two officers leaning back against head rests, rose to full alert as he pulled into the drive. He walked to the car and Officer Montrose rolled the window half-way down.

"Mario…you're right on time. Got all the evidence and prints. Sent them in with Jackson. They're working on it. Everything's been quiet here. Miss O'Donnell let us know that she was turning in, obviously very tired from the stressful intrusion, but all is good here. Need anything else?"

"No…thanks guys, good job. I'm staying here for what's left of the night. You can go back to the station and check in." Mario let himself into Maryanne's house and entered the bedroom where she slept soundly. He undressed, brushed his teeth and crawled into bed beside her. She didn't stir when he kissed her lightly and pulled the covers up around her. Soon Mario was asleep next to her.

"Wake up sleepy head. Time to rise. And don't look at me like that. I mean get out of bed kind of rise." Maryanne giggled and whispered in Mario's ear after she set a hot cup of coffee on the night stand beside him. Mario grabbed her and pulled her down beside him.

"You're not getting off that easy. Get in here. I don't have to leave for another hour."

"Maybe you don't, but I have an appointment at the office. C'mon, Mario, I need to talk to you before I leave." She made her escape from Mario's arms and attempted to touch up her make-up and made one final assault on her hair.

"Okay, I'll save it for tonight. I didn't tell you last night, but I have reservations at Q's restaurant for this evening, and a room as well. We'll wine and dine and have time for the finer things. Whattaya say? Are you up for it?" He was hoping last night's phantom intruder would not interfere with his well laid plans.

"Well, Mr. romantic, I didn't expect this, but I'm sure I can oblige." She chuckled and planted a kiss on his cheek before painting her final touch of lipstick.

"Okay. I'll pick you up after work. I don't have to go in right away since I worked late last night. Chief Olson gave me an extra perk, of time off this morning. I'll probably go wash the truck before I go in. Mario sipped on black coffee. "And thanks for the java, sweetie. It'll get my engine burning, since you won't," he grinned. "I'll take a shower and make a few stops before work." Mario climbed into the steamy shower and lathered his body, melting under the shower massage. Maryanne peeked in and threw him a kiss.

"Gotta run. Duty calls." She made a quick exit and headed for Pearl Street Mall, and her store.

When Maryanne arrived at work, a Russian couple who had called in a week ago waited by the entrance. Borislav Vasiliev and his partner Adriana Igmunov introduced themselves and extended handshakes.

"Hello, I Maryanne O'Donnell, owner and authority in antiquities. I am very pleased to meet you both, in person." Maryanne spoke as she cordially shook hands with the two anomalous patrons. "You had given me information on the phone of what you were looking for, and I have done some research on it for you. Maryanne unlocked the store and flipped lights as she entered. She gestured toward the glass door at the back of the store.

"Come into my office, please and we'll go over what I have found," she smiled as they entered and directed them to

easy chairs across from her desk. Maryanne could not help
but notice that they seemed oddly out of place. They were
extremely pale, almost to the point of appearing anemic, she
was thinking.

"Thank you, Miss O'Donnell. Appreciate diligence to this
matter. We were in neighborhood and decide to stop. We know
appointment is not until tomorrow," he spoke with his obvious
Russian accent.

"It's quite alright. I have a while before my first appointment
is due. Please take a seat." She picked up the file. "I have located
two of the items but I am not sure how successful I will be in
procuring them. The work is in progress. The third item; the
statue is not for sale at this time. I will not give up though.
The owner of the artifact sounded like he might possibly want
to deal but it may be very costly. I will let you know as soon as
more information comes to light." She filled them in on details
about their requests and they chatted on various subjects that
were quite enlightening. Maryanne got a feeling they were not
run of the mill clients. She couldn't put her finger on it, but
there was something very peculiar about the pair. She brushed
off her discerning thoughts and walked them to the door.
They had been planning on dinner and Maryanne pointed to
a very fine dining establishment down the street that served
ethnic dishes from several European countries. They seemed
quite anxious to try it and headed down the street toward the
Europa. Maryanne stood at the door watching the couple until
they disappeared through the doors of Europa Dining. Her
intuition was peaking and she planned to do a little research
on the couple. Hopefully it would all be good, but her curiosity
was getting the best of her. The rest of the day went smoothly
and she left a little early. Maryanne was anxious to get home
and hopefully finish more of the packing she had started in her
home, so she could be prepared if and when she got a buyer.
She returned home and called Mario.

Mario had been preparing for what he had hoped would be a night to remember; Dinner, dancing and romancing with Maryanne. What more could a man ask for? A dark-grey Armani suit and colorful silk tie Maryanne had given him for his birthday last month was the only thing he had that would be proper in such an exclusive restaurant. He wanted to meet her approval, of course. She had suggested he wear the tie, and that it would match her accessories very well, even though he didn't have a clue what she would be wearing. Style wasn't his forte', and to him, it wasn't a priority. Not that the eye candy wasn't, but trying to match up with a woman's attire was not one of his best attributes. When he finished shaving, splashing and brushing, he was ready. Maryanne had asked him to use the cologne she gave him for his birthday and he had no problem with that, since she had once told him that she was excited by its fragrance. That was reason enough. His cell rang. It was Maryanne.

"Hey sweetie, are you eager for our rendezvous?" Mario's voice was filled with anticipation.

"Of course I am. What time will you be here?"

"Should be there by six-forty-five. I'd like to be a little early."

"Sure, I'll be waiting. Don't be late," she kidded.

"Later sweetheart." Mario set his cell-phone on the night-stand.

Maryanne delved into her closet on an intense search for the never-ending task of fashion, even though her closet was bulging at the seams with countless styles and colors. He suggested she wear something sexy and sheik. She chose a perfect black, satin, over the knee, strapless that could be accented quite easily. She would top it off with a ruby pendant and earrings. That should do the trick. Black Jimmy Choo heels with a striking red ornamentation would complete the package. Maryanne slipped into the form-fitting dress and seasoned it with the exquisite Ruby, surrounded by gold. She would wait until just before leaving to slip on her posh, six-inch, pumps. She really didn't like wearing them, but this particular date demanded such painful pleasure. She had straightened her waves and her stunning auburn hair fell loosely around her shoulders against her naked back. She looked stunning, and the ruby stones emphasized her Irish-green eyes. Mario would be pleased. Her overnight bag was packed with new racy red lingerie that would knock his socks off; *and everything else*, she was thinking. Her recently installed door-bell rang out a four chime melody, and Mario was right on-time. She stepped into her pumps, and picked up her Louis Viton' clutch. A click of the key and three short knocks was enough to get her blood pumping. Only this time it was pumping in excitement for Mario and not in fear of some unknown phantom. Mario looked stylish and sexy in his grey silk pants and jacket, his intense dark eyes and thick black hair excited her. He had only worn the suit once before, to a wedding, and vowed not to wear it again unless it was another wedding; but not his own, he had expressed emphatically back then.

"You look amazing," Maryanne complimented before Mario had a chance to speak, when she saw his transformation. His face displayed appreciation as he smiled widely, exposing those pearly whites that she had first been attracted to. She had a thing for teeth, and dimples. He certainly had both, and then some. She shifted toward him, crawled her arms around him and they embraced. He held her and then stepped back, admiring her stunning attire from top to bottom.

"Wow! Turn around and let me look at you." Maryanne spun around in a flirty mode, and his eyes savored every inch of her from head to toe.

"You are lookin' hot tonight. I haven't seen that dress. Is it new?"

"Yes and no. An old dress with new accessories. Amazing what a gal can do in a hurry. Glad you like." Maryanne was stunning. She was almost head to head with Mario when she slid into the sexy Choo pumps.

"Let's get out'a here. I'm dyin' to get you on the dance floor and show you off. And later…well, you know what comes later. We have a special suite. Something we both need. A much needed escape from business for one night and we'll play in our own little world." Mario picked up her overnight bag, took her hand and walked her to the truck, playing the classic gentleman. He held her arm, while she lifted one foot onto the step side and scooted in, as she had done a hundred times before, but in obviously more casual attire. When they arrived at the Boulderado, he pulled into the Valet Parking and a well-dressed gentleman opened the door and assisted Maryanne. Mario tossed him the keys and they strolled into the hotel appearing to be a very affluent couple. Mario's eyes were glued to Maryanne, while her eyes were checking out every detail of the hotel.

"This is exquisite, Mario. Thanks for suggesting it." A lovely young woman approached the couple and offered to take them on a tour through the hotel. Mario was much more interested in Maryanne than the hotel and couldn't take his eyes off her. Every once-in-awhile she glanced at him and was aware of his obvious admiration. She blushed shyly, but his eyes excited her and desire was the only way to describe what Maryanne was feeling. She thoroughly enjoyed the tour, learning that the renovation had restored most everything in its exquisite eighteen-twenty-four décor. She listened attentively to the history of the Boulderado Hotel. When the tour ended, a well-dressed, young gentleman escorted them into Q's Restaurant and seated them at a table near the fireplace. A small Jazz trio performed a medley of tunes composed by some of the great musicians of the thirties, forties, and other genres. After ordering a four course dinner, they clicked glasses, and made a toast, sipping on a smooth Paloma Merlot. Mario took her hand.

"Would you do me the honor of this dance?" They hadn't danced for months and she felt a little awkward in her six-inch heels, but quickly adapted, and she managed to pull it off with the first two songs. When the music sped up, she decided to give it a rest. She wasn't about to push her luck. Her Choo pumps were not made for dancing.

Tasty appetizers made from chilled lobster had been placed at the table when they returned. A server brought crispy Caesar salads and French onion soup. Maryanne ate lightly, savoring every bite. The main course would be here soon and she wasn't about to spoil her appetite. Her real appetite was focused on the bedroom, though; as she made a comment that her desert would come later. Mario ate everything, as usual and joked that he needed the extra calories for the finale'. Another server brought the main course; Lobster Thermidor with béchamel sauce. It was the most amazing meal she and Mario had experienced in a Boulder restaurant. They would certainly be returning to Q's. Topped off with great music and incredible ambiance, the night was perfect. When the server offered desert, she ordered a take out. Mario finished his Tiramisu and smiled right down to the last bite as he licked his lips, eyes on the prize. The prize; sitting across from him so lovely, looking back. Her appetite still focused on 'desert'. Sparks flew between them as they locked in each other's gaze.

"You don't know what you're missing," He winked, auspiciously.

"Oh, but I do," she answered in a suggestive whisper. Mario caught the innuendo and grinned widely, giving her hand a squeeze.

Maryanne was secretly wondering when he would pop the question, but wasn't about to bring it up. She patiently waited, knowing that he would come around sooner or later. Hopefully, it would not be too much later. She reminded herself that her biological clock was ticking and she wanted at least two children. Little did she know; Dublin was coming up and so was her proposal.

"That meal was incredible! Mario sat back in the chair and savored the last hour of dining and fine wine. He gazed at Maryanne with affection. She looked stunning and he relished every inch of the eye-candy. The Jazz trio did their own rendition of 'The way you look tonight', a song originally from the thirties that had been handed down to many great singers, including Frank Sinatra. The rendition by Rod Stewart was one that she and Mario had danced to when they first met. It certainly set the mood.

"This one's for you." Mario took her hand and led her to the dance floor. He kissed her while they stood in the center of the dance-floor. Both were anxious to leave for their suite, intoxicated with a little wine, but mostly desire, and the rest of the night enveloped into perfect passion.

Morning always seemed to come too soon, and when Mario woke, Maryanne was in the shower. He eagerly joined her for a final romp. They called the front desk to pick up their bags, while they caught a quick breakfast. Coffee was first on the agenda, since they had been awake most of the night in their own little love-nest. Mario ducked into a small gift shop, while Maryanne sat at the table. He purchased a charming glass blown Orchid, returned to the table, and placed it in front of her on an empty bread plate.

Tears welled in her soft green eyes. "Thank you, Mario. I love you."

"Maryanne, I'm so glad we took this time together. I hope you know how much you mean to me."

"Yes, Mario *I do*."

All the while, Maryanne had been praying those two words would be coming out of her mouth in a wedding ceremony, hopefully soon. They both had a secret; one was planning a proposal and the other praying it would happen.

After an amazing breakfast of incredible omelets and fruit, they left their hideaway and returned to Maryanne's. They had another full day together before returning to work and made every second count.

3

Monday was already in full swing, and they were both over-run with work that needed attention. Time to get back to reality and work, as usual. First thing on the agenda was the robbery at Exquisite Jewelers. Mario was head detective on the case, organizing the evidence and witnesses in the coming week. No one had been arrested, but a few suspects were popping up via surveillance tapes along with their network of criminal behavior profiles and photos. Two particular suspects topped the list and Mario would be doing some heavy-duty investigating until something concrete turned up. He had a feeling the case would be a quick solve.

Maryanne rushed, arranging the office and making notes on pending schedules. Today, most of the time would be spent there. She had a new client coming in to discuss another acquisition. Business was good and the cash was flowing. Maryanne's cell interrupted her thoughts.

"Hello sweetie, I'm just callin' to check in on you and to tell you I had a wonderful time and to tell you again how much I love you."

"I love you too. I had the most wonderful time."

"Got'ta take-off now, hon. Talk to you later tonight."…
Mario was off to work into another busy day.

Maryanne was more certain every day that Mario was
the man for her. Life had been bliss since they met. There is
nothing she would do to change a thing. That was certain,
except perhaps, be married, she reminded herself.

Out of the house and off to work; brief-case in hand and
a fist full of mail she plucked out of the box on her way to
the car. She jumped into her ninety-eight Chevrolet that she
would be trading in on a new car, when she finished work. By
evening, a red ES350 Lexus; that had been waiting for her at
the dealership, would take up new residency in her driveway.
After trying out several cars in the last few months, the deep-
red Lexus had been her final choice. Business was taking off
and she could definitely afford it now. Her clientele were mostly
in the middle to upper class, and she wanted to look more
professional in not only attire, but every aspect of business.
Fortunately for her, that group of buyers had the money to
spend on things the majority of people only dream about.
She hoped one day to be included in that financial bracket.
Maryanne had great work ethic and tenacity, so it was only
a matter of time that she would be financially comfortable.
She hoped the Valencia Manor would in the end, be one of
those productive ventures that would help her to achieve the
goal. It would cost an arm and a leg to renovate it back to its
original condition, but the end result would be well worth the
investment. Especially since it was willed to her free and clear
and in the beginning had not been an expectation. When
the venture was complete and sold, she would certainly have
enough money to set Hanna up in a place of her own, and help
get her started so she would be economically sound. One of
her highest hopes was to see Hanna Michelle benefit from the
place that she had been imprisoned and abused for many years.
They had yet to actually determine how long ago, and who it

was that put her into that situation. Maryanne was positive that she would eventually have all the answers.

Maryanne had just opened her new store, which was in old town Boulder, where so much of the area had been restored. Most of the old stores and buildings still stood, reconditioned with historical aspects taken into consideration. New shops and activity had been resurging, making it a perfect shopping experience. It had proven to be one of Boulder's best developments, Maryanne thought. It was a perfect place for a shop like hers. The area catered to various unique and creative stores, such as art boutiques, gift shops and the like. She drove up to the front of the store, and she stopped to gaze at her newest upgrade; an artistic sign that read; '*Valencia Antiquities*.' A smaller by-line underneath read: 'Past, present and perfect.' A local sign company designed and hung it for her just a few days prior, and it was an eye catcher. A picture of the Valencia Manor had been reproduced from an old photo she had discovered in the box of pictures and documents left by Mr. Farthington. Mrs. Dirkshire had given them to her before she was brutally attacked. The picture on the sign was absolutely stunning. It was done in beiges and browns, with a touch of burgundy and muted greens. Jack Bancroft was the artist with a vision, she thought and it complimented the store perfectly. "*Valencia Antiquities*," she said quietly as she parked and gazed in reverie. Her store was next to an old book store that had been there for years. They had given it a facelift and were the owners of her building, as well. Maryanne was visiting the book store the day she found out about the lease coming up on the space. She heard a gentleman talking to the owner, about the lease on the building. She waited until they were finished and politely spoke to the man, who she knows now, as Earl Riley. He took her inside the store shortly after it had been refurbished. She fell in love with the space, and the price was too good to pass up. She took his card and left the store, trying to avoid looking over-anxious, hoping she may get an even better deal on the lease. She waited for two days, hesitating to return a call, when the phone rang and it was Mr. Riley. The rest is history.

Since then, she had transformed the space into a beautifully arranged display of treasures. She filled it with many of her already unusual and valuable collections. The store had such a unique ambiance and combined with her beautiful antiques, it made a hit with new customers, prospective clients and current connections. As luck would have it, the artist who made the sign had an office just across the street and down a block. It seemed like everything had fallen into place as though it were meant to be. The phone startled her while she was placing the open sign on the door.

"Hello, Valencia Antiquities, may I help you?"

"Miss O'Donnell, this is Carl Maguire. I was in the store the other day and you have a piece there that I am interested in. I am checking to see if you would be available. It is a little early."

"Of course I will Mr. Maguire. I open every day at eight o'clock, except on Saturday, when I open at ten. Come by and see me."

"Be there in fifteen minutes."

He sounded anxious. She remembered him looking at a few pieces, discussing price with her, and then leaving. He must have had a change of heart.

Not long after the call, the door-bell rang and Mr. Maguire entered; A tall, stoic and well-dressed man of about sixty.

"Hello Mr. Maguire. Nice to see you again." She reached out to him.

"It's a pleasure, Miss O'Donnell. I guess you know what it is I want. I think I was pretty obvious about that when I was in a few days ago. Do you still have the piece?"

"You looked at three that I remember. One has sold. Hopefully, not the one you want."

He made his way to the back of the store where the

African sculptures were creatively displayed. He picked up a rare, exotic-wood, hand sculpted Elephant from India, with a genuine Ruby gemstone embedded on its forehead. It was a stunning piece that she had acquired from an auction in Denver a few months ago. It was two hundred years old and very valuable. Mr. Maguire's eyes lit up when he saw it.

"That's the one! It's still here. I am going to make you an offer right now. You asked eighty-five hundred. I'll give you eight-thousand."

"Mr. Maguire, I appreciate the offer but the least I can sell it for is eighty-three hundred. It's worth every dime. Actually, I believe when I did a research on it, the last appraisal was ten thousand. I have the information here to certify that. I also have authenticity documents. That is my final price.

"You drive a hard bargain, but as you know; one has to try," he grinned and began filling out a check.

"Don't forget the tax." Maryanne handed him the receipt. Maryanne was good at sales and her ability to be confident and steadfast in her business decisions was an asset. He handed her the check. Joan had finished wrapping and boxing the statue and placed it on the counter. He gave her a firm hand-shake.

"I admire your business savvy. I'll be back again, Miss O'Donnell."

"Thank you Mr. Maguire. I appreciate your business. Hope to see you soon…and enjoy the statue."

"Oh, I will, without a doubt. I assure you it will be displayed with pride." He took the package and headed out the door. Maryanne was pleased. In the first hour she had already made a five-thousand dollar profit. Hopefully the rest of the day would be as productive. In the antique business it was always on again, off again. She would make it one day and then sometimes, nothing for days or even weeks. It all depended on the economy and a supply of affluent clients to keep you going when times were a little shaky. So far, she had both and hoped it would continue.

Maryanne had been interviewing applicants for a position as an assistant, associate, to help her run the store. So far no-one had qualified for the position that had any knowledge of the antique business. An applicant had made an appointment for three o'clock this afternoon. The chime sounded as the door opened, and an attractive young woman walked in. 'She appeared sophisticated and confident', Maryanne thought as she greeted the young woman and asked if she could assist her.

"I am Wendy Griffin. I called about an appointment yesterday when a friend of mine said she saw the ad in the newspaper about your store."

"Oh, yes, I have been expecting you, Wendy."

"I am an antique connoisseur with experience in the business, and thought this would be the absolute perfect job for me. I accompanied my Father to many countries when he traveled as a procurer for museums and antique dealers until he passed away a year ago. I am twenty-five and have traveled to many countries. I graduated from University of Denver when I was twenty-one after studying and majoring in World History, and the arts. Would you be interested in a resume'?"

"Absolutely. Sit down and we can discuss it." She directed Wendy to a chair in front of the desk in her office. She sat down across from her. The young woman seemed a little apprehensive as she began to speak.

"I am living in Denver right now, but I'm staying with a friend, Shelli Martin, who lives here in Boulder and I am looking for a place to live. Here is my resume'." She handed her a three-page, well put together resume' and sat in the chair with a look of anticipation. Maryanne took mental notes as she sat across from Wendy at the desk. Wendy was quite lovely with soft green eyes and straight, shoulder length brown hair. Her complexion was quite delicate as well as her small frame. She couldn't be over five foot two, she thought.

"My name is Maryanne O'Donnell and I am very pleased

to meet you, Miss Griffin." Wendy extended her hand. Wendy's hand felt small and delicate, as she greeted Maryanne in a formal handshake. Maryanne skimmed through the resume' and was very impressed with the contents. She skimmed over the documents and smiled as she looked up at Wendy's nervous half-smile.

"I am very interested. Let me check it out this afternoon and get back to you. I will call you tomorrow early in the day, if that would be convenient."

"Yes, anytime, my cell phone is always with me. Here is my business card. I am so excited. Thank you for taking the time and I will anxiously await your call. Have a wonderful day, Miss O'Donnell." She added.

"Bye Miss Griffin. Talk to you tomorrow." The young woman left the store. Maryanne took more mental notes and jotted down a few important facts. She was hopeful that Miss Griffin was as knowledgeable of the antique business as she had portrayed. She had all of the qualifications; educated, experienced and quite an impressive resume. Just what the doctor ordered, she thought. She liked her quiet demeanor and polite attitude. While at the desk, Maryanne combed through her resume. She had worked for the Museum in Denver for a year and began traveling as an assistant to work with her Father, Professor John J. Griffin. He was a teacher of World History and procurer of artifacts for the museum. It could not be more perfect a choice. One thing was sure; she was very informed on the business and if everything checked out, she may have found just the right person to take the burden off. If so, she could leave as needed and feel confident her store was in good hands. She breathed a sigh of relief and leaned back in her office chair, thinking this woman is just what she needed to help run the store. After a thorough check on the criteria, Maryanne had decided to talk to Miss Griffin, about the position; discuss the pay, stock options and commission and hopefully come to a feasible agreement. She however, would wait until morning to call, as promised. The rest of the day went smoothly and profitably. Maryanne was ready to close for the day. She quickly called Joan to follow up on her wedding plans. Joan said they set the date as November fifteenth, a Saturday, at their local Methodist Church. A reception would follow. Joan and Steve wanted a smaller more private wedding and planned on a honeymoon in December, in Florida, where they could spend a few days in the sun. They had some friends who had moved to Miami that had planned some exciting days for them.

Maryanne hurried home to kick back and spend time with Mario. He had planned to be home early, as had not been the case in the last few weeks. Lately his job had consumed his evenings and Maryanne was feeling the pangs of not having their quiet time together.

4

Maryanne and Mario retired early after a light dinner and discussions about the upcoming trip to Ireland. Plans were coming together smoothly, and they were both on pins and needles, looking forward to the excursion.

Mario had left for work early, allowing Maryanne to sneak in a few extra hours of sleep. She had been working very hard and extremely long days, as well. Mario was always so considerate of her, putting her interests at the top of his priorities most of the time.

After a quick shower, Maryanne rushed off to meetings with clients, and then the potential employee, Wendy Griffin at one-o'clock.

Another important consultation would be taking place at three o'clock with the contractor who would be making a bid on the renovation at Valencia Manor. She had recently acquired a bank loan for the upgrade, and the wheels were beginning to turn on her plans to restore the Manor to its near original condition. The dream of Valencia Manor would soon become a reality, after many months of a carefully executed plan.

Lunch came and went while Maryanne stayed in the office and grabbed a quick sandwich she had brought from home, playing catch up on work before scheduled appointments. The office door chimed and Wendy Griffin walked inside with a delightful smile. Her straight, dark hair fell to her shoulders, framing her face. Her green eyes seemed to dominate her presence. She was a striking young woman and Maryanne took an immediate liking to her. Fate happened to send this young lady to her door, just when she was in serious need of help. Maryanne had done her background check and was completely satisfied with the results.

"Hello Miss O'Donnell, How are you?"

"I am doing well, thank you. So glad you stopped by. I have decided to hire you if we can agree on the terms. You are very qualified and I think this will work out well for both of us." Maryanne offered Wendy a seat.

Wendy's face expressed relief and gratitude. "I appreciate your offer. This is a dream job for me, as you well know. It's as though a guardian angel sent me here. You won't be sorry Miss O'Donnell, I promise you."

"I feel very fortunate that you came in and applied for the job. Here are some papers to fill out; take your time and when you're finished I'll show you the store and we'll begin your training, although I have a feeling that part will be easy. I think you were made for this job." Maryanne laid the papers on the counter in front of her.

Wendy began filling in the information.

"Would you like to know what your salary will be?" Maryanne gave her an inquisitive smile. "I think you ought to know before you start."

"Yes, I guess that would be a good thing to know". She raised her head and looked up at Maryanne with a sheepish giggle.

"I was so excited about the possibility; it didn't even enter my mind."

"Well how does, six hundred dollars a week plus commission sound? Ten percent on every sale you make. It can be quite lucrative and I have very high end clients. You will be well compensated. On research travel, all of your expenses will be covered. We can start with that and go from there. We have insurance and stock options. As soon as the training is complete, I'll raise the salary. I have a feeling it won't take that long. Does that sound equitable?"

"I'm very happy with those arrangements and to let you know; I am quite good at sales, so I am positive I'll do well for you and myself. I appreciate the opportunity."

All the while Maryanne was thinking; '*This was a match made in heaven.*'

"Now that I have the paperwork, let me give you the grand tour of the store and get you settled in. I need someone to take over when I go on excursions for research and acquisitions and you fit the bill to a T. I'm thankful you stopped in when you did. I was beginning to think there was no one who would qualify for this job. I have an appointment with a contractor this afternoon at three o'clock and I'll try to get you settled in. When I leave, if you could stay, I would certainly appreciate it. I will completely understand if you have made other plans, though.

"I'm quite certain I can handle it and no, I have not made any other plans," her eyes spoke volumes as she waited for confirmation.

"Fantastic! You will be able to reach me on my cell with any questions that might arise. I'm sure at first there will be many, but as you get used to the job, you'll be fine. I hope I am not been too presumptuous in asking you to start today."

"Absolutely not, you have been very gracious. I have to make one call and I'm good to go."

Maryanne gave her a complete tour of the store and instructed her on the research program and filing system. She was a quick study, very computer savvy with data entry and already well informed about the business, so it was falling into place nicely. By then it was quarter to three and Maryanne had to leave for the Valencia Manor.

"Wendy, here's my card. Call for anything you need. You can reach me in an instant and I don't mind the interruption at all. Please don't hesitate, whatsoever. I know you will be just fine, but just in case; call."

"No problem, Miss O'Donnell. Everything is here, from prices to any data I have to look up. Don't worry. Take your time and do what you have to do."

"I am off then…and remember if you have any questions or problems, please don't hesitate to call me. I won't be gone that long."

With that Maryanne was off and running. She arrived at the Valencia just as the contractor was pulling into the drive. A tall, muscular man with thick, blonde hair climbed out of his new Ford Pickup. The sign on the door read; Prentiss Construction, Inc. The good-looking blonde approached her and introduced himself, along with a firm handshake. "I'm the one you spoke to; Donald Prentiss. Call me Don. You are Miss O'Donnell, I hope?" He flashed a casual smile.

"It's very nice to meet you, Don. I'm Maryanne O'Donnell and just call me Maryanne. Let's go inside. I've got a flashlight and lantern, since nothing has been repaired since I was here over two months ago. I wanted someone with expertise in all forms of construction and a friend of mine recommended you highly. The place is in shambles and needs a great deal of work. First of all, I want to have it wired and plumbed. I'm in a bit of a rush to complete this project as I'm trying to sell my home right now and not sure how long that will take. With this economy it may be awhile, but want to make sure I have a place to move into just in case. I really don't want to move twice," she laughed.

"I brought along a good flashlight, we'll see just fine. As far as recommendations, I have a great many satisfied customers in Boulder and Denver if you need any references. I've been in business for seventeen years. So far, there have been no lawsuits that could tarnish my reputation. His blue eyes lit up as he grinned. His tan face flashed an appealing smile.

"Guess I'd better knock on wood," he kidded and tapped his knuckles against the side of the house."

Maryanne's lips curled into a half-smile. "Come inside, and I'll show you around while I explain my vision. You can prepare a bid for me in a few days or so and get back to me; then we can talk business. Don flipped on the work-light. She slid the key into the lock; the door opened easily, with typical sounds infusing the room as the door opened, revealing the great-room. They began a tour of the Manor that was definitely in serious need of repair… As they moved carefully across the worn, dusty wood-floors, creaks reminded her that the house still had its share of ominous sounds, while light fell in sundry layers across the room as dust particles floated aimlessly around the room.

"This place is pretty creepy, have to admit." Don aimed his light up at the balcony. "But it does have a charming ambiance that I would love to bring back to life."

"Yes, to say the least. I could elaborate about the life part, but right now is not a good time."

"What's that supposed to mean?" Don's eyes narrowed as he gave Maryanne a questionable stare.

"Well, it's a long story and I'll fill you in when we're done here, how's that?" Maryanne tried to avoid the question for the time being.

"Sure, but I'm getting the feeling that there's something you're not telling me."

"You're very perceptive, but it's not as bad as you may think. I'll fill you in later. Let's get this out of the way first. Don shook his head with a reluctant grin and Maryanne knew his curiosity had piqued but wanted to keep focused on the renovation. She would introduce him on the paranormal aspects later, knowing full well that there would be some kind of unnatural activity without any effort from her. Then she wouldn't have to convince him. Maryanne would wait.

"You're a little squeamish, aren't you?" Maryanne queried.

"I'll explain that when we are finished here, if you don't mind passing judgment until you know why I'm asking these questions. Sound fair?"

"Sounds fair enough to me, Don," Maryanne chuckled under her breath, wondering what on earth Don could be thinking. She could hardly wait to hear his interpretation.

"Well, let's get to work and see what you come up with to for me, Don."

"I can tell you right now that I would definitely start by tearing walls out, replacing electrical wiring, put in the new fixtures and then work on the plumbing. Everything else will go fast from there, and we can get you moved into part of the house as soon as possible. It's not going to be cheap or easy. There's a whole lotta work here. We'll have to take off most of the wall-board and replace it with sheet-rock. More than likely have to replace some of the interior framing. There are years of deterioration here. The windows can be replaced but we'll have to take out some framework. All floors will have to be sanded, but there are a few areas where replacement is necessary." They walked through each room as he inspected, took pictures, made notes, measured rooms, doors, windows and anything that needed work.

"This will definitely be a huge undertaking," and he chuckled as he spoke. "Probably not the best word to use, huh? Well let's just say challenge." He looked at Maryanne with a slight smirk.

"Undertaking does have a grim connotation." Maryanne added to his dry humor.

"I'll have to come back again as soon as possible with my crew, so we can finish up the estimate. What's the next day you have available?" Don wiped his forehead and looked up at the second floor.

"Maybe finish examining the second floor then, and if there is a basement…oh, looks like there is," he said, when he opened a door from the end of the pantry and looked down at a dark, grungy stairway. Maryanne stood at the top, looking down.

"I have not been down those stairs myself, but the investigative team did a thorough check of the basement. I went down through an outside entry and it was pretty disgusting. I got the hell scared out of me and left in a hurry. I'll leave that part up to you." Maryanne glanced up at the contractor with a serious demeanor. "You've got a big job ahead. Hope you're ready for it." She expelled a deep sigh and then they walked toward the front door.

"Yes…you're right; but that's what I do best and it's what I love. Restoration is my specialty. Reviving the antiquity in a house intrigues me. I love the craftsmanship from back in the day. In many ways it was so much better than some current construction in the market now. Unfortunately today it's all about hurry and build. Back then it was about real craftsmanship. Guess that's what really turns my crank in the business. The products, tools and equipment today are far superior, though and when it comes to insulation, wiring, plumbing fixtures and in general, just about everything is much better. I like doing things well, so I can be proud of my work, which in the long run will speak for itself. Guess it comes from my Father, who was also a craftsman until the day he died. He was an expert, to be sure. I'll admit, a good profit is nice, but the finished product is worth so much to me; especially when I can sit back and revel in the accomplishment." His blue eyes lit up. He pushed his thick blonde hair back and a perfect tan enhanced an impeccable smile.

She had to admit, he was quite a specimen of manhood, but she was only admiring and not drooling. Maryanne was perfectly content in her world with Mario and had no other inclinations. '*No harm in checking out the eye-candy, though*' she was thinking. She was mostly impressed by his credentials and passion about the work.

They walked out through the massive front door and he studied the exterior portal. Looking up and around the overhang, he discovered more upgrades that would be needed. He set up the ladder, and scoped out the roof.

"I'm almost certain you'll need to recover the roof. Don't know how extensive that will be, but we'll give it a good going over and then I'll let you know." They walked down the stairway, which was in serious need of repair and looked at each other, breaking out in laughter as they descended.

"Don't say anything," she chuckled. "I know exactly what you are thinking." They walked past the concrete pillars in the yard and Don was admiring the external charm of the Manor as he wandered around the yard. She gave her usual military salute and he laughed, blue eyes full of energy and excitement and followed suit, adding his version of the salute and they left the yard. She could tell he admired the character and architecture of the Valencia more than most.

"Would Monday be a good time for you to bring in your guys? I could meet you here about nine a.m.?" Maryanne questioned hopefully.

"Sure, I can do that. I'll be here Monday morning at nine sharp with the crews, and we'll finish the inspection. I'll get you a price as soon as possible. It may take about five or six days to get it all together. We'll work fast. I'm kind of anxious to start on this one, if I'm lucky enough to get a contract. For some reason I feel a little kinship to the place already. It's going to be an incredible accomplishment, when it is complete, though. Thanks for the tour and hopefully, the opportunity. I'll speak to you in a couple of days. It's been a pleasure," he smiled and offered her a firm handshake. She acknowledged.

"My pleasure as well." Maryanne headed back to the office.

She was impressed with the contractor, and felt comfortable that his qualifications were up to snuff. His work ethics gave her confidence that he was quite possibly the right man for the job. His personality played a large part, in that she felt he would be easy to work with. His keen sense of humor was refreshing, but price would definitely be a prime factor in the final choice. The bank loan had already been granted, so she hoped the final bid would fall into her price range. The bid would be complete in a week or less, give or take, and she was chompin' at the bit. The project was soon to be a reality and Maryanne had many things to prepare. She would get started first thing in the morning. By the time she and Mario returned from Dublin, the work could be initiated.

5

Joan Bishop was about to meet the clients whom she had received a call from earlier in the week, and Maryanne had recommended. She had the list in hand and used her GPS to direct her into an area that she was not familiar. She had recently purchased a new Ford Fusion that had come equipped with the added luxury and she discovered quickly what she had been missing, not to mention the savings in fuel, compared to her older BMW. The property had been listed recently by another real estate firm and she had not previously viewed it. The house was not in good condition she could tell at first glance, but the client told her they were looking for an inexpensive fixer-upper. She thought to herself, *I hope it looks better on the inside than the outside. It will take a lot of fixing to make this one livable. However, the customer is always right,* she tried to convince herself as she climbed out of her car and retrieved the key from a lockbox.

A sleek, black Mercedes pulled alongside the curb and she waited by the front door for the couple to emerge. They were a strange looking pair, she thought as she gave them the once-over while smiling and making her introduction. The gentleman was quite tall, with salt and pepper hair and very pale skin.

"Hello, I'm Joan Bishop, from Bishop Real Estate." She shook his hand and handed him her card. His soft, cold hand gripped hers lightly.

"Hello. I am Borislav Vasiliev, and this is my partner Adriana Igmunov." We are Russian born and move to United States one year ago. We are in housing renovation, rent and sell. Always looking for something with good price. It is priced well, but we must take good look and inspect. Maybe we can make quick deal and get better price for cash." He smiled with squinted, beady eyes as he unveiled his reason for the possible purchase. He took out a pair of dark sunglasses and covered his eyes.

"Much better, I cannot look at sun. I have problem with eyes. He pointed to the short, younger woman and spoke. "This is my partner in business of real estate. She stepped forward. Her dark hair complimented her translucent skin. She wore an expensive pair of Armani sun glasses.

"I am Adriana," she said, with a paltry grin.

Joan eyed her smiling and shook her small hand, thinking that Adriana couldn't be over five feet tall and probably only about twenty-five years old. She was a beautiful woman, and seemed very pleasant but extremely reserved. Joan thought they both appeared as eccentric characters out of a storybook.

"Come inside." Joan opened the door, turning lights on while the couple followed behind.

"Not bad, for a fixer-upper. What are your thoughts on this one?" Joan walked through the house and did some inspecting of her own.

"You are right. This house has good potential from what I see," Borislav remarked. They walked through the small house checking it out room, by room.

"I would like to look at other two properties on list. You have time?"

"Absolutely. There is another one near here, a few blocks away. I'll take you there right now, if you wish."

"We appreciate. We follow you, Miss Bishop." Borislav very courteously took Adriana's hand as they walked down the steps. They left the property and Joan took them to view two more properties. One of them seemed to interest the couple. Joan made arrangements to allow their inspectors to go inside and do a thorough check. Her assistant would be there when they arrived on Thursday afternoon. She bid the couple good-bye and returned to her office, making a detour through Starbucks on the way home. She sipped a vanilla latte' as she made her way back, thinking that this could be a profitable day for her, even though they were not high priced properties. *A sale is a sale in this market*, she was thinking. Her cell rang and she quickly hit the Bluetooth connection, since she got the new car with the added luxury. She had already had one ticket and didn't plan on another. The agent had warned her, one more and the premium would be increased. Bluetooth was a savior for her business, as she often conversed while in transit from one property to the other.

"It's me Joan." Maryanne's cheerful voice was at the other end.

"I just finished up for the day and heading for the office. Want to have dinner? We need to catch up. I haven't talked to you much lately," Joan answered.

"Sure, I have some free time. Mario is working late, so it would be perfect for me. Where do you want to meet? I have made progress on the male dancer issue so I'll fill you in on that."

"That may have changed. I'll explain when I see you. As for where to eat?" She pondered a bit. "Hmmm…that's always a good question, Maryanne. Want to try the new bistro on Central? I've heard good things. Plus time is short because of all the meetings and I have to pick up my car, too."

"Sure. How about five o'clock. I can meet you there."

"Okay, see you at five."

Joan finished up last minute paperwork and after some headway at the office; she was on her way to Bistro Bella. Maryanne was there when she arrived. The two ladies enjoyed a light dinner, drinks and conversation.

"I met the clients today that you referred to me. The Russian couple." Joan said. "They seemed very odd, indeed, with names that were obviously of Russian decent."

"Good. I did meet them and they spoke with dialect, but very well."

Joan began describing the couple to Maryanne. "His hands were cold; gave me the chills when I shook his hand."

"I noticed the hands as well," Maryanne added.

"They seemed very sensitive to the sun, but with skin like that, I can certainly understand why. The young woman was quite reserved. Very odd couple, if you ask me. It takes all kinds you know. I shouldn't even question it, being a broker and all. I meet many diverse types of people. It's just that they seemed so out of place or something, you know?"

"Yes. It does take all kinds to make a world. I get that." Maryanne agreed.

"So tell me, Joan; how are you and Steve getting along?"

"We are still having some problems, and his temper is becoming unmanageable again. I was hoping to talk to you about it. We got into a terrible argument this morning, and he stomped out of the house raging. We have called off the wedding and of course the bachelor and bachelorette parties, as you might well imagine. He was clearly ready to blow up and who knows what then? Maryanne, I think it's truly time for me to face reality and just end it for good. It hurts a lot, but I think you were right when you said people don't change that much. He certainly hasn't. I'm worried that he could lose it completely and I don't want to be there when he does."

"I'm sorry to hear that, Joan. I did have hopes that with some counseling, things might have worked out."

"Let's talk about something else. I would like to forget it

for the night, if I can." Joan eyes had welled with tears and she touched a tissue to her eyes.

"You're right. This was supposed to be an escape for us to chat and forget our problems for a while, not dwell on them. "I told you the renovation should be starting soon on the Valencia Manor, didn't I?" Maryanne quickly changed the subject.

"No you didn't, but you said you had a meeting with a contractor."

"Yes, I met him a couple of days ago. He is very qualified and from what I have been told, he's somewhat of a perfectionist. He told me that his expertise is in restoring old properties and he appreciates the architecture and quality of craftsmanship houses like that are known to have. I haven't received the bid yet, but I'm hoping it's in the right price range. I really want him to do the job. He was quite impressive."

"Sounds like your plans are moving along as planned. Have you been to the Manor recently?"

"Yes, and when I took the contractor inside there were no signs of anything weird going on, if you know what I mean. Not a ghost in sight," Maryanne giggled. I expect to start the renovation very soon, probably within a couple of weeks or so, if it all goes well with the bid. I'm very excited about it and hoping my house sells quickly. Have you had anyone interested at all?"

"Actually there was one gentleman who wanted to look at it, and he is supposed to call me back when he returns from a trip overseas. He did seem rather interested when he called yesterday. Should be back in a few days, but I'll let you know as soon as I hear from him. Hopefully he calls back. In real-estate, you just hide and wait sometimes, and hope for the best. Know what I mean? I have listed it in the new real-estate brochure that just came out, so that will bring some activity."

"Yes Joan, I do. It works like that in my business as well. When business is hot it's hot and sometimes, it can be devastating. Hope I get lucky on the house and sell it quickly.

I still have some time, though. The renovation at Valencia should take at least two or three months to complete, give or take. Hopefully by then something will turn up so I can get some return back on the equity of my home."

"I have complete faith that will happen. Your home is priced right and you've done wonders with that house, Maryanne. It will sell quickly, I'm sure."

"The roof is supposed to be done next week," Maryanne added. "But I am going to have to cut and run. I'll talk to you a little later. Got'ta run over and pick up my new car. I'm so excited." Her new Lexus was waiting to be picked up at the dealership off Interstate twenty-five and County Road eighteen in Fredricks. She had already signed the contracts and set up financing.

After a short drive, she turned in her old car and was ridin' in style on the way home. Music playing, skylight open, hair blowing, she made her way back to Boulder, anxious to show Mario her new ride.

6

When Maryanne walked into her house, the phone
rang.
"Hello, this is Maryanne."

"Miss O'Donnell, this is Don from Prentiss Construction.
Hope I'm not calling at a bad time. Do you have a minute?"

"Of course. Just got in from picking up the new car."

"How do you like it?"

"It's incredible. So glad I got it. Put it off for too damn
long."

"Wanted to let you know that I'm doing a rush job on
the bid and have it nearly complete. I think it's going to come
out in the ball park. Actually it is over a little, but I know it
will be worth the extra thirty-five-hundred. I can meet with
you tomorrow to go over it if you have time. Name the time.
We can meet at the Manor so I can show you exactly what
each and every charge is and you can see for yourself. I only
use the best materials, so the extra cost will be well worth it.
As a matter of fact, I had some materials on hand in storage
that I can use and actually cut the price on those, which saves
a whole lot on getting first rate materials for half the cost on
the wood and wiring. Plus, I don't have to wait. Saves money
and time."

"Wonderful. Can you meet me at ten-o'clock in the morning at Valencia?"

"I'll be there. Thanks much. Talk to you tomorrow. Have a good evening."

"Same to you Don." Maryanne stood holding the phone momentarily. Her excitement was peaking. She flipped on the coffee pot. The price was over a few thousand but she still had some savings to use for emergency, so her gut was telling her to go for it. She let the coffee brew and jumped in the shower. After a short conversation on the phone with Mario, and telling him all about the car, she turned in early and was asleep before eleven o'clock. Mario was working late.

Morning snuck in without a hitch. Maryanne woke early, anxious to get the proposal and hopefully start the project. She was out the door after downing strong coffee and a bagel, hopeful the bid was in the ballpark. The Valencia stood proud against a perfect sky, its dormers cutting into the blue of the horizon. Morning sun always seemed to accentuate its design, Maryanne thought. The old Manor beckoned as she strode toward the portal and stood under its shield looking out across the landscape. Don Prentiss' Blue Ford pickup pulled alongside the curb.

"You're early, Miss O'Donnell," he said smiling as he ambled up the stairs. I hope that's a good sign."

"I'm not sure yet, but let's go inside." She politely shook his hand, and unlocked the massive door. Flashlight ready, she opened the door and Don took one from his tool belt and they entered. The door emitted familiar sounds, giving a slight reminder of past excursions. When they walked inside, light from the windows seemed to allow more light than usual. Flashlights searching, they looked around the eerie room.

"Let's get started, Miss O'Donnell." Don pointed to the fireplace. "This amazing piece of work would be completely restored, as it is the key feature of the room, along with the chandeliers, which will be stunning, when restored. Most of the fireplace will require refinishing and not replacing its original work. It has remained in quite good condition, except for the finish. When it's complete, it will be a classic masterpiece. We can recondition the stone and metal. There may be a few things to replace, but mostly refurbish as far as I can tell." He led her throughout the room, pointing out the most significant areas to renovate. "All of the wood floors will have to be sanded and finished. There are a few spots where we would replace boards, wherever needed and it will look completely original; bannister, stairs and doors as well." He flipped through the pages of his estimate, checking off what they had discussed as they continued the tour on the first floor of the grand Manor. She followed at full attention. The pantry and kitchen needed extensive work, and when he described his vision for design, she was very impressed. The back porch would be restored to its original Florida-room distinction.

"As far as the furniture is concerned, I'll leave it up to you, but what's here can certainly be restored if you are interested. I think it would be well worth the investment," he added.

The bathroom on the first floor near the end of the Grand room was pretty disgusting and they broke out laughing when they entered.

"I know it's pretty bad," Maryanne joked, "but let's face it, we're talking at least fifteen or twenty years of who knows what? Oh, that didn't sound so good." She giggled as they stood looking at its horrible state of decay and shamble.

"Don't worry; it's nothing I can't handle. The vintage porcelain, cast-iron, claw tub is in excellent restorable condition, and we can bring it back to life. It is over one-hundred years old. Some of your ghosts have more than likely taken a soak or two back in their day. There I go again, imagining this house in its prime."

"I'm getting the picture and identify with what you're saying. The history of this remarkable structure fascinates me, too. I certainly can visualize its inhabitants going about their daily lives inside its antiquated walls. If only walls could talk."

He smiled in agreement. "Yes, I'm sure it would make a great novel."

"Now there's an idea, I can play with," Maryanne noted. "If I can get some back-ground, with help from my friend, the psychic, I am sure it would be a best-seller."

"You have quite a back-ground on it already, as you had explained. Just get her to fill you in on some of the secret past of the inhabitants; I am sure you could create a great story."

Don returned his attention to the renovation and scanned the room. "The windows should be replaced in most of the house. They are in pretty bad shape. The first thing, though, would be to re-do the wiring and plumbing, top notch. Some of the fixtures are restorable. I have an electrician who does wonders. It would be just like new. He's truly an artist… Coming upstairs Maryanne?"

"Of course." She followed him up the wooden stairs, holding onto the banister.

"The upstairs is even creepier than the first floor," she commented. When they reached the top landing, a rat scurried across the floor in front of them. Maryanne jumped back, teetering on the top stair, and Don took her arm pulling her back from harm's way.

"Careful there young lady. It's only a rodent."

She fell against him, holding tight to his arm. He put his arm around her and looked down at her, smiling.

"Don't worry, I gotcha." She felt tiny pangs of guilt as she leaned against him. Still, she had no intention of any kind of relationship with any man. Her life was already perfectly happy, with a great guy, who she loved and felt complete happiness with.

"Thanks. Guess I should expect to see a rat once-in-awhile." She burst out laughing and pulled away a little embarrassed.

She thought to herself, *'It's a good thing it's dark in here, cause my face is probably bright red.'*

She followed him into the rooms, one at a time, as he pointed out each and every step he would take to bring the Manor back to its pristine state. Maryanne was impressed and convinced that this was going to be a feasible agreement. She showed him where the escape door was; inside the closet where she had been taken captive. They did not go down into the cell below, but he said he had already planned on that when he returned. She had instructed him to block it off and not to use the dumbwaiter. Knowing Don, he would definitely check out the cell below, out of pure curiosity. He would brick and mortar the entry to the dumbwaiter. She did not want any reminder of the horrible tomb she had been held captive in. The room gave her cold chills and she was eager to leave. They walked along the balcony that overlooked the grand room. Maryanne looked down, admiring the massive antique crystal chandelier that hung boldly into the well below. She imagined the room complete and took in a deep breath in anticipation of its soon to be, extraordinary restoration.

"The chandeliers are one of a kind and will be restored to mint condition, if you give me the chance to show you what I can do. I hope I am the contractor who completes the transformation of this fascinating Manor. You would not be sorry." He reiterated with a look of excitement in his sky-blue eyes. Maryanne could grasp the sense of how he loved this place and that is exactly what she wanted; someone who truly loved his art and would keep the integrity of the Manor as it was being restored to its original grandeur.

"I am seriously taking all of this into consideration," Maryanne interjected, and they continued the tour, reaching the attic door that had been left slightly ajar. Don pulled to expose the narrow, dilapidated stairwell. He took careful, wary steps.

"Coming?" he looked back at her as she put one foot forward, with caution.

"Yes I am. Taking my time. They are very unstable." She followed him slowly; one careful step at a time, haunting creaks echoing all around them as she ascended. The attic revealed a small room, where she had previously experienced manifestations and paranormal activity. A small window barely allowed light to steal into the room, highlighting the basinet and antique, wooden, rocking-chair. Don took great care to inspect every inch of the room. He had already been inside with his team when they worked on pricing out the bid. He took special interest in the ceiling and light fixture as he combed through the small nursery. On one wall, a window had been painted over with black paint.

"I found it odd that this location would be a child's room, here on the top floor of the Manor where no other rooms are adjacent. If it were my child, I would certainly want to be near, to hear its cry. The painted window is disturbing. But, I guess to each his own," he commented.

Maryanne found it rather charming that Don felt sensitivity when he commented on the nursery.

"I completely agree with you and I'm surprised to hear you say that. I didn't expect you to be such a tender-hearted kind of guy," she spoke, eyeing him credulously.

"Really? Does that mean I look like a mean and insensitive kind of guy?" He chuckled, and tilted his head as he looked at Maryanne with a half grin pasted on his face. "But it does seem weird that a nursery had been placed here."

Maryanne smiled, catching his humor. Don stood at the window and scraped the pane, revealing a view of overgrown trees, steadfast and proud from years of growth.

"There are three more attic rooms with dormers in each one, and then we should be nearly complete here," Maryanne added. As they were about to leave, the small, tatty rocking chair began moving slowly, back and forth, as if an eerie guest had just sat down. The basinet edged nearer the chair, as if an invisible hand were pulling it. Don and Maryanne were speechless at the manifestation. She moved closer to Don and held onto his arm. Though it was frightening, she was not as alarmed as before. Don was quite astounded, but watched the unnatural activity with intense awareness. This was a bit of second nature to Maryanne, since this was not her first vision of the apparition.

"Now, I understand what you meant by strange occurrences." he commented. "You mentioned spirits and haunting in a previous conversation. I think I'm getting the drift. It's definitely strange, and a little creepy, if I may say so." His eyes stayed fixed on the numinous movement.

"I warned you about this, Don. Maybe you didn't exactly understand what it entailed, but now can you see some of what we have dealt with?"

"I can, and though it's happening right in front of me, I am still skeptical. I've always believed there is an explanation behind every seemingly paranormal occurrence. It's definitely food for thought and I'm actually quite interested in the subject, and really not afraid. It does creep one out though, when you are not expecting it. I'll make sure I am expecting it next time," he joked. He took her hand and led her out of the room. They eased their way down the broken-down stairs to the main floor. Two more attic rooms that Maryanne had not previously entered were yet to be examined. The team of investigators had combed through the entire house though, and she was not extremely worried about unexpected live people showing up. Her main thought would be paranormal activity, as one might expect, but most of the time, that was something she seemed to handle rather well. When they were feeling comfortable again, there came a soft weeping from somewhere in the Manor; a childlike cry that seemed to get louder as they walked along the balcony toward the second attic room. Don stopped…trying to detect its origination.

"It sure sounds close, like there's a child in here for sure. Have you heard this before?"

"Yes, several times. It would come and go periodically, and then we wouldn't hear it again for some time. It always sounded like it was right here, though."

Don opened the door that revealed another attic-room, and they ascended another stairwell; deteriorated, with numerous missing boards.

"Be very careful here, this is a little worse than I thought." He opened the door at the top and inside it was completely dark." Have you been inside this room?"

"No, I haven't. What's in here?" She poked her head inside, behind Don. He walked around the perimeter of the room, scanning the light, and discovered that yet another window had been painted black.

"This is bizarre. Who the hell would paint so many of their windows black?" He ran his hands across the surface of the painted pane, and then took his screwdriver and began scraping a portion of the paint until it peeled it off in small patches where he could see outside. He peered through the hole and looked down onto the back yard overlooking the fountain.

"It was probably an incredible view many years ago," he added. "But apparently someone didn't think so."

Maryanne looked out over the yard, flashing back on the horrible rain storm and her first visit inside the Manor.

"Let's get out of here. I think I've seen enough for now. Agreed?"

"Well…there is one room that I haven't seen. The room at the very top…in front. I'm going upstairs to check it out and you can wait for me…but if you feel really brave you're welcome to come along. I don't think anyone has paid much attention to that room, or at least no one that I am aware of. You said you hadn't been up there. I can understand, since it's like four floors up. I'm dyin' to check it out. What's your thought on that?" Don eyed her curiously.

"Hmmm. Maybe I'll go with you. I don't really feel like staying here alone, for one thing. Yes… I guess I'll go," she agreed, hesitantly.

"Great! Let's get started. Take my hand and we'll brave the storm." Don grinned as if he had just won a bet. He took her hand and they walked to the other side of the well, where the door that was not so apparent, seemed to be awaiting their arrival. Don's firm hand took hold of an aging brass door knob that fell off when he rotated it. Maryanne scooted back, with a hint of hesitation. He took a screwdriver from his belt and jimmied the door open. He was thinking: '*It seemed anxious to let them in.*' It opened quite easily. Its eerie squeals seemed to invite them inside, while it generated unusual sounds, announcing its opening. Cobwebs clung, like ethereal curtains to its aged wood as he drew it open and peered inside. He took Maryanne's hand and made the first step, while squeaks and groans joined in unison as they climbed up the rickety stairwell. One…two…and on up the stairs, they carefully paced its unstable treads, a wobbly board here and there. Finally, Maryanne expelled a sigh of relief when they reached the top and opened yet another door. Maryanne's firm grip on Don's hand was a sure sign of her reluctance to enter. He pushed the door open, and again, a curtain of dense cobwebs seemed to hang as if put there by an eccentric, ghostly designer. Don swept them aside with his flashlight and pushed on, Maryanne trailing close behind. Without notice, Don's foot slipped into a hole, where a loose board had separated the floor and he went down, pulling Maryanne on top of him. She held onto his hand as if it were glued to his, and they lay there in the dark, his flashlight sliding across the floor until it came to a stop in front of an old trunk, the only thing they were able to see.

"Damn it!" Don broke the silence and Maryanne followed with added words of discontent.

"Shit! What the hell is going on?"

"Are you all right, Maryanne?" Don blurted.

"Yes, I think so," she babbled, in between a few words of profanity as they lay there; Maryanne finally letting go of his hand.

Don got up and brushed himself off, reaching down for her. The window allowed just enough light to make out their immediate surroundings.

"Take my hand." Don felt her hand clasp on even tighter. He pulled her up and they stood in the small room, not sure whether this had been such a good idea, after all. The window was dirty and half covered with a dingy cloth that in the past had seen much better days.

"Stay here, I'll grab the flashlight." He pried her hand loose from his and chuckled.

She reluctantly let go and he warily made his way to the light that shone against the deteriorated trunk. He moved toward her and grasped her hand once more. The tension had risen as they were both unsure of what was next. Don scanned the room; his light exposed an eerie setting of strange antiquities that lay here and there. A broken chair sat next to a small round table, where the stub of a half-spent candle had been placed many years ago.

"Wonder who sat here by candle-light, in waiting; for their price charming to come," he spoke, painting a mental picture of such a scene.

"It's hard to say…This house has exposed many secrets of its past and who knows what other surprises are yet to rise out of the rubble. It's definitely very eerie in this room, to say the least," Maryanne added.

They pushed on slowly, checking out every nook and cranny of the unusual room at the top of the house; the room that overlooked everything. Maryanne, still holding on, followed his every step as they examined its interior. A mirror that hung crooked on the wall surprised him when he pointed the flashlight into his eerie reflection, like that of a fun-house. A distorted face looked back at him, and he stumbled backwards, almost falling and Maryanne pushed against him, keeping him stabilized.

"Did you look into that mirror? It wasn't me I was looking at," he croaked. "Come here...take a gander."

She edged her way hesitantly in front of the crooked glass and backed up as a mangled concoction stared at her from its depth. A face, she realized was hers, but distorted as if the mirror were trying to play uncanny tricks on them.

"It's like a mirror in a fun-house."

Don stood in front of the bizarre reflection to see a scrambled and changed version of himself. "A fun-house would be similar, he was thinking.

"Now who would have a mirror like this back in the day?" He questioned.

"It's probably the age of the mirror that has ruined the back and caused the strange manipulation," she rationalized. "But it's crazy as hell." She began to contort strange faces and he quickly merged into the eerie game. They laughed, while playing like children watching grotesque reflections in their new discovery; a room-of-mirrors...quite happy with the unusual intrusion.

When the two regained a more serious composure, they moved toward a small closet, where the light revealed a long, black, top-coat. On the top shelf, a hat rested prominently. Maryanne imagined that it had been waiting for a chance to set atop the head of a now, long-dead gentleman. Don plucked the hat from its home in the deserted closet and placed it on his head, shining the flashlight under his chin, giving an eerie vision for Maryanne to view.

"Uhhggg! You look like one of the ghosts who used to live

here. Take that thing off!" She retorted, breaking into a laugh at the same time.

Don took the top-coat off its antiquated hanger and shook it vigorously. Dust filled the space, where the flashlight revealed particles floating aimlessly all around them. He placed one hand in the sleeve, as he handed Maryanne the light.

She held it, watching with unusual interest as he stood, donning the black coat and top-hat. He emerged, a very distinguished gentleman; in an odd sort of way, Maryanne pondered as she eyed him curiously.

"Why Mr. Prentiss, I would love to dance with you," she spoke flirtingly with a well-spoken southern draw, fanning her face with the flashlight like a perfect southern belle.

Don stepped forward, taking her in his arms and began a slow-waltz step to imaginary music as he turned her around the room, beams of light dancing with them. The two of them laughed as they played out their fantasy, until it was interrupted by a loud crash inside the room. Don took the light and searched for the source, where they discovered the mirror had fallen to the ground and broke into a thousand pieces.

"Does this mean seven more years of bad luck for this house?" Maryanne blurted out and they broke out laughing after fear from the crash had waned.

"I think it's time to go," Don said as he removed his gentleman's attire.

They left the room, half laughing and intense curiosity at the recent interlude. The couple walked down the stairs with caution and then made their way down to the main floor. Maryanne felt relieved and curious at the same time, not knowing which was most important at the time.

"I hope the work won't be too complicated a job and take too long," Maryanne commented on their way out.

"No, I'm sure it will be fine. I can take care of any of the repairs in good time…I mean if I get the contract," he laughed. "Sorry… getting ahead of myself."

"It's okay Don. I am seriously considering you for the job. I feel very confident you are qualified to handle this kind of restoration, in fact, I'm positive."

"I'm hoping that will be the case." He smiled and started toward the door motioning for her to follow. "What do you say we get out of this place and I'll buy you a late lunch?"

"Frankly I am famished and that's an offer I can't refuse." She trailed him down the rickety stairs. They were both relieved to exit the musty attic and take in some fresh air.

"Do you have a favorite lunch spot?" Don was anxious to please and determined to get the job.

"Surprise me," Maryanne quipped.

"Okay, but don't say I didn't ask. I think you'll like this place, though. He sped off to a popular spot on Pearl Street. They reached the Mountain Sun Pub, and indeed, Maryanne was very impressed, and it wasn't far from her shop.

"This is my first time here; thanks for bringing me. It's very nice. I have seen a few shops in the area, but haven't taken the time to visit all of them," Maryanne added. "There are definitely some great places to visit."

"You are welcome. Glad you came along. Don't like to eat alone." They enjoyed a pleasant lunch while chatting and getting to know more about each other before they dashed off for heavy schedules in the afternoon.

Maryanne was enthusiastic about the renovation. A move into the Manor was becoming a reality sooner than she had imagined. Her visions of the Valencia were extraordinary and she knew in the long run, a serious profit would be gained by her investment in the restoration. Even more than that, her love of the Manor had intensified, so just to live in the historical edifice was going to be worth every penny. Even adding in the eerie apparitions, her thoughts often wandered to the finished vision, and she was becoming more anxious by the day. Maryanne had considered that if her home hadn't sold by the time the Manor was complete, she could easily rent the house and still move into the Valencia Manor.

Back again, to Valencia Antiquities, where she would confer with her new associate. Wendy had been waiting to speak to her and quickly stood up to greet her when she arrived.

"I was just going to call you. Borislav Vasiliev came in today, looking for some specific items which I have a list of. I know you're going to be very fascinated by this one." She was beaming with excitement. She picked up the file and handed it to Maryanne.

After reading the list of items that were being sought, Maryanne sat down and began an intense search on the computer, followed by several calls for inquiries. When she had accumulated a significant amount of information, she called Wendy into the office.

"I was able to make great headway on the pieces Vasiliev is interested in. It will be a very unique quest. The artifacts are rare and I am not sure yet, how much luck I will have in locating them. I know the artifacts exist, but not so sure they are accessible. I discovered in one program that Bucharest, Romania has a dealer that is well known for these kinds of rarities. I'll contact the company and see what I come up with. You can go to lunch if you like. I'll be here working on this for a while."

"Thanks. I'm starving, but just running down the street to the sandwich shop and I won't be long. There is another message for you. She handed her the note." Wendy slung her overfilled, Prada handbag over her shoulder, brushed her hair back from her face and left the office.

"Be back soon. If you need me, I'm only a phone call away."

"Have a nice lunch and see you in little while." Maryanne became consumed in an online search for high-end dealers in and out of the area that could possibly help with the interesting new Russian client's requests. The dealer in Bucharest had one item and another company in New York City had given her some information she needed to advance her request. She may have to fly to New York in a few days to meet the dealer and put together an offer. This would be an expensive endeavor, so she planned on calling the client to make sure he was willing to sign a contract that could be rather expensive and include her expenses for travel. She would save the call for tomorrow after she had done a micro search of all such artifacts that could be obtainable. She became absorbed in the research and found two other locations that offered such antiquities.

The door of the office opened, setting off the new chime she had just installed, and surprised her. Wendy had returned quickly.

"I'm back! Had a great lunch. Sorry, I startled you."

"It's fine. I had been so consumed in work, that I forgot where I was for a moment. I get so wrapped up sometimes, but I'm getting a head start on good leads and beginning to have fruitful results. You have been such a help, Wendy. Now I have time to do what I do best and that's the part of my job that really intrigues me. To find such rarities and unusual artifacts is really my life's work. I know you of all people can identify with that. You had mentioned that your Father was quite the same."

"Very true. I think it's in my genes as well, because I am so fascinated with this job. Thank you, Maryanne. This is where I belong and I will make you proud. I feel fortunate that you have given me the opportunity to work at what I know and love, and that makes us a good team. I feel like you are the best thing that has happened to me since I lost my Father. He is probably smiling down on me right now, knowing I am at a place in my life where I am doing the very thing he spent a great deal of his life teaching me. You would have liked him, Maryanne. I know he would have liked you." Wendy smiled.

"Maryanne took Wendy's hand. I think you are perfect

for this business and for both of our success in the future. "I'm sure your father was a wonderful man. Just look at you. Anyone can see he did an excellent job bringing you up."

"Thanks Maryanne. Let's get to work then. I have much to do." Wendy sat down at her desk and continued her current project.

7

Joan had been busy showing properties for hours, and while she was in transit back to her office, a call came through.

"Hello, this is Joan. What can I do for you?" she answered.

"Miss Bishop, it is Borislav Vasiliev. I come to look for house with partner. We want to look again when you have time."

"Of course Mr. Vasiliev. I have some time tomorrow afternoon at one o'clock. Would that fit into your schedule? I have no more time today."

"It will be good time for us. I meet you at office by one o'clock. You have nice day."

"You as well. I'll see you tomorrow." Joan had already looked up three properties she thought the pair may be interested in that were more secluded, as they had preferred. She printed the listings and put them into her briefcase. Her day went smoothly with two more appointments set up, before calling it a day.

Her last client cancelled so her last hour was free. She headed toward Maryanne's office as she was about to leave.

"I got here just in time, where you headed?" Joan questioned.

"I am leaving for home, why don't you follow me and we'll catch up over coffee."

"I'm right behind you, Maryanne. See you in a few."

A few minutes later they sat at the bar, coffee mugs taking first priority.

"Maryanne, I got a call from the Russian couple; Borislav Vasiliev and his partner Adriana Igmunov. They are still interested in seeing more properties, and I'm showing them a few more tomorrow." Joan's face was all smiles.

"Wonderful. Hope you have good luck finding something they want. They have recently inquired about artifacts from Romania. I have been working with several antique dealers to find specific and unusual items for their collection. Though I enjoy the research and acquisition of such unusual artifacts, some of the pieces are quite bizarre, but I love every second of it," Maryanne's face was aglow. "They seem to be a very industrious couple."

"Yes. I think so too. Apparently, they are into buying, renting and selling property and want to settle in Boulder for a while to scout out some possible investments. I can't help thinking that they seemed rather an odd pair. In my business you meet so many different kinds of people, though. That's part of what makes it so fascinating to me, I guess," Joan elaborated.

"Good luck in that sale. Hope they find what it is they are looking for. I only wish they were interested in a small secluded house like mine. I'd say bring them on. You never know, they could be interested in it for speculation and rental. I've got it looking pretty snazzy now."

"I can't believe it! I am the broker. Why didn't I think of that? Damn, what the hell was I thinking; except I wasn't aware that you wanted to sell so quickly and you didn't tell me that you had completed most of the work. I'll bring them over to take a look and see what transpires. Thanks for reminding me, Maryanne. I feel ridiculously stupid for not picking up on that. Your house is exactly what they need. It fits their description perfectly; especially the secluded part."

"Thanks Joan. That would be terrific, since I have the contractor picked out and he is about to start on the renovation of the Valencia as soon as I give him the go ahead."

"Sure. I am meeting with them tomorrow and I'll set up a time for them to check it out. I'll file your listing today," Joan added.

"Just call and tell me when. You already have a key, so if I can't be there, go on in." Maryanne's plan was that she sold earlier than originally planned. Things had been moving quickly with the Valencia and she wanted to be ready when the time came.

"I'll see them tomorrow and if they are interested, I'll call you. I may bring them by tomorrow. Just make sure your house is picked up, if you know what I mean," Joan chuckled.

"Nothing worse than showing a house that has a too lived in look, like I have mine most of the time." She offered a quirky smile.

"Don't worry. I'll have it done and then some. You know how anxious I am to sell."

"I'll let them know the roof goes on next week as well as the final paint and finishing touches. You had better figure out an asking price, though," Joan advised.

"You should help me with that, Joan. You're the expert here, so tell me, what can I ask for this house?"

"If I were to make a calculated guess, I think it should be somewhere around two hundred fifty thousand.

"Hmmm. I like that, and if I have to do a little negotiating, I can drop a little off to keep them interested. You know the drill, Joan. I learned everything I know about real estate from you. Leaves me plenty of room to negotiate, and I still have quite a bit of equity there. I only have about a hundred twenty thousand in it."

"Okay then, we'll plan it for tomorrow."

"Call and let me know when, and remember; even if I am not available, go on inside."

Joan had received a call from Steve, wanting to discuss their recent argument and he planned to stop by to speak to her about a truce. Joan finished up at work and headed for home. After a light snack, a knock at the door made her heart jump and she to open it. She couldn't hold herself back and jumped right into his arms without thinking, and then they kissed. Suddenly Joan pulled away.

"I shouldn't have done that. I don't know what I was thinking. Things are not working out the way I had hoped and I think we really need to hold back and not see each other so much. We have too many ugly moments and they are beginning to come to the forefront of the relationship. It's ruining what we had, and that isn't much at this point." She looked down at the floor to conceal tears and then turned around to walk inside.

"You may as well come in and have a cup of coffee. We can talk about it. Have you eaten?"

"No, I mean yes, I have eaten and I'm just fine. Don't go to any bother. I had to see you. I am so sorry about the argument and I'm trying desperately to hold my anger and be patient. I don't want to lose you and I'm afraid that it's becoming a reality. I have made arrangements to go back into therapy and counseling, though. Thought you would want to know." He followed her into the kitchen. She poured the coffee and they sat at the table quietly for several minutes.

"I am glad you are going to see the therapist again. You really need to keep it up, Steve. You have a serious anger problem and it isn't getting any better. I love you and you know that, but I can't live that way…not knowing from one minute to the next when you will go off. It's too stressful and has made a big impact on my work as well. Let's just be friends for now, and not talk serious until you get yourself together. I need my space to think about my life and us."

"I don't blame you, and you're right in wanting that. I am humbly sorry about all of this. The last thing I want to do is hurt you. Believe me when I say I will do whatever it takes to make it right, Joan."

"I know you will. I think it's best for us right now. Please try to understand and be patient. I will do the same." After they had finished talking, Joan got up and looked sorrowfully down at Steve. He got up and put his arms around her, holding her tight for a moment. She backed away and took his hand, walking with him to the front door. Her heart was torn, but she knew it was time to let go.

"I love you, Joan. I always will and I will prove it to you, I promise. Don't give up on me yet." Tears trailed down his face as he walked out the door.

8

Joan woke out of a deep sleep, to a noise from the back of the house. She crawled out of bed and threw a robe around her shoulders. The unexpected racket had become intense and she took Steve's Ruger three-fifty-seven hand gun out of the drawer. Flashlight leading the way, she headed toward the kitchen.

"Whose there?" she slowly crept, Ruger in hand, edging toward the back door near the porch. The noise sounded as if it were inside. She dialed 911 while she moved toward the clatter, flipped on the light and a dark figure moved swiftly out the back door. She pulled to open it, but the door was locked. Puzzled, she unlatched the dead-bolt and flipped the porch light on, wondering how the intruder had left while deadbolt was still in lock position. Steve flashed through her mind. He had a key, but why would he want do something so ridiculous? It didn't make any sense. She stepped onto the deck and held the gun out with a threatening gesture.

"I have a gun!" she called into the darkness. The only thing visible was a cat scurrying off, and a flock of dark-colored birds take flight. There was at least seven large birds she observed rise from the lawn, and she followed with curiosity as their wings spanned across the inky moonlit sky. But that didn't explain the commotion in the room, or who had run out the back-door. No one was anywhere in the yard that she could see. She ducked back inside, locked the door and stared out the window for several minutes, but nothing was moving.

Two officers arrived. Joan peeked out and then opened the door.

Steve showed up immediately after officers Jackson and Montrose were inside. Joan had given them a quick run-down, when Steve entered.

"I heard the call. Came as soon as I could. Are you okay?"

"It was very odd. Someone was definitely in the house. When I got to the back door, someone left in a hurry and I rushed out, but found nothing but a black cat running and a few blackbirds, I think; flying away. I didn't know blackbirds flew at night, but then what do I know about birds? And why was the door locked, after the intruder left?" Joan looked at Steve. "Were you here? You are the only one I know who has a key besides Maryanne and we all know it wasn't her."

"I was on my way to meet Officer Jackson just before the call came in. You don't think I would come in and scare you like that, do you?" He eyed her questionably.

Joan looked at him apologetically and shook her head. The officers went outside, combed through the bushes, searching carefully for any evidence that might have been left behind. Nothing seemed evident except a few feathers here and there. The team would return and search again in the morning. As they were about the return to the house, Montrose picked up a silver medallion from the grass. It appeared very old and tarnished. Possibly antique.

"Maryanne O'Donnell will know, if anyone would, what this symbol represents, and if it is indeed antique. I'll take it to her in the morning." Steve commented.

"You are right about that. She is the expert and I feel

confident she'll know. Steve, will you call Mario and clue him in?" Joan asked.

"Yes, I was about to call him. Already dialed."

"What's going on Steve? I've been asleep for two hours?"

"Yes, Mario. You know I wouldn't call unless it was important. Wake up, grab some coffee and call me back. Got a problem at Joan's."

Mario had been sleeping and was about to speak when Steve hung up. He jumped out of bed where Maryanne lay sleeping and took his clothes to the other room so he wouldn't wake her. He was out the door and on his way as he dialed Steve.

"Where are you?"

"I'm at the station," Steve answered.

"Be right there."

In fifteen minutes, Mario arrived at the station and joined the trio, who were in the middle of a meeting. "Sounded urgent. What's up?"

Steve filled him in and showed him the medallion from the evidence bag.

"We have to get prints done and then take this to Maryanne for identification." Steve handed him the bag.

"Hmmm, looks pretty damned old if you ask me, but I'm not the one to know. You are right, Maryanne will. Let me know when you're ready."

"I'm taking it to the lab right now, so in an hour we'll have it for you. Steve left for the lab and Mario headed for the coffee pot. Time seemed to fly as he buried himself into paperwork. Steve was back with the evidence in less than an hour, which seemed like hours to Mario.

Steve handed Mario the medallion. "Let Chief Olson know ASAP."

"Will do." Mario put it into his chest pocket and headed to Maryanne's.

Mario unlocked the door to find Maryanne sitting at the counter, accompanied by coffee and yesterday's newspaper. It was almost five a.m.

"Morning. What was the urgency so early this morning?" Maryanne moved toward him, open arms.

"Surprised you're awake. Brought you something you may want to take a look at. Found outside Joan's house after the break-in early this morning. Chief wants you to analyze and research it, if you would. This is a real job, with pay, directed by the Chief himself. Interested?"

"Sure." Maryanne reached out and took the bag. "Is Joan all right? What happened?"

"She's fine, just a little shook up." Mario detailed the break-in." Maryanne studied the pendant.

"Has it already been processed for prints?"

"Yes. When you're done, give me a call and we'll set up a meeting with Chief Olson."

"I'm on it. Shouldn't take long. Maybe a day or so. I'll let you know. It looks like something from the eighteen-hundreds. Not sure… but won't take me long to figure it out."

"Appreciate that, Maryanne." A serious look covered his face. "I know this is business, and I shouldn't be asking you now, but can I pick you up and take you out for dinner tonight?" Mario's serious expression broke into a half-smile.

"I think I can handle that." She grinned and rose up to plant a quick kiss on his ever waiting cheek.

"Okay then. I'll pick you up at six-thirty?" He waited for confirmation and left for the station.

"Maryanne held the pendant, her gaze fixed. It was a striking piece, and very old. Of that she was positive. Now, she would verify its origin and date. This would be the most fascinating task of the day, without question. Later, after more research, Maryanne lay on the sofa for an hour. A catnap was all she needed to rejuvenate herself so the late night dinner with Mario would be more fun than forced. Mario showed up and dinner was quick, as he was in need of rest, as well. They turned in early.

The next day, after two hours of diligent exploration on the internet, Maryanne had discovered some interesting answers to her latest query. The symbol on the medallion had originated in Romania and had been used in cult ritual around the early eighteenth century. Many cults were originated, such as satanic groups and Vampire cults that had spread across certain parts of Europe, and the symbol was used in demonic worship rituals. Maryanne wrote up a complete history of the satanic and vampire practices in detail. Some of the rituals and cults were known as early as the seventeenth century and on through the eighteenth. Most reports she collected attributed vampire practices that were mostly clinical, meaning real humans were abducting people, and killing them by draining their blood and drinking it. There were other reports as well, that believed in the supernatural legends of real vampires, who were from the dead and came back to life to drink the blood of the living to survive.

Maryanne had become so engrossed in investigating this alleged vampire history, time had gotten away from her. With Wendy working, it had relieved her of opening every morning at eight. Wendy's expertise had given her an opportunity to work on the outside and accomplish so much more than ever before. She realized it was almost noon when her query had come to a halt.

Maryanne's phone rang and Joan was hoping they could have a quick lunch, which she obliged. She would pick up something for her assistant on the way back. Kill two birds with one stone, she thought and then chuckled to herself. *'Birds…hmmm.'*

At lunch Maryanne probed Joan for more details on the recent intruder. Joan also spilled her heart about the final break-up with Steve. After an assortment of information had been shared, Maryanne had to cut and run.

"Time to go…taking lunch to Wendy and finishing up research on the medallion. Seems it was from the eighteenth-century. Something to do with demonic worship and cults," Maryanne explained to Joan.

"Oooh…that's scary. I'm afraid to ask any more, I won't be able to sleep tonight."

"It is pretty strange. I'll keep you informed though. Call you later." Maryanne returned to the store with lunch for Wendy.

"You're a savior. I'm starving. Thank you." Wendy eagerly took the bag and dug in.

"Yummy."

"Glad I could do it. Thanks for covering again, I accomplished a lot. Without you here, it would have been impossible. I have another appointment and have to stop by the house, so I'll leave you alone again and if you need me, you know what to do."

"No problem Maryanne, I'll be fine."

Maryanne knew Wendy was a dream-come-true, and just in the nick of time for her trip to Dublin, which was coming up next week. She had previously planned on closing the store before she met and hired Wendy and felt very fortunate things worked out the way they had.

Tomorrow she planned to visit Hanna Michelle before she left on her trip. The Doctor said Hanna was doing extremely well, and anxious to see Maryanne.

She arrived at home, where Mario would be meeting her. She got out of the car, picked up her briefcase and started walking toward the front steps, when she heard a strange rustling behind her. She turned around quickly and Mr. Borislav was standing right in front of her. It startled her, and she almost set off the pepper spray, when she finally recognized him.

"What are you doing here? You scared the hell out of me!" Heart racing, she felt some comfort to see it was him.

"I am sorry Miss O'Donnell; I no mean to frighten you. I stop by to speak about house for sale. Miss Bishop tells me you want to sell house and she bring me to see today. I like very much. Maybe I buy from you? You interest?"

"Well, yes, but you must go through the realtor to make any kind of offers. I listed it with her, and she will do all the business until closing if we come to an agreement. Do you understand that?"

"I do, but I like to ask question about house. Can we have meeting soon?"

"Yes, I'll call Miss Bishop and arrange it. I have a meeting in a few minutes and have to go. I'll call you soon." She turned to go up the stairs and unlock the door, and Borislav stood at the base of the stairs, looking at her with a disturbing grimace.

"Again, I apologize. I no mean to frighten you." He forced a half-smile, tipped his hat and walked away. By the time she closed the door and looked outside, he was out of sight and she didn't have a clue where he had parked his car. It was not in front of the house, as one would imagine. Maryanne felt disconcerted that he would show up like that. She poked her head outside to see if his car was in the vicinity and looked down the street, but Borislav was gone. She didn't see a car. It was unsettling. Mario had pulled up in front, so she held the door until he reached her.

"Hi hon, we have to stop meeting this way," he chuckled. We seem to be going in two opposite directions lately. We really need to start meeting up more often. Come on, put your stuff on the counter and we'll grab some dinner."

"I'm all for that. Too tired to cook, that's certain. By the way, I did the research you were asking for and found some very fascinating facts. You'll be pleased."

"That was fast. I thought you said two days or so."

"Well, I got lucky. When I started investigating online, the information was fascinating and you know me; I love this stuff. It carried me away and I spent more time than originally planned. But it was well worth the effort. I'll tell you later. Let's go eat first." It didn't take much time for Mario to make up his mind and they were out the door, headed for Angelo's.

They arrived at their favorite Italian Restaurant and parked near the back entry. Maryanne was hungry. They found a table near the fireplace where it was quiet and romantic. Salvador greeted them. He was the manager now, but would sometimes serve them, since he had become close to them and they often chatted while he served.

"I am so happy to see you here tonight. I no see you for so long. How are you?"

"We are very well, Salvador. And you?"

I'm always very happy, especially when you come to see us." He broke out into a wide smile and pulled the chair out for Maryanne. "I serve you tonight."

"We are starved. What's the special entrée this evening?" Maryanne moved forward as Salvador pushed her chair in just right.

"Tonight we have one of your favorites. We have Chicken Parmesan with Pasta Marinara." He was brimming with his lovely Italian hospitality.

"You convinced me, Salvador. I'll take the Caesar Salad with that, as well." Maryanne quickly scanned the menu for a possible desert.

"Guess I'll have the same, sounds great to me, but I would

like a bottle of your best Merlot to start the evening, please."
He winked at Maryanne.

"I will bring it right away, Sir." With that Salvador left the
table humming along with the authentic Italian music, which
added that special ambiance to the charming restaurant.

"This is the perfect place to be alone with the woman I
love." He beamed.

"Thank you Mario. This is where we had our first dinner
date. Remember"?

"How could I forget, I spilled wine on your new dress. I
was so nervous that night. I was totally embarrassed. But all
in all, it turned out to be a great night."

"Yes, it was. I won't forget that." She took Mario's hand
and held it across the table.

"I can't wait for our trip to Dublin next week. We are
going to have a wonderful vacation," Mario remarked.

"I know, and I haven't done any packing yet. I may start
when I get home. There is a lot to prepare for. My new assistant,
Wendy is doing quite an incredible job. I think she is very
capable of handling most anything that might come up when
I'm gone. She can call me if something comes up. Speaking of
work, I want to give you the report on that medallion. I have it
at home. Don't let me forget. Are you staying the night?"

"Is that an invitation?"

"Since when did you need one?" She giggled.

"Just joking. Of course I am."

"Xcusa. Your wine, here. Sorry to bother." Salvador gave a
shy smile as he poured the wine. "Cheers to both. I return with
beautiful salad for you." He disappeared into the kitchen.

After a half bottle of wine and a dinner to die for, Mario
and Maryanne were ready to leave. Mario paid the check and
left a hefty tip for Salvador and they were off to Maryanne's
to finish up where they left off. The sex would come later for
desert, she was thinking as they sped off to her house. The

medallion took center stage at this point. Maryanne removed the documents from her briefcase that she had carefully researched and laid the paperwork across the table.

"I had no idea when this was discovered it would lead to so much history. Some of the research turned out to be down-right strange and unbelievable, but important." Mario read every word of the report.

"Why in Joan's yard? Who would have such an exquisite artifact and just drop it outside of Joan's house, during an invasion? Just doesn't make any sense. Very odd things seem to be happening that are not exactly run of the mill incidents."

"I know. These strange manifestations are beginning to pile up and there seems to be no rhyme or reason of who or why." Maryanne pondered.

"We'll get to the bottom of it, I promise you. Whoever is perpetrating these intrusions will come to light soon. I feel they are getting more careless as time goes by." Mario analyzed the strange apparitions as not supernatural, but maybe someone wanting them to appear as such.

"But how do you know they are even connected?"

Mario scratched his head. "We don't. Actually this one is a little perplexing compared to the others. There have been a few other connecting bits of evidence we have discovered, but when I get to that point, I will let you know. For now, let's enjoy the rest of the evening and forget the obvious turmoil that is rocking our lives."

"I am so glad you said that," Maryanne offered a toast, sipped wine, and lay back against the sofa. Soon, they were both asleep, lights on and clothes as well.

After a few hours, Maryanne awoke and checked her watch; five a.m. Mario was still asleep. She covered him, and hurried into the shower. She was facing a long day ahead and had to make the trip to Denver. Hanna was first on her agenda. She finished dressing and by seven-thirty she was out the door. Coffee was on and she was off. As she was about to leave, Mario woke.

"Hey you. Where you off too this early?"

"I couldn't bear to wake you. You looked so peaceful lying there," Maryanne answered.

"How thoughtful of you; my special lady."

"I'm going to see Hanna this morning. It will be the only chance I get until we return from Dublin."

"Be careful, and call me when you get back. I'll be at work by then."

"Bye now." Maryanne was on her way to the hospital in Denver, where she would meet Hanna.

An hour later Maryanne was sitting in the waiting room anxious to see Hanna, who had been under strict supervision and was not allowed on her own yet. She would be setting up in her own living quarters two days before Maryanne and Mario returned from their Dublin trip and Maryanne wanted to see her at least for a little while before they flew out.

The door opened and Hanna emerged looking more vibrant than ever. Maryanne was amazed at how lovely she had become. Her Auburn hair was the same color as Maryanne remembered her own, when she was a young girl. Hanna's complexion was second to none. What a change had taken place since they first discovered her at the Valencia Manor almost eight months ago.

A tall, thin, older woman with drab gray hair strode next to Hanna as she entered the room and Maryanne stood up ready to greet her, hoping she would be more receptive than in prior visits.

"Miss O'Donnell, I presume?"

"Y…Yes, I am Maryanne O'Donnell. Maryanne could barely speak."

"You two enjoy the visit. I'll be right outside." The matronly woman left the room and Hanna sat down.

"Hello Hanna." Maryanne spoke softly, remembering how cold and indifferent Hanna had become during the last few visits. I am so glad to see you again. I've been anxious to talk to you. How are you getting along here?" Maryanne nervously tried to communicate without being too prying or presumptuous.

"I am doing well, thank you." Hanna smiled, and Maryanne was relieved. Maybe Hanna had been going through a phase and her distant reaction had been a result of the new environment she had been experiencing. Maryanne's hands were beginning to sweat. She didn't know what to expect at this point.

Hanna's eyes were bright and seemed a deeper green than she remembered. Her face had filled out since she was able to put on the extra weight that she needed. She looked so much healthier now than when she had first been discovered and admitted into the hospital.

"Are you anxious to move into your new place?" Maryanne asked.

"Yes, I am looking forward to it. It's going to be a great experience. It is good to see you again. I feel so different now, than when I first came here." She smiled.

"You look wonderful, Hanna. They are taking good care of you I see." She still felt a little uncertain as to how receptive Hanna would be.

"Thank you Maryanne. They are taking good care of me. I have recovered a lot of my memory from when I was younger. I still can't remember my parents, though. I see it sometimes in little bits and pieces, but the Doctor says I will eventually remember all of it."

"That's good. You are so beautiful and well spoken. I am so pleased you are coming along well with therapy. I wanted to let you know that I am going on a trip to Dublin, Ireland with my fiancé, Mario Ramos, next week and will be gone for ten days. You apparently are scheduled to be released two days before I return. I wish I could be here to welcome you into your new home, but I will be back shortly after and we will spend some time together if you like. Had I known about your release, I would have changed the plans but they only informed me a week ago about this."

"It's fine Maryanne. They have everything all arranged, so not to worry. I will be fine. It is really good to see you. I remember you more than anyone else. Hanna stood up and opened her arms to offer Maryanne a hug. She could not hold back her tears, and tried hard to conceal them.

Maryanne was so relieved to see the reversal of attitude. They stood, embraced for a moment. Maryanne stepped back and smiled. There was no evidence of any hostility from Hanna and she was relieved.

"We are going to have wonderful times together, you and I. I promise you, Hanna."

Hanna broke into tears and returned to her arms. The matron entered the room and gestured that it was time to return to her quarters. She took Hanna's hand and they walked toward the door.

"I'll see you in less than two weeks, Hanna." Maryanne dabbed a tissue at her tears and stood watching while Hanna walked out of the room. She sat down and took a deep breath, feeling so much relief that Hanna had finally broken through her memory and showed great aptitude and attitude. In the back of her mind though, she flashed on the brief incident when Hanna had been so cold and disconnected, calling her Mother in a mean and threatening way. It was disconcerting and she kept that on a back-burner, wondering where it came from. Maryanne was on her way home, when a call came in from Mario.

"How did it go with Hanna?" Mario questioned.

"It couldn't have gone better. I am so relieved, Mario. It's like a big load has been lifted and I am so looking forward to spending time with her when she is out and living in her own place in Denver. She will be starting school for interior design classes as soon as she is released. By the time we get back from Dublin, she will be on her own for the most part, and will be monitored for a period of time until they are positive she will be okay."

"Sounds great. I'm glad she has made such progress. I know it's a load off your mind."

"I'm on my way home, Mario. See you in a while." Maryanne turned up the radio and listened to a classic rock station as she sped along the interstate.

She pulled alongside her house. It was a dark, sullen night and the moon was barely visible. Her breath shone like puffs of smoke, as she exhaled into the cold air. She had forgotten to leave her porch light on. The lamp-post was not much help. Walking toward the stairs, she noticed a flock of black-birds had settled all over the porch in front of her door. The temperature had fallen and it felt crisp, like snow was in the air. She walked toward the birds, waving her hands to scare them off. The closer she got to them, the more she realized they were not blackbirds, at all. Ravens had come to Boulder. She had done studies on certain birds in school and Ravens were one of the species she was quite familiar with.

"Shoo, get out of the way. Shoo…move." They didn't seem to care that she was coming near them. It was kind of creepy, she thought. Never before had birds ever done this since she had lived here and certainly not at night.

"Get away! Go! Shoo… go on!" Her cold hands waved wildly, trying to frighten them away. They just sat there obstinate, with beady eyes staring up at her. She backed up and took out her cell phone and dialed Mario.

"Hey. What's up Maryanne? You home?"

"Yes, I am and the strangest thing. A flock of Ravens are

sitting on my porch and they won't leave. I can't get in. Guess I'll go to the back door. I hate doing that at this late hour."

"I'll be right there. I'm only a few minutes away. Go sit in the car."

"Okay." She backed up and turned toward the car, clicked it open with her remote key. A huge swarm of birds came out of nowhere. She began climbing into the car, with flailing arms in an attempt to keep the birds off. They were quite aggressive and it was frightening. She closed the door behind her; heart beating quick in her chest, while she sat bewildered at what had just taken place. It was bizarre. She had never known any birds to behave in such a manner. When they finally flew off, she climbed out of the car and ran toward the front door. They were all gone except for one. It would not leave, but she didn't care; she was certain she could handle one Raven, if it got aggressive. She entered her house and slammed the door. Looking out of the window, steam formed a cloud as she breathed on the pane when she checked to see if the raven was gone. The bird sat stubbornly on the third stair, as if to taunt her in some uncanny way. She closed the blinds and heard Mario's car pull up.

She was relieved when he started up the stairs. When she met Mario at the door, she noticed the bird had finally flown off. Mario listened to her bizarre rendition of 'The Birds' as she unfolded the story. He was rather shocked himself. No one had ever reported a bird attack in Boulder that he knew of. When things had calmed down, they perched themselves at the bar, she had joked earlier; (like two birds on a branch.) each holding a glass of wine as they relaxed into the evening. Maryanne was still a little taken by the bizarre bird behavior, but she was trying her best to dismiss it from her thoughts. They discussed the trip to Dublin and later she began some of her packing, which was way past due.

"It will be such a relief to get out of here for a few days. I want to sit back and forget everything for ten days, except for you and me." Maryanne scooted closer to Mario at the bar as they chatted and made plans. "I forgot to tell you; that couple from Russia talked to Joan the other day and they went to see my house. I saw him yesterday and he said he likes it a lot. I hope they like it enough to purchase. When I get back I could begin the renovation at the Valencia Manor. *This* house is beginning to creep me out. Come to think of it, Joan said there was a flock of blackbirds in her yard the night she discovered her house had been broken into. There could be a connection. Maybe some kind of strange bird behavior has occurred elsewhere, and I will check that out tomorrow. Meanwhile, I want you to go over the research I did on the medallion. You will be astonished at what I found. Maryanne handed Mario the envelope and he began to read the reports. His attention was glued to the pages until the very last one.

"Hmmm. Very interesting. I have a feeling there are going to be a few more surprises. The fact that it is such an old symbol makes me wonder who would be so careless to lose such a rare piece of jewelry. Doesn't make any sense." Mario analyzed the information and filed it into his brief-case.

"I'm taking the medallion to the lab, and then to the Museum just to make sure of its origin and age. I'm not guessing or taking it at face value, but I am pretty sure it's older than one would imagine. Now let's get on with more personal matters." She smiled seductively at Mario and took his hand, pulling him toward the bedroom.

9

Mario had awakened, stretched out and lay awhile, thinking about all they had discovered in the last twenty-four hours. He was aware there would have to be much more investigative work done before it would come to rest. He finally pulled himself out of bed, careful not to wake Maryanne, and hit the shower. He managed to make it to the front door without waking her. She had another good hour to rest and he knew she needed it. He would call her later

Maryanne was at work by eight o'clock. Wendy had already arrived, and had the store and the register primed for sales.

"Morning, Wendy."

"Morning to you."

"Wendy, I wanted to remind you; Mario and I will be leaving tomorrow night, so you'll be on your own here. I know you will be perfectly fine without me here. You have already proven how valuable you are.

"Yes, I'm quite ready. You're a great teacher and I'm a quick study." Wendy's face lit up and she kept her pace at prepping the store. She loved the job and it showed. Maryanne was grateful to have such a well-informed assistant, who just happened to drop in one day, when she needed her most. Had it not been for Wendy, the Dublin trip would have been possible, but she would have closed the store down for the ten days, as formerly planned. Now she can keep the revenue stream flowing, and vacation at the same time. It turned out to be a perfect solution. Maryanne stayed late and worked with Wendy on more in-depth training on the store's computer program. She was positive Wendy was up to the job.

"Let's get out of here, Wendy. It's almost nine o'clock and you've done enough. I will be leaving early evening and won't be coming in tomorrow at all. Just take over like you have been and as I said before, I'm only a phone call away." She set the alarm, locked the door and bid Wendy good-bye. They went their separate ways. Maryanne returned home to finish packing.

Mario arrived and they set up final details of the trip. She prepared a quick snack for dinner and they turned in early. They were almost finished packing and all flight arrangements were checked, and in order. The flight was less than eighteen hours away and Maryanne was at a heightened state of excitement. She could hardly sleep, thinking about the trip.

The next day was a combination of finishing small business matters and messages to clients for Maryanne. Mario spent most of the day going over current files and bringing his assistants up to date. Officer Montrose would take over most of his case files while was on vacation.

At five o'clock a white limo arrived. A husky salt and pepper-haired driver loaded their bags into the car while they picked up their carry-ons, which included laptops, so they could stay in touch with business while they escaped to their romantic hideaway. The flight was long and a computer can only do so much. They watched a movie, ate twice and slept more than not. The first stop was New York City. Soon after, they were over the ocean and on their way to London where they would pick up a connecting flight to Dublin. It was about a seventeen hour trip, including the connection. They caught a few cat-naps on the way. When they were over DUB airport, Maryanne's eagerness was cresting. She looked out the window, pointing out familiar landmarks.

When finally landed, both were ready to embark on a romantic adventure that would soon top the list of their favorite vacations. Off to the beautiful Shelbourne Dublin, a Renaissance Hotel that had a reputation second to none, and their final destination. A limo took them to the hotel and a young concierge met them at the entry, with a cart for luggage. They were escorted into an elegant lobby. Maryanne was scanning every inch of the stylish hotel, while Mario took care of the registration. It was everything, and then some, from what she had read about. It had been exquisitely restored to represent its history. From the well-designed staircase in the lobby to the exquisite décor throughout the hotel, it was a masterpiece of interior design. In the front lobby a large Louis le Brocquy Tapestry, entitled Cuchulainn VIII, sat over the restored marble fireplace. The Shelbourne displays over five hundred Irish works of art. The renaissance in all of its unimaginable elegance was preserved beyond expectation. Maryanne was happy that she had purchased an expensive digital camera just for this occasion. She was not allowed to photograph some of the art works, however.

Later that evening, a dining experience would top off anything they had ever experienced at one of the hotel's luxurious restaurants. This was only the beginning of ten amazing days that they would never forget. Exhausted from the trip and anxious to rest for tomorrow's well planned excursions, they would turn in early. Little did Maryanne know; Mario had rented one of the plush honeymoon suites. When he opened the door she was overwhelmed with its extreme luxury. Admiring the plush, renaissance décor she walked through the suite from room to room inspecting its elegance as though she were hired to check out the room for a review. Everything was first class. If this was the beginning, she could not wait to see what else was in store. Little did she know about the main event of Mario's well planned excursion. The two of them spent an hour in the Jacuzzi, which relaxed them into a romantic rendezvous. Sex was unbelievable and it wasn't a quick 'Thank you ma'am' kind of romp. Sleeping well was just one of the rewards for such romantic activity and there was no rush upon waking, so they lay quietly talking and snuggling for an hour before hitting the shower. By eleven o'clock they were raring to hit the city and begin the tour. After a breakfast fit for royalty, they climbed into the limo and departed on a tour of Dublin's most treasured landmarks.

For three days Mario and Maryanne toured many historical sites. Dunsoghly Castle was one of the most interesting. It was constructed in fourteen-fifty, by Sir Thomas Plunkett, Chief Justice of the King's Court. They traveled across the River Liffey, which divides the city into north and south and the O'Connell Bridge, supposedly the most important bridge on the river. They were continually taking pictures of the rich landscape and gardens, enjoying lunches and dinners at many superior dining facilities, which included a traditional dish of corn beef and cabbage. Their days were filled to the brim with culture and entertainment. Every day was a new and different experience.

The seventh day they visited St. Patrick's Cathedral, which was spectacular. While inside the famous Cathedral, Maryanne got the surprise of her life. Mario bent down on one knee and presented Maryanne with the gorgeous diamond he had patiently waited to bestow upon her for so long, and proceeded to pop the proverbial question. There was a look of shock and a river of tears that followed. Maryanne was surprised, thrilled, and mostly relieved. After crying and laughing, Mario took her to an exclusive bridal shop and bought her an exquisite and very expensive wedding gown. It took several hours for the fitting and finishing touches. Mario fell asleep on the divan in the lounge where many a groom would sit patiently, waiting for the bride to be. He had all the coffee he could handle for one day and finally gave in and passed out for an hour, while Maryanne completed her most important task. When she entered the lobby donning the stunning dress, Mario was awed at what he beheld. She looked like an angel with devilish auburn-red hair. The dress fit like a glove and he thought she had just the right stuff to fill it. His eyes soaked in the vision as she slowly made her way toward him. She turned around whimsically three times, lightly lifting the train with her left hand. It was a stunning white satin strapless, form-fitted to the hips and fell into several layers of chiffon ruffles all the way to the floor. The train was about six feet long, the veil not too boisterous, but dainty with small light and dark green flowers that surrounded it perfectly in a circle at the top. The veil was sprinkled with tiny, emerald-green stones. Soft layers of chiffon fell to her waist in back. Along the top, against her alabaster skin, the gown was dotted with the same emerald stones. Her green-eyes sparkled as she moved across the room. Mario had never seen her look quite so lovely. He was speechless. His love for her had never been more apparent. He touched her face lightly and traced his fingers along her cheek, and then kissed her softly on her supple, red lips.

When they climbed off their cloud, she changed into her street clothes and they headed back to the Shelbourne. It would turn out to be the most romantic day and night of the trip, but the highlight had yet to materialize. Mario had all the plans laid out to have a wedding. She had no idea. First Mario took her to the spa and salon, where she had the total package from manicure, pedicure, massage, hair, makeup and everything in-between. She looked fabulous. He couldn't take his eyes off her and she felt like one of the royalty, who years ago lived here in such a lavish lifestyle.

"Mario, it is unbelievable what you have done and I am so overwhelmed, I can't put it into words. You have given me such a memorable vacation and the dress is beyond imagination. I can't wait to show Joan. We have to set a date now!"

"How does this evening sound?" He looked at her seriously and then smiled.

"It would be lovely, but I doubt anyone could put something together so quickly." She giggled.

"Well…I do think it's possible because I have done it."

"Right. You and who's army?" She laughed out loud and kissed him on the cheek. "Thanks for the humor though."

"Your hair and makeup is finished, and the dress is ready to wear. He handed her the garment bag. Just put it on."

"You must be losing it, Mario."

"Just humor me, Maryanne. Okay? Put the dress on. I want to see you in the wedding garb."

"Okay…Just for you. I'll be back in a few minutes." She retreated to the ladies lounge and meanwhile Mario ducked into the men's lounge where his grey silk suit waited with all the accessories, and he made the quick-change. Then he called the front desk to make sure they were ready in the specially prepared banquet room with the entire wedding ensemble. He informed them that they would arrive in a few minutes. He had commissioned a Priest, flower girls and a complete entourage that was included in the package. Several minutes later, Maryanne emerged into the room where Mario had been waiting, completely transformed into the handsome groom. When he saw her, he was in awe. She was in awe.

"What do you think?" She emerged more stunning than he had ever imagined. He stood there like a rock, mouth open and eyes glued to this beautiful woman that he would be spending the rest of his life with. He must be dreaming.

"Maryanne, you look amazing." He put his arms around her and held her tight against him and kissed her passionately.

"And look at you!" She took a few steps back and eyed him

from top to bottom. Mario, is it really you?" she kidded. "You look so dashing." The pair of them, a picture to behold.

"Let's go, we have some business to take care of." He took her hand and she followed him, questionably.

"So what's the deal here, why all this fuss tonight? She still hadn't put two and two together.

"Maryanne, come with me." He took her hand and they went through a door which led into a huge room that was laden with flowers, balloons and magical décor. She was stunned at the entourage that was waiting for their arrival. Music began playing and everyone clapped. Maryanne was in a world of illusion and fantasy and she had not a clue until that moment. It was hard to comprehend that Mario could put together such an amazing event without her knowing anything. She was still trying to get over the shock of the proposal. Now this unbelievable scene would be played out here in Dublin at the most romantic hotel possible. She was laughing, crying, and trying to keep her makeup from running at the same time. He had managed to get the proper documents completed for the license and it had all come together like a 'well-oiled machine'. The event went off without a hitch and they were officially married. They celebrated until wee hours of the morning, as they say in Dublin. When the affair had come to a close, he took her to the suite and another affair unfolded which turned out as the most unbelievable night of her life.

"Mr. and Mrs. Ramos; sounds pretty good, don't you think?" Mario chuckled as he carefully unzipped her wedding gown. He placed it on the divan, and unsnapped the emerald pendant that lay against her soft pale skin. The newlyweds were about to spend their first night together as man and wife. They spent the rest of the night making love. The ritual lasted for hours, until early morning. Sleep finally overtook the couple and they managed to sneak in few good hours of rest. Maryanne slept in his arms and neither one moved until eight o'clock. Mario woke, looked over, and pressed a kiss against her cheek. Her arms reached out for Mario, and she returned a passionate kiss hard on his yielding lips. She lay back against the pillow in complete contentment.

"I think I died and went to heaven Mario. I have to pinch myself to make sure I'm not dreaming. So glad you thought to hire a photographer, because no one would believe this." Her green eyes were sparkling and love was seething from her for the incredible man who was finally her husband.

"I love you too, Maryanne. Why else would I set up an affair like this from across the ocean? I wanted to surprise and wow you, and I do believe it worked." He laughed quietly. "This has to be the most memorable occasion I will ever experience."

When it was time to leave, Maryanne spent an hour visiting each of the staff that helped put the affair together thanking them for their incredible work. Shortly thereafter, they were off to DUB, on to London, New York and home to Boulder. It was a trip that she could have never imagined in her wildest fantasies. Joan would be so surprised at the news. She could hardly wait to tell her best friend and sister, as she referred to her, about the surprise wedding and unbelievable vacation that Mario had drummed up and pulled off without her knowing a thing. Mario was sleeping most of the way home and still a little groggy when they arrived. A limo escorted them home and now a long night sleep was all he wanted. Maryanne was quite acceptable to that. They were both completely exhausted and definitely needed to prepare for the real world, and a brand new day.

10

Mario was off by seven o'clock. He left Maryanne to rest. Being gone for ten days had taken a toll on both of them and his case files, but Officer Montrose had taken over and brought Mario up-to-date. They had a good case pending against the jewel thieves, but had not recovered the merchandise yet, so it was still up in the air, but the case was all but closed. Catching up on new activity would take some additional time, but the wedding and honeymoon had been well worth it. Mario was at the top of his game and happier than he had ever been.

Maryanne was out of the house by eight o'clock and ready for work. Her first intention was to call Hanna Michelle to find out about the move into the new apartment, away from the hospital where she had spent months recovering. When Maryanne arrived at her shop, Wendy was already two hours into the day.

"Hello Wendy," Maryanne entered the shop, surprising her. She had purchased a gift for Wendy and handed it to her before a special hug was shared.

"Maryanne! Thank you, you shouldn't have got me anything. I'm so glad you're back. I don't have to ask if you had a good time, it's written all over your face. I want to hear all about it."

Maryanne flashed her rings obviously, waiting for a reaction from Wendy.

"Are you kidding me? Oh my God, you are married! Congratulations, Maryanne. I know how you had been hoping he would purpose, but married?"

"Yes, how's that for a trip? Proposed to, wedding and honeymoon all in one amazing vacation. It was a perfect dream come true!" Maryanne went into detail about the surprise event and how Mario pulled it off without her suspecting a thing.

"That is the most romantic love story I have ever heard. I am so happy for you."

"Thanks Wendy. It was really amazing. He is an incredible man, for sure. I am a very lucky woman."

"Visa Versa, I am sure. You are an amazing woman yourself."

"Thank you Wendy. Well…I guess it's time to get back down to business, then. Did you have any problems? I didn't get any calls, so I assumed you did quite well on your own."

"Well, I have had some action in the store. The Russian couple stopped in, and I explained to them that you were away, and they want to meet with you about your house as soon as possible. I am sure Joan will be contacting you."

"Yes, she is going to meet me for coffee in an hour. The first thing on my list is Hanna Michelle. I have to find out where she is, so I can arrange another meeting. She should be moved into her own place outside the hospital. I have to call the psychiatrist. Meanwhile I'll give the prospective buyers a call right away. I would be ecstatic if they purchase the house and we could move into the Valencia Manor sooner than expected. The contractor said he would start working on it as soon as I returned. Thanks again for doing an excellent job, Wendy. We can go through the rest of the business after

I make a few calls." Maryanne went inside her office and took out the list. She dialed the doctor in charge of Hanna Michele. He informed her that Hanna was living in a house on Bayard Avenue where two other women lived and a house mother was sometimes present. She took down the number and address. Hopefully she would be able to meet her in the morning. The next call was to Mr. Vasiliev, since the sale of her house was her next priority. She hit speed dial and it rang three times, when Borislav answered.

"This is Borislav Vasiliev. Can I help you?" He answered with his obvious Russian accent.

"This is Maryanne O'Donnell, now Maryanne Ramos, from Valencia Antiquities. I'm returning the call about your interest in my home."

"Miss O'Donnell. You are back. You had good journey, I hope. I still have interest in your home. Miss Bishop, take me to your house as you suggest, and I very much like."

"I am so glad you like it. Do you have any questions about it?"

"I would like to meet again and discuss."

"I can arrange that with Miss Bishop as soon as I am able to call her. I will call you and let you know when she is available. I am sure we can all meet soon. I'll get back to you as soon as I can, Mr. Vasiliev."

"I wait for call, Miss O'Donnell."

"Thank you. My last name is Ramos, now. I was married a few days ago in Ireland. Just so you know." She finished the call and her excitement was building about the possible sale. She called the contractor to let him know he could begin the renovation of Valencia Manor in the morning, as they had hoped. Everything in her life seemed to be falling into place. She set up a meeting with Don Prentiss, at four o'clock. Now it was time to meet Joan and give her the rundown on her wedding and set up a meeting with Borislav. She hit quick dial on her desk phone.

"Maryanne, it's you! I've been dying to hear from you. How was the vacation?"

"Amazing, wonderful and eventful." She snickered. She could not hold back the news. "I am now Mrs. Mario Ramos."

"Get out'a here! Are you kidding me?"

"I am serious. Mario proposed, set up a wedding and bought me a dress that you would not believe, all in one day! It came completely out of nowhere. I had no clue. I was hoping for a proposal but the whole package was a real surprise. The real deal."

Maryanne described the marvelous wedding vacation from beginning to end. Joan suggested a reception in a week or two but Maryanne wanted to settle in before she planned anything else. The sale of her home was a priority right now and Joan had made an appointment to discuss an offer from Borislav Vasiliev and his partner for Maryanne's home. The Colorado trip to Denver and Cripple Creek had been pushed ahead so they could finish up the loose ends before getting another contract going. Maryanne's primary objective was the Valencia renovation. Don Prentiss would meet her at the Manor in the morning for final preparations. She could sign the contracts at that time, and then he could begin the project. The next few weeks would be extremely busy and she would be depending on the expertise of her new associate, Wendy Griffin, who couldn't have come along at a better time. The day was coming to an end. Maryanne let Wendy off early while she made several more calls and caught up on a few loose ends. She gathered up her current work and filled the briefcase, calling Mario on the way home. She was still floating on residual clouds from the vacation of a lifetime.

Mario was pulling into the drive when she arrived. The two of them were quite exhausted and planned to retire early. Maryanne had to meet the contractor in the morning and Mario, with the help of the team had come up with tight leads in the jewelry heist. His morning would have to be early, as well. They turned in at ten o' clock and went right to sleep, no interruptions and no sex.

11

D on Prentiss was taking advantage of the luxurious shower massage he had installed several weeks ago, and planned to meet with Maryanne at the Valencia Manor. One of the benefits of being your own contractor, he claimed, was having the ability to make anything you want at a much less cost than paying someone to do it. His property was quite unique and filled with expensive decor at a fraction of the cost. He had practically rebuilt everything in his three-thousand square foot home for the price of materials. He had a half story upstairs, open to the sixteen-foot ceilings and huge cherry-wood beams that complimented the space. A balcony was at least twelve feet high with skillfully crafted wooden railings of exotic woods that he had imported for a job he had completed at a five-thousand square foot mansion. He often used or added extra materials when ordering such exquisite wood. The house was a masterpiece of his talent in wood-craft. The floors were done in African cherry-wood that was a special order. He created his dream home with mostly his own labor and it would ultimately be worth a small fortune.

After shaving, he brushed his teeth, his curly blonde hair loosely framing his face, still damp. He brushed it back in its usual style, leaving it to dry on its own. Soft curls adjusted perfectly every time, which made his daily ritual easier than most. He looked at his reflection, his blue eyes looking back at him. Don didn't make too much a fuss getting ready. After all, he was a natural, who didn't need much more than what was already there.

After drinking half a pot of coffee and scarfing down a croissant with cream cheese, he headed out the door, tool belt in hand. His truck was parked inside the oversized-garage, loaded with tools that most carpenters would only dream about. He had mentioned to Maryanne; 'the best of everything was the only way to go. If you want to do it well, use the best tools you can find.' It was true when it came to his work, which was second to none and his reputation preceded him.

Don arrived at the Manor and parked in the drive on the left for easy access to his tools. Maryanne arrived shortly and parked in front. She hadn't been to the Manor for a few weeks and sat in the car, momentarily observing the extraordinary, but extremely rundown edifice. Don stood at her window as she rolled it down.

"How do you like your Lexus?" Don peered inside, admiring its interior.

"I love it. Seems to have everything I need and then some." She emerged from the car, looking up at the house. "I'm anxious to begin this project and I am almost certain I may have my other house sold, so it's all coming along well. Hopefully this project will be finished in time. I wouldn't want to store my stuff and then have to move again,"

"I'm eager to begin. All we have to do is sign the final contracts. I'll need a check for the materials. I think ten thousand will be quite sufficient for the time being and then I can order everything so it will be here in plenty of time to start. Meanwhile I'll begin by tearing out walls and flooring that has to be replaced, while the plumbers and electricians repair and replace everything. I plan on starting in the morning if we can complete this today. Are you in agreement, Miss O'Donnell?"

"Yes, I can live with that. Have to stop at the bank and get the construction draw this afternoon. I can have it for you around five-thirty if you stop by the office. Bring the contract and we'll get started." She shook his hand and looked him straight in his bright blue eyes. Honest eyes, she thought, among other things she didn't want to focus on, like how attractive he was.

"Check out the rock, Don. I almost forgot to tell you. I got married while we were in Dublin." She donned a sheepish grin and flashed the rings proudly.

"Congratulations, Miss O'Donnell. Oops. What do I call you now? Not Miss, I'm sure. The rock is impressive. I would like to meet your other half sometime. He is a very lucky man."

"I'm Maryanne Ramos now, and thanks. Oh and don't forget to change the bid offer to my new name. Just so you know. I'll introduce you to Mario very soon. We'll have you over for dinner."

"Now a home-cooked meal I couldn't refuse. I hardly cook and when I do, it isn't that great. I can throw a steak or a burger on the grill, but that's about it. Maybe a can of soup or hot dog, would be more like it," he laughed heartily.

Maryanne chuckled and they walked toward the front entry of the Valencia. The door opened easily. He led the way. As they scanned the lower floor, she could tell he was excited to get started. They took a small tour around the Manor, and he explained as they walked, more of what he would be doing.

"So, what's your guess as to how long until I can actually move in? I want to move in as soon as my house sells, so I realize it will be far from complete when I do. But hopefully enough for us to move into part of the house. Think that's possible?" Maryanne eyed Don seriously.

"I think the electricity, plumbing, walls and clean-up will

take about two months or a little less. I have a good size crew to do that part. It's the most crucial. Once the walls are covered on the main floor, and the floors are repaired, you could probably move in. At that point, we will be working mostly upstairs. It won't be easy and there will be some dust and noise though, and I hope that doesn't bother you too much."

"I can handle it. We are working all day anyway, and I'll have you put some plastic around where I'm going to be staying to help keep out the dust. I am sure that will help."

"Definitely. I'll take care of that for you. I'll keep the crews working as fast as possible so I can get the job done in good time. If all goes well, we may even beat that deadline."

Maryanne would stop by the bank on the way to the office, to pick up the first draw on the construction bid and then work on preparing for the trip to Denver, while she waited for Don to show up at five-thirty. Maryanne's assistant remained at the office to take care of any other issues that may come up. Her day went as scheduled and the bid was complete. The Valencia would be a project in the morning.

Anxiety was taking center stage and Maryanne was hoping the offer on her house would be within reasonable expectation. Borislav would probably come in pretty low, but she would counter if it was ridiculous. She knew he loved the house and the fact that it was a little more secluded added to his interest. He would not have to do any upgrades since she had completed most of the work. Her hopes were high, and tomorrow she would get her answer when she met with Borislav, his partner Adriana Igmunov, and Joan. The meeting was set for ten-o'clock in the morning. It would be a long night and she may have to take a sleep aid with her surmounting anxiety.

12

D on Prentiss was preparing for what he believed to be
one of his best and most historical renovations. The
Valencia Manor was a challenge he was certainly
up to, and he would meet his crew at the address on Valencia
Drive by five-thirty in the morning. Six of his best men were
ready to tear into the project. His main plumber Jay Sevato
was ready and waiting when he arrived. His tool-filled van
had whatever was needed to get the job started. The chunky
red-faced man of about fifty was going through the back of
his van to gather his tools to begin the tear-out. It would be a
challenge he was up to. With his expertise, there wasn't much
Jay had not done.

His cabinet designer and finish carpenter, Thomas
Caradonna, a dark haired New Yorker in his early forties
would assist in the job. He spoke with an accent you couldn't
miss, and was another one that specialized and took pride
in the finished product. He had one young apprentice with
him, Sammy Wade, who helped as a framer and laborer in the
demolition and restoration of walls that had to be replaced.
Some of the framing would be upgraded and all of the wall
boards would be completely new. They would begin with
the main floor. Thomas Caradonna would design and build

custom cabinets that would make most people drool. His artistic ability when it came to designing was second to none. While all of that was being done, Frank Danluk and his crew would work at replacing electrical wiring through most of the house. He was a top notch electrician in his late fifties, and would direct the electrical renovation. He was the best, as far as Don was concerned. He would bring in an apprentice as soon as the walls were opened up. Don Prentiss had worked with a lot of so-called experts that couldn't touch Frank's expertise. Another laborer was available as a gopher and all around help. Fred Cantrell was one of the most ambitious workers Don had been fortunate enough to find and had kept him employed for six years. He was learning all the time and soon would know most of the many facets of his business. He had impressed Don and was moving up the ladder in qualifications as well as salary. Don had considered appointing him as a foreman, trainee and job organizer along with his regular duties. He often trained new laborers that Don had hired and could be trusted to think on his own. That was one of the biggest qualifications in Don Prentiss' business.

"Alright guys, you know the drill. Let's get inside and get this job started." Before the next hour had passed, it was amazing how much had been removed and hauled outside. The city had supplied the large construction dumpster so they could begin loading up the debris. They worked until noon and he called three for lunch break, then three more left when they returned. The dumpster was half full by four o'clock. It would definitely be full by the end of the day. A significant amount of rotted and deteriorated wallboard and two by fours had been removed from the first floor. A lot of framing was still well intact. Frank Danluk was moving quickly behind the crew, removing the outdated wiring as the walls were being ripped off. The first day was turning out to be a huge success and Don Prentiss was proud of his team for a job well done. He sent five guys home. He kept the plumber back to go over the bathroom plans before he left. When they had all gone, and Don stood inside the main grand room that was lit up with work lights hanging here and there, he walked around the house and double-checked everything as he did at the end of every day, because *at the end of the day*, it was all on him. No mistakes could be made or he paid the price, and can take the profit out of a job real quick. His cell rang.

"Hello. Don Prentiss here."

"Hello Don, its Maryanne O'Donnell, or I mean Ramos. Can't remember to use my new name, sorry." She laughed. "Just checking in to see how things are going over there."

"Things are going better than expected. I sent the guys home a little while ago and I'm making a walk-through. You would be proud of them. They worked their asses off, if you'll pardon the expression. Didn't mean to sound so crude. In this business, you don't talk to too many women and some of those words sneak in now and then." He felt a little embarrassed.

"I'm a big girl. I totally understand. Good job…I'll keep in touch. If you need me I'm always available. Just call my cell. Thanks Don."

"You're welcome, have a great evening. I am checking out now, and hope to get some sleep and start at dawn."

"Nite."

Don walked through the house one last time and then turned off the main source for power that they had connected from outside. The house went dark and his large flashlight was the only source of light. He walked toward the front door, and the strange and eerie noises began again. Startled as he was, with fear in high gear, his curiosity took center stage and he scanned the light around the room. The sounds weren't recognizable and they encompassed him, coming from the belly of the house, he thought. It gave him a scare but he remembered another incident that he had experienced in an older home several years ago in Denver. The source had never been discovered, but at times, it became quite distressing. He managed to finish that job without incident, but there had been some very weird occurrences, non-the-less. Focusing on that earlier experience, he tried to calm his fears.

"Hey. Anybody here? Or is it just me and you ghosts?" He spoke into the empty room. The noises subsided for a moment and then his flashlight went dark. He shook the light and rechecked the batteries by taking them out and using a small pen light to see. It wouldn't come back on, and the house was pitch black…that is until a white light appeared at the back of the room, where a dark figure stood, gaping. Don took a hammer off his tool belt and waited for the man to make a move. The house became filled with cold freezing temperatures and a wind seemed to push the door open and rush through the house. He backed up toward the door and it slammed shut again. He tried to open it without success. The man walked toward him and a few chairs flew across the room, one almost hitting him. He stood by the door, and took the hammer to beat on the knob, hoping to break it and unlock the door. It would not budge. A loud deep voice screamed through the house, demanding him to stop his work and not come back. Don spoke very loudly.

"I am not leaving and I am going to refinish this house, come hell or high-water! The only way I'm leaving this house is on a slab and that's not going to happen. You are nothing! You are a miserable spirit whose passing probably was a blessing for those you hurt. What is your name?" Don demanded.

"Never mind who I am. This is my domain and I will not leave. We will see who wins this battle. You cannot hurt me here in the spirit world."

"You haven't reached the spirit world yet, I am sure of that. If you had, you would not be so miserable. You are in a world of hell and misery; the place evil stays and dwells until it can be released. I know that much about evil entities. This is not my first parade," Don spoke back to the manifestation with force and confidence. This seemed to calm the entity down and it began to communicate in a less angry demeanor.

"You remember I can hurt you if I choose to." Another chair flew across the room, barely missing Don's head. And then the huge table began to move back and forth, making loud scraping sounds that carried throughout the Manor. The light was beginning to dim around the entity. Don knew he was losing his power.

"I'll continue my work here until it is complete. I mean no harm to you. You should know that. Leave here and let me finish this work. Do not plan on scaring me, because it will not work!" Don tried to speak forcefully hoping the entity would not bother him again. He had experienced a manifestation in Denver once before and the people who helped him clean the spirits had done the same in a similar situation. They said that if the entity tries to frighten a victim, and the victim succumbs, they feed off their fear and become stronger. It is all a matter of will, he thought. Don would stay strong and not appear to be afraid, even though he had his doubts about it. So far, it seemed to be working. He would come back and continue the job, regardless. First of all, he needed the money and second the house seemed to be pulling him in to its endless mystery. He could not leave if he wanted to. Somehow it had a hold on him. He did not realize it at the time.

"Time to go," he spoke softly to himself. Feeling his way out of the dining room and back toward the front door, he made it all the way without a problem, until he tried to open the door again. A hit or two more with the hammer and it gave way. The door would be repaired tomorrow anyway, he thought. When he pulled open the door, it flew open and almost knocked him down. It was pretty freaky, and he quickly scooted out the door and pulled it closed. He checked the door to see if it was going to lock and it was secure, surprising to him, since he had beat the hell out of the lock. He knew it was time to get the hell out of there. On the way home, he shrugged it off and laughed to himself. He hit the bed after a quick sandwich and glass of milk. He was asleep as soon as he hit the bed.

Morning came quickly. When Don awakened, it was barely five o'clock but he was up and out the door by five-thirty. He pulled into Starbucks for coffee and a breakfast sandwich on the way, and sped off to work. The guys weren't there yet. It was still early and the sun was beginning to show its lazy head over the mountains. He got out of his truck and a flock of blackbirds swooped down out of nowhere and began pecking at his head. He began flailing his arms and cussing at them.

"Get the fuck out of here. What the hell is this?" He grabbed his tool belt and took the key out of his pocket, ready for the door as he ran up the stairs and into the house which opened without a problem. He turned on the electrical supply for the temporary lighting and hurried into the house and it lit up like a Christmas tree. He slammed the door shut and it immediately opened, startling him and Frank walked in. He looked at Don and asked what was wrong, obviously picking up on the momentary fright. Don shrugged it off and said that nothing was wrong and walked away to begin the restoration project. The rest of the team followed one by one, filing through the door with one extra laborer that would be moving debris out as they demolished more of the interior. Don didn't mention the weird manifestations that had occurred last-night, or the birds this morning. He was going to play it out and see if it continued. He didn't want the team to quit at this stage of the game. He knew sooner or later he would figure it out. Of that he was fairly sure.

Today, Jay Savato would begin tearing out pipes that were out-dated, rusted and some that had been dangerously contaminated. The job would be major, but with walls coming off the framework, it would be much easier.

The teams worked on the lower floor most of the day. A

lot of progress had been made but much more was yet to be done. A water heater had been ordered and arrived, along with several other bathroom fixtures that Maryanne had carefully picked out weeks ago. The floors would be the next project when walls, electric and plumbing were finished. He loved the art of wood floors. He could get very creative with the patterns and different types of wood. One thing for sure, with his finish carpenter, Thomas Caradonna, it would be perfect or he didn't put his name on it.

Maryanne and Mario woke bright and early, preparing for another busy day. A meeting had been set up with the strange gentleman she knew as Borislav Vasiliev and his partner Adriana Igmunov. Hopefully the offer they were prepared to make on her house was something she could live with. Maryanne showered, dressed, put on make-up, kissed Mario and was out the door by eight o'clock and heading for her shop. Wendy had opened and was taking care of a customer when she arrived. Maryanne, made her calls, took the title and house information from the file cabinet for the meeting. She briefly waved at Wendy and was out the door, off to Bishop Realty and Joan's office. When she arrived the couple was already there and going in the front door. Perfect timing, she thought.

"Hello Borislav…Adriana. She offered quick hand-shakes and took a seat at the table, where Joan had placed water, coffee and bagels on the table, ready to serve. Everyone took coffee except Maryanne. She was already wired and anxious, hoping to accomplish the sale and she didn't want to appear any more nervous than she already was. She had plenty of practice selling her services to high-end clients when it was necessary, so she wasn't too worried about that. But coffee would add un-needed stress and she sure didn't need it now. Plenty of time for coffee, later.

Joan greeted them. "Good morning everyone. I'm glad we

could all get together today, and hopefully we'll come up with something you both can live with. We have all met, so no need for introductions, as it were." Joan was quite a professional broker and knew how to move a property and take a sale to the closing quickly. She was one of the best, and her reputation in the business was highly rated.

"Mr. Vasiliev and Miss Igmunov have made an offer which we will present to you, Maryanne. Here it is. You may read it through." She placed the offer on the table in front of Maryanne. When she came to the price offered in the contract, she hesitated, and then finished reading it before speaking to them.

"I appreciate the offer but I cannot accept it at this time. The offer is nowhere near where it needs to be. I would be losing money and I would rather keep it and rent it out than lose to that degree. I have put extensive upgrades into the house and I do not feel that those considerations were met. I am sorry." She handed the contract back to Joan and waited for a response.

"Mr. Vasiliev, I am sorry, but your offer is being rejected. Is there anything you would like to add before we go forward? She looked at Mr. Vasiliev, hoping for a positive response.

"I want to know if she has other idea of amount to consider other than original price." He looked toward Maryanne.

"Mrs. Ramos, would you be interested in a counter offer?"

"You remembered my new name, thanks. I even have trouble with that." She smiled. "Yes, I would like to make a counter offer, and can do so immediately, if you would like." She smiled at Mr. Vasiliev. "Is that okay, Miss Bishop?" She responded.

"Yes, it is quite alright. Would you like to fill out a contract here and present it to him now?"

"I would, if that is proper procedure. I can do that now."

"Here is a contract. Fill out the appropriate blanks and sign it, please." She placed the contract on the table and highlighted the blanks to fill in.

Maryanne filled in the blanks and signed the paper and handed it back to Joan. "Here you are. This is the lowest I can consider. If you cannot live with this, I am afraid we cannot do business, Mr. Vasiliev."

He took the contract and read the pertinent information and then looked down, letting out a big sigh. "I do not like price. It is too high."

Maryanne's heart sank in her chest, and she sat quietly not saying a word.

Mr. Vasiliev leaned over and talked to his partner and after a few minutes he spoke.

"However, we accept offer, if you take out closing cost."

"I'll split it with you. I agree to pay half. That's my final offer." Maryanne's face was serious and showed no emotion.

"Mr. Vasiliev, did you understand that?" Joan asked.

"Yes, I understand. We will take house. I pay cash only. Will that be fine?"

"Of course it will. We can do that as soon as we set up the title search and insurance, which will not be too long. Maybe in a week or so. Most of the paperwork is quite current, since I was the listing agent when she purchased the house. She will need thirty days to move out of house when the sale is final. Will that be acceptable?"

"Yes that is fine. I wait." He forced a smile.

"I'll need the down payment on the contract of ten-thousand dollars to start. Can you take care of this today? I could meet you at the bank to make the exchange and when the contract's completed, not long after, the house will belong to you. Maryanne was feeling relieved and glad she held out, taking a big risk. She had a gut feeling they wanted the house badly, and went for it all the way. Turns out she did the right thing and thankfully so. She had been on the edge of quoting a lower offer, which at the last minute she changed her mind.

Breathing a sigh of relief, she stood up and offered a hand-shake.

"I do that today. I meet at Chase Bank on Pearl Street at two o'clock. Is that good?"

"Yes, I'll meet you there, Mr. Vasiliev, at two o'clock sharp." Joan Bishop shook both their hands again and they left the office. Miss Igmunov followed behind Borislav like a demeaned servant.

"Maryanne, I think we have done it. I'll congratulate you when it's final," Joan jested.

"I am so excited to move into the Manor. The contractor, Don Prentiss is working hard to get it ready for us. Remember, it's me and Mario now." She kidded. "If it isn't done, Mario and I will stay in his condo until its ready. Not a big problem."

"I'm having a time getting used to my new name, Ramos, also. It may take some time to soak in. I've been single way too long"

"I'll try to remember as well, but forgive me if I forget," Joan reminded. Maryanne left for the office, pleased that it went well.

13

On the way home at five o'clock, Maryanne accompanied Sir Elton, to 'Yellow Brick Road.' Stress was diminishing, her house was almost sold and soon the Valencia would be revived to its historical beauty, as she had dreamed about since she first laid eyes on the Manor. She made her way into the kitchen where she could multitask with calls and make coffee at the same time. She dialed the contractor, hoping for more good news.

"Miss Ramos, I have been expecting your call. We have removed most of the walls from the main floor and crews have been working on the electrical replacement and plumbing before we go any further. Tomorrow, we will be tearing out more walls, upstairs. Things are going well. I think with the crew I have, we'll get this job done in good time for you to move into the lower right section of the mansion when you are ready to move out of your house. How is the sale going?"

"Fantastic. I will be closing in about a week or two and they said I had a month to move, so it will work out well. Would you mind if I come over tomorrow evening and take a look at what you've done?"

"Certainly not. Could you be there around six when we are shutting down the crew?"

"Looking forward to it, Mr. Prentiss." She placed her cell on the table and made a dash for the refrigerator to see what she could scarf up for dinner that would be quick and simple. After searching, she realized there was nothing to fix and thought very seriously about ordering a pizza.

"Hey you." Mario snuck up behind her and put his arms around her, and she turned around. "How is my beautiful wife?" Mario had come in without a sound, and had given her a bit of a scare.

"Don't sneak up on me like that, Mario. I'm still floating on clouds and don't want to spoil the after effects of our romantic getaway. Life is good. The sale is a go and we will be moving in less than a month."

"That's quick. I like it, but I am going to have to put my condo up for sale as soon as possible. Will you let Joan know?"

"Sure. I'll talk to her later this evening. Meanwhile, I hope you don't mind if I order in Pizza. I don't have a thing to eat in here and don't feel like going to the market."

"I'm good with Pizza, you know me. I like food, any kind your heart desires. Just don't give me liver. That's where I draw the line." He laughed.

Pizza and company. What better way to end a long and tiring day.

The first thing on Maryanne's mind was Hanna Michele. Dr. Davis had given her a number where she could be reached and she could not resist the urge to call and she dialed.

"Hanna's mail box, you know what to do. Thanks for the call." Maryanne was disappointed she didn't answer, but left a message and would wait for a return call. She was anxious to set up a meeting with Hanna as soon as possible, so she could catch up on her progress since she was released from the facility. Maryanne had just put the cell back in her purse when it rang. She quickly retrieved it.

"Hello, this is Maryanne." She didn't recognize the number.

"Hi Maryanne. It's Hanna."

"Oh that was quick, I just left a message."

"I saw that you called and I'm calling you back on the house phone. How are you?"

"I am great, Hanna. I called to see how you are doing and would like to meet up with you… maybe take you to lunch?"

"Lunch sounds great, but I start school next Monday so we would have to do it soon. I'm open. Hanna sounded cheerful and seemed anxious to see Maryanne. "How about tomorrow at one o'clock? Would that be too soon?" Hanna suggested.

"Perfect! I was hoping we could meet soon. I can make a run to Denver and pick you up. We can go anywhere you choose. You probably have some favorite places in the vicinity. Tell me where you'll be."

"My address is at the Victoria Apartments on Chase Street, number sixteen. Just take the Boulder Turnpike to Denver and use your GPS. It's pretty easy to find. I would love to see you, Maryanne." She explained the directions to Maryanne.

"I'll call when I'm on my way. See you tomorrow." Maryanne was thrilled.

"I'm so glad you can come. See you tomorrow. Bye Maryanne."

"Bye." Maryanne was looking forward to spending some quality time with Hanna and give them a chance to get to know each other better. Things were looking up, she thought, and then she began reflecting on the day when she saw Hanna at the institution during the time she was being rehabilitated. She had gone to visit her, and when Hanna greeted her, it was with a hidden sense of anger and bitterness. She remembered how Hanna had embraced her and whispered very strangely into her ear. "Hello Mother." The way she said it sent cold chills through her and it took Maryanne off guard. She couldn't understand why or what had brought it on. Hanna had changed from a lovable young woman in just a few days, into a bitter and vengeful stranger. It seemed to come out of nowhere. Hanna had looked at Maryanne with an ice cold stare that sliced into the very heart of her. Maryanne left the facility feeling very estranged and bewildered. The Doctor had told her it was nothing to worry about and that it was part of the process she was going through in opening up and finding out more about who she was and where she came from. He said it was natural that she felt distrust and suspicion in everyone at this point. After all that she had experienced in her life, he said it was no surprise. But why did she say Mother? Was she remembering her own Mother, who had apparently abused and or abandoned her? Was she someone who she lost and is angry at the world? All of these questions plagued Maryanne's thoughts. She would try to be patient and find the right time to ask her if she remembered those words. Maybe not at this meeting, but perhaps the next. She would play it by ear. She didn't want to ruin what seemed to be a great reunion for the two of them. Maryanne was still bound and determined to find out who Hanna's real mother was and why Hanna was left at the Manor in such a state. However, it was time to make last minute changes so she could spend the time with Hanna. Maryanne realized that the meeting with Hanna could alter the time of her meeting with Don at the Valencia Manor unless she met him later in the evening after she returned from Denver, so she called Don and changed the time to nine o'clock. He was fine with that and said he would leave the job after work and then come back at nine o'clock to meet her. Everything was set and her day would be filled. Now only a few last minute details had to be made.

Maryanne's assistant, Wendy had received a call from The Cripple Creek Historical Association. The plan was still in place to visit the historical mining town, and she was hopeful they would make the trip soon. Established in 1890 during the gold rush days in the Colorado Mountains, the town of Cripple Creek had become a historical landmark and since then, had been developed from a run-down ghost town to a thriving gambling enterprise. Not too far from Colorado Springs, at the base of Pikes Peak, the town thrived now on modern day casinos that were created by preserving the old buildings that were left standing during the famous days of gold mining. She was taking a client to visit the famous mining town, where he was hoping to purchase certain historical antiquities. Because of its preservation status in the Historical Society she was not sure he would be able to obtain such artifacts. It would be a fun trip though, and she looked forward to the excursion regardless of the outcome. She would put that on the back-burner for the time being.

Mario called to let her know there had been another murder near the Boulder History Museum on Euclid Avenue. A young woman had been attacked and left for dead. Mario told her that he would be late getting back to her and not to wait up. Maryanne had plenty of work to keep herself occupied. She was used to Mario getting called out late at night for his work. That's what he did and she was fine with it, just as he was fine with her leaving now and then on an excursion for her antique shop.

Her attention would focus on locating a few artifacts for a new client. That would fill her time and she could get caught up on her rest, and a new novel that she had begun recently that she had not found much time to read.

Mario stood over the brutally assaulted body of a young woman who had been viciously attacked near the Boulder Historical Museum. It had happened sometime during the early evening hours. She was found behind the building, near a long hedge that separated the building and the alley-way.

From what they had put together, she had been walking home from a friend's house after a small get-together. The house was only a block east of where her body was found. Her cell phone was recovered near the bushes where she had died. After calling the last number on the cell, Mario discovered a witness who had given them the information of the woman's whereabouts prior to her murder. Mario knew from the blood found around the body, that the victim had been left alive and tried to pull her-self across the lawn, and toward the street, where hopefully someone would find her. No one came. She died alone, sprawled in a twisted pose on the grass, eyes still open, as if she were looking at her attacker before she died. She had suffered a brutal beating and gashes were apparent on the right side of her neck. Not sure if a sexual assault had occurred yet, Mario called in a full team to obtain all necessary evidence before the ambulance took her pale, lifeless body away from the scene for an autopsy. There were a lot of unanswered questions and only one witness that said she had been at her house for a small get-together. She had a few drinks, according to the woman who identified her and left the house around nine o'clock. The crime scene had been roped off and a team, evidence van and two homicide detectives were working with Mario collecting evidence and talking to potential witnesses in the area. Another detective would be canvassing the neighborhood for anyone who heard or saw anything during those hours. It was going to be a long night.

Mario called back to let Maryanne know that he would be much later than he thought.

"Be sure to lock the doors and check the windows too. The killer is out there somewhere and we don't have a clue as to who it is. I'll be home when I get through the first layer of the investigation. It could be awhile."

"I checked the locks. I hope they find the madman who did this. It's horrible. I'll wait to hear from you and plan on turning in at a halfway decent hour tonight. I love you. See you later."

"Love you too. Gotta go. Talk to you when I get home."

Maryanne completed her final paperwork. After checking the windows and double-checking the doors. She called Joan to warn her, but Steve had already called earlier and filled her in on bits and pieces about the latest victim of the Slasher. Joan was in the process of double-checking her locks as well, since the call.

"Thanks for calling, Maryanne. I appreciate you thinking of my safety."

"I'll change the subject then and ask you a question, if you don't mind. Are you and Steve reconciling?" Maryanne couldn't hold back.

"No, we are speaking but I really am over him at this point. I can't deal with any more of the rage he seems to exhibit when the least problem comes up. He is receiving counseling and that is good, but I am not capable of handling the stress from that kind of relationship. The not knowing when he will go off on a rampage is so hard to live with. I will always love him, but I guess it's finally time to move on," Joan answered decisively.

"I am sorry it didn't work out for you, Joan. I know it's been very hard on you but I know time will heal your heart. I wish there was something I could do or say that would help, but these things are left to each of us to deal with in our own way and time. If you need a friend, you know I'll always be here for you."

"Thanks Maryanne. That means a lot to me. Talk to you tomorrow. Think I'll go check my doors and windows again. So many strange things going on out there these days."

"I know. I'm going to bed early as well, so I'll call you tomorrow, Joan."

"Good night." Maryanne watched the news and climbed into bed. Morning came quickly.

14

The front door opened and Mario came in as Maryanne had just emerged from the bedroom where she had completed her morning make-up ritual. He looked like he had been out on a two day binge. Sporting a two day shadow, his clothes wrinkled and unkempt, he threw his jacket over a chair next to the door and walked in.

"Oh my God you look awful Mario. I'll run a bath for you and you can take a relaxing soak. I'll make you something to eat and then you go to bed for a while." She kissed him lightly on the lips. "You don't smell too good either." She joked. "Been a rough night, huh?"

"Yes, it was pretty gruesome. I haven't seen that brutal a murder in a long time, if ever." He sighed. "Beautiful young college student. Some crazy bastard is out there runnin' free after committing such a heinous crime. I'm gonna find the son-of-a-bitch, if it kills me. I won't rest until I do." Maryanne had never seen Mario so upset about a crime. But then those kinds of crimes were not a usual occurrence here in Boulder. He took a seat at the kitchen dinette and she poured him a coffee. He sat there staring at the wall…thinking. Thinking about Julia Bennett, lying in a pool of blood, her neck sliced near the jugular vein. The more he thought about it, the more he realized there wasn't really much blood at the scene. It may not have been the cut that did her in. If she had died from loss of blood, it sure wasn't evident. He was anxious to get the forensic reports to determine what actually killed her. There was something very strange about this one. He needed rest so he could think more clearly. It appeared that the killer managed to clean up the scene quite meticulously. He had ordered the detectives and evidence team to check the perimeter of the crime scene and all garbage cans in the vicinity before he left. This was not a run of the mill kind of murder and there were a lot of unusual, unanswered questions.

Maryanne had drawn the bath, turned the bed down and returned to the kitchen. "Mario, eat something, and the bath is ready for you. You'll feel better when you get some rest." She had heated a bowl of potato soup and set a roast beef sandwich in front of him.

"Thanks hon. I appreciate it. He picked up the sandwich, took a few bites and sipped on the soup. It was too late for breakfast and Maryanne had planned to see Hanna Michelle, so she made a quick lunch for him, instead.

"Not too hungry. I'll hit the bath and try to catch some zees. Have to go back to work today later on. A lot of work to do on this one." His face sullen, he kissed her on the cheek and left the room.

Maryanne was worried about him. She left Mario to sleep and prepared for the trip to see Hanna Michelle. Maryanne collected her files, picked up her brief-case and headed for the store to touch base with Wendy, who was covering the shop. By eleven o'clock, she inserted a cd into the slot and was serenaded by Chicago and Little River Band as she sped along the Denver Turnpike. The GPS was set. In about an hour, she would be having lunch with Hanna, who had been released from the facility and staying in her own apartment. This would be the first time she would actually meet her alone without guards and matrons present. Hanna would be free to come and go mostly as she pleased. Maryanne wanted to take advantage of this time with Hanna, as she would be starting school next week and there would be little, if no time to visit, except week-ends off and on. She felt confident she and Hanna were on their way to a closer relationship. Mulling over all of her plans, she sped along the interstate. The Valencia was under renovation and Hanna was starting school. The only thing that worried her was Mario. He was embarking on a new and troubling case that had put him in a very depressing state of mind. She had never seen him quite so unsettled but imagined a scene like the one he witnessed must have been horrifying. She would try to help him in whatever way she could. The voice from the GPS interrupted her thoughts.

A clinical female voice instructed her get off on Federal and go east until she reached Clay Street where she turned, and it was only a few blocks from there. *Easy when your GPS does all the work,* she thought. She parked in the lot next to the Victoria Apartments, climbed out of the car, looked around and stretched. Almost to the front door she dialed Hanna.

"Hi Maryanne. Where are you?" Hanna sounded excited to hear that she had arrived.

"I'm right at the front door of the Victoria. Which one is it?"

"I'll be right down. Maryanne opened the door and Hanna was fast-tracking down the stairs to meet her.

Hanna ran and threw her arms around her, giving her a strong hug. "You're here! I'm so happy to see you." Hanna's face showed such exuberance; like she had never seen.

"Me too. I've been counting the minutes and finally you are out and on your own. Now we can spend time together and get better acquainted. I'm so happy things are going well for you Hanna."

"Thank you, I really like it here. I feel like a normal person again. The two room-mates are quite nice. When we get back from lunch I'll introduce you. They'll be back by then. Well I'm ready to go if you are."

"Okay then, where are we going?"

"It's not far. You like Italian. I remember you telling me that once when you visited me at the facility. I found a great place not far from here." Hanna brimmed with smiles.

"Come on, we'll take my car." They climbed in and Hanna gave directions. Maryanne was very comfortable with Hanna. She had certainly made a change since she had visited her in the past. This was the best Maryanne could have hoped for. The restaurant was only three blocks away.

"It's called Spagos Ristorante," Hanna pointed at the sign.

"That means spaghetti in Italian." Hanna interpreted, giggling.

"Brushing up on your Italian, are you?" Maryanne smiled.

"Well-not so much. A little, I guess. I have been busy preparing for school and getting the apartment set up. It's fun…living here and meeting new friends and all. I think it will be good for me, Maryanne."

"As long as you are happy. That is my main concern. If there's anything you need, let me know and I will do whatever I can to help."

She parked the car in the lot and they went inside the smartly decorated restaurant. It was very typical Italian décor, and the music was perfect. Maryanne was quite impressed. After a hostess seated them, they went through an appealing menu that made it difficult to choose.

"I give up, you've been here…you choose. There is so much to pick from and I love all of the foods listed." Maryanne set the menu down and looked at Hanna smiling.

"I suggest the Spaghetti and Meatballs. It really is their specialty, thus the name, I presume." She giggled again.

"Good choice, Hanna. I was actually leaning toward that. Would you like to have a Caesar Salad, as well?"

"Perfect."

A middle aged woman who Hanna introduced as the owner, Rosaria, came over to greet Hanna. She was very pleasant, and asked if Maryanne would like a glass of wine. Of course Maryanne had to decline, since she was driving back to Boulder in a while.

"Now, I am interested to know more about your school," Maryanne questioned Hanna.

"I am so excited. I am very good at art and design, so I am discovering. As you know, I decided to study for a career in interior design. It is only an eighteen-month program and I can intern in one year. I would love to help in designing the Valencia Manor. I have so many ideas that you may want to hear." Hanna's exuberance filled the room.

"That would be such a helpful and exciting challenge for you. Of course, I would love to include you on the final décor. That way it would have a much more personal touch along with its historical theme." Maryanne beamed.

"Here are your salads and bread, ladies, with a spicy garlic olive oil dip." A young male server brought two crisp Caesar salads and a hot plate of bread wrapped in a checkered napkin and placed them on the table.

"Bread; My all-time weakness. Especially hot and Italian." Maryanne smacked her lips. "Yum." She started laughing, "Now that didn't come out right, sorry."

"It was pretty funny, though." Hanna joined in her laughter and then she snatched up a chunk of the crisp bread and tore a piece for dipping. "Yummy. Dig in, Maryanne." She still had a lingering giggle over Maryanne's last comment.

Spaghetti came shortly, and Hanna was right. It was second-to-none, as far as Maryanne was concerned. They thoroughly enjoyed the meal and conversation. It was the best she could have hoped for. On the way home, she was already planning the next visit, and was pleased Hanna had come around. All she could think of now was Hanna's future and making sure it turned out in the best possible way.

They enjoyed almost two hours of laughing, good conversation and food. It was an exceptional visit. When they returned to the apartment, Hanna introduced her to the young women who shared her space. They appeared to be intelligent and well-mannered young women. The apartment was incredibly decorated and when complimenting them on the décor, the room-mates, Sherry and Carla told her that Hanna had done the decorating. Maryanne knew she had a knack for design after seeing what she had accomplished with the small apartment and very little money.

It was soon time for Maryanne to leave. Hanna gave Maryanne another strong hug, and thanked her for coming. It was great to finally gain the trust of the young woman that no one knows from whence she came. '*Hanna Michelle Smith*', Maryanne was thinking, '*A twist of fate had brought the two of them together in a bizarre episode at Mysteerie Manor, where Maryanne had become Hanna's victim. Now, everything had changed and they were closer than Maryanne had imagined they could ever be.*'

Maryanne hit the Turnpike and headed for Boulder in a much better frame of mind than she had left with. It was almost four-thirty and she still had work to do at the store, make dinner for Mario and meet with Don Prentiss at nine o'clock. She arrived home around six o'clock, and a red sun was on its way to setting soft against the mountains. She loved this time of year. Even though it was very cold, Maryanne appreciated the crisp mountain air and watched it, as it made little white puffs when she exhaled.

After stopping at the store to check in with Wendy, preparing dinner and Mario's absence again due to the case, she made a few phone calls and prepared to meet the contractor at the Valencia. The night was pitch-black and the moon was only a sliver. She approached the Manor as it stood staunch and mysterious against the night sky. The cold air hung suspended in foggy mist, from the freezing of particles when the sun went down. Don's truck was parked in the drive, and she pulled up next to the curb in front. He was sitting in his truck with the interior light on, and she could see that he appeared to be reading when she approached the pickup. He opened the window and she leaned inside. He had been studying a floor-plan of the Manor.

"Jump in. Take a look. You can get a better idea of what some of the changes will be."

"Sure. Love to." Maryanne climbed inside his Dodge pick-up and he flipped her overhead light on. He showed her the drawings and they went inside the Manor to complete his interpretation of the interior.

The room was cold, as the furnace had not yet been completely installed. White puffs of breath blew out from their mouths as Don guided her through the drawings of his exceptional vision. Maryanne buttoned up her jacket, shivering from the cold, but loved every minute of it, regardless.

"Check it out. Here's the great room. That's where the beams will be placed to accent the ceiling. The chandeliers will stay, obviously, but I am having them reconditioned. They will look just like new. There's the arch we are enhancing, where the room expands into the dining area." Don was excited about his work and she was catching on. She was even more anxious now to see the finished product.

Her eyes reflected the lights that were hanging here and there. She was filled with enthusiasm as she walked through the main floor while he explained to her; his mission. She was astounded at what had already been accomplished.

"You work fast. The place is coming along nicely. Even though it's freezing in here, I want to see all of what you've done so far.

"Thanks. I try. Got a good crew. That's half the game." He looked down at her and smiled. Blue eyes that were almost irresistible and a smile that most women would revel in, Maryanne found him so appealing, but then she climbed back into reality and they continued with the tour.

When he had finished describing the highlights of his envisioned work, they were ready to examine the upper floors. Lights had been placed expediently for the crews and seeing was not a problem. He had already begun replacing sheet-rock on some of the walls downstairs but they hadn't quite started on the upper floors. It would be a few days, he explained and they would begin the second floor and then the attic rooms. She would soon begin to realize her dream of residing in this grand old Manor. Hardly able to contain her excitement, Don continued to explicate the project, room by room. When they got to the door of the first attic room, a light was visible in the upper landing. Don led the way as they climbed to the top. Stairs still creaking, he assured her they were safe. Inside the small chamber, where a black window used to shroud light, he had replaced it with a new pane. She looked down at the yard, where the exquisite antique fountain and statues loomed in the darkness. Only light from the moon illuminated the eerie setting. She got a cold chill. A rocking chair in the corner began to rock slowly, and she stumbled back away falling into Don's arms.

"I'm so sorry," she apologized. "Let's leave this place. I'm cold and it's kind of creepy, don't you think?"

"Yes…a little. C'mon, let's get the hell out of here." With that, he took her arm and escorted her to the door, down the stairs, and finally out of the Manor. He turned off the main switch to the lights as they left the house. Don walked her to the car and opened her door. She took one more look at the Manor and pointed up toward the attic room.

"Look, there's a light inside the room…there. Do you see it?"

"Yes. It looks like a candle. Very weird things happen here, and I am beginning to realize what you said is true. I think it's time for us to leave, though. I'll talk to you tomorrow." She thanked him and hurried off to her home, realizing she had not even called Mario. Preoccupied most of the day, she felt half-guilty and she finally dialed his number on the way home.

"Hello Maryanne. Where are you? I was just getting ready to call you and the phone rang; it's you. Everything all right?"

"Yes… I'm fine. A lot has happened today. I met with Hanna and it went extremely well. I am just leaving the Valencia for home. Where are you?"

"Just getting off work. Long day. It's gonna be a tough case. I'll see you when I get there."

"See you in a little while." Mario had just walked inside when she pulled into the drive. He stood by the door and waited for her. They embraced.

"Good to be home." Maryanne set her briefcase on the table and sunk into the pillow laden sofa. "I'm exhausted but I want to hear about your day and if you've had any luck on the case."

Mario sat next to her, moved his arm around her and leaned back, also waning from a trying day.

"Not much yet to go on. They picked up some DNA on the body and a few belongings, but haven't finished testing it. There are some clues, but at this time, I'm not allowed to divulge anything. He's still out there somewhere and I want to be there when we get him." Mario was still enraged by the horrific crime and intended on solving it quickly. The stress showed weary as it masked his face.

"I'm glad you spent time with Hanna and apparently it was positive, from your call."

"Yes, she has made a hundred percent turn-around from then and now. We had a wonderful chat at lunch. She starts school Monday at a Junior College, to study Interior Design.

I am so impressed at her progress. You would be amazed." Maryanne's eyes emitted the contentment that was a long time coming.

"I have an early morning, so think I'll turn in right away." Mario was ready to hit the bed.

"Sure you don't want a snack? I'll heat up the leftovers from earlier, if you do."

"No, I'm good. Thanks sweetie." He gave her a peck and took off for the shower.

"You coming?" He asked with an inviting smile.

"Yes, give me awhile to catch up on my computer data and I'll be in." She opened her laptop and closed a current work file and made a few notes for tomorrow's schedule. She was definitely ready for a good night sleep.

"Get in here, I missed you. We're becoming strangers. Let's make better use of our time." He stepped out, and she was excited as his muscular body stood wet and inviting. He took her arm and pulled her inside the shower where they played out a romantic rendezvous and then climbed into bed. Sleep took hold quickly.

15

Maryanne woke during the night, long before dawn. She had been restless, with haunting nightmares that were on replay. She gave in and went to the kitchen for a cold drink of water and stood by the window looking over the yard, while the cool liquid quenched her thirst. A sudden rustling and a flock of large birds swept down onto the back yard and landed. There must have been at least twenty or more. They looked like Ravens and not Blackbirds, as had been reported recently. Maryanne was familiar with Ravens since she was a young girl and had completed a biology project on a pair of them, so she knew more than most. The yard was covered with the beady eyed Aves. She opened the door and they immediately took flight, causing a loud whirr as their wings flapped against the eerie moon-lit sky. A ghostlike -figure appeared in the yard when the birds ascended into a black cloud of feathers. A tall, white-haired, man shrouded in darkness, stood in the yard, his beady eyes peered; shining, glowing and frightening. She tried to communicate with him, but unable to speak, she cautiously backed away and ducked into the house. The dark visitor seemed to vanish into a mist and was gone. There were no signs of the stranger or the birds. She pushed the door closed with a forceful slam and locked the deadbolt, but couldn't help looking again through the window into the yard. It had become quiet and still, as if it were nothing at all. She was thinking of Poe's famous poem, The Raven, and a phrase in the poem came to her thoughts; '*Quoth the Raven*', "*nevermore.*"

"What are you doing up at this hour?" Mario startled her.

Maryanne turned around in panic, and a mask of shock had crawled over her pallid face.

"Hey, it's me, Maryanne. What's wrong? It's Mario."

Maryanne stood frozen with fear until Mario put his hands on her shoulders. She was absorbed in a nightmare, colliding with reality. When she recognized Mario, she came to her senses. It was not the dark stranger.

"I had horrible nightmares and got up for a drink of water, and when I looked out into the yard;"…she went on to describe the ghoulish man and the birds. She had calmed down but was still shaking from the abhorrent aberrations that she had experienced; not sure whether it was real or her primed imagination. Mario was bewildered as he glanced into the yard to see that it was quiet and no one was apparent. Maryanne began to question it as well, thinking she might have been sleepwalking. Mario agreed. He escorted her to bed and she climbed into the pile of covers that had been mangled during her bizarre nightmares. He pulled the covers up around her and she quickly descended into a deep sleep. He was quite surprised, because Maryanne was a light sleeper and once wakened it was usually difficult for her to relax.

By then it was almost dawn and Mario brewed coffee, and plucked the paper from the front porch, after he heard its proverbial thud when it was thrown against the door. A story about Jennifer Bennett's murder had taken top billing, since the young coed had been killed in a savage act of brutality only days ago. It was on Mario's top precedence. He vowed to capture the brutal killer, whatever it took. Mario had been working close with homicide and he was going over the current research on his laptop, when Maryanne entered the room looking like a *'second hand rose'*.

"Morning." She yawned as she picked a mug off the hook, filled it, and sipped the morning pick-me-up.

"And to you as well. I thought you'd sleep a little longer after the disturbing visit from your unwelcome guest." Mario tried to make light of it.

"I was probably sleepwalking, though I have never done it before. Or at least I don't think I have."

"I hope it was only your imagination, and not a recurrence of the Valencia ordeal." Mario responded dubiously.

"Hmmm. Very strange." Maryanne looked out the window and then opened the door, ambling into the yard.

"Checking out the yard just for the hell of it," she explained to Mario. Donning a pair of fuzzy slippers, her favorite robe and hair mangled to the extreme, she shuffled across the porch and down the stairs. There on the railing of the deck, was an unusual amount of bird droppings and several black feathers, of which she collected a few. She walked across the yard where many more feathers and bird-droppings dotted the landscape. She was positive they were of Raven derivation. Hurrying back up the stairs, she pushed her way into the kitchen, holding the feathers.

"Where do you suppose these came from?" She waved them proudly in front of his face.

Mario looked in astonishment. "I should have gone outside to check. Now I feel like an idiot, not believing you. I thought you said it was a nightmare."

"Apparently not. They were on the deck and around the yard. There's a ton of bird crap there too. I've never seen that before. Guess I'll have to do some checking just to see if any more unusual bird activity has been reported in Boulder, recently."

Mario went outside to witness the strange setting. "Hmmm. Very odd. I am baffled at this."

"Well, Mr. Detective, more for you to ponder?" She giggled. "But it is very weird and I am confused as hell now. I think I am going to call Vivian Gilbreth. I'm sure she can give me some insight."

"Who?"

"The psychic. Don't you remember? Vivian Gilbreth. She's the woman who came in and performed her rituals to help clear the spirits from the Valencia. She's quite informed about bizarre, paranormal activity and I don't have a clue. Do you?"

"No, can't say that I do. But why a psychic?"

"Why not? Got any other suggestions of anyone who wouldn't think I was losin' it?" She questioned.

"Well, now that you put it that way, I see what you mean. Go ahead and ask her. She is as good as anyone I guess." He scratched his head and smiled. "I sure don't want going through any more of the unnatural phenomena that the Manor was exhibiting."

"You're tellin' me. I am so, not wanting that to happen. I'll give her a call and see if she can put some light on it. Who knows? She may have a perfect explanation. I hope so, anyway. The strange, dark, man is enough to rattle anybody's chains."

"Maryanne toasted some frozen waffles and they had a quick breakfast. Mario headed to the shower and she followed. After a little romp and a lot of steam, they emerged from their liquid love-nest and prepared for another long day.

New clues had been unveiled concerning the murdered coed, and Mario combed through the data. It seemed the DNA did not match with anyone in the system. The forensic detective met with Mario and said she had been beaten with some kind of wood club, possibly a bat. During the struggle her throat had been cut with an unusual tool or rough instrument. It did not resemble anything they had ever seen before. She actually died from blood loss, but what did not make sense is that the blood left at the scene was hardly enough to die from. Someone would have had to drain her blood, in a questionable manner, or carried her from another location where the blood was let. He had teams working non-stop, searching remote areas that could have been strategic to such a crime and nothing had turned up. Mario questioned why would they take her somewhere, kill her and bring her back to the place they abducted her? None of it made any sense. Plaster footprints had been taken at the scene. There were no fingerprints other than the girl and a few others which they had already identified and cleared. Prints had been taken from her bag and the cell phone. They matched the girls that were at the small get-together on the night she was killed. They had strong alibis, since the parents and a brother were home all night. Nothing unusual was found and she was not raped. Not raped, or robbed. Brutally beaten and killed. So what was the motive? Jealous boyfriend? That didn't make sense either. Mario was putting a list of suspects together.

Meanwhile, the Exquisite Jewelry heist was taking a back seat to this brutal crime. He put Officer Montrose in charge of that case. He had already worked with him on the case, so he already knew the drill. Mario would focus on Jennifer Bennett's killer. He would not rest until he solved the crime. Steve appeared at the door of his office, held up the search warrant and gloated.

"I got the warrant from the Judge Grant, so you can interrogate the wacko-janitor at the museum. He has a rap sheet a mile long. Can't figure out why anyone would hire someone with that kind of history without checking him out better." Steve was anxious to get the case moving. At this point everyone in the department was on full alert.

Maryanne made the phone call to Vivian Gilbreth, the

psychic medium, and she agreed to pay a visit the following evening. Maryanne was lucky to call her when she did. The Psychic had planned to leave for Winchester, England in one week for a yearly convention of psychics, mediums and parapsychologists from all over the world. She would be gone for ten days while attending workshops where she would be studying, working and conferring with other psychics and mediums. Mrs. Gilbreth was looking forward to the experience but she agreed to oblige Maryanne's request. She looked forward to returning. Maryanne was pleased to have her aboard again, even if it was temporary. She was available for two days, prior to her attending the convention. Maryanne was primed for her visit and informed Mario and Joan.

Maryanne picked up Vivian at the Hilton Hotel. She was pleased to see Maryanne, and the feeling was mutual. Maryanne filled her in on the bizarre episodes of unnatural phenomenon that had taken place in the last several weeks. The Raven incident was right up her alley. She already had some ideas. As for the other activity, she wanted to visit the Valencia again to get a feel for the current state of activity there. There was a lot to do in a short time. Maryanne took Vivian to her home so she could get a feel for the house. When Vivian entered the house, she picked up some vibrations that were quite uncomfortable and very unusual. She felt a strong force trying to invade the space, but felt that whatever the entity, it was having trouble penetrating.

"This phenomenon is not unusual in that it can be stopped, but it takes strong will and perseverance," Vivian explained. "I can feel the presence but it cannot come through unless I invite it in. I can summon bad entities and if they are willing to come through, as they will in most of my cases, we can make some headway here. At least find out why it's here and what its intentions are. Where is your new husband? I like Mario. You did well." She smiled.

"Mario should be here soon. He had to work late. Thanks for the kind words, Vivian. So should we start now or wait for Mario?"

"Was Mario here when the activity was happening?"

"No, in each case I was alone. I hope I'm not imagining it all." Maryanne had a bewildered look on her face.

"Then let's give it a whirl and see what we get. Do you have some candles?"

"Hmmm. Oh, yes I do. In the kitchen. Received them for a gift and never used them." Maryanne brought the candles and Vivian set them in a circle, on three tables in the living room area. She lit each one and turned off the lights.

"I will meditate to contact the entity. If it was truly from the other side, I will more than likely be successful. If not, I could get messages from outside entities that might help guide me. A spirit guide, so to speak…but not always. I'll give it a try. Sit down on the sofa and relax, Maryanne." She sat back into the sofa, quiet and morose. Vivian shifted a chair to the center of the room, sat down, inhaled deeply, and then exhaled very slowly. Her hands, placed on the arms of the chair, palms up, she continued deep and slow breaths. Maryanne sat in silence, watching…listening. Vivian seemed to be slipping into a trance. She had not moved but her eyes were closed and her breathing had slowed down. Maryanne watched, calm and curious, not missing a thing. Distant crying began to emanate from inside the house. It sounded far-away, yet felt so close. A breeze whispered through the room, causing the candles to flicker. Vivian began to speak in a man's voice. Maryanne became frightened and anxious, leaning back against the sofa, heart beating loud in her chest.

"Why are you calling me?" The deep voice came from Vivian. "I don't want to be on the earth plane." It spoke again through the medium. He seemed to be upset at being summoned.

"Why are you calling me?" He pleaded through Vivian.

She answered him in her own voice. The entity continued to communicate with the Psychic. She then began to ask a spirit guide to assist with the communication.

"Please spirit guide, help me to understand what entity is bound here and why it is entering this home. What does it want? They are victims of harassment from a spirit who has left this plane and who has not yet crossed over. What does the spirit need from this place?" Vivian was becoming agitated and began deep and heavy breathing. Then the voice spoke again.

"I may be able to help you, but if I do, I need your help to cross over. I want to go on, and something is holding me back." The strange man's voice kept speaking through the Psychic.

Vivian returned to the conversation in her own voice. "I can help you, but you must tell me who you are, who is entering this home and for what purpose."

"My name is Fredrick Holmes. I died in nineteen seventy-three. I was a friend, mentor, and attorney of John Farthington, and I helped him with an adoption. I was killed in an attempted robbery after the adoption was completed. One of the spirits is a young woman who wants to communicate with someone in the house." He spoke through Vivian. "She wants to warn her about someone who is a possible threat. That person is from this world. He is dangerous and she must be vigilant and careful. I cannot identify him, but only warn her of the danger. He is out in the evening hours and very early morning, but spends most of his days inside. On occasion, he is out during the day. He has been inside this home and is looking for something she is connected with. As I said, he is from this world and not from the other side."

"Thank you for helping me, and I will do what I can to assist you in reaching the other side."

"I will perform a ritual that will help you to move on." Vivian began to recite a prayer ritual, which was sometimes helpful in such cases.

"Since you are willing to cross over, you must pray with me

and the catalyst will be your will. God knows what is in your heart and you must ask for his help." The man did not return to the room or into Vivian's body. She was confident that he moved on to the other side.

Hearing the words of warning through Vivian, coming from the spirit, Maryanne questioned her about its validity.

"Should I be afraid?"

"I would be vigilant, though it's not to say for sure. I am going to research the name Fredrick Holmes and see what I come up with. I am sure there is a connection here with John Farthington, the former owner of the Valencia Manor."

"I have never read or heard anything about John Farthington adopting a child. It was not ever mentioned by Mrs. Dirkshire. This Valencia family tree is beginning to bear some very strange fruit. I think there is much more to uncover about the Valencia Manor and its past."

"I'm going to make some hot chamomile tea and we'll relax and discuss the matter, if you don't mind." Maryanne put on the tea-kettle and Vivian took a seat at the kitchen table.

"You are becoming thick-skinned when it comes to paranormal entities, Maryanne." The Psychic sipped tea and set the cup in its saucer, eyeing Maryanne with a portentous smile.

"It's a good thing, though. The less you are skeptical and afraid, the more you will be able to perceive and sense entities that are not on this plane. It's the process in which most psychics begin development."

"That's good to know…I guess," Maryanne answered dubiously.

"It's definitely not a bad thing, Maryanne. However far it develops is up to you. Just take it for what it's worth and let it happen. We all have the ability to a certain extent, but busy lives have taken over most people's sensory capabilities. If you ignore it, as in any skill, it becomes dormant and stays buried in the subconscious. Those who practice developing their abilities become more aware and able to connect to the spirit world, or the other side. Some cannot ever get there. It depends on the individual, and there is so much to learn. I have been studying and developing for most of my adult life and have connected many people to loved ones who have moved on. It has been most rewarding. I am working steadily to improve my abilities and that is what perpetuated my interest in the convention at Winchester, England. I am looking forward to the experience." Vivian held up her tea-cup and Maryanne filled it once more.

"Vivian, there is another question that puzzles me. There were at least three incidents where Blackbirds or Ravens were involved. Do you know of any significance to the birds?"

"There have been many paranormal activities that involve birds, especially Ravens and crows. I wonder if there is a connection to anyone from the Valencia." When I return from Winchester, I will definitely look into that possibility. I am rather tired now and must leave for the hotel."

Maryanne's phone rang. Mario informed her that he was working late on the recent murder of Jennifer Bennett. A recent lead had generated new developments and he wanted to follow up. Maryanne hung up and turned to Vivian.

"It's Mario…working late on the Jennifer Bennett murder case. He said there were some new leads. He's like you, in that he really gets into his work." Maryanne smiled at Vivian. "Why don't you stay here tonight? You know I have a spare room with all the accommodations that you need."

"It's an invitation I can't refuse. For one, I don't like the idea of you being alone tonight, with Mario gone, and I am a little tired as well. Sure, I appreciate your hospitality." Vivian Gilbreth had decided to stay.

"Wonderful. I'm happy to have you and I really don't want to be alone." Maryanne's face broke into a wide smile. "I'll fix something to eat and you can use the room on the right." She pointed out the room. "Come on, I'll show you." She led

Vivian into the room, showed her the bathroom and placed a set of towels on the dresser. "Anything you need is here. I'll go prepare a light snack since it's late, and you can freshen up, if you like."

"Thanks dear. I'll be out in a few to help you."

Maryanne went through the refrigerator and rustled up a roast chicken she had purchased the day before, and chopped lettuce, cucumber, carrots, tomato, avocado and onion to create a beautiful fresh salad. Chicken breast and boiled eggs topped the impressive, green creation. She served whole grain flatbread on the side, toasted. A glass of Merlot was placed in front of each plate and they enjoyed dinner and conversation until they could not keep their eyes open.

"It was absolutely wonderful Maryanne, and the salad dressing was incredible. I saw you whip it up. I'd like to have to have the recipe." Vivian picked up the plates and took them to the sink.

"Certainly. I'll copy one for you before you leave in the morning," Maryanne answered.

"Now, you go freshen up and do what you have to do and I'll finish cleaning up, Maryanne." Vivian gave her a friendly pat on the back and indicated for her to leave the kitchen

"Thanks Vivian, but I'll help, and then we can turn in early and get a good night's rest. I'm sure we could both use it." Half an hour later, they were sleeping soundly. Mario returned home at three a.m., crawled in beside Maryanne and she didn't even stir.

16

The most sadistic murder case Mario had ever encountered was consuming most of his waking hours. He left at seven o'clock, before Maryanne or Vivian woke. Maryanne found a sweet love-note on his pillow when she climbed out of bed at eight. After a shower and coffee, Vivian wanted to visit the Valencia before she left. Maryanne was excited to return to the Manor. Normally the contractor worked at least six hours on Saturday, but he had to take the day off and they would be alone. Maryanne hadn't been there for five days and knew a lot had been done, and she was anxious to see the results. When they arrived at the Manor, they stood in disbelief at what had been accomplished. The roof work had begun and a lot of the exterior had been revived. Don Prentiss was working at a very fast pace. Maryanne led the way and Vivian followed as they climbed the renovated rock stairway to the front door. The once ramshackle Manor was beginning to take on a very different appearance. It was beginning to resemble the pictures when the Manor had been constructed in the early nineteen-hundreds. Both Maryanne and Vivian were amazed at the changes. The door opened without a hitch. When she pushed on the door it no longer wailed its usual melody of groans and squeaks, as it had in the past. The overhang on the portal had been refurbished extensively. It was a marvelous transformation from its decayed and decadent state just a few weeks ago. Maryanne was very surprised that he had completed so much on the exterior. She stuck her head in first, out of habit. Carefully, she moved into the room, Vivian close behind. They were ready for anything. Light from the new windows streamed across glossy cherry-wood floors. A far cry from their previous condition.

"You have chosen an excellent contractor. The place is beginning to look like new again. I am very impressed at the work he has done," Vivian complimented.

"Thank you, I am very fortunate to have found him. His reputation is well earned," Maryanne responded.

"Have you picked up anything yet? Any spirit activity?" Maryanne questioned.

"No, I haven't felt any unknown vibrations yet. Can you turn the lights on?"

"Oh, I guess I can, let me see. I had almost forgotten that he had repaired the electrical wiring and fixtures," Maryanne giggled and went to the new wall-plate that had been installed next to the main entry. She flipped two switches and the room came alive with streams of light from stunning chandeliers that were more impressive than she could have imagined. Hanging crystals glistened and reflected sparks of light that moved across the room, painting patterns along the walls and high up into the ceiling that towered above them. Maryanne scoped out the room, not missing anything. Don Prentiss had worked above and beyond her expectations. The fireplace at the back of the room was the focal point and both women were enthralled at the restoration. Don had started work on the stairwell, repairing the once decrepit stairs. He had refurbished them as if they were new. The charming carved-wood bannister was remarkable. He finished each post about half-way up the stairwell. The second floor did not have electricity yet, and not much had been done there, but the renovation on the lower floor was almost complete. They went from room to room on the first floor, where most of the work was done. The kitchen and pantry remodel had begun and looked amazing, though it had a ways to go. The dining room was finished, but the table and chairs were not back from the refinishing studio, where he had a crew working to bring the furniture back to life. A large buffet and other antique furniture were also being worked on at his studio. Maryanne was becoming more anxious than ever to move into the transforming edifice.

"I am so glad you suggested visiting the Valencia today. I had no idea it had come this far." Maryanne stood in awe, looking up at the chandeliers and scoping out the masterpiece Don and three crews had created in just two short weeks. He had three crews working day and night, knowing how anxious Maryanne was to move in.

Then, as if the house just wouldn't stop its pesky behavior, the lights began flickering and then went completely out. The house was dim. Light from outside still fell across the floors from the brand new windows, so they were not in complete darkness.

"Good thing we came early. I might have freaked out, otherwise." Maryanne jested.

"Wait. I am getting some activity. An entity wants to enter the space. Let me communicate with the spirit. Be very quiet." Vivian stood silent, looking up toward the top landing of the stairs. The lights flickered again and the figure of an older man was looking down. He spoke telepathically to Vivian. He told Vivian he was the lawyer of John Farthington and that Maryanne had a key that she found while going through a dresser when she first visited the Valencia Manor. The skeleton key would unlock secret information about the adoption of a child.

"It was that attorney, Fredrick Holmes that communicated to me at your house. He helped John Farthington with an adoption. He said you found a skeleton key in a dresser here in the Valencia. What did you do with it?"

"I put it into the effects of the estate in an envelope. Do you think it's important?" Maryanne was puzzled.

"You must get the key and we have to find out what it unlocks. That is unless I can get Mr. Holmes to tell me. Let me see if he can tell me." Vivian began to meditate until his figure again appeared, this time on the main floor next to the bannister. She asked him to tell her where to look. He told her there was a safe under the floor in an upstairs bedroom, and then he disappeared.

"We have to get the key and search the upstairs bedrooms for a safe. I don't have much time, so get the key today and we can come back tonight. I have to leave in the morning to prepare for my trip." Vivian was insistent.

"I'll check in at work and then we can pick up the key at my house and come back. We have to see what's under the floor." Maryanne and Vivian hurried for the door. On the drive back, Vivian informed Maryanne more about the Raven connection.

"As for the birds you saw, Ravens are a symbol in certain societies; such as living beings who practice vampirism. Although it started many years ago, those types of cults have been reported to be alive and well in this country. You would be surprised at how many unsuspecting people can be drawn into such activity. Those people are alive on the earth plane, but there are also those who are dead, and living on this plane; walking dead…They suck the blood from living beings to sustain their existence. Personally I have never encountered one, dead or alive, but many people have confirmed their existence. I doubt the Ravens you saw are related to such activity. I think it is a coincidence that they landed in your yard. I would not worry too much about that…Unless it happens again, of course." Vivian looked at Maryanne with a sinister smile.

"Seriously, I doubt such evil is actually true. I will meditate and see what I come up with." Vivian patted Maryanne's shoulder in an effort to reassure her.

"That's too creepy for me to digest. It's impossible, as far as I'm concerned." She was somewhat reluctant to believe in the idea that such things could exist today. Maryanne chuckled.

"Vivian, let's change the subject."

"Sure. No problem. Actually, I'm quite hungry, how about you?" Vivian broke out in a hearty laugh. "Would you believe I'm hungry at a time like this?"

"Yes, I can. I'm famished myself. We can grab a late lunch and stop by my store. There's a small deli just a ways from there."

When they reached the Pearl Street Mall, Maryanne backed into a spot in front of her store. They walked to the small deli from there and enjoyed food and conversation.

After lunch and checking in with Wendy, they headed to Maryanne's house to pick up the skeleton key. The envelope was just as she left it on a shelf inside her closet. She dumped the contents across her bed and the key fell out and landed on the floor.

"There it is. I wondered if I would ever find a use for that key. Leave it to you, Vivian. I have a feeling we are on the edge of a big discovery about someone in the Manor."

"I am positive the revelation will be well worth its discovery," Vivian concurred.

Maryanne took a moment to call Mario and let him know where they were going. He was not sure it was such a good idea but he knew there was no changing her mind.

"Call me when you're done. I'll be home by then. Love you, sweetie," Mario added.

"Love you too, hon. Call you soon. We're on our way back to the Valencia Manor now."

Maryanne pulled her Lexus into the driveway and the amateur sleuths anxiously approached the Manor, hoping to find answers to a question that had not yet been determined. The Valencia seemed as though it were eager for their return, and not in a good way Maryanne was thinking. As they approached the huge portal, the door opened right before her key slid into the lock. Maryanne pushed in on the door, moving forward head-first, entered and then gestured for Vivian to follow. Vivian, not the least bit apprehensive, audaciously strode into the room.

"I wish I could be so brave," Maryanne teased.

"If you had been doing this as long as I have, you wouldn't even raise an eyebrow," Vivian replied, smiling, her green eyes filled with enthusiasm.

"I guess you're right. I should be getting used to it by now, though it isn't half as bad as when I first encountered strange activity in this house," Maryanne chortled.

"I'm anxious to get started, let's go upstairs. Turn the lights on, though. I'm not that brave," Vivian chuckled as she led the way up the staircase.

Light flooded the room when Maryanne flipped the switches and she swiftly caught up with Vivian, not wanting to be alone, just now. They climbed the staircase, eyes scanning the landing ahead and Maryanne checking out for new upgrades as she ascended the long flight of shiny, refinished stairs. When they reached the top, lights on the main floor began to flicker off and on. Maryanne took hold of Vivian's arm and held on tight. They moved ahead fearlessly until they came to the third door on the right.

"I think this is the bedroom where I discovered the skeleton key inside the dresser." Maryanne pushed on the door and it opened easily, emitting low eerie squeals. Obviously the contractor had not worked on much of the upstairs renovation. Before entering the room, Vivian turned back and looked below to see the lights flickering off and on. Finally they stayed in the off-mode, to their dismay.

"Did you bring a flash-light?" Vivian asked hopefully.

Maryanne scrambled inside her leather bag to retrieve the flash-light she had become accustomed to carrying for moments like this. She felt a sudden rush of relief when she felt the cold metal and pulled it up as if it were a fish on a line.

"I found it!" she expressed eagerly. The light flickered a bit when she powered it up but then it remained lit, and both women were instantly calmed. She scanned the light back and forth until she found the dresser; a drawer slightly open.

"There…that's where I found it," she remarked, like a child eager for praise. Scanning the light around the floors, they searched for what would reveal a safe, or hiding place, where valuable documents were left years ago by a man who was obviously keeping a dark secret. As Maryanne carefully aimed the light, they were checking out every inch of the time-worn wood floor. Nothing seemed to have changed in the room since Maryanne had been abducted months before. They inspected every area of the room and then went into the small closet. Nothing indicated such a hiding place existed.

"Let's go into the next room," Vivian suggested. They warily left the bedroom and moved back along the balcony as they looked down at the lower level where the lights had suddenly become active again. The chandeliers cast lovely patterns against the burnt-red, newly-painted walls and refinished floors. The next room awaited them and they entered boldly, not affected by the groans and squeals of the dilapidated doors. It was the room with the bed; the antique bed that had been covered with tattered blankets and repulsive odors. It was the bed where Maryanne had been captured and held prisoner by an unknown phantom…a phantom who turned out to be a wonderful young woman that had been held captive in the Valencia Manor for years. No one knows for sure, even now, how long.

Memories flooded through Maryanne's psyche, like a tornado churning around her. For an instant, she was intensely overwhelmed and wanted to leave…to run away from the fear that had suddenly enveloped her. Vivian felt the emotions and embraced her with a comforting hug. She knew Maryanne was on the edge.

"It's fine Maryanne. It's going to be all right. Don't let the past intrude on your life now. You have passed through the fear and terror. Now it's about understanding and knowing in your heart that you are in a different place. A place that was partially created by what you experienced in this Manor. It was hurtful and difficult, but it also gave you a whole new person to share part of your life with. Hanna Michele is the product of that experience here. Had you not gone through this, you may have never met her.

Maryanne's eyes welled up and she took in a deep breath, then exhaled slowly and took a step back.

"You are right. Thank you for reminding me that I am very fortunate to have her in my life. I had been so consumed by the memories of the experience, that I let it overcome me. I feel so much better now that I think of in a more positive way. Thank you Vivian."

"You're welcome."

"I am also very thankful for having you in my life, Vivian. I have so much more than I ever imagined could be possible. But now, I guess it's time to get down to business," Maryanne joked. She moved her flashlight to the floor and began the search, taking in every inch of the unkempt wood. When they moved to the closet, her light illuminated a spot on the floor that made them both take notice. Boards had been cut in a square and placed back down into their space. It was not very apparent unless one knew to look. Maryanne handed the flashlight to Vivian and got down on her knees. She looked into her bag and found a nail file to help dislodge a board and pull it up. Once it came up, the rest were easily removed. There, below the floor was a silver box. Maryanne's heart raced full-bore. She reached down into the hollowed vault, pulled out the strongbox and set it down beside the makeshift safe. Vivian held the light as Maryanne searched into her purse and pulled out the skeleton key…a key that would change everything, little did she know.

"Here goes nothing!" She placed the key into the lock and turned it. Nothing happened. Her heart sank. She tried again. This time the lock unlatched and she pulled at the lid, which had obviously been closed for years. After nudging, tapping and knocking against the box, it finally opened. Inside was a very well preserved manila envelope, which she instantly pulled from its tomb.

"Let's get the hell out of here and check it out." Maryanne put the envelope back inside the box and carried the box, key and papers out to the balcony. They moved toward the landing, Vivian still holding the light and leading the way. Maryanne held the box close to her chest, following behind in an anxious, but uneasy effort to hopefully discover a secret that had been hidden for many years. Down the stairs and toward the main floor the two women treaded. The lights suddenly went out and Vivian dropped the flashlight. It rolled all the way to the bottom, but oddly the light remained on. The room went pitch-black for an instant until their eyes became adjusted and they held onto the bannister with fear at the sudden darkness. The sun had gone down but some light was showing through the new and much clearer windows. Yard lights that had been restored sent patches of light throughout the room. They made their way down the stairs, cautiously one slow step at a time. When they reached the bottom, Vivian picked up the flashlight and held it up toward Maryanne until she reached the bottom.

"Do you feel any activity?" Maryanne questioned.

"No, I don't feel anything right now. Earlier I felt a presence of a good vibration, but kept it to myself while we were in the room upstairs. I didn't feel it was anything to be concerned about. Friendly, I can handle," She jested. "I tried to communicate but nothing came through. I feel it could have possibly been the lawyer who worked with John Farthington on the alleged adoption. I hope these papers reveal something of importance."

The front door opened effortlessly and the anxious sleuths darted outside into the crisp night air. Maryanne locked the door and they rushed down the rock stairway into the yard. Anxious to inspect the contents of the strongbox, a mad dash for the car and Maryanne and Vivian were well on their way to her house.

While coffee was brewing, the ladies sat at the table anxious to expose the treasure in front of them. Once the box was opened, a manila envelope was about to have its contents revealed. Maryanne meticulously withdrew the documents, careful not to tear the delicate papers that were in a fragile condition. With utmost care, Maryanne separated the documents and laid them in sequence across the table. Four sheets, one by one she placed them, but when the last one was pulled out, a picture fell onto the table. Maryanne's heart raced and she glanced at Vivian with a propitious smile. Vivian returned an emotional glance.

"It's the picture of a child…a baby. It's only an infant. Maybe a week old or less. Let me see, the first document is an adoption certificate. It's old but well kept. John Farthington adopted this child when it was first born. It says two days old and a girl, but there is no name for the child. It goes on to say the agreement was that the Mother not see the child and gave it up immediately after it was born. "How awful! I know just how that feels. I had to give up my child because my Mother thought it was the best thing for me. I was barely sixteen years old."

"Let me see the document," Vivian requested. Maryanne handed them to her, tears welling up, but trying to conceal them.

"Maryanne, when was your child born?"

"January 14th, nineteen-eighty-seven. She would be twenty-two now. I was still in school and didn't graduate for two years after. I had a terrible time after that happened."

"I am sure you did. It's not easy to give up a child, let alone having one when you were so young. Your Mother probably thought she was doing the right thing at the time. I would imagine she was sorry after the fact." Vivian consoled her and then took the papers and began reading the information.

"It says here that the adoption took place in nineteen-eighty-seven. Do you know the local of the parents who adopted your child?"

"Mom told me the people were not from the Denver area. I vaguely think about it now. It was a very painful experience. I always wondered where the child was. I felt so guilty about it. Don't know why. I wouldn't have done it if it wasn't for my Mother. Could we talk about something else? It's getting to me." Maryanne dabbed at the corner of her eyes.

"I am trying to figure out where the child of the adoption is and who this information pertains to? The Farthingtons did not claim to have any other children after the one child fell years before that, except for Edwina Rafael, who they said left town because of a family dispute of some sort, and never came back. That's what Mrs. Dirkshire told you. Edwina had a birth certificate so she would be about thirty-two or three, if I'm not mistaken from the information you had given me." Vivian kept the questions coming.

"You're right about that. No one ever found Edwina. I wonder if she is ever coming back," Maryanne pondered.

"All I'm saying is that there should be some kind of evidence of the young Farthington child, other than this adoption certificate. Where is the child now?"

"I wonder too. I had no idea about it until your visitation with the Farthington attorney. I guess we've got some serious work to do. Or at least I do. You will be leaving tomorrow night for England, so I'll be busy doing the investigative work while you are gone. Hope it's productive," Maryanne smiled and picked up the papers. "Let's eat something and get some sleep. Mario should be home soon, too. Haven't seen much of him since the Jennifer Bennett murder last week. It'll be good to see him and spend a little time."

"Maryanne, I really have to go back to the hotel and pack some things. I'm a day late and a dollar short, with all these latest revelations," she laughed. "I can call a cab to pick me up." You get some dinner together for you and Mario. It's getting late and I am tired as well."

"I wouldn't think of it! I will take you myself. You don't need to be calling a cab. Why don't you eat something with us first and then I'll take you?" Maryanne responded.

"Okay. If you insist, but let me fix dinner, or at least help."

"Vivian, just take a rest on the sofa and I'll whip something up quick. Mario will be home soon. I'm going to throw together some steak wraps and hot soup. Sound good?" She was already cutting up a roast she had purchased on the way home from work the day before and had a salad already chopped in the refrigerator, to add. She put the soup on to heat and dinner was served. Mario walked in the house just as the table was being set.

"Evening ladies. How was your day? Meet any ghosts at the Manor?" He chuckled, while coming in behind Maryanne and wrapping his arms around her.

"I missed you sweetie," he said as he planted a kiss on her cheek.

"I always miss you, Mario. You are hardly ever here anymore. But then neither am I, so I guess we had better start making more time for each other." She turned around and returned a kiss. "Dinner is served and I know you're hungry. Sit down, you two and let's dig in."

The three of them scarfed down the wraps and soup, and then chatted while sipping on coffee. Vivian began cleaning up the kitchen and Maryanne joined in. Mario turned on the TV and lay on the sofa watching one of his favorite cop shows.

"Vivian, let me take you back to the hotel and you can get some rest. I'll settle up with you when you get back. I'm sure there will be more work to do anyway." Maryanne got her bag and keys, kissed Mario and they left.

When Maryanne returned, Mario was sound asleep on the sofa. He didn't stir when she came inside. Retreating into the kitchen, she slid the papers from the envelope, and read every word once more. What if Vivian was right? After all, it was possible…but not very probable. All of the information could match up, but still, it could be anyone. She tried to convince herself it was too far-fetched to have anything to do with her own child and didn't want to get her hopes up, to have it all go up in smoke. Besides, the girl was missing. No one knew where she was and after twenty-two years, how would anyone find her? Maryanne put the papers away. After a lot of nudging, Mario finally opened his eyes, yawned and sat up. He took her hand and pulled her down next to him. The sex was good and they both needed it. An hour later they were in bed, sleeping soundly.

17

Sunday started out with a phone call, first thing. Chief Olson informed Mario that they had found another young co-ed murdered near the museum, and the MO fit the Jennifer Bennett crime. Mario kissed his wife and left for the crime scene. When he arrived, the place was already roped off; crawling with detectives, reporters, an evidence van and Chief Olson was standing near the van, waving Mario in. An ambulance was standing by waiting for the detectives to finish with the victim.

"Mario, come over here. Take a look at this." He led Mario around to the back of the stone-building, where three forensic detectives, a police photographer and a blood-spatter expert were working frantically, gathering any and all evidence that could give them answers to this gruesome attack. The battered woman, sprawled across the grass, was covered in blood, neck slashed, indicative of the methods used in the prior murder. Her face, frozen with fear, eyes wide open as if she were still looking at her brutal attacker. Mario thought about the horror that her last moments must have been. Chief gave the order to move her body to the lab. Mario checked the scene, making sure nothing was overlooked before they left for the station.

"Chief, I'll see you back at the office." Mario climbed

into his truck and sped off. He felt sick and rolled the window down, leaning toward the fresh, cool air. He sucked in a few deep breaths, exhaling slowly. When he arrived at the station, he was feeling better and went inside, where three detectives were mulling over the case. The murder was a positive match for the first case just over a week ago. She had lost a lot of blood, which is probably the cause of death, as in the first murder. A serial killer was at large, and Mario was preparing for some long days and nights. He called Maryanne, informing her that he wouldn't be home until late in the night. She was used to his unscheduled hours and would keep busy while he was working. If there was one thing that stood out about Mario, it was his dedication to the job. She could live with that. Mario delved into the case and Maryanne sipped on coffee, thinking about what had taken place the last three days.

The phone rang, and her concentration quickly switched to matters at hand.

"Hello Joan," She answered after glancing at the caller ID.

"How's it going? Checking in and wondering why you haven't called," Joan answered in a concerned manner.

"The last three days have been unbelievable. Would you like to come over for a late lunch? I have much to tell you." Maryanne breathed deep.

"Sure, I'm kind of laying low today. Steve and I are still on the outs. I'll be over in a little while."

"Talk to you when you get here. I'll prepare something yummy." Maryanne added.

A half hour later, Joan arrived, clad in white-washed, straight-leg jeans and sneakers. She strolled into the kitchen, holding on to her half-filled coffee mug.

The ladies exchanged a quick greeting and sat at the table where Maryanne had just served a healthy lunch of tomato bisque soup fresh from the Health Food Market, and a chef salad filled with fresh veggies. Joan was impressed and famished.

"I wish I could whip up a lunch like this in half an hour."

"It's easy when you get it from the deli," Maryanne jested. "With the help of the Market, it's a snap," she chuckled.

"Don't be so humble, Maryanne. You always had me when it came to preparing food. I just never was that interested in the culinary arts, I guess," she kidded. "Though, if someone else makes it, I'm all about eating," she smiled and tasted the soup. "It's very good, Health Food Mart or not," Joan grinned as she took another sip.

"Thanks Joan. Enjoy."

"Believe me, I intend to. So clue me in on the latest. I'm having gossip withdrawal."

"You're too funny, Joan. Well it's not exactly gossip and a little spooky, at that." Maryanne went into detail about everything from ravens, the skeleton key, finding the information about the adoption, and the recent murder of the co-ed. Joan sat in astonishment while Maryanne elaborated.

"You're right, it's not gossip. My God, you've been a busy girl. Who knew? John Farthington adopted a child? There was no record of that anywhere. The raven thing is a little weird, too. Guess I'd better start keeping in better touch. By the way, how's Vivian Gilbreth?"

"She left for Westchester, England on a psychic convention. Two weeks and she'll be back."

"I'll say one thing," Joan retorted. "She's a hell of a good psychic. If anyone can solve the eerie manifestations, it's her. You're in good hands."

"Yes I do believe I am. Still a lot of unanswered questions, you know. So what's new with you Joan?"

Not a lot, but you'll be glad to hear that your house will be closing in two weeks and you'll have to prepare to move. Are you ready?"

"Don't worry about me. I'll be ready. I'm so anxious to move into the Valencia that I've been counting the hours. I'd like to show you what the contractor has done, mostly on the first floor. It's really more than I could have imagined. You'll be surprised. I think Mario and I could actually move in right now, and the contractor could continue working on the upstairs while we are there. We're not home all day anyway." Maryanne's eagerness was obvious, even though there were still plenty of unanswered questions.

"Great. Good to hear things are moving in the right direction." Joan gave her a thumb's up.

"So tell me, Joan. How are you and Steve doing? Any progress on your relationship?" Maryanne questioned.

"I am pretty sure I'm not going back to Steve. He really scared me the last few times he flipped into anger mode. It was like he changed his whole personality and became this other person that I don't like. You know, like a split personality. He seems to be getting worse. I hope he gets some help. I can't help but love him, but something isn't right and it's going to take a lot of therapy to get him where he needs to be. I guess I should be more patient but the violence was getting out of hand. I didn't want to become another statistic." Joan was on the edge of tears.

"I'm sorry Joan. I do know how much you love him. Has he agreed to therapy?"

"He said that he would do anything to get me back, so I have insisted, but I am really not going to try again. Just told him I would be here for him, and hopefully he might get some help…I pray." Joan was perplexed.

"Let's talk about something more positive. I forgot to tell you how well Hanna Michelle was doing since she started classes and is living on her own. I am so happy. We are getting along fabulously," Maryanne added.

"Finally. I know you've been hoping she would have a break through. Glad it finally came through. I wish you both the best of luck. And not to change the subject but do you think you could give me a tour of Valencia?" Joan questioned.

"Sure, we can go right now if you want to. Mario is tied up all day and I have nothing better to do." The two of them hustled to clean the kitchen, and Joan would soon get her debut of the updated Valencia Manor.

An hour later Maryanne parked in front. She took a moment to look at the aging, but rejuvenated edifice. "So what do you think, so far?" Her face was glowing with pride and anticipation.

"This is remarkable. The contractor has transformed the outside into its almost original design. I can't wait to go inside." As Joan and Maryanne ambled into the yard where fences had been restored, decrepit stone pillars were in mint condition, and crumbling rock pathways had been revived, Joan was overwhelmed at such a transformation. Maryanne chuckled to herself and couldn't resist offering her charming salute to the stone pillars that stood proudly defending the yard, as she had always done. Don had not yet begun the back yard renovation, so they climbed the front stairs leading to the portal and entered through the massive door in front. No squeaks, groans or moans were present when they peeked inside. Maryanne piloted as they walked into the great-room, Joan scanning from top to bottom, the charming ambiance of its antique décor.

"You have done well in choosing the contractor. This is some of the best work I have seen. I will definitely pass the word," Joan complimented.

"I agree, and I'm sure he would appreciate that." Maryanne escorted Joan through the Manor, and she was impressed at the dynamic renovation that had been perfected to a T.

"Let's go upstairs, Maryanne." Joan was eager to see the rest of the Manor. "Can you turn the lights on upstairs?"

"Sorry, they are not working yet. Only the main floor seems to be working at this point. He still has a lot to do up

there. Joan stood in awe at the magnificent chandeliers that
hovered above, with sparkling crystals glittering and casting
reflections around the room. She went to the fireplace and ran
her hand across the marble accents that he had brought back
to life.

"It is truly magnificent, Maryanne. Your vision is
incredible. What you envisioned in this house has virtually
unveiled itself. Good job."

"Thanks, but I owe it all to Don Prentiss' expertise. He is
a genius when it comes to this work," Maryanne smiled.

The lights began flickering, as they had at the previous
visit. The top floor had become fully lit once more. They were
perplexed, but gutsy, and immediately made their way up the
staircase. Joan led the quest, while Maryanne followed close
behind. They did a quick-step all the way up the spiraling,
staircase. When they arrived at the top, they glanced at one
another and then trudged along the balcony, peeking in the
first room and entering, somewhat apprehensively. The next
room, and the next, the ladies audaciously forged through
chambers that were awaiting their chance for regeneration. Joan
opened the attic door, and the rotted stairs looked as if they
were begging to be part of the mix, she thought. Up the stairs
she climbed, cautiously, one careful step at a time, until she
reached the top. Joan pushed the door open to reveal the tiny,
once nursery that seemed out of place in its existing condition.
The painted window had been scraped half-way clean when
the contractor was inspecting its curious facade. Joan looked
out over the back yard and the surrounding landscape. The
fountain and statues remained in poor condition, again waiting
for their turn to be a part of this refurbishment. The tattered,
timeworn bassinette began to move, as usual, as if it were being
rocked by an invisible hand. The cry of a baby emanated into
the room. Joan's heart jumped into full-gear and she backed
away from the apparition. A ghost ridden rocking chair began
to move back and forth, while the floor uttered its remorseful

groans. Maryanne called from below. The ghostly figure of a young woman had appeared on the opposite side of the room, clad in late seventies attire, and engulfed in a white cloudy mist. She began to speak.

"I was murdered in this house. My body is still living within the walls of Valencia Manor. Please help me to escape this hell and go to the other side." And then she disappeared.

"Hello. Joan, are you up there?" Maryanne had been calling out to her but she was unable to speak.

When Joan finally snapped out of her trance-like state, she peeked out the door and looked down toward Maryanne, who stood at the bottom, with a color of worry on her face.

"I'm right here. Be right down, Maryanne." Joan quickly stepped through the narrow door onto the rickety stairs and pushed the door closed behind her, escaping the ghostly phenomenon, before she edged her way back down.

"That's got to be the strangest room in the house. The rocker began moving and a baby was crying. The ghost of a young woman appeared and said she had been murdered in this place and was still living within the walls of the Manor. She disappeared and I don't know who she was. When she reached the bottom, she shook her head. There's some bizarre paranormal activity going on there. Why would anyone put a nursery there in the first place? What were they thinking?" Joan looked back in a state of confusion.

"I have to agree. Strange place for a nursery. Everyone has wondered the same thing. And…who was the murdered woman? Maryanne added. "I say let's get the hell out'a here." She closed the door behind them. "I want to know more about the ghost, but I'd like to wait until we get out of here before you get into that."

"The contractor will return tomorrow and continue the renovation. It should be complete in a few weeks, give or take." Maryanne led the way down the staircase to the main floor. The lights began flickering, and then completely went dark. It was as if the house was urging them to leave. The ladies charily made their way out the front door and to their car.

"That was bizarre. We must find out who the ghost is," Joan remarked.

"Yes, when you give me the details I will go into the history to see who there is that we haven't uncovered, yet," Maryanne responded. "C'mon, let's get out of here." They hurried out the front door and to the car. In a few minutes, Maryanne pulled through Starbucks where they treated themselves to a daily fix of their favorite brew. After much consideration, Maryanne would plan a strategy to solve the identity of the unknown phantom that seemed to be caught between the now and the hereafter.

When Maryanne arrived at her house, Joan had to leave for an appointment. "Before I go, I want to let you know that I'm going to set up a meeting with you, Vladimar and his partner to prepare for the closing on your house. I'll call you tomorrow and give you the details. Thanks for a wonderful and strange day." Joan jumped in her BMW, and harried off to meet a client for a showing in North Boulder.

18

Mario called to let Maryanne know he would be home late, except for the constant updates on the recent murders. The murder case had taken an unexpected turn. Maryanne worked on her client list, coffee in hand as she sat in the easy chair and watched the news. Nothing new, as usual and Maryanne nodded off until she was awakened by a loud racket outside. She pulled herself up and ran to the window in the living room, but all was quiet, and then hurried to the back porch, pressing her head against the cool glass, trying to get a clear view of the back yard. Her warm breath fogged the window, but she rubbed it clear and saw Ravens, dozens of them, planted across the lawn and perched along the bannister of the deck. She flipped on the lights and half of them took flight in a whirring cloud of black feathers. The rest of the beady-eyed creatures seemed to taunt her, and did not move, holding fast to their perch. Maryanne was not brave enough to go outside, but knocked on the window in an effort to scare them off. A few more took flight but about ten ravens staked a claim to her yard and would not leave. She wasn't normally afraid of birds but the strange manifestation was a little too much to trust, especially after the confrontation in the front yard not so long ago. She opened the back door and made sure the screen was locked and stood yelling out to the birds. A flock of the black creatures swooped down across the yard, and then one crashed hard against the door and fell to the deck. Maryanne screamed in terror. There were several ravens, but when she looked closer, she saw at least six large, squealing bats. Some of the Ravens flew off. Their large wings flapped against the moonlit sky. Several bats were flapping and flailing around the yard. She had never known of bats to be that close in the area, and why would they be flying while Ravens were present?

"Shoo! Go away! Get out of here!" She screamed clapping her hands several times. On the other side of the yard near the fence a figure stood draped in black, still and quiet. His eerie eyes glistened in the night as she looked at him eye to eye. It was as though she was being compelled to emerge into another dimension, and then she turned away from the face of the dark stranger until she got control of her senses again. She backed away, slammed the door and locked both deadbolts. She could not resist another look into the yard from the window, and pressed her head against the glass, while the ravens began to take flight, one at a time, until they were gone. A loud crash! Something hit the window, followed by an uncanny howl bellowing its loud scream into the night. Something was out there. Petrified with fear; her eyes focused on the yard. A dark figure crossed in front of her. She was mortified; unable to move. The moon shifted from behind the clouds and light fell across the landscape. A dark, hooded creature crept across the yard and then seemed to rise up and disappear. All was silent. She stood at the window for what seemed like an hour, but when she finally emerged from her spell of darkness and moved into the front living room, it had only been a few minutes. She managed to dial Mario and when he answered, she pleaded for him to come home. He arrived in less than half an hour. When he walked inside, Maryanne was curled up on the sofa, TV blaring, covered with a blanket over her face. He removed the blanket to reveal a frightened woman, who under normal circumstances wouldn't have been so upset. It was definitely beginning to take a toll on her. When she explained the entire scenario, he went to the back yard, searching every square inch of the landscape, picking up a few feathers and a piece of black cloth that had gotten caught on one of the bushes, apparently ripped from the intruder, to leave evidence of its reality. Now, someone had to take her seriously. And… try to explain the feathers. When Mario came inside, she had managed to compose herself and was sitting up, blanket draped around her shoulders.

"Did you see it? A bat! It hit the window hard and fell to the deck. I thought it was dead. Was it still there?" Maryanne questioned Mario incessantly.

"No. I didn't see any bat or birds out there. He handed her the feathers he had collected from the yard. She walked to the back door with Mario and showed him where it had hit the window. Outside, on the glass there was a splat of a dark blood-like substance. He went outside to scrape a sample, which he carefully put into a small plastic evidence bag. Mario couldn't remember when bats had been a problem in Boulder. He thought she may have made a mistake in the darkness and it was probably the ravens, after all. The lab test would verify its source.

Mario made hot chocolate to help her relax. He would soon return to work for a few more hours. The phone rang.

"Hello, this is Mario. What? Another one? I'll be there right away." He hung up. The Moonlight Slasher had claimed its third victim. "Maryanne, there's been another murder. Same MO; another co-ed. Got'ta go now. Lock the doors tight. Better yet, call Joan to come over. I've called a team to watch the house, so you'll be okay. I'm gonna be out most of the night." He kissed her, picked up his hat and was gone. The squad car parked in front and Mario spoke to them before he left. They were there for the duration. Maryanne felt safe with protection and did not call Joan. She fell asleep in bed with the TV in full mode.

At four am, Mario returned, exhausted from the never-ending saga. He lay across the bed and was asleep within minutes. Maryanne was still sleeping when he woke at eight am. The cover had fallen off Maryanne and he picked it up, gently placing it across her. She stirred, but remained asleep. Mario showered and had a crew already scouring the yard for evidence of last night's phantom expose'. He took a shower, made coffee and Maryanne sauntered in, looking quite unkempt as she rubbed her eyes and yawned.

"When did you get home?"

"Early this morning, before five a.m… Didn't want to wake you. Obviously you needed to sleep. Feeling any better?" Mario reached his arms around her and held her. She felt safe.

"I feel much better now. Sleep can do wonders. How's the investigation going?" Maryanne queried.

"Not good. Just when we think we have something, it's up in smoke. There's a maniac out there, slashing young women's throats and letting their blood. It's unimaginable what's going on out there. And we don't have much to go on. The guy is careful and precise. Not leaving any prints or DNA." He sat down at the kitchen table, trying to make sense of all the evidence to date. It seemed like they were running in circles on a road to nowhere

"I have to stop this monster before any more women are killed. Sorry, but I'm gonna have to leave now. I'll grab a sandwich on the way to work." Mario rushed out the door.

"I'll call you in a while. Love you." He looked back apologetically and hurried to his truck. He pulled into Wendy's on the way and scarfed up an egg, sausage and cheese breakfast sandwich and another large coffee. He was going to need the buzz. It would be a long day.

When he walked into the station, there was a commotion near Chief Olson's office. He emerged from a group of detectives and walked up to Mario. We had a breakthrough in the case. At the last murder scene, there was a medallion, quite like the one you had Maryanne analyze. If I didn't know any better, I'd say we had vampires in Boulder, but I know better so we have to figure out who wants us to think it is vampires. Am I making any sense?"

"No, you're not," Mario answered, half laughing.

"I'm serious Mario. It has to be a vampire, wanna-be." The Chief actually believed someone could do such a thing, and Mario couldn't wrap his head around it. It didn't make sense to think anyone would be crazy enough to pull of something like that, especially in Boulder, Colorado. The blood-letting was pretty far out though, and there could be someone out there just crazy enough to do it. But how? They hadn't left a fingerprint, shoe-print or DNA. A crazed maniac would not be so calculated and careful. As bloody as some of the crime scenes were, the guy had to have some kind of help to pull this off, with no trace to anyone, and very little blood. Mario and Chief Olson had decided it was probably more than one person to execute such a crime with that much precision. That is, unless someone could fly, Mario chuckled to himself. Then he flashed back on the scene at Maryanne's and the description she gave of the bats and ravens. The dark hooded stranger sounded a little far-fetched too, but after hearing the crime description, just about anything made sense at this point. It had become more visceral, than logical at this point and Mario was willing to explore an alternative theory, even though it made no sense to him. He would definitely speak to Maryanne about getting in touch with the psychic when she returned from England.

Mario was about to leave the office when another call came in. This time it was Officer Montrose, who had just been called out to another crime scene. Only this time it was an attempted murder. The Chief and Mario sped off. An ambulance was arriving when they pulled up. Two police cars and a fire-truck were already attending to the latest victim. Same MO, same lack of evidence, but there was one huge break. The victim was still alive, but barely hanging on. The ambulance transported the victim to Boulder Community Hospital.

"Mario, you stay here and work on the crime scene, I'll go to the hospital, stand by, talk to the family and hopefully be there if and when she wakes up. We have to put a lid on this one, quick." Chief Olson walked out of his office.

Mario worked with the evidence team gathering anything that was even remotely important and could possibly help to find answers. The city of Boulder was on full alert and six teams had been added to the night shift since the second murder. Everything possible was being done to curb the gruesome murders and attacks that seemed to be relentless. Mario called Maryanne to check in and make sure she was safe, warning her again to keep all doors locked and security system on full-time. The squad car was still outside on watch.

Back at the station, Mario waited for any kind of news that may help solve the bizarre attacks. He was at his desk, downing a third cup when Officer Jackson showed up.

"We got a print on this one but can't find it in the data base. There was some kind of animal hair on the victim. Looks like dog. We'll know a lot more in a few hours. Have you heard how the victim is?"

"Waiting…hoping. She has to survive. This has got to stop. The city's in a panic." Mario was exhausted and looked every bit of it. "I'll talk to you soon. Let you know when I hear from the Chief."

"Later Mario. I'll keep you informed." Jackson returned to the lab.

Maryanne had spent most of the day working with Wendy

at the store. Several clients had stopped in to shop, which made for a productive day. Joan had set up the closing for her home sooner than planned. Since the purchase was a cash offer, it went through with flying colors, and they would be moving in ten days. Maryanne and Mario had already packed most of their house, except what they used daily and a few clothes to get them by. She was anxious to move and spoke to the contractor, who said he had begun to work on the upstairs at the Manor. He had removed some of the wall-boards in the first two upstairs bedrooms. First thing in the morning he would finish the third bedroom and then go to the library and attic rooms. Maryanne was pleased at his progress. He had heard more of the strange voices in the attic again, but he didn't seem too worried about it. He told her jokingly that it wasn't the dead you have to worry about. She related with that. Maryanne was getting used to it, as well and expected as much. When the psychic returned, she would ask her to perform another cleansing at the Manor before she finished decorating.

Hanna Michelle called Maryanne to let her know that she had been doing well in her classes and grading high. She was hoping to help Maryanne with more of the décor at Valencia Manor. Maryanne was elated to hear the good news and hoped to bring her over soon, to see the Manor's transformation.

She was excited that Mario would be coming home early for a change, and they planned a quiet dinner, where they could spend a little quality time on just being in love and hopefully not so many diversions. She left the store an hour early, leaving Wendy to clean up and close the store. Wendy had been doing a remarkable job.

Maryanne and Mario arrived one after the other, Maryanne taking the driveway and Mario in front.

"You look like you need a week of sleep." Maryanne knew he could use a good rest. The recent murders had taken their toll on him, and it was beginning to show. She darted to the kitchen where she had the slow cooker going with a juicy pot roast with carrots, potatoes and onions. All she had to do was make the salad and they could share a meal and talk. In fifteen minutes, she walked into the living room to find Mario sound asleep on the sofa, in a sitting position. She nudged him gently and he woke.

"Come on Mario, you have to eat something. You're letting yourself go and it's high time you let me take care of you." Mario didn't hesitate to scarf up two servings of roast beef, vegetables, and a piece of chocolate cake.

"Just like mother used to make," he kidded.

The night ended with cuddling and sleep. The sex would have to wait for another night. Sleep had definitely taken top priority.

19

Mario received a call from Chief Olson, informing him that the Gem Jeweler's heist had been solved. It was just as he thought. The buyer had set the whole scam up for insurance money. His girlfriend was the accomplice. Mario was relieved that was out of his hair, now and he could devote all of his energy to the Slasher serial murders, which had the entire city on high alert, let alone the State of Colorado.

The young woman last attacked was still alive and critical. She had just slipped out of a coma and the diagnosis was promising. She hadn't become fully conscious enough to speak, but Mario placed full-time guards on the room, just in case the killer tried to silence her. There had been no further murders or attempts by the unknown assailant, since she had been admitted into the hospital. Mario kept in close contact with Doctor Delucia, in case he would be able to speak to the victim, should she improve.

Evidence had been piling up and laying out a very bizarre crime. Forensics had collected DNA that had not been identified and had some unusual traits associated with it. It was taking top priority at a lab in Denver. An in depth study of the DNA was being done to identify a particular strand that was very unique. The results were atypical of the normal patterns that they were familiar with. The lab informed Mario that it could take a few more days to provide results. The lab had considered that the test could have possibly been contaminated. In that case the results would be incomplete and insufficient to deliver concrete evidence, unless they could secure more of the same DNA sample to test further. At this point they were still hoping for good results.

Not much later, Mario's cell rang and Dr. Delucia, informed him that the victim was awake and improving. He suggested Mario make a visit to hopefully get some useful information on the serial killer. It only took Mario half an hour and he was at the hospital, face to face with the victim, who looked much better than he had last seen her sprawled across the lawn covered in blood.

"Hello, Miss White," Mario quietly spoke. "I am Detective Mario Ramos, from Boulder Police Department." He held out his badge. "Are you feeling strong enough to talk to me about your recent attack?"

"Yes Detective Ramos, I am feeling much better. The sooner they catch him, the better. I am ready to tell you all that I can remember," she spoke softly. "Go ahead and ask what you may."

"Thank you, I appreciate the help. Anything we can get at this point will be valuable. We have to stop this maniac before anyone else is hurt or murdered. You are one of the lucky ones, to be sure," he took a deep breath. "Can you give me an account from beginning to end of what you remember? I would like to tape it, with your permission." He had a small hand-held recorder which he showed her. He turned it on and asked her the question. "Miss White do I have your permission to tape this conversation?"

"Of course I don't mind being taped. Whatever it takes to get that bastard off the streets," she answered quickly. "Oops, I didn't mean to use that language," she responded sheepishly.

"It's fine Miss White. I understand. Now if you would, in your own words, please take it slowly. Tell me what happened from the time you left the party and all you can remember."

"I left the party around ten-thirty and started walking home. I live a few blocks from there. When I was close to the museum, I heard a rustling in the bushes as I walked. I remember distinctly, there were some black birds, or dark colored birds that swooped down and all around me. It was pretty weird. I had never seen birds do that before and I've walked that same path many times." She took in a deep breath and exhaled slowly, as if to prepare herself for what she didn't want to remember, but knew she must.

"I remember stopping and looking around…looking at the birds flying down and settling on the ground and bushes. There were quite a few. Some flew away immediately and some just stayed there. I was pretty scared by then. Suddenly I felt the breath of someone behind me…close. I turned around and no one was there. I must have been imagining things at that point. But then the breathing sound became louder and there in front of me a man appeared quickly, as if he had been hiding in the bushes or something. I am not sure why," she stopped and took another breath. Her face was covered with distress.

"Can you give me a description of the man?"

"I looked right into his eyes. It was as if they drew me into a spell. They peered at me… almost right through me, I was thinking. He was not old, maybe about forty or fifty, I am guessing. He had a jacket; a long black jacket. I think a hat too…no, it was like a hood or something. Very bizarre. I just stood there for a moment staring at him, like I was frozen or something. And then he spoke to me. He told me not to be afraid. By then, I was freaking out, and there was no chance I wouldn't be afraid. I remember trying to run, but something held me like a force that would not let me move. I was in pure panic mode, I guess. He looked right through me, and then I felt the weirdest feeling of a sudden calm sweep over me. It was almost as if I could trust him or something; like I was being seduced. Very strange. I can't explain it any other way. That is the last thing I remember until I woke up here at the hospital. Sorry, but that is all I can tell you." Her face expressed relief that it was over. "I am glad to get the story out so you can find the pervert who did this. How many others are there?"

"There are three others that weren't so lucky. They were murdered." Mario's eyes darted away. "He knew she might be upset to hear that, but thought it best she knew."

"Oh my God!" she retorted.

"Sorry you had to hear that. But at this point I thought you should know. Did you get a good look at his face?" Mario questioned.

"I did, but it was dark. I do remember he was thin-faced and had very piercing eyes that seemed to have a strange kind of eeriness about them. The hood covered part of his face so I didn't get a good look. It was dark. He had longer hair, maybe a little grey, I think."

"Maybe when you are feeling better we can get a sketch artist to work with you and try to get a picture of what he looks like. You just let me know when you are up for it. No hurry. I want you feeling better and out of the hospital before that happens," Mario responded.

"Thank you so much for your help, Miss White. I know it will be of great importance in the case. You are very brave. I wish you the very best and quick recovery so that you can get back to your family."

"I have no family, Detective. I have school friends, but my parents were killed last year in an automobile accident and I have no brothers and sisters. I think my Uncle and Aunt live in Utah somewhere, but don't keep in touch."

"I am sorry to hear that. I know your friends will be very supportive, though, as I have spoken to some of them and they are very concerned for you. When you are ready to be released, we have services that you can utilize to get therapy that can help you get through this."

"Thank you Detective. I just may do that," she held out her hand and smiled shyly.

Mario left the room feeling very depressed after hearing her story. For now, he would return to the station and go full steam on the case. The description was odd and slim to none, but when he thought about it, he reflected on Maryanne's story and realized there could be a definite connection. He called Maryanne and she refreshed him on the details of her experience with the man who she thought was standing in her yard before disappearing into a mist. She thought possibly she was half asleep and had imagined or dreamed it. It made sense, in that the stories were similar. The birds were definitely an issue worth checking into.

Mario left the hospital and returned to the station. Chief Olson was in his office closing out the jewelry case when he knocked on the door and entered.

"How's it going, Chief?" Mario asked and waited for the signal to take a seat.

"Good, Mario," he motioned for him to sit down. Guess you know we nailed the perp in the Gem's Jeweler's heist. You were right about that one. But then, you have a good sense and that's why you're top dog here, next to me, that is," he kidded.

"Thanks Chief. I try," he chuckled. "I wanted to discuss the latest info about the serial murders."

"Shoot, if you'll pardon the pun," he laughed. "Want some coffee?"

"No thanks, I'm tryin' to cut back. Can't seem to sleep. I think it has something to do with the murders, though. I have a few theories and I'd like to run through them with you."

"Sure, what you got?"

"I told you about the incidents with birds recently... it

would seem that the victim who is in the hospital remembers birds…black birds; before she was attacked. I think there's a lot more going on here than we have been thinking. Something a little unusual, or maybe paranormal. It's just a theory, but worth looking into, don't you think?" Mario had a look of uncertainly painted across his face.

"Not another one. I sure hope not! It tends to stir up more crap from the media than we already have to deal with. Keep this under your hat. I don't want more back-lash from the press. I already have more than I can deal with as it is. They are eating us alive since these murders started. It just pisses me off the way they feed like vultures when we have a hard case. This one is a whopper." Chief Olson scratched his head and leaned back in his chair. "Ya know, I think that if you just keep doin' what your doin' we'll get our perp. I'm with you all the way, Mario. Just keep it between us, okay? I mean the paranormal stuff."

"Gotcha. I'll follow the leads and keep you informed. He filled Olson in on the details and signed out a little earlier than usual. He would try to piece a few elements together and hopefully bring the case to an end." Mario signed out and left for home.

It was early and Mario drove by the Valencia hoping the contractor was still there. He hadn't seen any of the current renovation. A blue pick-up sat in the drive with the obvious 'Prentiss Construction, Inc.' sign on the door. He hurried up the front stairs while observing the surprising changes on the exterior. The door was cracked open and he pushed it in. At first glance he was astounded at the work that had been accomplished in such a short time. Don Prentiss called from the top of the staircase.

"Hello. I'm Don Prentiss. What can I do for you?"

"I'm Mario Ramos, Maryanne's husband. Nice to finally meet you. I've heard nothing but praise for your work and now I can see why."

"Good to meet you for sure." Don started down the stairway to greet Mario.

"My pleasure," Mario answered, eyeing the good-looking contractor, with a slight pang of jealously.

"It's looking great! You've come a long way since I was here last," Mario complimented.

Don reached out to Mario and offered a handshake. "I was just about to start upstairs tearing out the final wallboards. I'll show you around down here first." He gave Mario a tour of the fruits of his labor as they walked from room to room. Mario was very impressed.

"This is much more than I could have imagined," Mario complimented Don.

"Thanks, I appreciate that," Don answered humbly. "Come upstairs and I'll show you what I've done. Tell you a little about what's left to do." Don sprinted up the stairs and Mario followed, but not quite as fast. Don seemed to be in a lot better shape. Mario was thinking he had better get back to the gym.

Don showed him the results of a new wood floor in most of the rooms and some which had already been dry-walled. The floors were not at final finish yet, but even without the finish it was incredible.

"I'll put the finish on the floors last thing. Don't want any dust at all. Can really mess it up, you know," Don chuckled.

"Here's where I'm at right now," he pointed to the walls, where he was ready to start the tear out.

Mario was amazed at the excellent quality of work the contractor had completed in such a short time.

Don took a hammer and knocked a hole into the wall where he was about to tear off more wall-board. Mario thanked him for the tour and started back down the beautifully finished stairway. On the way home, he dialed Maryanne to let her know he was on his way home and expressed his compliments on the work.

20

D on Prentiss returned to the area where the walls were being torn out, and was about half-way finished with the bedroom where Maryanne was once a prisoner. It was the room that had originally housed the old brass bed where she had mysteriously ended up after falling down the stairway when the railing gave out. Don knocked at the wall with his hammer and tore several boards off with the crowbar, when a disgusting smell permeated the room. He began to gag, and turned away, trying hard not to throw-up. He managed to control the urge. He took a red handkerchief from his pocket and wrapped it around his lower face from the nose down. With the crowbar, he began pulling the wall out from the studs. The wall gave way and the ghastly remains of a human skeleton fell out of the wall, hitting Don full force. He backed up in shock and there was no holding back his physical impulses. He spewed vomit like a geyser. When he was finished he wiped his face with old rags he had used for cleaning, freaking out about the bones touching him. *He was tough, but not that tough,* he was thinking. After he finally got himself together, he braved the bones and looked inside the wall. There were still remnants of the skeletal remains beneath the wall where he hadn't finished taking off the wood slats. He called 911.

"Hello, this is Donald Prentiss. I am owner of Prentiss Construction and I am at the old Valencia Manor, refurbishing the house. I pulled off a wall from the studs and skeletal remains fell out onto the floor. There are still some remains inside the wall. You'd better get over here," he gave them the address and turned off the cell. Don stood there, without a clue of what to do next. He was perplexed, and sick at his stomach. It had to be the most shocking discovery of his career in renovating older homes. He left the room and went down the hall to the staircase, while dialing Maryanne. She was all over it and in her car before he could finish the sentence. He kept talking and she kept driving until she arrived at the Valencia, where she pulled into the drive next to Don's truck.

"I'm here now and the police just drove up. I'll be right behind them." It was Detective Corolla and Steve Tratnik, Joan's ex fiancé.

"Hello Maryanne. Looks like we have another body to add to the list." Steve's face was covered with a somber mien.

"Yeah, it never seems to end…right?" Maryanne answered. She followed the detectives up the stairs and into the house. Don was standing at the foot of the staircase. His face was sullen and pale.

"I got the hell scared out of me today! I can honestly say, nothing can compare to that! C'mon upstairs and I'll take you to the room," Don spoke in a serious tone. The three followed him up the stairs and down the hall to the last room on the right. Maryanne was anxious. When they came to the room she had been held captive in, it brought a flood of memories back and she had to stop at the door and back up.

"I don't think I ought to go in there." Maryanne stood by the railing on the balcony holding on tight. She couldn't wrap her head around it, and decided to wait outside the room.

They went in while she stood thinking; re-living the horror she experienced in the room, not so long ago.

'*Why now?*' she was asking herself. She had been inside the room a few times since the abduction. What was making her so upset tonight? It couldn't be the bones. She studied forensics in college for at least a year. She had no problems with a few bones here and there. It was a pretty gruesome discovery, nonetheless. After mulling over it, her curiosity won out, and she took a few steps closer where she could see inside the room. The two detectives were inspecting the scene carefully, while Don Prentiss stood wide eyed, watching every move. A team would be coming along to gather evidence and study its derivation, hopefully able to identify the skeletal remains. She edged in and watched the detectives as they carefully secured any evidence they could find. A voice from downstairs rang through the house.

"Hello! Where are you?" The head forensic detective called out from the landing below. Maryanne went out to direct the team upstairs. She waved them up.

"Up here, Detectives," she called down to them. They began to ascend the stairs and when they were half-way up, the lights in the house went out. It was black as pitch! The detectives turned on their flashlights and kept moving slowly up the stairs. Maryanne was becoming more apprehensive as she waited for them to reach the top. Soon with the help of the flashlights, and her eyes becoming adjusted, she felt more at ease.

"What just happened? It can't be the wiring. I had an expert electrician do this job. It can't possibly be the work. Maybe a storm is coming?" Don stuck his head out from the room and held the light on Maryanne. The two detectives followed suit and stood outside the room, waiting for the forensic team.

"It figures. Now that we need light, the damn ghosts are going to play with us," Maryanne quipped.

"What ghosts?" Officer Jackson questioned.

"Never mind," Maryanne quickly tried to shut the subject down, but now the door had been opened and she was responsible. "It's all good. Don't worry about it. You don't have to worry about the dead…only the living. Didn't you know that?" she responded, trying to make light of a bad situation.

"Sure, I knew that," Jackson retorted, nervously.

"Okay then, let's get to work," Steve responded quickly. They all went back into the room, except for Don and Maryanne. They stood dumbfounded at the bizarre, morbid scenario.

"Is this for real?" Don questioned? "I'm beginning to get a little worried here."

"Calm down Don. They are dead and can't hurt you, so get over it," she chuckled quietly.

"You're right… they are dead. That's what has me worried."

"It could be worse. They could be alive and dangerous, hello!" Maryanne kidded.

"Okay Maryanne. You got me now. I am gonna get the hell out of here."

"Oh, you're gonna let a little ghost scare you off?" she quickly came back.

"I'm not scared, just a little maybe. I haven't really seen or heard any ghosts yet, so it's probably just a light malfunction, right? But I know that electrical job was well done. Doesn't make any sense."

"It could be a blackout in the area. It's been known to happen off and on around here. Let's not jump the gun and get too frenzied. We'll go inside and see what the guys are doing," Maryanne answered.

"At this point I feel safer in there anyway," Don quickly affirmed. "Let's go in." Not two seconds after he spoke a loud growling pierced through the darkness. It seemed to encompass the entire house, '*as if the house were alive again*,' Maryanne was thinking. '*As if they were back!*'

The two of them entered the room where the detectives and forensic team were diligently working to get everything they needed. Everyone was on edge, but no one believed in ghosts, except Maryanne. She had first-hand encounters that would freak even the experienced medium.

She knew the paranormal aspects of the house and what could happen here. She was ready, almost to the point of hoping to make contact with someone on the other side; to find out who this corpse belonged to. Who was locked inside the wall, either dead or alive and left to die there? What an awful thought. Her mind was going in circles now, imagining the most bizarre scenarios. The house seemed to be coming alive and ready to communicate. She wanted to be there when it happened. Maryanne was ready to delve into the unknown phenomena of the mysterious Manor. This time, it would be the final step, she convinced herself. Maryanne stepped outside the room, dialing Vivian Gilbreth on her cell. A quick answer from the Psychic and she breathed a sigh of relief.

"Vivian Gilbreth here. Is that you Maryanne?"

"Yes...Vivian it's me. I'm in the middle of a dilemma at the Valencia Manor again. Are you in town?"

"Yes I am. I returned yesterday. Had an unbelievable experience in England, and learned so much from so many. It was very worth the trip. It will help me immensely in my work. So what's going on over there?"

"I am having the house renovated, as you were aware. It had been going well, with a little activity here and there but nothing really to speak of; that is until now. My contractor was tearing out walls inside the upper bedroom. The bedroom where I found myself after the fall. It's the room where the secret dumbwaiter was...that led to the hole under the house. He had been tearing off a wall and a skeleton fell out of the wall, right on top of him. The forensic team is here now and detectives, working to get evidence and secure the corpse for lab testing and DNA. Don't have a clue of who it is; whether its man or woman, you know the drill. When the forensic team arrived a horrible growl encompassed the house and all of the lights went out after the electrical had been restored to like-new condition. It is so bizarre. I know you can help me. Can you come?"

"Of course I can. When would you like me to be there?"

"How about as soon as possible?" Maryanne was hopeful.

"Sure. Give me about fifteen minutes to get myself together and I'll drive on over. Take me about thirty minutes, or so."

"Thank you so much Vivian! I'll be here waiting for you. Just come on in." Maryanne added.

"See you in a few…don't worry." Vivian hung up.

For the time being, the house had become quiet again. All Maryanne could hear were the detectives working diligently to extricate the boney corpse out of the wall with all of its parts. She entered the room where Don stood; eyes wide open with a look of bewilderment. When she touched him, he jumped back, startled.

"Don't scare me like that," Don snapped and then chuckled. "I was totally absorbed in the forensic team performing such unusually inordinate duties. Incredible work. It's fascinating to see what they do to secure a scene. I hope they figure out who the boney captive was, or is, I should say. Kind of creepy. That thing fell on top of me," he sneered. "I nearly had a heart attack. Ugggg! I feel like I have worms crawling all over me," he said, with a disgusted look on his face.

"It looks like a worm crawling on your shirt," Joan pointed down under his chin.

"Oh shit!" He jumped and swiped at his shirt almost falling backwards against the wall. "Is it gone?" he frantically questioned. Maryanne stood laughing, trying to keep it under wraps, but he got the gist of the joke and joined in, with another dubious look.

"Damn you woman. I'm gonna get even with you. Just wait."

"It was just too good to pass up," she answered, laughing. She could see he was a little embarrassed. "I'm kidding Don. Couldn't resist that one. Sorry," she sheepishly apologized, still with added laughter.

"Like I said, I'll get you," he kidded, trying to hide his embarrassment.

Maryanne moved closer to where the team was working. "So how are you guys coming along?"

"Looks like we'll be done in a few minutes. Then we'll get to the lab and hopefully discover who this unfortunate person is, or was." Steve Tratnik answered, peering inside the wall. Within minutes, the team began gathering up their wares and headed out the door and down the stairs to their vehicles. As quick as they left, the lights turned on again, and the house lit up in full bloom.

"Now wouldn't that just beat all?" Jackson remarked, shaking his head as he walked out the door

The detectives left, while Maryanne and Don lingered, checking the house to determine why the power had suddenly failed.

"It shouldn't have happened, I can tell you that, unless it was a neighborhood thing. I had a top notch electrician restore all the wiring and boxes, like new. There has to be more to this than what's obvious. I sure don't like to say it could be paranormal, but I'm beginning to wonder." He smiled at Maryanne. "And you just watch out, Maryanne. I still owe you one. I'm gonna pull a fast one on you one day and you won't see it comin'," he teased.

"Are you still mad that I got you good?" she ribbed Don.

"No, not mad. Just gonna get you good," he mocked.

A knock at the door startled both of them and Vivian Gilbreth walked inside.

"Hello Maryanne. I'm back." Vivian teased as she sauntered inside; her usual calm, collective attitude written all over her. "And who might this handsome devil be? Pardon the pun, but you are a good-looking man." Vivian was not afraid to say what was on her mind. Maryanne loved that about her.

"This is Don Prentiss, the contractor…Vivian. The one I told you about."

"I figured that, just had to throw a punch or two to get this party started," she grinned. "Looks like the lights came back on."

"I've heard great things about you Miss Gilbreth," Don reached out to her.

The Psychic took Don's hand. "Hmmm…one of these days I would like to read you. I am getting some very interesting vibrations," she eyed him curiously.

"So, what am I thinking right now?" Don kidded.

"You are thinking, 'who the hell's this crazy lady?', and she laughed, her magnetic charm spilling over. "But what you are really thinking is…oops, I think I'd better keep that thought to myself." The Psychic chuckled again. Her green eyes sparkled as they reflected light from the chandeliers. After an exchange of small talk, they were ready to check out the crime scene.

Don watched Vivian curiously, wondering whether she was kidding or if she really knew that he had been thinking about Maryanne. He hoped it didn't come through that obviously. He hoped it was only his conscience getting the best of him and he would not want to make a bad impression on Vivian. Besides; as much as he was attracted to Maryanne, he would never do or say anything that would interfere with her fiancé in any way. Of that he was positive.

The lights magically came back on after the team of

forensics and two detectives left. They had been forced to work diligently by flashlights and construction fixtures, while they labored to clean up the scene.

"Someone didn't want them up there, did they?" Vivian answered. I'm eager to get started. I thought this place was clean last time I was here. One never knows about the supernatural, though. One day here, next day there." She ascended the stairs behind Maryanne, and Don followed close behind and when they approached the end of the hall, Maryanne stopped.

"This is it. The bedroom." She opened the door and led them inside. Vivian went straight to the gaping hole, where the remains had been unsuspectingly discovered and reached inside with both hands held open. After a few minutes of quiet, she turned around.

"There's definitely something going on in this room. I can feel an extremely strong presence. Someone is very angry. A woman. She's trying to tell me something. Keep very still." The Psychic went into a trance-like meditation and stood with her hands open and palms up. The lights began to flicker and a freezing cold breeze swept through the room. Maryanne and Don stood wide-eyed and quiet, taking in every move. The Psychic began speaking in a strange dialect, and then in English. Her voice changed to that of a younger woman.

"My Father put me in this wall. I knew too many secrets about his past and another child that Mother had given birth to. We had a terrible argument and he began hitting me with the poker from the fireplace. He became very hostile. I wanted to leave the house and run away, but he wouldn't have it. He made sure I didn't leave and tell any of his dirty little secrets. I was only seventeen years old. My name is Edwina Rafael Farthington. My Father did this and I want to find him. I have unfinished words to discuss with him." The voice stopped and Vivian stood still, taking in long, deep breaths, and was exhausted from the experience.

"Edwina Rafael. That's the child of John Farthington that

his sister Irene Dirkshire told us had run away after a family disagreement. I guess she didn't run away. That's why we could never find her and or any record of her death. He murdered her and put her in the wall. My God, that is tragic. The poor child. She never even had a decent burial. A tragic ending for such a young woman."

"I guess that answers one question, but what did Edwina mean secrets?" Maryanne pondered.

"I must speak to her again. We need more answers to those questions," Vivian said. "I wonder if she will materialize for me. Do you still have those candles that were in the room before?"

"Don, do you remember a box of candles that I left downstairs?" Maryanne asked.

"Yes. They're in the pantry. I'll get them. Be right back. He hurried off, down the stairs and was back in a few minutes with the candles.

"Let's get started." Maryanne set the box on the floor and the three of them began placing candles in a circle under the Psychic's direction. They formed a small circle and Vivian sat inside them, on the floor. When the candles were lit, Don switched the lights off. Vivian began her ritual and the chanting. After about ten minutes, a light mist appeared across the room, near the hole where Edwina had been walled up after she was murdered. The mist became brighter until a lovely young woman appeared within. She had dark brown hair and her eyes were almost a sky-blue. They had such a magnificent exuberance. She was truly a beautiful young woman. Maryanne and Don were speechless and in awe at the manifestation.

"Edwina Rafael, can you tell me what I need to know about the secrets of John Farthington? I must get the information in order to right some wrongs that were done to many people." Vivian spoke softly to the spirit.

"My parents had another child that was killed by my father. It was a boy and he was two years old. No one knew they even had a child. He had been born at home and my father would not let my mother out of the house when he found out she was pregnant. The child belonged to another man. My mother was abused so badly, as I had been, and she met a man who she fell in love with. She became pregnant and that's why no one knew about the child. He kept her inside until he was born. He was born with a deformity; he had only one arm. My father didn't want him and kept him inside the Manor until he was two. At that time, he pushed him off the top floor where he fell to his death. I know he was probably better off than being treated with the cruelty that our father had put him through for those two years. I tried to get away but finally when I was ready to leave, he started screaming and ranting. He picked up a poker from the fire-place and beat me with it until I lay dying on the floor, covered in blood. He buried me in the wall to keep me from telling the truth about the horrifying experiences and the murder of my brother. He was a little Angel. I woke up inside the wall and began screaming, praying someone would find me before my demise. No one ever came. The last thing I remember is my baby brother, Samuel coming to me and taking me with him. That's when I died. My father drove my mother insane and she finally died, after giving birth to another baby girl that fell from the top balcony to her death. My mother tried to save her but she could not. She was never the same after that. My spirit stayed inside the Manor since then. I wanted revenge on my Father. I only wish my father had to pay for his crimes. I want to find him but I don't know where he is. I did not want to cross over until I saw that he paid for his crimes. Now, I don't know how to get to the other side. The hate and discontent I felt about my Father has kept me from passing through into the light. I only want to go and be with Samuel, my Brother and my Mother." The apparition was beginning to fade.

"Edwina, in order for you to find peace you must cross over. John Farthington will pay the ultimate price as everyone who has done wrong pays. You must not let it keep you a prisoner here, between heaven and earth. It is more of a hell than anything else. Let me help you go to the light." Vivian persuaded Edwina.

"There is one more thing," Edwina began to speak softly and much weaker than before. "John Farthington adopted a child long ago, who is about twenty-three years old now. He abused her and locked her up in this house. He kept her in a hole under the house most of the time. There is a dumbwaiter that he used to bring her food and sometimes he let her come upstairs. Not very often. She was schooled by John and well-educated. He was not in a right mind. He did make sure she had an education, even though she was abused. He adopted her from a family that had a young daughter that became pregnant and made her give the child up before she ever saw her. The child is still alive. I am very tired now," Edwina spoke softly. "I want to go. I think I am ready to go into the light. I can see it now. Thank you for releasing me from this hell." Edwina Rafael disappeared from the mist that had been surrounding her.

The three of them stood in silence after hearing the most gruesome story ever connected with the Manor. Maryanne was sick at her stomach. She had been crying while the tortured soul had poured out the horrible story of her past and beyond. Don was so overcome, he could not speak. Vivian was at the point of exhaustion and she sat sullen on the floor. She began to speak.

"I really don't think I could take too much more of that kind of revelation. It was so overwhelming. It took a lot of energy to complete this task. God bless poor Edwina Rafael and the two other children whom we had known little or nothing about. Where is the child who was adopted? It has to be Hanna Michele. While I was in trance, she came to the forefront of my mind for just a second. I am pretty sure it's her. We had suspected that all along and now it seems evident. Now we can understand where the education had been administered. At least she has that, and the good thing so far with Hanna is that she doesn't remember him and let's hope she never does."

"I think I'm going to be sick." Maryanne ran out of the room and down the stairs to the bathroom. The lights were still on downstairs. When she was finished she splashed cold water on her face and stood looking into the mirror that had been beautifully restored and hung over the basin. The face of a woman flashed into the mirror and she did not recognize her. It was a woman of about forty five or so, with dark auburn hair. She looked like an angel and was gone within seconds. Maryanne backed away from the sink and left the room. She met the others in the great-room, where they had just returned from up-stairs.

"Oh God. This house is so unbelievable. How could so much insanity prevail in one lifetime?" I must get out of here for now. It's too much to digest." Maryanne slowly made her way toward the front door. The others followed in silence until they were out on the grounds.

"Vivian, I can't tell you how much you have helped to clear paths for those who have gone and helped us to understand what really happened here. I will be eternally grateful. We will keep in touch. I will call you next week and we can make plans so I can take you to dinner and spend time just being ourselves. Thank you again."

"It was my pleasure, Maryanne. Anything I can do to help you just call. Yes, dinner sounds absolutely wonderful. Let's plan that." She wrapped her arms around Maryanne and embraced her. Don opened the door to her car and she was off.

"Maryanne, this was probably the most unbelievable thing that has ever happened to me. I still don't know if I believe what I just witnessed. The ghosts, I can handle but to have a

skeleton fall from its tomb in the wall was a bit overwhelming."
Don looked down at her with his seductive blue eyes that
went right through her. She felt a weakness but held back,
knowing it was only because of all the emotions that she had
just experienced that had made her more vulnerable.

"I understand, Don. I feel quite similar about the entire
ordeal, but I've realized that as time goes on it is much easier
to believe. I guess it's, 'To each his own'. Thanks for being
here, it certainly helped to have a man around the house", she
kidded.

"You are quite welcome, but I should thank you for
bringing Vivian Gilbreth in to solve some of the dilemma.
Bones have a way of telling the tales that get buried away. Now
at least the young woman can get some peace. And I was pretty
freaked out in the beginning but I'm getting a thicker skin,
too," he replied, smiling.

Maryanne walked toward him and gave him a friendly
squeeze, thinking how easy it would be to let go and take this
into another direction. He walked her to the car and opened
the door. She shifted into the seat and rolled the window
down.

"Thanks again, Don. Talk to you tomorrow. Are you okay
going into the house tomorrow to work?"

"Sure. No problem now. I'm good to go," he smiled and
waved her off. But was he? He would soon find out, once he was
back to work at the mysterious and ever-changing edifice.

21

Mario sat at his desk, going over details of evidence from the Slasher case. He hadn't made too much headway since he spoke to the only survivor, who was still a patient at Boulder Hospital. A visit to her was next on his list. She had asked to speak to him recently and had been improving greatly. Forensics determined the DNA samples must have been corrupted, since they showed an undecipherable code. They had never before experienced these kinds of results and put that on a back-burner, until tests were completed at a high tech lab in New York City. Meanwhile, Mario had a complete scenario of all incidents and evidence in a well-organized file.

There were many tight leads of how the crimes had taken place but still nothing concrete as to why there was so little blood at the scenes. He was hoping to get some answers from the only surviving victim.

When Mario walked to the victim's room, an armed guard was outside the door, which he had insisted upon. He spoke quietly to the guard and then made his way inside the room. She was sitting up in bed, looking quite well, considering the last visit. Her face had regained its color from the pale greyish tinge it had when he last saw her. The doctors had given her three separate blood transfusions to get her to this point. When she had arrived, she was at the point of death, with an extremely low blood count. From first look, he was pleased that she had improved as much. He greeted her.

"Hello, Miss White. I am Detective Mario Ramos. Do you remember me? I last visited you when you had only been in a few days." He took out his badge and showed her. She looked scared and apprehensive when he spoke. After what she had gone through, it was no wonder.

"Yes, I do remember seeing you. I can't remember much of what we talked about but, yes," she meekly answered.

"I just got the message that you wanted to speak to someone about the case and if you feel like talking about it, I am here to listen. Hopefully to get any kind of clue as to who this vicious person is and get him off the street before anyone else is hurt or worse. Can you go through it with me, the parts you can recall? Do you approve of me recording this conversation?"

"Yes, I will tell you anything I can remember. If you will ask the questions, I will answer as best I can, and you may record anything you feel is pertinent to the case." She spoke in a soft, quiet demeanor.

"Thank you, Miss White. We'll start from the top. When you left the party, just go on from there as you walked down that street. Can you do that?"

"Sure. I remember walking down the sidewalk, and then crossing the street on the corner where I usually walk." She took in a few breaths, as if she were remembering more clearly, the tragic attack.

"First, I heard a fluttering of wings. Then it became more intense. When I looked up to see where the sounds were coming from, the whirring and fluttering intensified and a cloud seemed to be moving in the darkened sky, toward me. It was a flock of black birds in frenzy, it seemed. As they approached, some of them began landing on the ground all around me. It was uncanny. Their beady eyes seemed to be staring at me as if they were there for a reason. A reason that felt eerie and supernatural, if you will. Not that I am familiar with that subject, but nonetheless, my interpretation. I felt as though someone, a person, was watching me as I stood there in fear. It wasn't just the birds. It was as though someone could see my every move and I could almost feel the eyes on me. It was an uncomfortable feeling; like I had never experienced before. I remember looking back and all around me, but there was no one there that I could see, except the birds who seemed to be part of the whole scenario. I felt fear begin to surge through me and began to walk faster, looking back once or twice before approaching the museum. The birds followed and landed here and there as I walked along. I stopped quickly to see if I could hear anyone but the birds were making so much noise. Then, the birds lifted and flew off and I heard a distant sound, almost like breathing. It was all very unsettling. Then I began to walk again, slowly, carefully past the bushes and I felt a presence, even before I saw him. It was as though he just appeared right in front of me. I know it sounds weird, but this is the way I am remembering it. His eyes…they are the one evil and strange thing that comes to my mind. They were piercing, like he was looking right through me. I couldn't move a muscle. I stood still, wanting to run but for some reason, could not. My eyes were drawn to his like a magnet. I felt a strange feeling that I can't even describe right now. It was a feeling of helplessness, but then again it was mixed with some kind of trust. I know it doesn't make any sense to anyone. Not even to myself. I have gone over it a thousand times in my mind and none if it seems to make any sense at all."

"It's okay. Take your time and don't try to force yourself. Just take it easy and tell me what happened. Do you feel like talking any more about it?" Mario was very gentle in his approach. He knew she had been severely traumatized and used delicate measures to question her. She was in a fragile mental state and Mario was a professional who knew how to handle even the most unusual circumstance when dealing with a victim.

"After I felt the weird sensation of almost beginning not to fear him, I remember him speaking to me, but it is more like a dream-state at that point. It was as if he was speaking to me telepathically. I am sure it's just because of the trauma that I remember it like that, but it's the only way I can describe it." She began to tear up, and Mario knew it was time to stop. He didn't want to push her any more.

"I am going to leave you now, Miss White. I think I've bothered you enough today and I apologize that it has made you upset. When you are more able to talk and only if you want to I will be glad to return."

"No, don't leave. I want to finish this. The horrible person has to be caught and if I can help in any way, I will. Now I will finish telling you what I remember."

"Only if you are positive it is not making you too upset. I don't want that to happen. We have plenty of time. In your time; when you are ready," Mario spoke softly.

"I am ready. Please just a bit more," she urged him.

"Okay Miss White; just a bit more then. But only for a few minutes," he sat back down beside the bed.

"Detective Ramos, if they don't catch him, there are more to come. This I know. Now I will finish." Miss White sucked in a deep breath and exhaled. "When I was almost under his trance-like stare, I tried to pull away but was unable to. And then he came close and his breath was hot and peculiar sounding, like one would expect a ghost to sound like; if there were such things, and if that makes any sense at all. His mouth was next to my ear, breathing ever-so-slowly, and then he touched my face with his hands. His nails were long, like a woman's. I could feel them lightly brushing against my face and down to my neck. His mouth touched my face and it slowly made its way down to my neck. I became almost excited with its intimacy. Never before have I even known such a feeling. It was almost sexual, yet not at all. I was consumed by then and the rest is blank. I cannot remember anything after that until I woke in my hospital bed. Even then, I don't remember too much of the hospital stay. Like bits and pieces of nurses, doctors and even a time or two, it was as if I saw him again and again. I am so perplexed by this and not even understanding what it is I am trying to say. That's why I wanted to speak to you. To see if you can understand more of the details that I have told you since the last time we spoke. Now I am finished, Detective Ramos. You may leave now. I appreciate you coming and listening to me. I had to tell someone soon," she let out a deep sigh, as if she had a subconscious memory that was bubbling to the surface and not yet able to recollect. She seemed relieved in a sense, and unconsciously trying to warn him of something to come.

"Thank you so much. I appreciate all you have told me. My heart and prayers are with you. If you want to talk more, just let the doctor know and I'll return. There will be a guard posted at the door. You are safe here," he comforted her. "I hope that you'll soon be able to speak with a therapist. It will help you greatly." Mario left the hospital and now he was inclined to take a new approach to this crime. A new direction, that Chief Olson would more than likely not be in agreement. He would speak to him today and relay his find.

Back at the station, Mario entered Chief Olson's office, carrying the Slasher file.

"Mario, come on in. I've been expecting you. Coffee?"

"No thanks, I'm good. Want to run this by you and get your thoughts on it. Some very odd things have been going on and the more I add them up, the more it becomes unbelievable. I know you're not going to like what I have to say upon conclusion, but nevertheless I am going to tell you now," Mario looked down at the floor.

"Okay Mario, spit it out. I know your look and something is brewing. Let's have it," the chief offered a slight smile and then became serious.

"Remember when I told you about the birds and the strange man in Maryanne's yard? Then there were the issues at Joan's with more birds and strange visions as well. Now I have a whole new event that has just been described by the surviving patient of the Slasher serial case."

Mario went on to tell him the entire scenario and then played the recording. Chief Olson was riveted by the story and even though he was not in tune with paranormal theories, the information just presented, gave him more of a consensus with Mario's conclusions. When they finished going over the recent findings, Chief Olson was more acceptable to visiting other theories. Now Mario was ready to pursue an indubitably, non-conforming direction. He returned to his office leaving Chief Olson in a very anomalous state of mind. He knew the chief would have to chew on this one for a day or two before he was totally on board with Mario's new theory, but somehow Mario knew they would both come to agreement in the scheme of things.

Mario's phone rang, and Maryanne informed him that Vasilev, the buyer of her home was meeting her at Joan's office, hopefully to close the deal on the house. She told him to stop and get dinner somewhere, so she wouldn't have to prepare anything. He would be late coming home anyway, as he intended to call on Vivian Gilbreth to ask her a few questions concerning the current case and its paranormal twist. Two hours later Mario arrived at the Psychic's town-home.

"Mario Ramos. It's a pleasure to see you my dear." Vivian opened the door and directed him to her office, den where she offered him some tea and cookies. The room was remarkably decorated with unique items relating to the paranormal, spiritual and supernatural aspects of her special gift; communicating with the afterlife, so to speak. The Medium was very informed on all aspects of unusual phenomena. She was just what the case needed. Mario never thought a year ago, that he would ever agree to collaborate with a Psychic in his work as a detective.

"You are a remarkable decorator, Miss Gilbreth. The room is very interesting, to say the least," Mario complimented.

"Why thank you. I am delighted that you are beginning to become more open-minded about such things," she chuckled, her hazel-green eyes vibrant. She seemed to have an aura of well-being and her eyes were warm and kind. Mario had not noticed too much about her in the past. He felt quite comfortable in her presence, though. She had the "it" factor, which to him meant that people automatically were drawn to her positive energy.

"You are certainly welcome. When I called I explained why I wanted to see you. I hope you can help me. This case has taken a serious turn in a direction that I am not familiar. You on the other hand, are the only one that I know who might have some answers," he spoke directly and more seriously.

"Yes, you are probably correct since you are not familiar with the other side, or should I say the unexplainable?" Vivian smiled warmly. "The incident you are describing is complex. I have some books here that I will show you as we proceed. There could be a presence of one of two things. A cult inspired person or perhaps more than one, who practices a form of vampirism which is modern day and are alive on the earth plane. They sometimes use animals for their practices and have many kinds of rituals. Usually they don't kill humans to feed on. The other is described as the walking dead. They are not of this world but have been known to inhabit the earth plane for a time, causing chaos and death wherever they can. These are the real vampires. You don't want to know one, trust me on that. Now I think I can help you. Will you take me to Maryanne and Joan so I can talk to them and hear every detail of each apparition? I want to know everything. It is important so that I can examine all the facts that we are dealing with here."

"Yes, I can take you there and you can ask all the questions you need. When will you be able to go?" Mario was anxious to get to the bottom of the strange phenomena.

"I can be ready in an hour if you want me to go right away. I have to put a few things together so if you'll hang out a while, I'll get ready. How does that work for you?" Vivian began getting things together. She placed a book in front of Mario, and continued to get ready, while he caught up on some very unusual information.

The book, Parapsychology; The Controversial Science, by Richard Broughton, Ph.D. was something he knew nothing about. Thumbing through the worn pages, he read a few paragraphs and it seemed rather easy to follow and very enlightening. He became buried into the pages, when Vivian came into the room.

"I'm ready Mario. Let's get the show on the road," she kidded.

"I got sidetracked with this book. Interesting stuff," he answered. "Sure, I'm ready. Let's get going."

"Take the book with you and if you get time, give it a read. It's easy to follow and you'll be fairly surprised at what it's all about. Just remember where you got it," she chuckled.

They left the house and on the way back, he spent time asking more questions about the practice of vampirism in America and abroad. He had a lot to learn in that department. He would have never given it a second thought until the strange materializations began.

Fifteen minutes later, they pulled up the driveway. He jumped out and opened Vivian's door.

"Chivalry is not dead, after all," she joked, smiling.

"I guess I still have a few good habits," he responded, with a slight grin.

"I am glad for that. The house looks great since I was

here last. When I was here, you and Maryanne weren't even married yet. She was working on the house then, but it's come a long way."

"Wait until you see the inside. It's gone through some big changes and the house is currently under contract. She is supposed to have the closing tonight. Hopefully it goes as planned with no interruptions. As soon as it's done, we are preparing to move into the Valencia. Both of us are obviously quite anxious."

Mario opened the front door and let Vivian enter first.

"It looks incredible. Good work, whoever did the decorating."

"Thanks. It was mostly Maryanne. She has a knack for it." Mario took her through the house and showed her the recent changes.

"The next time I want my house decorated, I'm calling on Maryanne," Vivian added.

"Would you like something to eat? I haven't eaten since breakfast. I'll order some Chinese if you like," Mario asked.

"Sounds wonderful. Wonton soup and fried rice for me," she answered.

"You got it. I'll order something for Maryanne too, and she can have a snack when she gets back from the closing." Mario was eager to please. He called the order in and made coffee and tea, remembering that she loved green tea. He directed her to the comfortable easy chair where she could relax. He slid a small table near the chair. Vivian sipped on tea and they spent half an hour going through everything Mario could remember about the apparitions. The delivery was here and Maryanne arrived in time to enjoy the food while it was still hot.

"Hello Vivian. Always good to see you. I've got great news!" She went on to explain that the closing was complete and they could now move into the Manor.

"We can move whenever you want," Mario exclaimed throwing his arms around Maryanne.

"I called Vivian so she can speak with you about the apparitions you had experienced; the birds, bats, and strange man. I think the recent murders could be connected. Sit down and eat something and we'll talk about it," Mario urged.

"Mario wanted my expertise, and I'll let him explain what we are dealing with and then I can ask some questions. But first, you must sit down and eat some of this wonderful Chinese food Mario ordered for you."

"Mario you are a sweetheart. I am famished. Thank you." Maryanne kissed Mario quickly on the cheek. "I have a lot to tell you now, but it can wait until we're done. Be right back." She laid down her brief-case, went into the kitchen, washed her hands and then took a seat on the sofa next to Mario. The three of them enjoyed the best Chinese take-out in the area.

"Thanks for dinner, I certainly enjoyed it," Vivian complimented. She got up and picked up the plates, taking them to the kitchen and then sat down again, ready to discuss the matter at hand.

"Now I'll let you two discuss the important stuff and I'll be finishing up a little paperwork until you are done." Mario went into the kitchen where he spread the Slasher file across the table while the two of them were in deep discussion about the strange birds and the mysterious dark stranger, who had appeared in her yard.

When Vivian had heard all of the pertinent information from Maryanne, they sat for a while chatting about various subjects, not connected with the supernatural. Maryanne insisted that Vivian stay the night. It had been a trying but fruitful day for all of them. By eleven o'clock they were all sound asleep.

It was three o'clock in the morning when a loud banging began to emanate from the back yard area. Mario jumped out of bed, threw on a robe and grabbed his gun. He opened the door to the back yard deck and walked out onto the porch with his thirty-eight in front. Vivian came to the back door and pushed it open.

"What's the racket?"

"I'm not sure. Stay there, I'm checking it out. I have a gun." Mario stood on the deck, flashlight scanning the yard. There were birds as before, sitting in various places on the deck-railing and around the yard. He didn't see anyone at that point. Several black-birds took flight. Some stayed, *as if to mock him*, he was thinking. When he stepped onto the deck, he noticed a dark figure on the other side of the fence. He couldn't tell what or who it was. Vivian followed behind, stepping outside the door onto the deck and stopped. She held out her hands, palms up, chanting unusual verses. The rest of the birds took flight and the dark figure stood peering at them with ghastly eyes from behind the fence. He wore a long dark coat or jacket, and a hat; maybe a top hat or the like, he was thinking. He became anxious as the figure seemed to shift closer. Vivian had made a connection and was telepathically communicating with him. Mario moved back away from the railing and stood next to Vivian, watching. She was in complete trance at this point and making sense only to herself. Then, without any indication, the dark stranger seemed to vanish from his spot near the fence. Only a white mist remained and all was quiet again. Mario took Vivian's arm and directed her into the house. She seemed to be out of trance and aware of what had been happening.

"Who the hell was that?" Mario questioned excitedly. Did you get anything from that, Vivian?"

"Let's go inside. I have made some connections and I'll explain." They re-entered the house and he locked up tight. Maryanne had awakened and they gathered in the living-room.

"I have some information from another entity; one who is an enemy of the man in the yard. A friendly spirit-guide gave me information about the stranger in black," Vivian expounded, slightly out of breath. "The man is apparently living on this plane and a modern-day vampire, as I had explained before about the different types or species, if you will. They have evolved and are able to live as we do, for the most part. He is actually dead, but living as a normal man by day and prowling by night to find feeding grounds for the group of them who inhabit a few locations in the area. They have not been here for long and want to expand their reach throughout the state. So far, they live in Denver and Colorado Springs. The guide told me there are six of them here in Boulder. They have graduated to a state of being where they can mix with society, as long as they keep their eyes covered when the sun is bright. It harms them when they do not wear special glasses. They feed on human blood and we can fight this, if we do everything the guide has told me. We have no time to waste. There have already been several casualties that I will be informed of soon. The spirit-guide will be in touch with me. Do not go outside the house at night. They are harmless during the day and you can't recognize them if you aren't looking. If you are an informed person, such as yourselves, you may be able to spot them. Keep yourselves on high alert." Vivian was exhausted. "I'd like to rest now. We can talk more about it in the morning."

Mario and Maryanne were in total disbelief that such things could be manifesting here in Boulder, Colorado. After an informed discussion, they all went to bed and made an attempt at sleep until seven a.m.

22

Maryanne, Mario and Vivian slept very little and were ready to become more actively involved and take on a whole new outlook of the perpetrators in the Slasher case as quickly as possible. Mario would speak to Chief Olson at work. He called to make a special appointment so he could inform the Chief of recent developments. Mario was almost certain there was a connection to the Slasher murders. Vivian had given him enough to go on for now and she had offered to assist in any way that she could. If indeed, Vivian's communication was valid, this evening she would take them through the complete breakdown of what they must do to eliminate the vampire-like creatures from their midst, before anyone else was murdered.

Maryanne drove Vivian back to her townhouse after treating her to a nourishing breakfast. They arrived at the shop where Wendy was already busy with inventory. Maryanne didn't want to upset Wendy, but she had to inform her of the looming danger that had become fore-front in their community.

Meanwhile, Vivian would collect some things together, that would help protect them from the unknown creatures, should they return. They would meet with the psychic later, when she would educate them on current measures that would hopefully keep them safe.

At Boulder Hospital, Julia White, the latest victim of the Slasher, sat in bed re-living the gruesome attack. A constant replay of the incident repeated itself like a broken record. She could virtually feel the assailant's hot breath, and the strange sensations as cold fingers traced along her face and down to her neck. No matter how many times she tried to ward off the memory, it would repeat itself only to make her more aware of a feeling that she was not able to comprehend. She began to feel different physically and mentally since the brutal assault. It was as if she were becoming someone that she didn't recognize. When she looked into the mirror, it was as if her physical appearance had changed in some odd way, but it wasn't obvious to others, and she was becoming more confused and afraid. Could she be going through some kind of metamorphosis caused by the attack? She wondered if that were possible. She pressed the nurse-call button.

"A barely audible, complacent voice answered, "Nurses station. Can I help you?"

"Can you send a nurse please?"

"Right away," the voice confirmed. Julia waited what seemed like half an hour when a stern-faced nurse appeared in the doorway.

"What is it you need?" she questioned impatiently.

"I want to talk to the Detective again. Detective Mario Ramos. Can you let Boulder Police Department know that I want to speak to him?"

"I'll let the supervisor know." She turned and walked out of the room, without another word. Julia slid back down into the bed as she lowered the head, and would try to get some well-needed sleep. It seemed like she was always tired during the day and when night came, she felt restless much more than usual. She hoped Detective Ramos would come soon. She needed to speak to someone about the strange feelings she had been experiencing. It was one o'clock in the afternoon when she finally slipped into a deep, sleep.

A dark figure stood in the doorway of her room. She could not make out the face and then as it walked toward her bed, and she recognized him. The attacker came close to her and leaned over, whispering in her ear.

"You belong to me now. You must let yourself go. Follow me into my world of ecstasy. You will know an everlasting life that will not change you. You will remain young forever. Follow me now"…the voice drifted off and someone was calling her name.

"Julia White. Wake up Julia. Are you all right?" Detective Ramos was standing over her bed as she opened her eyes. Even though it seemed so real, she was thankful that it was only a dream. She was relieved and moved the bed into its upright position. Somewhat disheveled, she gained her bearings before speaking.

"Hello Detective. Thank you for coming. Sorry about that, I was having a bad dream. I wanted to speak to you about the way I have been feeling since I saw you last.

"Feel free to tell me what is bothering you," Mario pulled up the chair next to her bed and sat, while Julia began describing the strange feelings and the dreams. Mario was very worried and concerned that she could have a relapse.

"I know you are not feeling right, but it hasn't been that long since you were attacked and I am sure that for some time, you are going to feel and remember dreadful thoughts about the experience. You must not let your imagination get the best of you though." Mario didn't want to alarm her, but felt that by comforting her and giving her reassurance, she would not tend to be so worried. He also knew that there was a more sinister side to the story. A side that he did not want to let her know, but one that he wanted to explore.

"I have a friend who is experienced in many things about what you are telling me. May I call her and have her come in with me and you tell her your concerns. She is not a shrink. She is a medium and studies parapsychology and the many different aspects of it. Would you like to have her come and speak with you? She is a wonderful person and I think she can help you," Mario reassured her.

"Sure. If you think it will help to clear up these confusing thoughts I am having. I would like to meet with her. When can you bring her? Soon, I hope."

"I will try to call her now. I'll step outside your room to call her and be right back." Mario dialed.

"Nice to hear from you Mario. What can I do for you? We are due to meet later this evening, right?" the Psychic answered.

"Yes, that is correct, Vivian." Mario explained the recent feelings that Julia White had been experiencing and she was very interested in speaking to her. She offered to come right away, if he agreed. Mario would wait for her. He re-entered Julia's room to let her know that Vivian Gilbreth would be arriving in about half an hour. He sat by Julia's bed and she expounded more about the feelings that she had been experiencing. Mario let her go on, knowing that she would be less anxious if she talked about it. When the Psychic arrived and Mario left the room so the two of them could talk privately. He sat in the coffee shop, going over everything in his mind, worried that these manifestations were more serious than he thought. He was thankful Vivian had come over and was sure she could answer the questions.

Vivian spoke to Julia for an hour, listening to her concerns and what she had interpreted to be manifestations. Julia was thankful Vivian had come and felt more assured that there was an explanation for her fears. Vivian would be back to see her the next day to keep up on her progress. She called Mario and he returned to the room. The three of them chatted for another half hour and Julia was beginning to get very sleepy. Dinner was soon to come and then she could get some rest. Mario and Vivian bid her good-by and would leave for separate destinations. They would meet later in the evening at the Valencia Manor, where Vivian would bring some of the *tools* of her trade and share more information on the subject at hand.

"I put a talisman under the mattress that may help ward off her assailant, should they return. It is supposed to help protect her. I'll let you know more about it this evening when we meet." Vivian got into her car and drove away. Mario returned to the station.

At five o'clock, Mario left for home to shower and prepare for the meeting at Valencia Manor. Maryanne was already home, getting ready for the meeting when Mario entered.

"Hey sweetie, glad you're home. Missing you today," Maryanne gushed and wrapped her arms around him like she hadn't seen him for a week.

"Wow, what brought that on?" Mario responded while holding her. He kissed her and then stepped back, looking into her eyes.

"Are you all right?"

"Yes, I seemed to miss you today more than usual. Don't knock it," she chuckled.

"Oh quite the opposite; I love the attention. Are you kidding me?" he smiled. "Do you want to eat something before we go, or wait until after and take Vivian to a late supper?"

"Late supper, if I have a choice," she replied, matter-of-factly. They finished dressing and left for the Manor.

The Manor seemed unusually dark. There were no lights on at all, inside. That was unusual, since the contractor always left two on at all times. He had worked until five o'clock. Mario dialed his number.

"Mario, what can I do you for," Don answered.

"Did you leave any lights on when you left the Valencia?"

"Yes, they were on when I left. The two downstairs, as usual," he answered. "What's going on over there? Don't tell me the power is off again?" Don grumbled.

"Haven't gone inside yet but we're about to. I'll call you if there are any problems."

"Okay. Later." Click.

Mario and Maryanne walked up the stairs to the front entrance. It was already dark and the moon was partially hidden by low hanging rain clouds. Maryanne unlocked the door and they entered as she flipped the wall-switch to no avail.

"It's the power again. Damn this house," Mario muttered. "Let's check a few others before I call Don." They walked with flashlight to three other switches, none of which worked. The front door opened and startled the duo, when Vivian poked her head inside.

"I'm back," she chuckled. "Lights not working again, I see."

"You scared the hell out of me!" Maryanne bellowed, followed with a deep sigh.

"Sorry. Thought you would be used to strange interruptions by now," she laughed.

"I am, but it's been a long, weird day."

"You're tellin' me," Vivian responded.

"Okay then; make sure your flashlights are on," Mario reminded the two. "Follow me." They followed him up the stairs, with slow, chary steps. When they reached the top, their attention was diverted to strange sounds from the main floor. A radiant figure suddenly manifested in the center of the room. A beautiful, dark haired woman wearing white stood looking up at them. She began speaking to Vivian telepathically. Vivian made a gesture, to let Mario and Maryanne know what was happening. They stood silent, while Vivian channeled, and then spoke.

"You say you are Maryanne's Mother?" she looked at Maryanne and put her hand to her lips in an effort to let Maryanne know to stay silent. "I will tell her that for you." And then the manifestation disappeared.

"Vivian, was that really my Mother?" Maryanne questioned apprehensively.

"Yes it was her. She wanted to let you know something about the adoption, but will return to explain. She told me that she loves you and is sorry about what she did; making you give up your child."

"Oh my God; it is my Mother. I have tried to forget that horrible day, and never forgave her before she died. I know that I should have forgiven her, but at the time I couldn't bring myself to tell her. She only did what she thought was the right thing. I was very young, and she knew it would be almost impossible to raise the child myself. But then, why didn't she just let me keep it and help me raise it? I can't wrap my head around that." Maryanne was in tears.

"She will return to explain more at a later time. She said very soon," Vivian tried to ease her mind and comfort her. "I think it's time you went home Maryanne."

"Yes, you're right. Let's go. I need to get away from here," Maryanne agreed as they headed downstairs and out to the cars. Vivian bid them good night and she drove away. Maryanne held tight to Mario, as he reached his arm around her shoulders and walked her to the truck.

"I wonder when Mother will return to finish her explanation," Maryanne questioned, a tear trailing down one side of her cheek.

"Try not to worry about it. She will let you know when the time is right. Trust in that," Mario comforted.

"You are right, Mario. All in good time, I am sure. I will wait until she is ready to speak to me. Until then I can only say I am sorry too, and hope she knows that."

"I am sure she already knows," Mario expounded as they drove to Mapleton Avenue.

"Not to change the subject but we have a lot of work to do if we are moving into the Manor in a week, Maryanne." Mario interjected, hesitantly.

"It will be a job well worth the trouble though. I'm anxious to finish packing. Hanna Michele said she wants to help with the design, and I know she will be amazing. I'll call her tomorrow to let her know."

"Great. She'll be pleased," Mario agreed.

Minutes later they were in the kitchen where Maryanne prepared a light snack before bed. The two of them made plans for the next day and turned in, only to be awakened again at three a.m. by a loud noise from the back of the house. Mario peered out the window and there on the lawn, another flock of birds had dotted the lawn and perched along the fence. This time he took his pistol and walked outside onto the porch. He would be ready for the stranger who usually accompanied the birds.

"Who the hell's doing this?" he yelled. His temper was brimming and these endless interruptions were getting the best of him. Edging toward the end of the deck, his gun was on safety, but ready and loaded, waiting for the dark stranger to appear. He called out several times and the birds flew off except for a few, and the shadow of a man was there and then it was gone. He was frustrated and angry. Maryanne approached the door and called out, startling him.

"I was ready for him and he came and went like a flash in the night. He's gone now." Mario was disappointed and turned to go inside. Then off in the distance a gruesome scream pierced through the murky, night sky. He hurried into the house and locked the door behind him.

"This is some weird shit, to say the least," he grumbled. "I was ready and he was like a ghost in the night. I don't know what the hell it is."

"Don't worry about it tonight. We must get some sleep. Got so much to do tomorrow," Maryanne tried to appease his anxiety. "I wanted to begin preparing the move. Do you think you'll have time to help tomorrow," she queried with a pleading look and a half-smile.

"Yeah, I can take a few hours off to help get the job started. When can we move the stuff inside the Manor?" Mario questioned.

"The contractor told me we could start bringing it in any time now. We can put some boxes in the rooms that are finished that we won't be using. That way, when we are moved, we can unpack at our own pace," she responded.

"Hmmm. Sounds like a plan and I'm looking forward to it, even though we will be sharing it with unknown phantoms and the like," he joked.

"Yes, it certainly is a possibility but I'm up for it. So far, it's not been that bad, a few ghosts here and there. I am not too worried about it. The bad spirits are gone, so far as we know, except for the strange man who keeps appearing with the birds, but he is usually away from the Manor", Maryanne added. She and Mario returned to bed and slept well for the rest of the night.

23

Dark clouds loomed overhead, and rain was gaining momentum. Mario had left a note on the table that he had been called in to interrogate a suspect for the Slasher serial murders. He would call her later. Maryanne began packing more boxes of remaining kitchen supplies, except for the most used, like the coffee pot and a few minor essentials. She kept two plates and a few utensils. Just enough to get through the week, and by then they should be out of the house and setting up the Manor. When she had almost finished, Mario called to let her know he was on his way home to help. By then there wasn't too much left, and they escaped for a late lunch at Salvador's.

Rain had started drizzling when they arrived at the restaurant and soon, it was pouring down. Just the right setting for a visit to the Manor, Maryanne was thinking out loud as she kidded Mario.

"Hey, I'm up for it if you are. We have some boxes we could haul over and move them inside. Get a head start on the move. Wada ya think?" Mario questioned.

"Are you serious? It's definitely not on my list of favorite things to do. I'm not crazy about moving in the rain," she answered.

"Ahhh…it'll stop by the time we get home. If it's still raining we'll stay home. Agreed?"

"It's a deal. If the rain doesn't stop we'll crawl in bed and watch the tube. Sounds like a winner to me, or I'll finish the book I've been trying to get to." Maryanne chuckled, half-hoping the rain would not quit, but still anxious to complete the move.

They hid under the umbrella to avoid the drowned rat look, as they emerged from the restaurant. The rain had subsided by the time they arrived home, and Mario was grinning with the look of a man who had just won a bet.

Mario loaded the truck while Maryanne set the boxes on the porch. When most of the boxes were loaded, they were off to the Valencia.

The house stood gloomy and dismal, with gloomy rain clouds hovering overhead. Mario was hoping it would remain dry until they finished. They worked fast to get the job done before that happened. By the time they took the last two boxes inside, the rain was pouring down in buckets. One thing was in their favor. The lights actually worked. Mario's cell rang and Don called to let them know they found the trouble with the lights; a wire had been loosened from the outside of the house. Don thought it was too strange to be a coincidence. He assumed some kids were messing around at night when the place was deserted. It seemed to be a favorite place for kids to hang out prior to the Manor's upgrade.

"Well at least we have some blankets if we want to stay here and sleep on the floor. What's your poison? Mario laughed.

"No poison for me, thanks," Maryanne quipped. "I am not sleeping on the floor. Besides I have to work tomorrow and I have no work clothes here. My clothes are the last thing I'm bringing over. I am not prepared."

"Yeah, I guess you're right. Let's get the hell out of here then. He took her hand and they dashed to the front door, where he pulled on the handle only to discover that it was jammed. He yanked and prodded several times but it wouldn't open.

"What else could happen?" He gave it another try but it wouldn't budge. Then the lights went out and a deafening scream rang through the house.

"I guess I'm still not used to these bizarre interruptions," she jeered.

"I'm not either and don't plan on ever being used to it," Mario resounded in a serious tone. "Come on, let's try the back door. The door opened easily and when Maryanne glanced outside, memories flooded her mind and instant replayed the horrific experience that she had suffered when she first entered the Manor over a year ago. She flashed back on the ferocious rain storm and her first encounter with supernatural entities. It was all coming back in a pool of memories that swirled through her psyche. When she looked into the back yard, the fountain and statues were still abiding; regal, aged and dilapidated. Mario jolted her out of her flashback.

"Maryanne, are you all right? What's wrong?" he questioned, as he bent down and took hold of her shoulders, looking at her eye to eye.

"What…oh, yes, I'm fine. Just thinking about the night I was stuck in here with a storm similar to this. It was an awful experience. For a moment there, it was as if I were back to that same awful night. Don't you remember? It was right after you and I met. Funny what the mind can do to a person. Just memories, that's all," she answered, putting herself back in command.

"Come on, let's get you home," he took her hand as they stepped out into the yard and braved the storm. The rain pelted them as they made their way around the house and into the truck.

"That was very odd…the feeling I mean. I really felt that I was back there again." Maryanne wiped her face with a semi-clean towel that Mario kept in the truck. She turned and looked back up at the Manor. The lights were on and all seemed well by then. She looked up at the attic and a young woman stood in the window, looking out, the curtain pulled aside.

"There she is again! The woman we have seen looking out of the attic room window. I haven't seen her for quite some time, but she's there tonight. I would give anything to know whose ghost she really is."

"Let's not worry about it tonight," he urged. It seemed as if both Mario and Maryanne were getting thick-skinned and dealing better with strange and unexplained manifestations.

When they were back inside their house, Maryanne was hoping that moving would not be a mistake, but it was too late to worry about it now and she knew that it was all a matter of your own frame of mind. She knew that she had to stay in control of her thoughts and not let past memories cloud any future plans. The first thing on her agenda was to call the contractor in the morning and get him to start on the back yard as soon as possible. It would be the final renovation of the project, like the cherry on top, she thought. She was soon in a much better frame of mind and realized that it was just the storm that made things seem so dismal and dark. She would tuck it away in her memory bank, where many other unexplainable events had been saved, and hopefully not check in there any time soon.

Mario entered the living room, where Maryanne had been sitting and served her a plate with grilled cheese and a steamy cup of hot-chocolate. All the unpleasant thoughts disappeared as she sipped, her tongue tasting the marsh-mellow topping that floated on top of the frothy, hot beverage.

"Yummy. Thanks sweetie, you have saved the night!" She giggled and sank her teeth into the crispy sandwich, soft, creamy cheese oozing from its edges.

Mario sat next to her while they chomped down the delicious snack. It was a great finale to a cold, rainy-night. They would turn in soon, so they could get an early start on moving of boxes. The plan was to move the furniture the day after.

"Mario, we have to meet with the Psychic tomorrow. She was going to help with your Slasher case and the elements needed to fight off the alleged vampires, or whatever they are. I should call first thing and make an appointment."

"Call her. I'll fit it in. Let's get some sleep now, unless you want to play," he answered, eyes lighting up and his inviting smile taking her over.

The night swirled into passion, taking them into another place. A diverse facet of love, ecstasy and unity as the two of them, spiraled into a sexual experience that seemed to surpass all others. When the pleasure had ended, they lay fulfilled, bodies glistening in sweat as light from the upper windows reflected against their naked bodies.

Maryanne had to spend time at work, as appointments were piling up and she had a list to fill for the next two days. She was surprised to see Carl McGuire back so soon. He was pleased with his past purchases and back again for another look. She had acquired new artifacts and he was carefully examining each and every treasure. She knew he would be a long-time customer. His collection must be amazing, she thought as she watched him so fervently take notice of several different pieces. After he had asked many questions and carefully browsed, he chose two lovely antique vases that were from Egypt, and very expensive. He obviously wasn't concerned about the price, as he didn't blink an eye when she quoted twenty-thousand for the pair. He handed her the credit card as though he were buying a vase from Target. This of course made another day for Maryanne. She had Wendy carefully wrap and box the artifacts for him while she chatted with Carl. He invited her and Mario to his home for a cocktail party and art show. His home was a huge mansion on the edge of town near Pearl Street, where some of the older and nicer homes were located. Of course Maryanne reciprocated and thanked him as she walked him to the door and stood waving as he climbed into his Silver Ferrari. She had gotten to know him better and was thankful to have him for a loyal client. It seemed they would be good friends as well.

It was getting late in the day and clouds were beginning to form. It looked like a repeat of yesterday's squall. Maryanne was helping Wendy change a layout of the African sculptures, when the bell sounded and she looked to see Borislav Vasilev coming through the door, dark glasses covering his eyes. She greeted him and told him that they were moving out of the house and would be completely done by the end of the week. That gave her three days to complete the move. Mr. Vasilev seemed anxious to move into her house. It was earlier than expected but that was good news to him.

"Where is Adriana?" Maryanne questioned.

"She is not well," he commented. "But fine soon," he answered in his slightly broken English. We ready to move into house when you finish. I have someone help to do this for me. I have storage with much furniture to put in house." He forced a half-smile.

"Great Mr. Vasilev, I am glad you are prepared and have help. I will call you as soon as we are out of the house so that you can notify your movers.

"Thank you, Miss Ramos. I will expect call then. I go now. Adriana ask me to get medicine, so she feel better. I hurry now to help." He turned and walked out of the store and Maryanne walked to the door, looking out to see which way he went. He was nowhere to be seen. He must have had a driver pick him up," she reasoned.

"Wendy, we accomplished a lot today. I wish every day could be so easy and fruitful. But I should never complain, as it has been unbelievable business for the most part, since I opened."

"Yes it has, since I have been here I think business seems to be improving all the time. Of course, I didn't mean just because I was here," she blushed. "Just that it is increasing."

"I am sure you have a lot to do with it since you are a great sales representative. I could not have done better and I appreciate all you do. You have no idea how important you are to me, Wendy. A Godsend, that's what I call it. A Godsend," she smiled.

"It is also for me," Wendy beamed.

"Then let's go down the street and have a sundae and call it a day. It's nearly time to close anyway. I'll treat you." Maryanne closed out the register and Wendy did the usual closing tasks and they walked down the street to Plato's Ice Cream Parlor to enjoy a treat and chat. They had become close. Wendy looked up to Maryanne as a mother figure, since her family was gone and Maryanne cared deeply for Wendy. After a pleasant visit, Maryanne left for home while Wendy took some time to check out the shops in the area of Pearl Street Mall.

Upon Maryanne's arrival, she called Mario to let him know she was home and remind him that Vivian would be arriving at their house around nine P.M. Vivian had remarked earlier that she actually enjoyed the rain and did not mind going out to see them during the storm, which had mostly subsided by now, anyway.

Mario arrived at seven o'clock, grabbed a late dinner and Vivian showed up a few minutes later. She brought a leather satchel filled with information about the practice of modern day vampirism and a book on the study of traditional vampirism, as well. They sat around the table as she explained about other items and customs that were used to ward of such creature. The very well informed Psychic began to explain in detail about the practices that she thought could be harbored in Boulder. It was Vivian's belief that a cult of modern-day-vampires had taken up residence in several towns around the area, and some had been trying to move into Boulder. There were about thirty in total that she had knowledge of, from other areas. Vivian had done research and contacted several of her colleagues in the other locations, who filled her in on the latest phase. There had been similar attacks, such as the Slasher murders in two other locations, not long before they occurred in Boulder. Rituals and cult meetings had been discovered. Apparently, the attacker had left the other vicinities before he or she had been apprehended. Her informants said that the recent attacks in Boulder had mimicked or were possibly perpetrated by the same cult. It had been considered that more than one member was doing the killing, as there had been some witnesses who thought they may have seen three different suspects, and Vivian was considering that information. At this point, only one person was still alive that could give the best description, and she was still in the hospital in Boulder under heavy guard. It was reported to Vivian that the police in other areas were not taking the cult mentality of the attacks by vampires seriously. They were looking for a killer but did not believe the strange clues given about any such cults existing. Mario had one thing going for him. Chief Olson had an open mind and would have some backing when manifestations and other activity took place, as had been the case at Valencia Manor.

The recent victim, Julia White, was the only possible witness that could give as good a description as anything that had been reported. It was vague but there were a few important clues that could help the team locate and hopefully arrest the suspect. Vivian was almost certain the person was linked to the cult. It would be her job to connect the dots. With her expertise, it looked as though she had been making progress in that determination.

"Alright…now that you have the information you need,

I want you to read it and study it well. It will help in your evaluation of the kinds of people we are dealing with. They have no scruples, and if I am correct, they seem to be in the living category, practicing blood-letting ceremonies as one of the cult traditions. Most of them do not drink the blood, but use it for rituals. If they do consume blood, it isn't out of necessity for survival, but for a bizarre fantasy. There is murder involved and disgusting rituals that would turn your stomach. You read up on it. If any of the criteria fits, you can determine that for yourself. If I am right, we should be able to win this battle. But if I am not, and it is from beyond the grave, we are looking at a more sinister dilemma. I am aware of more unconventional means to deal with such entities." She held up the book. "In this publication, there is more data of the actual walking dead vampires. That is a more complex challenge and will take a particular effort to counter. We can begin by starting on the cult analogy. Remember, I could be wrong, so be ready for anything." Vivian was *dead* serious and urged them to take careful precautions. She handed each of them an amulet, a silver cross and a mirror.

"These are your best weapons to identify the species if it is not from this world. Keep these with you at all times. If you have a visitation from one of the creatures or vampires, if you will, use the mirror to identify its origin. A real dead vampire will not reflect from the mirror. The crosses of course, will tend to keep them away. The amulet will protect you, so wear it around your neck; visible at all times. They cannot hurt you if they see the symbol on the amulet. It sounds ridiculous but I assure you, it's better to be ready and safe than sorry. They cannot thrive in the sun at all. They only move about at night." Vivian went on for an hour or more.

"In the event that it is cult related, you will know at once. They can be killed by traditional methods. Hopefully you will not have to deal with that. They are usually very light skinned and wear glasses, as they are sensitive to sun and it will not kill them, but the sun causes serious illness. It must be the way they live that causes these reactions. They usually only go out at night or when it is gloomy, so they have little sun exposure. They however, can be seen during the day. Remember they are alive, and not from the grave. Some of those cult practices include the drinking of blood and some feel that they are unable to live without it. Most of the cult followers use blood in their sacrificial rituals. One, who is attacked by a living vampire, will not be changed into a creature, such as the result from an attack of the walking-dead." Vivian stood up with a look of extreme gravity.

"You have the ammunition, and now it is up to you to find and identify the origin of the species. If they are from this world, it will be much easier to find, track, arrest or kill, if need be. It is much more difficult to kill the creatures of the dead. They can be killed by the sun, sprinkling of Holy Water onto their bodies, a stake through the heart while in deep sleep, or if you happen to get lucky while they are up and active. It is easier though, to attack them at their dwelling, but we are not always aware of their place of inhabitance. Crosses, if pressed onto the vampire will take its powers and it will die with the emblem embedded into its skin. It's all in these books. Please study them. If you have any questions or need me at any time, call at once. I will be on stand-by. I must leave now. I have a meeting early in the morning and must rest. I wish you the best of luck. May God be with you." Vivian left the books and 'tools of the trade'. Maryanne walked her to the car. When Vivian started her car, a huge flock of birds encircled it and began settling in the yard. Maryanne stood motionless in the center of a black haze of feathers. Vivian opened the window of the car.

"Get inside the car, Maryanne!" Maryanne edged her body close to Vivian's car and tried to open the back door while seemingly ravenous birds began to swoop down upon her making her anxious and afraid. Vivian urged her to move quickly. Maryanne finally succeeded, slipping inside, her arms flailing in an attempt to scare off the birds. Taking in a deep breath, fear finally loosened its grip and she leaned back against the seat.

"Calm down. It's going to be fine. Vivian took out her cell and dialed Mario.

"What's up Vivian? Where are you?" Mario questioned, while looking for Maryanne.

"We are out front inside my car. The birds attacked and she is here with me," Vivian explained. "Can you come outside and see if you have any effect on the birds?"

"Yes, I'm on my way." He opened the door and birds were flying and banging their wings against the door, as if they were trying to prevent him from exiting. He pushed hard on the door and it finally opened. The birds continued to swoop down upon him and peck at his head. He backed up, took his gun from his holster and opened fire. The blast of two shots rang through the night sky. The birds began to depart momentarily and he rushed to the car, carrying a blanket and his gun. The birds were still flying up above them, with several still standing on the ground and perched on the roof. Two or three would land incessantly on the car, as if to taunt them in an uncanny ritual.

"Whew! This is getting ridiculous," Mario remarked, looking through the window and up into the sky. The birds are hovering above like vultures waiting for dinner.

"Vivian, what do you make of this? It doesn't say anything about the birds in the information you gave us, does it?" he questioned, while breathing hard and quite disturbed by the odd manifestations.

"There are some studies that have associated Black-Birds and Ravens with occult practice. I have not heard of too many incidents around Boulder, in my research. I am sure we can check it out quite easily, if and when we get out of this car." She tried to add a small gesture of witticism in her vociferous comment. The noise was quite disturbing and she spoke very loud.

"I think you should shoot the gun again a few more times," Vivian suggested. Mario had already called the station, informing them of the unusual incident, and his intent to use gunfire to scare the birds, just in case any calls came in from curious neighbors. Mario then took his gun and opened the window, carefully aiming his weapon into the sky and let go with three loud shots. The birds finally began to disburse. Mario, Maryanne and Vivian took advantage of their departure, and made it safely into the house. Vivian wasn't going anywhere. She would stay the night and hopefully daybreak would curb any more abnormal behavior from the birds. When they were inside, Mario looked out to see that more of the birds had returned to the yard. Mario called Chief Olson updating him on their bizarre predicament and he was perplexed, but definitely on the bandwagon to explore possibilities of paranormal aspects pertaining to the case.

Daylight took hold and first thing on Mario's agenda was to check the yard for any remaining birds. They were gone and it was quiet on the home front. He woke Maryanne and then made coffee while she and their guest prepared for the day. Vivian emerged from the guest room, all smiles and took a seat at the bar. Coffee was sending inviting aromas throughout the house and was enough to get anyone moving. Mario served her a cup of the black magic and she sipped its stimulating brew.

"This is all I needed to get my day started," Vivian commented. "Thank you so much for the hospitality and great company; both of you.

"You are very welcome, but I am not finished here, my dear. Breakfast is soon to come." Mario had been preparing pancakes, bacon and egg sandwiches, which he set on the bar in front of her. Needless to say, she was deliciously surprised and grateful.

When she finished, she bid them good day and hurried away, while the birds were busy bothering someone else, she was thinking on her way out.

"I will be in touch shortly and bring you up to date on any facts I can dig up pertaining to the birds. Bye now." Vivian was off and running with many things to catch up on, including a meeting with a local psychic that she had never met, but the woman was anxious to exchange information.

Mario and Maryanne went about their usual day at work. Maryanne made several trips to the Manor, finishing minor moving and storage details. The contractor was busy working with the completion of upper attic rooms. His next and final task was to completely renovate the back yard and its extraordinary fountain, statues and pool. He informed Maryanne that it would be complete in a week or so after they had moved into the Manor. It was becoming a spectacular design that had captured its antiquated mystique and was going to be a sight to behold. A reporter from the newspaper had contacted Maryanne about doing an article when the house was complete. They suggested a public viewing to allow its magnificence to be shared with the community. When the masterpiece was finished, she looked forward to the opportunity of showing the Valencia Manor in full bloom, but they would definitely wait until the paranormal manifestations had ceased, before presenting the historical Manor to the public.

Meanwhile back at the station, Mario was in conference with a team of detectives and forensic specialists, going over the Slasher case. It had gotten extremely complicated and some of the evidence was conflicting and inconclusive. There was, however, one piece of evidence that could tie in a suspect, if and when they found the perpetrator, who had seemed to be illusive up to this point. One suspect had been interrogated, but they had insufficient evidence and had to release him, reluctantly. The surviving witness was near recovery and would soon be released. They planned on a twenty-three-seven guard until the case was solved. She was the one tight link that could solidify the case, if the perpetrator was apprehended. They couldn't afford to take any chances. She had recently remembered more details about the assailant and it looked as though the suspect would soon be apprehended. They had provided Julia with a psychologist who had been diligently working on her mental state, helping her to cope with the horrific crime. It helped her significantly and her outlook was very positive. The depression and visions had started to decline. The doctors assured her that she would have a complete recovery, mentally and physically.

Moving was on the agenda when Mario returned home and final few boxes were waiting to be moved into Manor. Electricity was functioning well; the contractor had almost completed the attic bedrooms, and all seemed to be quiet and peaceful at their future home. All aspects of the renovation were coming together in unison, and soon the project would be perfected.

Maryanne returned to her home after several appointments and picked up a few suitcases which would complete the move. Returning to the Manor, she worked swiftly to put things in order. She had called Hanna Michelle earlier, to set up a time for her to visit the Manor and begin her design illustrations. Hanna would make the trip to Boulder by Friday. This gave Maryanne two days to finish the unpacking and new furniture move. It was all coming to a grand-finale' as the project was coming together like a well-oiled machine. Before Maryanne left the ever-changing edifice, she stood admiring its stunning revival. Soon, she would be breathing its historical effervescence, and living as part of its legacy. She could not be more exhilarated.

Home again and Mario still at work, she opened the car door, carefully eyeing the landscape and overhead, just in case a bird invasion was on the horizon. Nothing was apparent, and she scurried up the stairs into the house, feeling relief to have no strange feathered-friends welcome her arrival. Her usual duties came natural as she went from one room to the other, checking for anything left un-done. There was not much left in the house, and not much to do. Coffee would be one ritual that she would keep until the last piece was removed. She pulled herself onto the bar-seat and enjoyed the brew. Mario rang.

"Mario, I'm at home. Forgot to call, but I'm reading the paper, that I have been neglecting. Oh, and did I tell you that a reporter is interested in doing an article on the Manor when we move in and complete the interior design?" Maryanne went on in her anxious chatter.

"Great! Wanted to tell you I will be home in a couple of hours. There are lots of good things happening with the case. Finally making some headway," he replied. "See you when I get there."

Food was next on the agenda and simple was her favorite solution; an organic Pizza with whole grain crust from her new favorite; "Amy's. She took out the pizza, set it on the counter and then turned on the oven. She wanted it to be hot upon Mario's arrival.

After pizza and exchanging information of the day, Mario and Maryanne turned in, for a hopefully, restful night.

24

Daylight and delicious is the only way to describe breakfast, when Mario was in charge of the morning dine. He had created veggie omelets, pancakes and bacon, before Maryanne awakened. Her senses were primed when she awakened to tantalizing aromas as they drifted through the house. Aromas of Coffee topped off the invitation as it crept lusciously through the room, her stomach grumbling in anticipation of a feast at hand. A quick shower and she poked her head into the room, licking her lips with a satisfactory smile. He had a plate sitting in front of her within minutes and the hot coffee steamed, pleasing her senses.

"This is impressive, Mario. I'm famished and you know just how to satisfy the ever-waiting stomach," she giggled.

It didn't take her long to devour the delectable breakfast. She sipped on coffee, satisfied and content; looking at the newspaper Mario had placed conveniently in front of her.

"I owe you one," she chuckled. "This was so delicious. I'm ready to take on the day."

"I'll remember that," he joked. "How about tomorrow you make your legendary breakfast burritos?"

"Glad to do it, sweetie. Count on it!"

"Duty calls now, so I have to run…talk to you later." Mario pecked her on the cheek and left.

"I'll call you later, maybe we can meet for a quick coffee?" Maryanne responded as Mario disappeared through the front door.

"Bye." Maryanne wasn't ready to move from her perch at the bar. She poured another cup of java and sat enjoying every last drop. When she finished the newspaper, she made a quick call to Joan. They had not spoken for a few days.

"Hello Maryanne. What a surprise. I was going to call you. Hadn't heard from you. Glad you called. How are you?"

"I'm well, thanks. Checking in to see what's new with you?"

"Not good, I'm afraid. Steve has been acting very strange lately and even though we aren't living or sleeping together, he keeps checking in constantly and I have seen him following me three or four times. I'm beginning to get a little paranoid about it. Do you think I should be worried?" Joan sounded quite concerned.

"I think you have every right to be worried. It's not natural to be that obsessive. Should I tell Mario to have a talk with him?"

"I hate to get him involved. Steve may really get pissed if he knows I even told you. I'm not sure what to do. I know something isn't right, though. On second thought, tell Mario and get his opinion, but please tell him not to let Steve know I said anything. Okay?" Joan pleaded.

"Sure. I can do that. Meanwhile, you be very cautious. People can do weird things when they become obsessed and jealous." Maryanne tried to warn Joan, without being too pushy. "I'll let you know what he says after I call him. I'm a little worried about you."

"Thanks Maryanne. I'll be waiting for your call." Click.

Maryanne dialed Mario and explained what was happening

and he suggested she call in a stalking report. Maryanne knew she wouldn't do that so Mario would have a talk with Steve, just to get a feel on how he would react when he mentioned Joan in conversation. It may trigger something and Mario was good in detecting behavior patterns. He would call Maryanne after the meeting.

Maryanne informed Joan what the plan was and told her to be on guard and hang tight. She would get back to her soon.

Mario set up the meeting at Dots for coffee in an hour. He would feel him out then.

Steve's squad car pulled into the parking lot where Mario had just parked. They shook hands and walked into the café, exchanging small talk. They took a booth near the window in the back.

"Hey Steve, how's everything?" Mario grinned.

"It's all good. Going okay, I guess," Steve answered, with a bit of somberness. Mario noticed he was not acting his usual self.

"You seem a little down. What's goin' on, Steve? I can sense you are worried about something," Mario used caution to get him to talk.

"I guess I'm upset because Joan has been putting me off. I told her I would give her some time, but I'm sure she doesn't feel like she used to. It's killin' me. Maybe she has a new boyfriend. I think I saw her having coffee with that new detective, James Melbourne, the other day. Man, it tore me up. It could have been just a simple meeting but I love her so much, I can't get it out of my thoughts. If she leaves me for good, I'm not sure I can handle it. It's good to get it off my chest though. I've been going to talk to you but didn't want to bother you, ya know," Steve let it all out.

"Hey man it's gonna be okay. Sometimes things just aren't

meant to be. We don't always have control of everything. Be patient. It's all gonna work out for you. Even if you guys split for good, it's not the end. Shit, we all got'ta go through things we aren't happy with sometimes," he tried to smooth it over, but Steve seemed overly distressed.

"I guess so." He looked down and sat quietly for several minutes.

"Hey, I got an idea, Steve. Let's you and I go out tomorrow night and play some pool, have a beer and just hang out. I need to get away and let loose too. I'll meet you after work at the Blue Mountain Pub over at the Pearl Street Mall."

"Yeah. I guess it sounds good. Might help me get my head out of my ass, for sure," Steve unconvincingly tried to make light of it. "I'll meet you there.

The server had delivered coffee to the table and they shared conversation for another half hour. On the way home, Mario reflected on Steve's peculiar behavior and was seriously concerned. He had never known Steve to be that depressed, but understood that when it comes to women, men can do some very strange things.

At dinner, Mario and Maryanne discussed Steve and the plan. She agreed it may be good to get Steve out and about; have a little fun. Meanwhile, Mario had more serious things to do with a report on the Slasher murders. Maryanne was packing the final clothes she wanted to move and Mario would pack his when the report was finished.

By Monday they would be living at the Valencia Manor. That too, was weighing on Maryanne's mind, since the ghost of her mother had spoken to the psychic. She gave Vivian a quick call to find out when Vivian wanted to meet again at the Manor in an attempt to contact her again. Maryanne wanted answers now; that had been stirred up on the issue of her child's adoption. Vivian agreed to meet her the next night. It was perfect for Maryanne, since Mario would be out with

Steve for a few hours. The plan was to meet at seven o'clock in front of Valencia Manor.

Another day came and went. Mario was off to meet Steve, while Maryanne left for the Manor to meet the Psychic.

Maryanne entered the Valencia, turned on the lights and prepared for answers to questions that Maryanne had never resolved, since she was a young girl of sixteen.

Most of the furniture that belonged to Maryanne and Mario was already in place. The rest of the furniture had been purchased from several different stores, and was to be delivered starting at nine a.m. tomorrow. Some selections were antiques of significant importance when it came to the historical décor of the Manor. The contractor had done some of the refurbishing of the antiques that were left inside the Valencia. Maryanne had been picking and choosing numerous charming pieces, since the contractor began the renovation. The antique and furniture dealers had all agreed to deliver the furnishings in the morning. The Psychic would then have ample time to implement the communication with Maryanne's Mother, without interruption.

Vivian pulled one of the chairs from the exquisite dining set that had been flawlessly refurbished by the contractor. Maryanne took another chair and pulled a small table next to Vivian, where she could place candles for the communication that was soon to take place. Today, she would hear from her Mother if all went well, and she may possibly get the answers she needed about the adoption of her baby; the adoption her mother forced upon her; and she had been angry about for twenty-three years. Vivian was solemn as she opened her bag and withdrew candles, a book of incantations and incense. When all had been situated in its particular order, Maryanne lit the candles and turned the lights out. Daylight still tossed rays through tall windows as they sat quietly waiting for a signal that the entity had been contacted. A cool breeze swept through the room like a miniature tornado as dust swirled about and danced across the wood floor. The pair remained quiet and Vivian sat in trance, hands extended and palms up. She began chanting, until a mist began to form at the back of the room by the fireplace. It settled quietly and the aberration began to materialize in the misty cloud. Maryanne's heart was pounding. This could be her Mother and she hoped to keep control of the emotions that had been pent up for so many years. Vivian had warned her to stay quiet unless she was being directly spoken to and heard the communication herself. The Psychic began to breath deep and discontinued her chant. Someone was speaking to her. The manifestation began to materialize in the midst of the fog. Maryanne was able to visualize its formation. A beautiful young woman in a dress that Maryanne recognized stood at the center of the mist. Bright and luminous, the aberration was impressive and brought many unresolved emotions back to Maryanne. A voice became apparent and Maryanne recognized it as her mother's and she stood in awe, not able to speak for several moments.

"Maryanne, I have come back to apologize to you for a mistake that I made, unknowingly when I was attempting to be a good Mother to you. I made mistakes that have put unnecessary burdens on you and the child that I forced you to give up. I was not aware at the time, what a devastating mistake it would turn out to be. By the time I started to realize it, I had become ill and did not attempt to let you know. I regret that I kept it from you. Hopefully you can find it in your heart to give me some kind of forgiveness. If not, I may never be able to forgive myself and pass into the light."

Maryanne was becoming emotional, and tears had begun to well, as she tried to hold back the flood of tears and emotions. She contained herself and listened.

"I wanted you to know who adopted the child in hopes that you can find a way to change the outcome of such a terrible disservice that I have perpetrated against you and the child.

Had I known it would turn out like this, I would have never let it happen. At the time, I only did what I believed to be the answer to a problem; you being so young and inexperienced, and a child that I wanted only the best for. The family that took the child seemed of good breeding and well-off. I thought they were a kind and decent couple, who had another child as well. I felt it was best for you both. I know now it was the gravest mistake I had ever made. It changed lives of two beautiful people who I loved dearly. But it changed them in such an appalling way that I grieve for the pain that you two have suffered because of my error in judgment. If I could do anything to change what happened, I would."

Maryanne could not keep silent any longer. She spoke to her mother among the tears that were flowing. "I told you I loved my child and didn't want to let it go. I still don't even know if it was a boy or girl. Who did you give the child to? What happened to it?" All of these questions that she had mulled over in her mind a million times before overflowed into a dialogue of hurtful, emotional seething that she could not control.

Vivian touched her shoulder to calm her and spoke. "Maryanne please be patient; listen to her. She is not finished. Let her tell you the entire story. You must know all of it before you judge, regardless of your anger."

Maryanne settled down. The entity continued to explain, while Maryanne contained composure as best she could.

"I will answer your questions if you will give me the opportunity. It may help you to go on and find peace with what has happened. I only hope it will. The child was a beautiful little seven pound baby girl. She was only with you for a moment when I had the nurses take her from you, so that you would not see her and hurt even more. I thought it was the right thing to do to protect you. I was wrong. The couple who adopted the child was John Farthington and his wife, Sarah. According to the background check I had done, they were a highly respected family of good breeding, in Boulder. We, of course were living in Denver then, and I thought it be best to have the child raised in another city, away from you. Your father had already passed away and I was alone and having hard times. I knew the hardship it would have placed on another child. I wasn't thinking rationally, I guess.

"Are you saying that John Farthington, the former owner of Valencia Manor adopted my little girl?" Maryanne was devastated by the news. "How could you? He was a cold, calculating, evil man, who murdered his own child. Oh my God! Where is she now? Is she alive?" Maryanne was shaking and Vivian held her, trying to comfort her.

"She is alive. I know that he kept her a prisoner in the house, like a criminal, after his wife passed away. He must have gone insane. These things I found out after my death. The things he did were shocking and unbelievable. She had been educated quite well, through John and his wife, who were both highly educated people. After his wife passed away, he changed and turned into an evil, despicable person. She was kept in the basement where no one knew she existed. People in the town obviously had no idea of what had taken place. Because of his social status, he was not held suspect to anything. She lived inside the Manor after he moved to his sister, Mrs. Dirkshire's home when he became very ill and more mentally unstable. Mrs. Dirkshire knew nothing of the child. He had never divulged to her or anyone else in the family of the adoption, so I think the town was oblivious to the child's existence. The child is now a beautiful young woman, who by God's intervention somehow gave her back to you. The child is who you now know, as Hanna Michelle Smith."

Maryanne gasped for breath and stood up. She was shocked at the revelation. Her emotions exploded and she sobbed uncontrollably. Vivian held her as she tried to grasp the story that had unfolded.

"My baby! My baby! Oh my God! Is it true?" Maryanne

sobbed mournfully, trying to make sense of it all. Vivian held her, and led her to the chair where she sat, rocking back and forth for what seemed like an hour. Vivian comforted her. The ghost of her Mother had vanished. All that was left was a mist where she had stood in the light. An eerie silence consumed the Manor and the two of them sat for a time, until Maryanne had collected herself and began to speak.

"Vivian…what do I do with this? I am so hurt. I can only feel sorrow for Hanna and her terrible life because of my Mother. What can I do to help her? I knew that Hanna had a terrible life before, but in a million years had no idea she was my own child; my own flesh and blood."

"Yes you knew she had a terrible life. Start with that. You have already given her a new life because of what you have already done to help her. You are the reason she is free and now has a chance at life. Had it not been for God leading you to her, she could have spent her life in an institution or worse. The police would have assumed that she was a criminal and not a victim and killed her or had her incarcerated. You were there because of divine intervention. You saved your child. Think of it that way. You had no idea of what had happened but because you were her Mother, you had a sixth sense when you were held captive in the Valencia. You knew the perpetrator was not an evil person. It was you who gave her back the life she now can live." Vivian tried her best to make Maryanne understand what had been completely out of her hands.

When Maryanne regained composure, they walked out of the Manor into the sunlight, where a new day had emerged that would change her life forever.

"Maryanne I have only one thing to tell you now. You must start by forgiving yourself and your Mother. If you hold anger and judgment it will cloud any good that could come from this knowledge. Hate, anger, blame and guilt are not part of a good heart. It can only bring more pain. You must let go of those feelings and let yourself move forward to a better place. Can you understand what I am telling you?" Vivian emphasized.

"Yes, Vivian. I am beginning to understand that. I do forgive my Mother, as she only did what she knew to be right. I hold no blame. I also know that it was not my fault and thank God for leading me to her so that I can make up for some of her misfortune. I will make sure that she has everything it takes to fulfill her life."

"Maryanne, you already have. The love and caring that you have bestowed on her since you first met her in the Manor, under deplorable conditions, shows the love and compassion you have for her already. She is already there. She has you and you have her. Her life will be fulfilled, as will yours." Vivian's wisdom was more apparent now than ever.

"Thank you Vivian for leading and guiding me through a most difficult time. You have shown me that love and compassion can conquer all. Even in death. You are so important to me. I love you like a Mother and will always be here for you, whatever you need." Maryanne hugged Vivian and held on tight, thankful for her insight and friendship. She stepped back and looked at Vivian.

"I don't know what to say to Hanna. Should I tell her? Now?" she was confused at how to approach Hanna with the knowledge.

"All in good time. Hanna is still in delicate condition, so feel her out when you are with her and you will know when the time is right to explain it. I am sure it won't be long," Vivian smiled, her eyes sparkling in the midst of her kind aging face. She emitted more love from her being than Maryanne had ever known. It was like God gave her a gift; the gift of love and understanding through Vivian's presence. Maryanne had much to be thankful for and much to prepare for with Hanna's future. Maryanne remembered something that Vivian had once told her. Vivian said that in life, your teacher will appear. She believed that certain people who you come in contact with during your lifetime, are your teachers. It is up to you to gather the knowledge from those whose paths you cross, and to decipher which information will be a good influence on your life. Maryanne knew that Vivian was the most important teacher she had ever met. Her influence would forever change her life. Vivian's heart was full of goodness, and Maryanne was aware that God had placed Vivian in her path for good reason.

The two of them left the Manor, to go their separate ways. While Maryanne drove home, she pondered the last few hours with much more awareness of her life and what her reason for being had become. Life was good and her plan was to improve upon it. She felt free; really free, for the first time in her life. She was free from the past guilt and anger that had embedded itself into her since she was a child; free from the pain of wondering and hurt that had filled her every moment, until today.

Maryanne was brimming with excitement, waiting for Mario to arrive from work. It was all she could do to keep from calling him, but she managed to hold on until he was there in person to tell the story.

Mario was surprised that Maryanne had finally been given the answers that she had so long waited to hear. He knew this would be life-changing for her and was there to support her in every way.

They would be moving into the Valencia Manor tomorrow and were both looking forward to their new life together in the enigmatic Manor that had changed Maryanne's life.

25

Movers from several different companies where she had purchased new and antique furnishings for the Manor would begin transporting furniture at nine o'clock a.m. When Maryanne arrived, one truck had just pulled up in front with the living room collection; coffee- table, end-tables and accessories for the grand-room. The appliances arrived immediately after they had placed the sofa and chairs. All new stainless appliances were installed in the new kitchen and laundry room. The Manor was being transformed into its former elegance, modernized, but still enhanced with spectacular antiquity. Another truck arrived containing three bedroom sets. The master bedroom would be first in line. Maryanne had decided to use the room at the top of the stairs, first door on the right. Maryanne walked them through every room, making sure each piece was placed exactly as she and Hanna had imagined. Hanna had done most of the preparations for placement of furniture on a design plan that she had completed and sent to Maryanne. The school she was attending seemed to have greatly advanced her in the art of design, even though she had only been a student for a short time.

The next bedroom to receive its adornment was the room

across the well opposite the master bedroom. The third would be the next room on the right. Soon, another mover arrived, carrying a stunning antique Wurlitzer baby-grand piano that would be the focal-point of the grand-room. Maryanne had vowed to take refresher classes to play again. She had also purchased an easel and supplies for a complete art-studio, including sculpting tools and a pottery wheel. Their offices would be on the main floor, where an antique desk and bookshelves were carefully situated to make each room cozy and nostalgic. More antique lamps and accent tables were placed strategically here and there, to add depth and character to the renovated edifice. It was truly magnificent and came together like a giant puzzle that Hanna had meticulously designed, with Maryanne as her assistant.

Maryanne was anxious for Hanna to see first-hand, the end-result of what she had created from her artistic vision. She would call her in the morning to plan the visit. Hanna had worked on the design while in Denver, using only the floor-plans to set the stage. She was familiar with the structure, since her memory had returned and recalled the interior as it used to be, when she lived at the Manor. She had incredible artistic vision and the end result was proof of her aspiring ability as an interior decorator. Maryanne knew Hanna was going to be successful at her trade. Anyone who observed the results of this creative project would be impressed.

After several hours of staging rooms, Maryanne was alone, and basking in the spectacular results. She perched herself in the grand-room on the new sofa, gazing at the wonders that had made the Manor a work of art. Maryanne had shopped meticulously at several galleries, which would be delivering more amazing works to be displayed on the upstairs walls of Valencia Manor. Artworks on the main floor were perfectly placed to spark any connoisseur. That was the icing on the cake, she was thinking. When she finished admiring the results of their labor of love, she proceeded to test out the new coffee maker as it sat on the luxurious marble counter, waiting for its first task. Later in the evening she sat at the piano and plucked at the keys, with surprising skill, considering she hadn't played since she had first left Denver several years ago. She thought, 'it's like riding a bicycle.' Once you learn, you never forget. In half an hour, she was playing the Vienna waltz like she had been practicing for days. The house had perfect acoustic quality for the Wurlitzer, and she would be using it often. It was the perfect end to a long, productive morning. Maryanne's head was still spinning from the revelation about her Daughter, Hanna Michelle. She was beginning to work through it and had a much better outlook today than last night.

A local reporter had contacted Maryanne in hopes they could do an article on the Manor for a magazine. They wanted pictures, historical information and a bio of Maryanne. Maryanne would contact her when the final renovations had been completed, including the back yard. That would be the crowning glory. The fountain, statues and pool were almost finished to perfection and it was more than she had ever expected.

Mario called to check in. After a quick conversation, Maryanne left the Manor and finished her day at the store. She couldn't get her mind off Hanna and waited until closing to call her about a meeting to see the Manor with all of its furnishings in place. Maryanne had decided to keep the information about her being Hanna's Mother under wraps until she was positive Hanna could handle it. She did not want to disrupt the progress that Hanna had made in the last several months and would speak to the psychiatrist about her newfound information. He would be the one to make the decision. Meanwhile, it would be hard to keep it under wraps, but Maryanne would do it for the sake of Hanna Michele.

After Hanna had moved into the apartment and started classes at the design school, she took several weeks of driving lessons and became a very good driver, passing the test with flying colors. Maryanne had subsequently helped Hanna purchase a small compact car, and she would be driving to Boulder first thing in the morning. Maryanne would meet her at the house on Sycamore and then take her to the Manor. Mario and Maryanne would be finalizing their move by evening. They would be residents of the Valencia Manor at long last. Maryanne was excited. She had decorated one of the bedrooms especially for Hanna, without her knowledge, bringing in an interior designer and giving them a list of many ideas that she knew Hanna would love. The stage was set and Hanna would be making her first visit back to the Manor since she had been rescued almost a year ago. Everything was perfect.

Maryanne woke early; before the sun had risen. Her excitement was bubbling over and there was no way she could sleep. Into the shower and dressed by six o'clock a.m. and having coffee, all before Mario woke. While she was reading the paper, Mario sauntered in, rubbing his eyes and yawning.

"How long you been up?"

"I think around five or earlier. Couldn't sleep. Too anxious, I guess," she answered, her face revealing obvious enthusiasm.

"I am sure you are," he kissed her on the top of her head and poured coffee into his personal oversized mug that Maryanne had given to him as a joke on his birthday, "World's hottest Detective". And she meant every word of it!

"Hanna should be here around eight o'clock, she informed me yesterday."

"Good. I hope you two have a wonderful time. I'll get over there later to take a peek at what you two have accomplished, since I have been doing way too much overtime and haven't even seen it myself," Mario sat down across from her at the table and snacked on a bagel with cream-cheese and jelly.

"Hopefully you can make it over before Hanna has to leave, unless I can convince her to stay the night. I'm going to work on that, but not sure of her schedule. Didn't think to ask when we spoke."

"I'll call and let you know when I get to work; see how the case is going," Mario answered, and snatched up the newspaper that Maryanne had already browsed.

"Someone's at the door; probably Hanna, I'll get it." A Fed Ex delivery showed up, with a package. It was the final set of documents on the house. It was a joyous moment. Now, the house was officially sold. The new owners, Borislav Vasiliev and his partner Adriana Igmunov would be moving into the house within days of their leaving. Maryanne scurried into the kitchen, waving the papers, grinning.

"It's done. We are officially out of here. The house now belongs to the buyers. All we needed was the final paperwork. I think we ought to crack a bottle of that excellent Merlot you brought home last week. Are you up for it? Hanna will be here in a few and we'll make a toast." No longer did the words come out and the door-bell rang. Maryanne opened the door to see Hanna's smiling face. She threw her arms around her, giving a hug that told more than Hanna understood. Maryanne was secretly thinking that this was her own Daughter. Not able to relay the information to Hanna yet, she relished again on the good news. She would soon tell her; when the time was right.

"We were just going to break open a bottle of Merlot, if you would like to join us in a toast. The house we are now in has been sold, and we are set to move tomorrow," Maryanne filled her in on the details.

"I'd love to. And then can we go see the Manor? I am so excited!" Hanna's face lit up as she smiled with anticipation.

"Mario popped the cork and served the wine. After the toast Maryanne took Hanna to the Valencia. Maryanne was a little apprehensive about how Hanna would react to being back at the place where she spent her devastating childhood. As they walked up the stairs, Hanna seemed in good spirits and commented on how beautiful the landscaping had been upgraded.

So far, so good, Maryanne was thinking. She opened the door and flipped the switch that brought the chandeliers to life. The look on Hanna's face was one of elation and not apprehension, or sadness, that Maryanne had been somewhat expecting. She was relieved. The lights scattered diverse patterns in various paths around the room. The furnishings were spectacular and Hanna was more than pleased at the results. She looked around the room, eyeing every piece of art, furniture and accent pieces.

"Maryanne, I could not be happier how it all turned out. It's perfect. More perfect than I could have ever imagined."

"It was you who did most of the design work, so you should be very proud. Your talent is extraordinary. Thank you, Hanna, for the work you have done to help us put this place back together again. Just like in Humpty Dumpty, right?" Maryanne kidded.

Hanna laughed loudly. Maryanne could see she had come such a long way from when this place was a place of torment and misery. It was a remarkable recovery. The doctors had done extremely well with Hanna. Maryanne walked up the stairs and Hanna followed; eyes full of wonder. Its nostalgic atmosphere illuminated, as the ladies toured the rest of the Manor. When they neared the room at the end of the hall, the door flew open, and then slammed suddenly, frightening them. They stopped short and Maryanne took hold of Hanna's hand.

"Hanna, don't worry, it gets kind of weird in here every now and then, but it's quite safe, I assure you." She tried to convince Hanna and herself, she was thinking.

"Hanna seemed to remain fairly calm and spoke softly, "I am fine. I understand what you are saying. When I lived here, many odd things happened. After a while, I became immune to it and began to accept it as the norm. I am all good with this, don't worry," she reassured Maryanne.

Maryanne was relieved, knowing that Hanna too, had experienced the phenomena and was comfortable with it.

"Well…let's go inside the room, then," Maryanne suggested.

"C'mon, I'm ready. Let's go," Hanna started for the door. She took hold of the handle and pulled, but it wouldn't budge. She tried again and then Maryanne took hold but still it was not going to give up the ship.

"We'll wait for Mario to open it later. It's just stuck. New door and all, you know the drill," Maryanne reasoned.

"Yes…okay. Let's look at the room that I'm going to be sleeping in when I stay the night," Hanna grinned, excitedly. Maryanne was surprised that she wasn't the least bit upset by the unnatural occurrence. She reasoned that being a captive in the house for so many years would probably be enough to make anyone immune to its mysterious environment. Maryanne wasn't completely comfortable yet, but presumed she would soon become adjusted to it, since it would be her and Mario's home starting tomorrow. Hanna and Maryanne entered the room that Maryanne had decorated especially for Hanna. The door opened quite easily and they felt much more at ease. Hanna was overwhelmed at what she saw. A beautiful crystal chandelier hung from the center of the room, its glowing sprays of light dancing around the ceiling and on the walls. An antique brass bed, tall posts reaching toward the ten-foot ceiling had been placed at the corner of the room. It was covered with a fluffy, white and gold quilted, satin comforter. A canopy of lace and satin reached across the top posts. Lace swooped downward in swags around the top. Tall windows were dressed in similar fabric that hung in swags along the valance and down both sides. Beige colored blinds covered the glass. After taking in all of the amenities,

Hanna ran to one of the windows, pulled the blind halfway up and looked out across the yard. Enormous trees with overhanging branches seemed to reach out toward the house, as if trying to grasp at the ever changing edifice; as if they were in communication with its bizarre supernatural complexity. Hanna stood for several minutes, quiet; as if she too, was in tune with its unearthly emanation.

"Hanna." Maryanne spoke, trying to distract her from what seemed like an odd fixation; possibly of something many years ago, as a child.

"What?" Hanna answered, reconnecting to her surroundings. She seemed quite oddly distracted, and then she turned to Maryanne with a perplexed look, as if she had momentarily been far-away in thought.

"Are you all right, Hanna?"

"Yes…I mean…I am now. For a moment, it was as if I were elsewhere, and not really sure where. Unusual feelings had come over me as I looked out into the yard and the trees. Someone was calling me from far away. I am not sure what happened, but I am fine now. Can we go now? I feel like I could use some fresh air." Hanna started toward the door and Maryanne followed.

"Sorry Maryanne. I was feeling a little faint for a moment. I didn't eat this morning and I am sure that's the reason. As soon as we leave, I'd like to have something to eat." Hanna hurried down the stairs and out the front door, Maryanne not far behind.

When they were in the car, Hanna apologized again. Maryanne was very cordial and understanding. The Manor would take some getting used to, she was sure of that.

"Let's go eat. What are you hungry for?" Maryanne made an attempt to change the mood. "I'm famished as well."

"Hmmm. Let's see…what sounds good?"

"You choose; my treat." Maryanne countered.

"Let's eat Chinese. I would love to have a bowl of good

won ton soup and I love lo mien. How does Chinese sound to you, Maryanne?"

"Yummy. I'm for it. I know just the place, not too far from here. They steam vegetables using no additives at all. Totally fresh and healthy." Maryanne headed for China Gourmet, on Broadway. Soon they were munching on egg rolls and chatting, while the main course was being prepared.

"I hope you weren't thinking that I didn't like the room. It was so beautiful and I loved every inch of it. You did a spectacular job! Thank you, Maryanne. You picked out everything I love and then some." Hanna tried to explain her eagerness to leave the bedroom so quickly.

"You are welcome. I knew you loved it when you walked into the room. No need to explain anything to me. I think sometimes I almost know what you are thinking. It's strange but true. It's as if I have known you forever. You are a huge part of my life now, and I want to make your life perfect in any way that I can. Just say the word and I will come running, no matter where I am or what I'm doing. You are very important to me." Maryanne affirmed.

"Thank you. I feel very much the same way. You are the most important person in the world to me." Hanna's eyes welled with tears, and she blinked several times, to conceal her emotion and distract the tears.

"Let's eat! It looks wonderful. I'm so glad you chose Chinese. Mario never wants to come here. It's always Italian or Spanish for him! We are going to have great times together." Maryanne poured the tea and they devoured the food. The two of them got along famously as they talked about everything under the sun. Two hours later it was approaching time for Hanna to leave. Maryanne had tried to convince her to stay, but she had a class in the morning. She promised to return in a week, when she had a three day break. Maryanne took her back to the house on Mapleton avenue and Hanna was off to Boulder. It had been an incredible day for both of them. There was so much more to be shared and there would be much more to experience at the grand Manor on Valencia Lane.

When Maryanne arrived at her budding store, Valencia Antiquities, Wendy was carefully unwrapping and preparing to display new artifacts that had just arrived from New York City. Maryanne joined in, scanning the merchandise and entering it into the database. Nothing could make her more enthusiastic than to inspect incoming artifacts when a shipment arrived. This was what Maryanne was born for, she always claimed; to find and admire what had been a treasure in its time, and was still greatly sought after today. Learning the historical aspects of each piece had always been where her interests had seemed to lie. She loved the work and knew she would stay in the field for years to come. Many of the pieces she had placed inside the Manor were items that she had discovered through research at the store.

26

The Slasher murders had taken another wrong turn. The latest victim, a young woman had been slain and found on the edge of town near the highway that led to Lyons. They found her blood-soaked body in a clump of bushes half covered with old branches left by an assailant who was obviously trying to hide the body. They had not succeeded, because the corpse was discovered after lying there for just a few days. The MO was not as indicative as the last four murders. Only one victim still remained alive and recovering at Boulder Hospital. The recent discovery had taken on a more sinister plot, in that the attacker had changed its habits and now detectives in the homicide squad were ready for anything. The latest casualty was a twenty-five year old nurse from the hospital where the one surviving victim remained a patient.

Mario was headed to the hospital to meet with Julia White. She had been recovering well but emotionally and mentally, there were some unsettling questions. She had not disclosed to anyone, how she had been experiencing the feelings of her changes and what she had interpreted as metamorphoses. Today, she would make an attempt to explain it to Detective Ramos. Mario was perplexed and uncomfortable with what she had disclosed to him and immediately called Maryanne to update her. He left the hospital in a confused and bewildered state of mind, hoping that with the help of Maryanne and Vivian, there would be some insight to the bizarre revelation.

Later after dinner, the primary discussion focused on the Slasher murders. Julia White was indeed the key to it all, if they could find a way to make her remember more of what had taken place. Being the only survivor, it was mandatory that full-time guards remained with her at all times. The murderer was a silent and vicious predator. His victims were all taken without any suspect of what was happening. According to Julia White, it seemed to have an uncanny ability to mentally draw her into a spell, where she did not reject its aberrant assault. Vivian was consulted, and joined the two of them for a discussion. She had done further research on the peculiar behavior. The lab had confirmed that the blood DNA was an unknown strand that seemed to deviate from any known pattern. This led the Psychic to interpret it as a possible unearthly form of vampirism. In the modern day cult behavior, the DNA would be a distinctive type, associated with human blood. The DNA of unknown origin, is what Vivian was concerned about. If indeed it was what she suspected; her conclusion was to have the DNA of Julia White retested since she had first been admitted, to see if her DNA strand had changed at all. Mario called the request into the station. Chief Olson would send his top forensic specialist to the hospital, to acquire another sample of the surviving victim's blood.

A few days later, the test was confirmed. Julia White's DNA had changed significantly and showed the same unusual metamorphosis as the attacker's sample. They had a new lead, but the lead was not in the usual conformity of interpretation. They immediately had it sent to the top blood analysts in New York City to unravel its complexity. They had not seen anything like this prior to its discovery and were working 'round the clock to unravel its anomalous origin. The latest victim had been tested to show the exact DNA on a neck wound. As time had passed, the attacker had become more intense and careless in its need to kill, which added to the dilemma.

A report was received, showing that the test from the survivor had changed again, which was very unusual. The blood DNA was beginning to mutate. The puzzle became more complex each day. Mario met with Julia White at the hospital once more, to discuss the theory at length, and its unusual mutation. Mario had summarized her behavior as she had described; a metamorphosis. It was all beginning to make sense now. She was changing; possibly into the creature that the Psychic had described. A creature that lived by ingesting human blood and was forced to kill for survival. The only other way to survive this horrible disorder was to obtain blood from blood banks, unless she would be released to find her own supply. Of course that meant she would be allowed to kill for survival and we all know the answer to that one.

Until now, Mario had not even given a second thought to the connection of a recent blood-bank break in. A huge quantity of human blood had been stolen, and now everything was coming together in a bizarre circus of strange consequences. He consulted the Psychic. Vivian agreed with his conclusion and warned that the surviving victim, though still alive, may succumb to the exact needs of a vampire. She had suggested testing constantly to determine if they needed to supplement her with blood to sustain her life; and hopefully to halt any more changes that she would otherwise experience. If not, perhaps in the end she would revert, though unwillingly, to the same practices as those of the living dead. Such ghoulish interpretations started to almost make sense, even though it seemed literally impossible.

A team of scientists were working diligently on the blood samples, but so far had come up empty-handed. They tried to make a connection that would make scientific sense, but came to a dead-end. Chief Olson had put his top forensic detective on the case to investigate and try to connect the dots with the earlier victims. Something had to give, and soon. Time was against them and Julia White's life hung in the balance, of this world and the next, according to the Psychic. If they could find an antidote for Julia before the change was complete, they could save her from a fate much worse than death itself. The word spread quickly in the scientific community. Three top labs in the country had come together to decipher the unnatural blood connection. If that didn't work, Julia was in for a rough ride. They may end up keeping her in protective custody stop her from hurting herself, or others. The other issue was the most disturbing, since they were aware that if she were on her own, she may revert to the behavior of her attacker to sustain herself. They had decided to keep her in protective custody until hopefully someone could come up with a solution that would save her and answer the most likely questions; how many of these vampire-like creatures are out there and how do we exterminate them. Are they already dead and unable to be stopped? Many scenarios had been thought out, but no one had the answers that were needed. It was going to be a complicated and subjective case. The fact that some did not believe that it was possible for a vampire to be dead and walk among the living, was inherently a stumbling block. Trying to convince someone to believe in the dead coming to life was like trying to change life itself, one scientist had been reported as saying. He said that it was virtually impossible, and we must find out the real truth before we get on the vampire wagon

When full reports had come in on the latest victim, it had been determined that she was drained of blood at the scene of the crime. It looked as though the killer or killers were getting desperate and taking bigger chances. A full scale alert was still active, and they added ten more officers to the case. Denver PD had sent eight of their own to assist in the hunt. In Denver, three murders had taken place, but a slightly different MO was discovered. Two of the victims had been cut or torn in the neck. One had wrists cut, but they were all drained of blood. The difference was not only the wrist being used as the point of blood loss, but two of the victims were young men. Police in the entire State of Colorado were on high alert, working day and night to unravel this supernatural quandary. The siege of murders was becoming rampant and diverse in nature. The one common denominator was blood-letting.

Mario had a meeting with the Psychic and two detectives to obtain any new information that was possible. The Psychic would attempt another communication, to see if she could connect with the master of the cult, if there were such a creature in the midst. The meeting would take place this evening.

Mario would not be able to help Maryanne finish the move, but the contractor had been willing to assist her. Most everything had been completed in advance. There were only a few small items to contend with. They had nearly finished by six-o'clock and Mario's meeting was at eight o'clock at Chief Olson's office.

Vivian Gilbreth would attempt mediation and telepathy to communicate at that time. She did tell Mario that only two other officers should be present. Too many would cause an adverse reaction and she wanted to have a successful connection. They agreed. She was prepared with the ritual, chant, candles, incense and other usual items she used in such rituals. She felt very confident this would be successful. Eight o'clock came and Vivian began by reciting an incantation. One that she had used years ago and that she had been given instruction on when she was in England, recently. The psychic convention she had attended had given her much more knowledge and ammunition, if you will, on similar activity. Though, she had never been involved with this kind of unnatural entity in the past, she felt it would be successful if the entity were on another plane, and not of this earth. If on the other hand it turned out to be modern day vampirism, they could be looking at real living beings that had been changing for some time, in the same way Julia White seemed to be transforming. This communication would tell the tale, she was positive of that.

It was eight o'clock, and Vivian began setting the stage; lighting candles and burning incense. Three detectives including Mario, sat around a large, round table; candles placed tactically around the room. She instructed them to be silent and sit; hands on the table, palms up. Lights down and candles flickering, the Psychic began to recite an incantation to summon the evil entity and communicate telepathically. She spoke softly, but demanding. The room was quiet except for her words of summons to the unknown entity.

"Whoever you are, I demand that you speak to me. I summons you from the depths of hell to come out and show yourself. Let us see who you are. Speak to us. We want to know you and understand what it is that you want. I demand that you materialize at once!" she spoke with an assertive, commanding boldness. She continued the chant, trying to motivate a connection with the undetermined entity.

"Show yourself! Speak to us. What is your reason for the evil you perpetrate? We are not afraid of you. Are you a coward who cannot show your face?" she tried to anger the unknown spirit to materialize. Nothing was happening. She began reciting another incantation that had been used in séance rituals. A freezing wind blew through the space and a vase was thrown across the room. The candles were blown out and two chairs turned upside down, while objects seemed to fly effortlessly across the grand-room. The detectives were terrified at the sudden manifestations. Jackson pulled the gun from his shoulder holster and stood up in a threatening manner.

"I have a gun! I'll use it if I have to. Come out and show yourself, you cowardly bastard!" He waved the gun around the room, as he turned to find the entity.

The noise continued and a candlestick holder flew past his

head, just missing him. A thundering voice bellowed through the room.

"You cannot hurt me. Sit down. Nothing but bad can come of this if you don't control yourself, Detective Jackson. What do you want from me? I have done you no harm. Why are you summoning me?" The voice seemed to emanate from the walls as it echoed throughout the house.

Vivian urged the Detective to sit and be still. He reluctantly sat back down and laid his forty-five on the table in front of him. Vivian continued the chant and ritual to summon the spirit to materialize.

"Make yourself known," she urged the entity. "What is your name?" Another bitter gust of wind blew through the room and the temperature dropped quickly. As Vivian spoke, her words came out with puffs, like smoke from freezing vapors in the air. The group was fixed in trepidation at such unnatural phenomenon.

"I summon you to appear, now! I demand that you make yourself known to us. Speak to us about the killings. Are you afraid to speak?"

The voice answered in its low-pitched resonance. "If I materialize, you must promise me that you will find the killers. I have nothing to do with the murders that have taken place. Your killer is not I." And then in an instant a fog formed and then the dark figure appeared in its midst.

Vivian spoke gravely, trying to appear sympathetic to the creature of the night. "If you are not the killer, then tell me who is responsible. We must find the one who is responsible for these brutal murders and put a stop to it. Helpless, innocent, young women are dying in a most brutal way to satisfy someone's thirst for blood. That seems to fit your pattern in the past, I see," she taunted. "If not you; then who?"

Your killer is not on my plane. He and his followers are living on the earth plane and using vampire rituals of new modern-day cults. If I were responsible, you could not catch me. I am illusive. That is all I can tell you. I must leave now. If and when I return, you will be well aware of our powers." In an instant he was gone. The materialization had diminished and only the fog remained.

"There is your answer," Vivian spoke. "We must look elsewhere for the killer or killers. They are stalking people and walking in the streets at night, waiting for vulnerable victims to use for their blood-sacrifice and rituals. The Police will have to be more vigilant, as well as the community. An article should be posted in every newspaper, warning people against being out at night, and to watch for strange signs of possible cult activity.

"As far as I'm concerned, that makes a whole lot more sense than something sub-human or supernatural," Jackson reasoned. "Officer Montrose, what's your thought on that?"

"Guess I want to think it's a human suspect, cause I can't say that I'm really one to believe in the supernatural vampire thing, but after tonight, seeing the manifestation and hearing the voice, I'm inclined to feel a little more open-minded. Just hoping it is a living, breathing killer. That one we can destroy. I don't know how easy it would be to kill or destroy a vampire who is already dead," Montrose commented, his face sullen and serious.

The meeting had come to an unexpected end, but not a dissatisfied result. They were all in agreement on one fact. They were not the walking-dead, as a few had formerly concluded; very few. The group left with a new plan of attack; one that they had been following, but they had still left room for the supernatural aspect. Now it was determined that a full-scale alert for cult activity be on every agenda. The Denver PD was alerted, leaving out the comments from the Psychic. They were not sure the Denver PD would appreciate hearing that they had worked with a psychic to determine what kind of killer they had been searching for. Mario walked Vivian out to her car and thanked her again. When she left, he contemplated the information, but one question remained. Why was the blood of Julia White mutating? There had to be more scientific studies done to determine what the unusual strain was caused from. He would meet with forensics in the morning to discuss all possibilities. Could it be that there was an evil entity who took part in some of the murders and a distinct possibility of the real vampires as well? He spoke to Chief Olson on the phone and briefed him on the results of the meeting.

It was time to get murder off his mind. Mario jumped into his Rumble Bee and sped off to the Manor, where Maryanne waited eagerly for his return. It would be their first night together at the Valencia Manor.

27

Morning greeted the Manor, and Maryanne opened her eyes to see tufts of light peeking in from the partially covered windows. Their first night at the Valencia had gone surprisingly well. The morning was serene and peaceful as she puffed up two pillows and sat back watching the morning news on her laptop, quietly thinking and planning her day. Mario was still sleeping, but stirring as if he might be dreaming. It seemed to be a positive one at that. She noticed his lips curl a time or two. After a shower and make-up, a quick cup of coffee and one for the road, she left for the store. A reporter would be finishing up the details on the story for the Sunday Newspaper; Valencia Manor, property of the month. The photographer would be taking pictures this afternoon.

When Maryanne arrived, the reporter was browsing her store with great interest.

"Hello Maryanne. Nice to see you. I have been admiring your inventory; you have impeccable taste. I am sure I will be coming back to spend money here at a later date when I have more time to focus. I was not aware of the incredible artifacts you had acquired. I would like to do a story on the store in a few weeks, as well, after we finish the Manor. I think it would be of interest to many who are not yet aware of what you have here."

Why thank you, Miss Henning. I appreciate your compliments and I would be more than happy to work with you on a story when you are ready, if you wish," Maryanne said, her eyes showing eagerness at such interest.

"We can do the photo shoot for the Valencia now, if you are ready," Maryanne offered.

"Certainly. I'm ready if you are."

"Maryanne and Miss Henning left the store. When they approached the Valencia Manor, Miss Henning, with camera in hand, snapped a few shots of the exterior and landscape. Maryanne took her inside and gave her a grand tour of the interior. The reporter was impressed at the décor and her photography savvy was second to none. She had an incredible eye for placement and the pictures were of excellent quality. The article would definitely be an eye-catcher. Fortunately, no ghosts were playing today. Maryanne had held her breath a few times, hoping that nothing too quirky would take place and scare the woman off. 'The spirits were taking a break,' she was thinking. When they were finished, Maryanne drove her back to the store and shared interesting facts for the article before Miss Henning departed.

"Here is my card; please call me Sherrie. Call me anytime. I'll get back to you with the proofs, so you can approve them." She left, pleased that it was a productive interview and successful shoot.

Maryanne stood in the entry as she drove away, thinking that an article about the store would really help business and she was pleased that Sherri was interested. A call from Marshall Hanover came in on her cell. She had met Marshall, the well-to-do gentleman who had been interested in certain aspects of the paranormal. He had been looking for a property through Joan's company last year and through that connection, Maryanne introduced him to Jonathon Livingston. Jonathon was about ten years Marshall's senior and a paranormal enthusiast, as well. Both men were wealthy, with similar interests. Through the connection, they had become friends last year, and it turned out to be a romance that blossomed quickly. They had referred to Maryanne as 'Cupid', since the relationship had budded into such an affair.

"Maryanne, its Marshall, remember me? You are the one who introduced me to my now partner, Jonathon Livingston. How have you been? It's been a long time since we've spoken."

"Hello, Marshall. I am well, thank you. Mario and I recently married. I ended up inheriting the Valencia Manor, after all of the turmoil and weird manifestations. Opened up a new store and have been all kinds of busy. Wondered how you two had been doing and thought of you often. We have recently restored the Valencia, and there's going to be a write-up in the Sunday paper, so check it out. You'll have to come to the house warming when we are ready. We've barely moved in. Now tell me what you have been up to, and how is Jonathon doing?"

"We are both fine and still living together, as you may have imagined. I still appreciate your playing cupid that brought us together. Congratulations Maryanne, on the marriage. I too have been busy. Since Jonathon and I have been together, we started our new business, Ghost Chasers, Incorporated. We specialize in helping to clear houses of evil entities, as you've probably guessed. We have purchased every machine possible that is being used today in research of supernatural and paranormal phenomenon. I'll give you a rundown soon, perhaps lunch; my treat, of course. We can exchange information and catch up. After all, I would not have met Jonathon had it not been for you. I owe you one, my dear. I would like to meet with you soon. I have some interesting data and equipment that you may want to see."

"How about you meet me at my store tomorrow? Valencia

Antiquities; in the Pearl Street Mall shopping district. I'd love to show you the store and we can have lunch then. Can you make it at noon?"

"It's a date Maryanne. I know exactly where that is. Looking forward to it. See you at noon then." Click.

"Maryanne felt almost guilty not getting in contact with them, but a lot had happened and she was sure he would understand. 'Friends always understand,' she mentally noted.

The day was winding down and Mario was actually coming home early for dinner, so she picked up some of his favorite food at the market and headed for home. First meal at the Manor. She planned on making it a good one. She made a quick call to Joan, to see if she could join them. Maryanne had neglected Joan in the past couple of months as well. Now that she was moved in, she would plan much more time with friends. Joan eagerly accepted the invitation.

On the way back home, Maryanne almost drove to the wrong house, while she had been thinking and on automatic pilot. As she passed her old house, she pulled in and turned around, feeling a pang of nostalgia, but not for long. She was quite content in her new abode. She noticed Borislav's black Mercedes in the drive when she backed up.

Dinner was ready, Mario was in the shower and Joan rang the door-bell. Perfect timing. She had already set the large dining room table; candles and all. Joan was very impressed at the décor when she entered. Maryanne showed her through the first floor while they waited on Mario. He stepped out, dressed in his casual slacks and one of her favorite shirts. 'He looked very sexy.' Maryanne made a mental observation.

"Joan. So nice to see you again." Mario pecked her cheek and escorted her through the grand-room.

"You too Mario. I've missed you guys. We seem to have gone into our own separate lives for a while and it's time we got together a bit more often. When's the house warming?" she questioned eagerly.

"We haven't figured it out yet, but soon. We spent our first night here last night. Quiet and peaceful, too. No strange visitors at all," Maryanne chuckled.

"That's something to be thankful for," Joan agreed, exposing a sinister look.

"So far, the place looks incredible! I am really impressed," Joan scanned the room.

"I'll show you the rest of the house after we eat. I don't have a maid, so I'll do the honors," Maryanne giggled, hurrying away into the kitchen. Joan followed, offering her assistance.

They enjoyed standing-rib-roast, surrounded with roast potatoes and carrots. An organic mixed green salad was served first. The roast had been cooked to perfection. Maryanne was thankful, since she hadn't made a rib-roast for at least two years. Maryanne served chocolate cake with vanilla ice cream after everyone had enjoyed the main course. She served frothing cappuccinos while they sat at the table and chatted for an hour.

Joan filled them in on the recent incidents where Steve had been stalking her. She had to make a formal complaint and he went in for counseling, but served no jail time. She wanted nothing to do with him and was still a little apprehensive about what he might do. He had made a few calls to her, trying to apologize as in the past, but she finally blocked his calls. For two weeks she had heard nothing from him.

"I used to see him at work, but he was suspended when the formal complaint was filed against him. He is still on probationary leave, as far as I know," Mario explained. "It's sad that it all turned out so badly for both of you."

"I am seeing someone now. I like him a lot, but taking it slow," Joan confided.

"I don't blame you," Mario agreed. "It's not something you would take lightly now, for sure."

"Yes, I hope he doesn't get wind of it. I don't know what he would do. He went into some pretty serious rages. I am being quite discreet, so please don't say anything to him if you see him." Joan's eyes were tearing, and she dotted them with her napkin. "Well, we can't all have the perfect love, like you two incredible love-birds," she chuckled. "Soon, I'll introduce you to the new man in my life."

"Oh, we have our problems too. It's not all perfect," Maryanne grinned at Mario. He smiled and pulled her close to him," brown eyes sparkling.

"But we don't stay mad for long. And making up is always the best part of our arguments," he added. "We'd love to meet your new friend."

"I would like to see the rest of the house, so I can get going and you lovers can be alone," Joan stood up, taking her plates into the kitchen. When they cleaned the table and filled the dishwasher, Maryanne gave her the grand tour. Joan was truly enthralled at the finished product.

"It's unbelievable," she complimented. "But I do have to leave. Early clients are arriving at seven and I have a desk of paperwork to complete tonight. Looks like another good sale for me. I have to get my rest, you know," she giggled on her way out the door. Mario walked her to the car and she was off.

Mario and Maryanne would use the master bedroom to its full extent this evening. They were hungry for passion and ready to express it. It would be their first sexual encounter in the Manor; and one that they would remember for years to come.

While the couple were in perfect sexual unison and ready to experience the peak of ecstasy, strange noises began to emanate from somewhere within their sanctuary. The orgasmic encounter had been shut down cold, and they withdrew from the embrace, to fix their vision on piercing eyes glowering at them from near the window of the room. No light was apparent, but for the moon that sent a few traces from the top window, high up above the others. Certainly not enough illumination to detect what creature stood before them. Eyes reflecting a hint of green, watching the couple who had been at the peak of ecstasy; now their eyes fixed on the evil creature, they were at the edge of terror. A voice sliced through the silence, piercing the darkness, cutting into their psyche. They lie motionless, unable to speak. Maryanne held tight to Mario, not moving, only watching the shiny, green-cast emitted from unnatural eyes that seemed to dominate them. Mario forced words, unable to move.

"Who are you? What do you want from us?" Still there was silence. Clouds moved away from the moon, and a luminous glow snuck through the small window. The creature shuffled quickly away from its path. The moon was full, and they were beginning to decipher what looked like a human, clad in black. Silver-white hair flashed from underneath its dark hood. It spoke with an ominous gurgle.

"Why are you here? This is my domain. No one will inhabit the Manor, unless I command it. It is my realm, and not to be interfered with. You have entered my sanctuary; one that you will not be able to endure. I will haunt you to the ends of the earth. If you are able to survive what there is in store for you, then I shall leave willingly to find another place to dwell; among the dead." It suddenly disappeared into a fog that quickly diminished. They lay there still, hearts beating fast, unable to move or speak. When they reclaimed composure, early morning light had begun to make its way into the room. They were embraced, holding fast to each other as they tried to escape the feelings of terror that loomed over them. After what seemed longer than it was, they climbed out of bed and rushed through their morning ritual and hurried through what was usually a relaxing shower. Everything was done quietly, and quickly. They did not speak much, still feeling the ominous presence that had threatened them. Finally Maryanne spoke.

"What are we going to do?" She spoke quietly as if to conceal her voice from the unwelcome predator.

"Are you kidding me? We aren't going anywhere. We are going to fight this entity with everything we have. I'll call Vivian first of all. If we need a priest we will get one. You said you spoke to Marshall Dunn yesterday. We can consult with him and his partner Jonathon Livingstone, as well. We can beat this thing. There is no way in hell we are leaving this place for a frickin ghost! I hope they can hear me now, because they just picked a battle they will not win." Mario was angry and serious.

"Then I'll speak to Jonathon and Marshall right away. I was going to have lunch with him, and I'll tell him then. You call Vivian. This can be stopped. Mario...I'm scared; but I believe we can do this."

"Today is the first day of the battle. A battle we will win hands down. Bring it on!" Mario bellowed loudly. His voice echoed throughout the house. If the entity was truly listening, it would be aware that they weren't about to give up without the fight of their lives.

Maryanne spoke to Marshall and he was quite excited to join in the quest to end, once and for all; hauntings at Valencia Manor. He volunteered his partner Jonathon, as well. Since they had created their ghost hunting business, they had acquired specific machines and equipment that could aid in the success of this mission. He would use a thermal imaging camera to photograph spirit activity, a static night vision camera, and use spirit voice recorders. They had acquired a new piece of equipment that had worked well in the last encounter they had made in Denver. It was called a spirit box and could scan spirit activity when present. They were well equipped for the job. Along with Vivian Gilbreth, the gifted Psychic; the team would have every advantage possible, for their latest endeavor.

Maryanne set a date for the meeting at the Valencia. Saturday night would be the test. They would all meet at nine o'clock, so by midnight it would be primed for activity. Mario and Maryanne were anxious and a little apprehensive, but well prepared for the encounter. Now they would patiently wait; only one more day. They were pumped and ready for the major leagues of ghost hunting.

Later, Maryanne called Joan to let her know what was about to take place; and to see if her problems with Steve had ceased. Joan was depressed and worried, because Steve had forced his way in to see her last night and it got pretty violent. She called the police and he was incarcerated. If he continued this way, he would certainly end up in jail for assault, stalking and the works. He had definitely taken a wrong turn in his relationship with Joan. She was quite disturbed.

Later, Maryanne stopped by to see her. She had several bruises and a black-eye. It had evolved to a very critical stage and Maryanne was worried. If Steve got out again, it could be much worse. Court was coming up and Steve made bail today. Joan was terrified. Maryanne tried to convince her to spend time at the Manor with them until court. She had an assistant working at her real estate firm, so business would not suffer. Joan did a lot of work by phone and email, anyway. Her computer was her best friend in that respect. Joan agreed to stay with them after the team had finished their ghost-quest. It was all set. Sunday Joan would move into the Manor temporarily, until Steve was hopefully behind bars. Mario had not spoken to Steve, as Steve had made himself scarce since he was put on probation at work.

28

Plans were moving along; the Psychic had been contacted and the team of Ghost Chasers, Incorporated were ready to start on a new and intriguing venture. They met in front of Valencia Manor. Marshall Dunn and Jonathon Livingston arrived in a black Cadillac Escalade. Maryanne and Mario were inside and Vivian had just driven up, parking behind the escalade, in her BMW. Jonathon had not changed much from his stoic, and somber demeanor. Underneath it all, he was a very charming man though. Tall, staunch and attractive for his age; about fifty-five, Maryanne had guessed, and sometimes overbearing. All in all, Maryanne and Joan had formed a quick bond with him and his partner Marshall. Marshall; still as flamboyant as ever, and much too good-looking to be real, one would think. Maryanne had always kidded him and mentioned a time or two that he should be a model. Man candy was not a bad thing as long as it was kept in perspective, she had thought to herself. Even though he was gay, many a woman would enjoy such a feast for hungry eyes.

Vivian Gilbreth, the Psychic that had impressed Maryanne from day one, showed up in all her glory wearing a multi-colored one-piece silky gown, she liked to call a muumuu that fell loose around the body. She had always liked the style because she had jestingly mentioned that they leave a lot of imagination to what's underneath. She looked amazing in the dress and her green eyes were sparkling with enthusiasm.

The team was assembled and the equipment was being set in strategic areas on both floors. Night vision cameras, EVT recorders and other useful devices had been tactically placed to capture photos and communicate with the entity. EVP recorders capture sounds of spirit voices. EMF and Thermal detection equipment was also installed. These devices were being used now, main-stream. Psychics and ghost hunters were able to collect much more evidence in the field of strange phenomenon, making much headway in proof of its existence.

It was as if the weather would change when these events were planned surrounding supernatural activity. It seemed to link up, adding its eerie and dismal elements as if it were staged purposefully. Its compliance with dark elements made it even more unsettling.

The stage was set, candles were lit and the Psychic tuned in, making an attempt to connect with the unknown entity. It didn't take long. Right away the weather began to emanate its bizarre thunder ritual, as if a switch had been pulled; as if the creature actually had that much power. Pictures began to fall off walls and chairs did their usual dance until they fell over. A table slid across the floor, just missing Vivian. Lights were out and it was dark, except for the candles that flickered from the circle that she had assembled. A loud grumbling voice shot through the dark, spewing blasphemous warnings and sinister messages.

The creature was enraged and beginning to materialize. The special cameras and voice- recorders were activated; devices that in the past would have been laughed at were ready to capture evidence of its manifestation. Vivian began her incantation to summon and take away the power from the entity. It was angry and causing serious upheaval. Its voice was raging and they covered their ears to bear the intensity. Words of pure evil emanated from the walls of the house. It had not materialized yet, but the Psychic was chanting and summoning its presence to do so. The room had become freezing cold, and a cloud of fog began to form. Finally, the creature made its debut. Let's just say that there would be no show without its presence. It became more violent; moving furniture and breaking glasses as they flew off the counter with the supernatural forces at work. The noise was unbearable. Vivian sustained her chant without interruption. She had stood her ground, giving the creature back as much as it could deliver. Finally, they could see a dark figure, white hair protruding from its hood. Its eyes were eerie and ghastly as they pierced through the darkness, reflecting a green hue and specks of flickering candle-light.

The recording equipment was taped securely so that it could not easily be moved by supernatural forces. Each device was set to activate at the presence of any activity, upstairs and down.

The evil entity fully materialized and stood in the fog, anger seething from its core. Eyes that took on a color of blood-red and they could feel the hostility emanating from within it. It began to rant an evil incantation, causing the house to shake from within. It was communicating.

"What do you want with me? I have not yet spread my wrath against your mortal souls. I am not the one you want. If you do not leave me alone, I will begin a rage that you or no one could even begin to contain. I have the power to send an evil fury that you would not be able to endure. If you do not let me be, I will carry out a vendetta that would destroy all that you love.

"Who are you?" Vivian questioned the dark visitor. She had not yet spoken to this entity that she could remember. "Why are you at this place? These people are innocent and do not deserve your anger and retaliation. What happened to you that you want them to leave this Manor?" They have every right to be here. This is their home now."

"I was once like you, a mortal human, who visited this Manor many years ago. I was attacked by one of the living dead and now I am included in their world; a world of darkness where blood is the source of life, where these creatures such as I, roam the earth. We must have blood to survive and flourish once we materialize and take root on the earth plane. I have not yet taken that step. If you summon me again, I will. I did not choose my world, it chose me. I was a mortal good human and lived only to love and be loved while only a visitor here at the Manor. I am the lover of Sarah, who was married to John Farthington. He was a cruel and desperate man, who had much hate in his heart. Sarah was miserable and we became lovers when I was staying here as the grounds keeper. I lived in the house next door. We had a beautiful relationship until John had driven her to the edge of sanity. She died and I left the house to live a lonely existence without her until I died, five years later. I had been attacked by a group of vampires who lived an earthly existence, though they were the walking dead. They fed on my body for hours and then I died and crossed into emptiness where I still exist. I only wanted to find Sarah when I died, but have not been able to, because of the way I was killed. When you are killed by a vampire, you can no longer be in contact with the other side; with the good people who have crossed over. I live in a cold, empty grave and when I materialize, it is only to see if I can find my dear Sarah. I am evil, but for some reason, there is still a part of me that is good. If I hold on to my memories of her, I am in control of the evil side of my nature. Until now; until you summoned me, I was living a lonely existence roaming the rooms of this Manor. Now, it has been taken from me and I have nowhere to go except to hell itself. If someone could find my coffin and pierce my heart with a stake carved from the old wood of this Manor, I could be free and able to cross over with my Sarah.

Until that happens I am a lost soul, full of rage, wandering the earth, never to be at peace. I do not want to live on the earth plane, or terrible things could happen. Many people would be hurt or killed, because once here, I would not be able to control myself in order to sustain this being with blood from mortals. Do you know what it is to be locked in a world of death and hate? Having to kill for blood to support your horrible existence? I do not want that. I want to go on to the next world; a world where my lovely Sarah awaits me. Can you help me to cross over? I will show you where my coffin lies. At dawn I will return to my earthly grave. You can drive the stake into my heart, so that I may be released into the light. I still have goodness in my soul, and I do not want to continue the spiral downward into the depths of hell."

"Where is your coffin? I will help you if it is possible for me to find it. I feel some goodness coming from you. For some reason you were not completely changed into the unfeeling, undead, vampire creatures. I think the goodness in you prevailed and you won over the evil that dominated you. Show me where your coffin is and I promise you, that when the dawn has risen, I shall drive the stake into your heart and release you from your hell."

"In the basement, there is a hidden door. I can show you if you will follow me."

"Let me speak to my associates here and then I will answer your question," Vivian spoke, out of breath. She explained what she had to do and Mario would help her through the process.

"We will follow you to the basement and find the coffin. When the dawn is up, we will fulfill your wishes."

The entity seemed to be in a state of calm, unlike before. The green cast in his eyes had diminished and they took on a silver, grey glow. He forced a smile showing grossly misshapen teeth, sharp and pointed. He still emitted a calm that changed the energy in the room. He was truly showing appreciation and hoping to be saved from his life of agony and wrath. He was obviously a good man when the creatures used him for their blood gratification. Vivian could hardly believe what she was hearing. The others were not able to hear his words and she explained to them what he had asked of them.

"It would be several hours before dawn would come, but Vivian and Mario were willing to follow the creature to the room. The entity began moving to the basement door and they followed; Mario first and then Vivian. It was a dark, gloomy stairway, with only a small bulb illuminating the way. They could see the white fog-mist that surrounded the creature as they descended the stairwell. At the base of the stairs, the creature stood silently pointing to a corner that was barely visible. Mario turned on his flashlight and they followed. Hearts palpitating, the pair followed this dark entity to the door of an undiscovered room; a cold, earthen dungeon that had probably been there since the house was first constructed. The door had been indistinguishable, until the entity had moved toward it and wiped away years of cobwebs and debris without a single movement of his- own.

The creature was using its seemingly limitless powers. The room was pitch black, and when Mario stepped inside, he aimed the light into its midst. Only darkness was evident in this cavern under the house. Mario reflected back on the room that he and Maryanne had been held captive. For a moment the thoughts were so vivid, that he had to close his eyes and take some deep breaths, or be sucked into oblivion, he imagined. Composure took hold once more and he sent the light rays wandering through the cavern. The entity stood in the corner, the mist surrounding him. There on the ground in the corner, were three coffins. They were open and all three were empty. He pointed to the first one next to the wall, and looked back at Vivian, eyes still radiating, but only the white was evident and the green-red cast was gone. He began speaking to Vivian in telepathic communication.

"I will be here at dawn. Please help me to escape my hell. I would be ever-so-grateful." His eyes were solemn and showed a tear-like reflection. Sadness was surely a part of his being. Vivian and Mario agreed to a dark-deed that would forever embed itself into a small corner of their memory. The entity was gone and they stood silent in the cold, damp cell. Mario took Vivian's hand and led her to the exit, where they emerged into the gloomy basement, and then made their way to the top of the stairwell. They sucked in deep breaths to clear their lungs of the pungent air that permeated the room; a room where three coffins had been placed long ago, in the graveyard under the house. This would not be the last trip to the eerie chamber that was on the other side of the world. A world of darkness and depravation, unlike anything they had ever seen. They would have to wait until dawn emerged to complete this unnerving task. When they returned to the great-room where Maryanne, Marshall and Jonathon waited anxiously for their return, they described what had taken place and what they must do to bring an end the creature's suffering in order to find peace at the Valencia Manor.

It all seemed so bizarre and unreal, but nonetheless a reality. Vivian prepared for the final ritual; a ceremony to release the walking dead into a realm where it could eventually find peace. From there, hopefully the creature would be rejoined with Sarah, the love of his life.

Marshall and Jonathon gathered up the equipment and brought it to the grand-room, where they hooked it up to reveal the uncanny, ghostly, aberrations and voices that were captured digitally, so that they could use them to understand more of what most do not comprehend or believe exists. Maryanne and Mario expressed extreme thanks to the team who helped to bring the spirit to materialization.

"I am glad you thought to call us, Maryanne. It was wonderful seeing you again, even in such an uncanny atmosphere. Mario, congratulations to yours and Maryanne's marriage, and to think I just found out. I really don't think we should leave, but wait until the deed is done. Are you positive you don't want us to stay?" Marshall asked.

"Maybe we should wait until after the morning is here and the vampire has been exterminated," Mario answered.

"Then we will stay and assist, if you need us," Jonathon spoke seriously. "It is a huge undertaking you are dealing with and we can help, if needed."

"Then, we've got some serious work to do," Mario answered. "I thank you very much for your concern and assistance."

"That's what we do best, Mario. We are masters of our trade. I am sure we can help," Jonathon confirmed.

"Okay, we'll all go to the grand room, relax and talk shop," Marshall joked.

"The team was uptight but willing to follow the instructions of the entity.

"Meanwhile, let's all go into the dining room and I'll make some hot-chocolate and we can discuss the gory details of what we are here for. I doubt that anyone is feeling like desert." Maryanne waved toward the long antique table and they all took a seat. Who would have guessed it would be a ghostly encounter that brought us together at my new dining table." she joked laughingly, trying to lighten the mood.

In a few minutes, she was filling their cups with hot chocolate and sat down to join them.

"Now, let's relax and try to calmly discuss how we will execute our plan, if that is even possible." They sipped their chocolate and sat back, discussing their soon to be venture in the basement. When they had combed the subject thoroughly, Maryanne directed each of them to take a seat in one of the easy chairs or couches in the great room and make an attempt to rest until dawn. She took some small blankets out of a closet and passed them around as the ghostly inspired sleuths wrapped up and eventually nodded off. Mario and Maryanne went to their office, where they opened a futon that served as a chair, when not in use for sleeping.

A few hours later, Maryanne tapped Vivian on the shoulder gently to wake her. The time was right and this was the hour that would tell the tale. Vivian went to the sink and splashed water onto her face, and then wiped it with a paper towel. The others followed suite.

"Let's go do it. Sun's just poking its head over the mountain." She stood looking out the window. Vampires cannot sleep during the night. Only when the sun comes up, can they rest." Vivian gave a sinister look at the paranormal team and they set out toward the basement door.

"Hold on." Vivian stopped. I need a stick of wood from the old part of the house. Where are all the scraps of wood you tore out? Surely there are a few lying around somewhere."

"Oh. Yes…I know where it is. I had Don save a stack for what he called useful furniture rehabilitation, if I remember right; in the back yard." Mario ran to the back door and into the yard, where a pile of old wood was stacked just for such an occasion, he thought. He rummaged through it until he found what he thought were the perfect weapons. At the same time he was thinking how bizarre this was. He returned to the house and held up three pieces of wood like a little boy who had found his lost toy.

"Such a kid," Maryanne was thinking, and giggling under her breath. Even though the matter was serious, she managed to find humor now and then. She thought how strange the situation and became a little more serious, if not worried; worried that it might not work and that it was indeed a trick to lure them down to the basement, so he could do away with all of them. But she was only thinking and knew after what she had seen and heard that this could not be a trick. They boldly descended the dark stairwell once again. Cautiously and without hesitation, they moved as if they had a plan; and what a plan they had. Vivian followed Mario as he led the way into the mysterious sarcophagus and they walked slowly, hanging onto one another as they moved boldly toward the archaic wooden coffins. Jonathon and Marshall were last to descend. Three coffins, all in a row; lids closed tight. Was it the one on the right, or on the left?

"Vivian questioned herself as she prepared to open what she remembered him telling her. One hand held the piece of wood, and the other took hold of the wooden lid of the coffin. Mario reached down to grab hold and lift the lid that hopefully housed the corpse of an entity that promised to deliver if they could manage this one last gory deed. It was heavy and it took both his arms and Vivian's to pry it open. Marshall stepped up to the coffin and assisted. As it was being pulled up, the stench became horrifying. Maryanne, restraining her urge to vomit, held the flashlight while the three of them struggled to open the decaying oblong box. It finally gave way and struck hard against the earthen wall, breaking apart as it crumbled into the coffin. Inside was a rotting corpse. Not the corpse that they had been speaking to, but one that was in a decayed condition, as if it had been dead for many years. Did they just open the wrong coffin? Or is this what happens to vampires when they sleep? No one had an answer to that question. This was a first for the entire group.

They discussed the possible error and decided to open the next lid. Pulling hard at the dusty wooden relic, they exposed the second sarcophagus. It too had a decayed corpse that seemed even older and more decrepit but was that of a woman. The team felt pangs of nausea as they stood in the dungeon encompassed by the stench of death.

"Third time is a charm," Mario tried to joke, unconvincingly between chokes. Marshall helped them pull and pry until the lid opened to reveal the creature they had spoken to. He looked more human than beast or creature. He looked evil and angry as he lay there. '*He could be sleeping*,' Vivian was thinking.

Though his skin had the pallor of death, he still seemed as if he were alive.

Vivian took hold of the wood and hammer that Mario had provided. She set the stake, hesitantly on its chest and looked up at Mario. Mario shook his head yes, and she hit the stake with the large hammer as it started to sink into the chest of the vampire corpse. Immediately a loud agonizing scream began to come from the vampire's carcass as he lay squirming in the box. She hit the stake again, this time harder and it sank deeper into its chest. Blood squirted out and covered Vivian with splatters of a warm, thick, red, ooze. Amidst the blood were screams of agony and ghastly gurgling. The noise filled the room and echoed through the night. Vivian thought that it must be like killing a real person. She felt queasy and sickened by the uncanny, cadaverous experience. Groans that filled the room were blood-curdling and chilled her to the bone. Mario and Maryanne stood, eyes fixed on the horror, unable to move. Marshall and Jonathon watched as Vivian made one more last attempt to finish the job and hit the stake, as it made its way through the corpse into the wood below. It screamed once again, a chilling low gurgle, and sat up straight, giving them the fright of their lives. And then it lay back down uttering one final gurgle, as if to give up and hopefully go to a place where it could find the peace it had sought after, for so long.

Vivian was exhausted. She fell back on the floor holding the bloody hammer. The sticky blood dripped down her face as she sat, bewildered and stunned at what she had done. Maryanne handed her a rag that she found lying on the floor. It was dusty, but anything to get the blood off. She was sick, to the point of throwing up. The five of them had come to help a creature of the night. A creature that most people would not dare believe existed. A creature that would change the way they thought about death forever.

Mario went to the next coffin. "Do you think we should run stakes through these other two?"

"He never said anything about them," Vivian answered, between the gagging and holding back the vomit.

"What if they are vampires? Why are they here? Where were they earlier?"

"Good question," Maryanne answered. "Why, Vivian? Why are they here?"

"Your guess is as good as mine; and if there's going to be any more killing of corpses, it's someone else's turn. I'm over it," she gagged again.

"I get that," Mario resounded. "I should do it this time. Need to go get more stakes though. Let's just get the hell out of here and discuss it upstairs. Sound like a good idea anyone?"

"I'm for that." Vivian held out her hand in a gesture to help her up. I thought this was going to be easy but I've never experienced anything this gruesome in my life."

"Let's go," Maryanne agreed. "If you want to come back and finish the other two off, Mario it's on you. I'm all out of nerve and frankly don't give a damn right now."

The group of bungling ghost hunters managed to make their way to the exit and up the stairs to the main floor, leaving the corpses in their coffins, as they were. Vivian headed for the bathroom and shower. Mario had commented that she looked like she worked at a slaughter house. When Vivian came out, she felt sick but at least the job she had been asked to do was over with. Now the spirit could regain its life on the other side and not remain with the undead. In the back of her mind, she thought that after they had time to rest, they should go down stairs and finish it up. Who knows what else could happen, should they be of the living dead. The fact that they were not present when the entity took them to the room, gave caution that they could have been out on a hunt, perhaps. Hunting unsuspecting victims for their blood? Maryanne pondered.

It was only six-o'clock in the morning and they were

totally exhausted. Time to sleep... '*Perchance to dream?*' or nightmares?

Three hours passed as they slept; not even stirring until evening fell upon the Manor. It must have been around six o'clock when Mario was awakened by a loud banging coming from the kitchen area, he thought. He climbed out of bed, and went into the great-room flicking the lights on and then on to the kitchen, where the banging noise seemed to emanate from. The door of the basement was open and slamming as if someone were knocking it against the wall. He looked down from the top. A shadowy figure moved about at the base of the stairs causing the hair to stand up on the back of his neck. Cold chills ran through him, as he stood, eyes gaping into the basement. A mist appeared below the stairs and the figure of the creature was looking up at him, eyes glowing. Only now, his face had lost the anger and he spoke to Mario.

"You have released me from my hell. I did not want to leave without telling you how much I appreciate what you have done for me. I must tell you what you have to do now. I should have told you before, but there wasn't time. You must take two more stakes and drive them through the corpses inside the coffins that remain in the room below. When you do this, you must tell Vivian to recite the chant that she is well aware of. This will protect you from any more harm from these night creatures. The two remaining are vampires that have been sleeping for many years. They need blood to survive, and are about to begin their hunt for blood from humans, as you are probably well aware by now. When the stake went through my heart, blood was spattered into their coffins and they have regained some of their strength. You must get to them before they get out and find a victim to revive themselves. Do it tonight. Do it now. I must go. I am passing into the light where I can escape this hell I have been in for years. Thank you for helping me. Tell Vivian I appreciate what she did. Without another word, the manifestation was gone and Mario stood there in trepidation, knowing they had to finish this job before the night fell, and the creatures regained their ability to hunt. He hurried to where Vivian slept and then told Maryanne. Jonathon and Marshall were awake and ready. Mario searched the yard and found two stakes and another hammer, in an effort to kill both creatures. They were well on their way to another gruesome kill.

Five curious ghost-hunters were prepared for the final task. Into the basement, two flashlights streamed through the dark stairwell. Two stakes would end it all. They would be free from the menacing vampires when the job was complete.

As they cautiously descended the narrow stairway, a rustling noise was coming from down below. They continued, knowing this had to be done soon or it may be too late and two more creatures would be wandering the streets of Boulder, attacking and killing innocent victims to sustain their existence through the drinking of blood. They too, could be among the victims and they could not let this happen. One step at a time, carefully and purposefully, they made their way into the basement and toward the door where two coffins housed the decaying corpses.

Their light found the coffins still open. The creatures had regained some of their material bodies, but were still in a dead sleep. Literally speaking; of course. Mario leaned over the first one and placed his stake against the chest of a decaying woman that was in a state of reconditioning herself, he observed. The woman had started to regain a distinguishable face, which had not been the case when they were here earlier. The skin on her face had begun to revive and become more human-like. He wasted no time. He held the stake against her chest and aimed the hammer, making a strong movement toward the stake. He could feel the wood tearing into its chest, as it sunk into the boney decaying flesh about three inches. A ghastly, high-pitched scream filled the air and echoed through the house.

It seemed to go on forever. He pounded the hammer down once more and it finished its journey, blood gushing up and all around it. It was as if the heart beat sent huge streams of blood gushing out into the darkness, and into the other coffin where it splattered across the corpse and onto Mario. He felt the thick warm ooze of blood clinging to his face and hands. One last hit and the stake reached its destination; all the while the decomposed corpse screaming and gurgling until at last it was still. The carcass in the next coffin began to awaken and move. Mario had to work fast. This beast could be powerful and if it took hold, he may not have a chance. Blood was still oozing from the corpse, but there was no sign of movement, so he moved aside and to the next rotted, oblong box. Jonathon and Marshall watched, with wide eyes, the unbelievable scene playing out in front of them. Even though they were official ghost hunters, nothing had ever compared to this gory scene. Kneeling down, Mario placed the stake onto its chest where it had reclaimed some flesh. Bony arms flailed at him, attempting to restrain his actions. He slammed the hammer at the stake, and the corpse let out blood-curdling screams, and seemed to have more power than before. He fought the boney creature, and held tight to the stake, knowing that it was their only chance to rid them of this being from beyond the grave. Once more, he flung the hammer at the stake but this time it went in deep. The corpse had regained much of its strength but Mario was at his best physically and making headway with the struggle. It was an unusually strange scuffle, fighting a bundle of mostly bones, he was thinking as he took one more swing at the stake until it reached the wood below. A wailing, spine-chilling squeal, almost like that of an animal, resonated through the night. The frightened ghost-hunters backed up and waited to be sure the deed was done. When the cadaver stopped squirming and lost its strength, it slowly transformed back into a decaying corpse, and then into nothing but dust. The final blow had finished off the last of the undead creatures.

The team was finished and exhausted, ready for showers. Blood soaked, they trudged up the stairs. Mario stepped back for a moment and slammed the lids. He took nails from his pocket and with the hammer, sealed the lids on tight. He re-joined the team as they made their way upstairs and then he nailed the door to the basement, in one final effort. It was over. At least the vampires were gone. Now Mario had to find out who the killer or killers are, of the students. He was pretty certain it was not of the living dead. Although, there was a distinct possibility that a victim or two could possibly have been attacked by these creatures, Vivian believed that the serial killings were of this world and not of the undead. There would be more research and investigation before they could be absolutely positive. But for now, they breathed a sigh of relief at what they had accomplished. They had done well. Undoubtedly, no one would believe them. The story was so incredulous; they hardly could believe it themselves. One thing was certain. It would be a long time before they could sleep well without wondering if the night creatures were still out there somewhere, waiting, for their next victim, so they could gain the strength to become once again, earthbound.

29

Mario called the station and spoke to the chief about the current status at the Manor on Valencia Drive. They organized the Forensic team, who would be combing the basement for anything and everything. Mario waited until they arrived before he left for work. While he was in transit, a call came in about another murder; this time at the University of Colorado, Museum of Natural History on Broadway, near Euclid. A twenty-three years old man, who was leaving the Museum after spending early hours doing research on a college project had been attacked, throat sliced and bled out. He had been left sprawled across the walk near the rear entrance of the building. Unlike the others, there was a lot of blood at the scene, as if they had performed a ritual right on the spot. It happened early in the morning, they estimated at around seven a.m. He had been spotted by a night watchman, who was leaving from his shift. A full team was disbursed immediately. Mario headed for Broadway. After an hour of going over details and analyzing the MO, he concluded that the attacker had used most of the same MO, but now men or women both were targeted. They always picked young adults that were students, but usually women. He returned to the station to work on the case. Whoever the killer, he was becoming more brazen in his attacks and seemingly not caring how or where he picked his victims; as if in desperation.

Maryanne was at work most of the day and Wendy took a few hours off for some shopping. While she sat at the computer, the door chimes rang and Borislav Vasiliev walked into the store. Donning his dark shades, and dressed in his mostly black attire, not much had changed.

"What can I do for you, Mr. Vasiliev?" She reached out to him, his hands clammy and cool.

"I stop by to say hello and tell you I enjoy house. We like very much."

"I'm glad you are happy about the purchase. Has everything been working well? No problems?" she was hoping no strange birds and weird apparitions had shown up on the property, as had been the case prior to her leaving. He seemed to be quite content and she breathed a sigh of relief. They chatted for a few minutes and then he left quickly, just as he had appeared. Maryanne walked outside, to see if Adriana had been in the car so she could say hello, but saw no evidence of them, anywhere. She got a cold chill and stood thinking back about the beginning, when she first met the couple. She realized that it was a very gloomy day and he still wore dark shades. Thoughts were beginning to spin through her curious mind. But the day was full and customers were coming and going. Soon, thoughts of Vasiliev disappeared quickly. That is until she closed and began to reflect back to the beginning. The beginning; when the couple had entered the store for the first time and they had seemed so out of place, so unusual.. She had never thought of any odd bizarre behavior, only a little off-the-wall. Now she had definite thoughts that would keep her up thinking about it; keep her awake trying to understand why the strange couple had moved to Boulder. Sometimes Maryanne's intuition got the best of her and led her to places she would never visit. Places in her mind, where strange and disturbing thoughts were swirling around trying to find a spot to rest. She would discuss it with Mario when he returned home.

She arrived at the Manor just as the sun was beginning to fade behind the mountains. It was cool and cloudy with rainclouds on the horizon. It would be another long night. Mario was going to be tied up with the recent murder investigation, so she put in a TV dinner and curled up on the sofa catching the news. Coffee was her friend tonight and she had at least three cups before she realized it was getting very late. Time had flown by while she read her latest mystery and now, wide awake, it was way past midnight, which is when she usually retired. Standing at the windows out of habit, there on the lawn a flock of ravens had decided to take up residence again. There were at least twenty of the beady-eyed corvids perched on the fence, pillars and here and there around the yard. She switched on the yard lights to scare them off, but they were not the least bit concerned. Maryanne was aware of the high intelligence of the birds and also that in some historical depictions; they were associated with the dead or evil. In Germany they had referred to them as 'souls of the damned.' With this kind of reputation, she was a little apprehensive of their visits. One sat right in front of her on the window sill, staring at her curiously. She stood still, curtain pushed back, scanning the landscape. The Ravens had taken hold, and weren't about to leave anytime soon, she thought. As she was ready to close the curtain, a figure moved across the yard near the left side of the Manor; a dark, shadowy figure of a man, similar to the others that she had seen in the past. She moved stealthily to the door, pulled it open, hand firm on the cold steel light, aiming at the shadow there in the yard. Quiet dominance with eyes of steel, slicing through darkness, its eerie eminence drew her to it. She felt as if an invisible hand were gently pulling her. It stood, quiet and still, his gaze fixing onto hers.

"What do you want from me? Say something. I need to know what it is you want." She screamed out, no thought of danger. She was losing control; a soft, sweet, smell permeated the air and she began to take on a comfort with the apparition. The entity stood tall, gazing at her, moving closer as she was being drawn into its essence. Closer he came, until she felt the cold chill of his consciousness, as if it were running through her veins. Still she was not afraid. He was face to face with Maryanne and she stood motionless, with a deep need to bond with him. His eyes were intense, dark, and powerful, seething her into her consciousness. His breath was cool and it brushed through her as he moved closer. She offered no resistance as he reached out to touch her. She took his hand as if she were in trance, or another dimension. He spoke telepathically, which calmed and soothed her. Oddly receptive sensations crawled through her and she was submitting to this creature as if it were in her nature. It moved closer and touched her hair, sliding its white, clammy hand to her face and caressed its softness. She felt an arousal take over her and emanate into her psyche. Willing to allow the encounter, she moved toward him and he embraced her. Even though he felt cool to the touch, he awakened her cravings and intensified the desire, allowing him to caress her. She was helpless to resist his advances and joined in a rhapsody of erotic carnal pleasure, like she had never experienced. He carried her to the grass and dropped his cape. She stood while he removed her clothing and kissed her body, pulling her down where he continued an intoxicating ritual, until she was ready for him to take her. He placed his mouth on hers and then down to her neck and she seemed to be at one with the uncanny dance. The arousal was intensely passionate and she moaned with uncontrolled desire until he brought her to an extraordinary level of intensity. When it was over, she lay there on the ground, not hurt, not bloodless, only simmering with an afterglow of the intense unnatural union. The stranger was gone. The only thing that remained was a black cape that he had used to cover the ground where he had seduced her. He did not force himself on her and the horror of what she had done shot through her like a bullet. She grabbed her clothing and picked up the cape, covering herself with it as she ran into the house and to the shower. She stayed in the shower for what seemed like an hour, trying to wash away the unnatural memory and comprehend its reason. She relished it and hated it with equal intensity. She couldn't tell Mario. He would never understand. When she came out of the shower, she began studying herself in the long mirror. Her body had not been bruised or scratched, but when she looked at her neck, there were two marks, where a trail of deep-red, blood was dripping slowly down to her shoulder across her alabaster skin. She moved in closer. There were two puncture wounds; not torn or ripped like victims she had heard described from Mario. She wiped the blood and put a bandage across the wounds. Mario would be home soon. What would she tell him? Maryanne was horrified at what had just occurred. She then remembered Mario describing the victim at the hospital, where Julia White had mentioned an intense sexual arousal and then blacked out. Could this be the same predator? She was terrified. How could she ever tell Mario? Would she also begin to change as Jennifer White had described? Maryanne stood staring into her face, the mirror reflecting a bewildered woman who had no idea of the consequences or the reason. She began to sob uncontrollably and crawled into bed. She finally succumbed to the night, and escaped into dreams.

Mario unlocked the front door. Lights in the house were on and the house was in disarray. He had never known Maryanne to leave things in such condition. He thought she must be ill.

"Maryanne. Hello, you up?" The house was quiet and he realized that she must have been feeling extra tired and gone to bed. He checked his cell to see it was well after three a.m. Time had passed quickly for Mario. The case was beginning to take a toll on him. Long days and sleepless nights were a normal occurrence. He flipped switches as lights disappeared and went upstairs to the master bedroom where she was curled in a fetal position, fast asleep. He reached down and pulled her hair aside and kissed her on the cheek. He saw the bandage on her neck. She did not stir. He undressed, brushed his teeth and climbed into the shower. Her clothes were strewn all over the floor and he picked them up. The cape lay across the hamper and he reached down taking hold off its heavy black fabric, holding it up curiously. He smelled it out of habit; it was a detective thing. A stale, musty odor and a man's scent were apparent. He threw the cape over the hamper and climbed into bed beside Maryanne and cuddled next to her with his arm across her. She did not stir. He speculated where the cape had come from, and knowing Maryanne, she probably found it in an old trunk, he reasoned. He trailed off into a deep slumber.

Maryanne's dreams were charged with bizarre elements of the unnatural encounter in the yard. The dark stranger would stay with her for the night.

Daylight again, and Mario had awakened to see Maryanne dressed and ready for work. She barely spoke to him as she finished her make-up. She explained that she was late for an important meeting in a few minutes and then left the room.

She could not bear to speak to Mario. The guilt of her rendezvous with the strange visitor was weighing heavy on her mind. She knew that what had taken place was an uncontrolled action, but her guilt would win over and she felt responsible, as if she had welcomed it. And in a sense she did. But she could not understand why she did not resist his temptation. She would ponder most of the day with questions that she was unable to answer.

"Wait a sec Maryanne. I have to talk to you."

"Can't it wait until later?" she abruptly answered.

"I need to talk to you. Are you all right?"

"Yes, I'm fine. Why do you ask?"

"You are acting very strange. What's going on?"

Maryanne took in a deep breath, trying to keep it all inside. "Sorry, just in a hurry. I'll call you later today from work." Maryanne hurried out the door. On route, she hashed the memories through her mind, not knowing who she could talk to. 'Maybe Joan,' she thought. Talking to someone would be the best way to help deal with it, and try to understand how its unearthly power could dominate her like that. It was so uncanny, so bizarre that she didn't know if anyone would even believe the story, let alone herself. When she focused on what had taken place, strange, intense feelings stirred within her. It was more than she could handle. She dialed Joan.

"Hi Maryanne. What's up? Kind of early to hear from you." Joan kidded.

"I must talk to you as soon as possible. I have to talk to someone. Can you come to my office right away?" Maryanne pleaded.

"Sure, something wrong? You sound upset. Are you and Mario fighting?" Joan tried to understand the urgency.

"No, we are fine. Just please come."

"I'll be there in half an hour, Maryanne."

Maryanne sped to the store and went straight into the office, barely speaking to Wendy. She sat in her chair and stared at the wall, waiting for Joan to arrive.

Mario got up and went to the bathroom. It had been cleaned up and the cape was gone. He figured she was embarrassed that the house was in disarray and that would explain the mood swing. She had made up for the mess by cleaning everything in sight before she left. Mario was still a little put off by her strange behavior. He made coffee, which usually was already made when she woke first. He drank a quick cup and then headed for the hospital to speak to the only surviving victim of the Slasher, Julia White.

He knocked on the room before entering. She motioned him to come in. He pulled up a chair and they talked again about the attack and how she had been feeling. She looked well but somewhat pale. He noticed her personality had become more aggressive and outgoing. Not like the girl he had spoken to many times before. She must be feeling better Mario reasoned and hoped to be true. They spoke for a few minutes and she went over the attack clearly and carefully, noting the part in particular about how she had been feeling a change coming over her since then. He attributed it to a delayed reaction to the brutal attack. She seemed oddly changed, Mario thought. But then, he had not known her before so he ignored his intuition. She was to be discharged in two days and would have protection until the perp was caught. He could not afford to take any chances with Julia on the outside. If the attacker knew, he might try to kill her to avoid a witness against him. He left the hospital and drove straight to work. His urge to call Maryanne was strong, but he decided to wait until she called. She seemed unusually upset and he knew when to leave well enough alone. The day seemed longer than usual. He had not received a call from her and decided that he would take a ride to the store on one of his rounds…later on.

***

Joan arrived at the store and greeted Wendy, who pointed to the office with a cheery smile, and Joan knocked on the door.

"Maryanne, it's me, Joan."

"Come in Joan."

When Joan entered, Maryanne was sitting at her desk with her jacket still on and briefcase still in tack; unusual for Maryanne. She hadn't even turned the computer on yet, Joan noticed. She sat in her chair, a sullen look on her face.

"Okay Maryanne. Let's have it. What the heck is going on with you? Something is wrong? Tell me."

"I…I don't know if I can. I don't know if I can tell anyone. I have to talk to someone but it is too painful. I don't know how to tell you." Maryanne began to cry and Joan moved to her side and comforted her.

"You know you can tell me anything. We are sisters, you and I. What is wrong? You must talk to me." Joan pleaded for Maryanne to let it out.

"It's awful and disgusting. Even you won't understand," Maryanne sobbed.

"I will. I will not tell anyone, but you have to tell me or you are going to be worse off than you are now, I promise you. I tried to hide things about Steve too, and look where it got me."

"Joan, it's much worse than anything you could imagine. I will never be able to tell Mario."

"Did you cheat on him?" Joan tilted her head and look eye to eye with Maryanne.

"It's worse than that. It's so bizarre I don't even know how to explain it."

"Well, just try. Start talking and let it come out any way it comes. I'll understand and help you. Please Maryanne. I'm worried about you."

Maryanne began to lay out what had happened the uncanny way she remembered it. She told her everything. Joan's eyes were wide with disbelief and fear for Maryanne's safety. She suggested speaking to a psychiatrist; the one she had used previously. Maryanne would not have it. She was embarrassed and humiliated, not to mention full of guilt. Joan comforted her as best she could. They talked about it for some time, and Maryanne did feel a little better. She still could not tell Mario. Joan insisted she tell him, thinking she was right; that it was the same assailant who seduced the surviving victim, Julia White.

Maryanne would ponder the situation and call Joan later. She told her under no circumstances could she tell anyone. Joan promised, and told her she would be there for her if and when she needed her.

Joan left and Maryanne made an attempt to work. She apologized to Wendy for ignoring her and explained it off as feeling ill. Wendy was understanding, but concerned.

The day took way too long, Maryanne was thinking. She wanted to get out of the office and didn't know where she wanted to go. Home was not her idea of a place to be right now. She couldn't face Mario. She drove to the mountains where she loved to get away from it all and pulled into a small camp-spot near the road, got out of the car and started walking. She walked for some time before realizing that it was getting late and the sun had started to lay its head down and hide behind dark mountains. The evening air was beginning to chill, so she turned back and headed to the car. Maryanne didn't want to think about anything right now. Her IPOD was tuned to her favorite music and 'Your Song' by Sir Elton seemed to fit her mood. Tears rolled down her cheeks as she tried not to think, without much luck. The only thing that came to her mind was; how would Mario react if and when she was able to talk about it. Speaking to Joan had helped lift some of the guilt, but she knew it would be a lifetime before the memories would ever leave her.

When the car was about twenty yards away, a dark figure appeared off to the right. Terror took hold and she bolted out into the trees to find protection, knowing all well there was none. Night was closing in and a cold breeze pushed through the pines. Up ahead, the stranger stood in her path. There was no getting away from him. Frantic and afraid, she turned back and ran faster. Stumbling on a rock, she fell; sprawling across the forest floor. She lay for a moment, stunned and confused, and then a cold hand reached down and took hers. She started to panic and then looked up to see the dark stranger's piercing eyes gazing into hers. He pulled her up and she stood frozen and frightened. He spoke to her in a silent telepathic message. His face looked sorrowful and sad. He too, had been sorry for what he had done. She could feel the anguish he harbored for taking advantage of her. He spoke sorrowful and with passion.

"I am not the beast you make me out to be. What happened was out of love for you, and not out of lust and viciousness. Though I am not able to exist on the same plane as you, it doesn't make me love you any less. When I saw you for the first time, I couldn't help myself but to return just to see you again. I want nothing more than your love, but realize it is impossible to have. I never wanted to hurt you in any way. What I did was unforgivable but doesn't change the fact that I will love you forever. I will erase the memories from your mind so that you will not be in agony and guilt of what took place between us." He stood sorrowful and full of regret.

Maryanne felt an unusual rush of calm overtake her. She began to question the dark stranger. "First of all, I want to know if it is you who perpetrated those vicious crimes against the women who were brutally assaulted and then left for dead. Except for one. She spoke about a similar experience, during her encounter. Were you the one who seduced her? And what about Joan? I told her everything. Can you take those memories from her mind as well?" Maryanne questioned him with anger and confusion.

"I am not the perpetrator of those crimes, but one of the vampires that your husband killed, attacked the young woman Julia White. He seduced her, not I. I am not like the others. I have taken blood from victims, but never killed anyone. I know it is wrong, but in my world it is survival. Yes, I will take the memories from Joan so she will not remember what you revealed to her. I can do that and consider it done. I only wish to say that I am sorry and I will not return to bother you." He disappeared, as if he had never been there at all. Maryanne stood bewildered among the trees, wondering how she ended up there. Just up ahead, the car was parked and she walked slowly to the camp-spot. When she was inside the car, she felt that something had changed, in a good way. On the way home, she was excited to see Mario. She reflected on her drive into the mountains and how beautiful it had been.

When she pulled into the drive, Mario's truck was home and she hurried inside to see him. The only trace that was left of her strange experience was the black cape, and Mario was waiting to ask her about it. His curiosity had gotten the best of him.

"Hello sweetie. I'm glad you are home. You seem in a much better mood than before. Are you feeling better?" Mario asked.

"Yes...sorry if I acted different. I wasn't aware that I did. Guess I was in a hurry...sorry." Maryanne did not recollect what had happened earlier. She did not recall anything about the bizarre encounter in the yard the night before.

"I'm feeling great. Are you ready for dinner? It's ready now." She kissed him and smiled and he followed her into to the kitchen. A bowl of hot spaghetti and meat-balls was waiting on the counter ready to be devoured. A mixed green salad donned the table and hot tasty garlic bread was fragrant and ready. They enjoyed a delicious Italian feast, chatting and laughing through the evening. Mario brushed off the odd behavior of Maryanne earlier as they enjoyed each-others company even more than usual. It was evident that Maryanne and Mario were still very much in love. As long as the encounter did not return to her memory, all would be well. Mario would find the right time to ask her about the black cape. Tonight was not the night.

Their night ended in passion. They had been starving for each other's affections, but the love they shared seemed to endure whatever circumstance had befallen them.

30

Mario faced another day of complications at the station. The young woman, Julia White had been released from the hospital the night before and guards were placed at her residence. During the night, she called the station screaming when someone accosted her in her apartment at two a.m. She said it was the same man who seduced and attacked her. The station contacted the guards outside the building who quickly came to her rescue and stopped the attack. Mario was going to set up a new location for Julia that no one was familiar with in order to prevent another attempt. He must keep her safe; not only for her own sake, but she was the main witness for the case against the attacker, once he was apprehended. She gave a thorough description of the assailant and said that he had attempted to hypnotize her, as before. She recalled what had happened in the last attack, and kept her gaze away from his, which prevented him from gaining any mental control of her. He had entered the apartment without a key. The doors were still locked and the detectives were unable to detect how he accessed the apartment. One piece of evidence, a talisman that Julia had torn from his neck during the struggle would help. A strange symbol was embedded into the silver; one that Mario had seen before when unnatural aberrations had appeared at Joan's. Mario would compare the two. At this point any kind of evidence was critical. These attacks had to be stopped. The city was in a panic. More serious warnings were spread out across the media. It would help to limit the killer's targets and would certainly decrease the crimes, until they could apprehend the maniac, who had been attacking and killing people for months. A state wide alert had been posted. Mario would be on twelve-hour shifts until the perp, could be apprehended.

A call came in from the south end of Boulder. A family had been startled by a figure in their back yard when their teen-age daughter had been out with the dog for a few minutes. She said several birds had landed in the yard, and then a dark shadow ran across the lawn by the trees. She immediately ran inside. A full team had been dispersed to the location. The perp was becoming desperate, Mario thought, since people were aware and not taking any chances at night. He would make a mistake soon; and then his bloody rampage would be stopped. Another call came in immediately after the first and a team was sent to a location near the first call. Two large dogs had been severely ravaged and drained of blood. A woman, who had been walking with them in her back yard, was startled and ran inside when the birds came, but the dogs went crazy with all the birds and tried to bite at them. They managed to overcome the dogs and when the father went outside, they had been left for dead. Throats had been slashed, in the same manner as the human victims. The perpetrator was desperate and obviously hungry, he was thinking. The news had been on for hours warning all to stay inside, but there were always those who took chances. One more victim had not heeded the warnings, and they found him near his bicycle on the street at the end of Maple, near Maryanne's old house that was now owned by the couple from Russia. The young man was barely alive, and slashed as in the other cases, but he was injured by blunt force trauma and had some blood taken but they didn't have time to finish him off. They had fled when officers had been in the area and scared him off. The victim was awake and talking. He said there were two attackers. One had looked very much like a woman. He couldn't be positive, but he knew there were two.

Mario called Maryanne and updated her with the latest information about the Slasher assaults increasing as well as becoming more brazen. It only made sense that desperation was driving the evil creatures to go after anyone, anywhere.

"They seem to be more desperate; getting careless," Mario explained. He would be spending every waking moment on the case now. Time was of the essence. Maryanne knew she would be seeing a lot less of Mario until they had aprehended the assailant.

Hanna had called to arrange another visit with Maryanne while Maryanne was still trying to conjure up the nerve to let Hanna know that she was her birth-Mother. She would wait until Hanna was present and make her decision when the time was right, just as the Psychic had told her to do. At this point, she felt it was due time that she knew the truth. She went over in her mind how she would explain it, hoping it was not too soon and that Hanna would be able to handle the information without an emotional setback. Maryanne called Vivian Gilbreth to find some comfort and advice on the matter.

"You will know when the time is right. Go with your instinct and it will be fine." The Psychic commented, assuring her that she would instinctively know. Maryanne already knew the answer but wanted Vivian's wise conformation before she made the final decision.

On Saturday afternoon, Hanna would come to the Valencia Manor, where Maryanne would prepare a lunch, and later on a dinner for her. They would spend the day together.

Sometime during the visit, she would find a way to tell Hanna the story. Hanna was looking forward to spending the night again and anxious for the visit. Maryanne made plans most of the day preparing just the right touches to make the visit comfortable and special. She arranged Hanna's room with a small box of expensive chocolates, a fragrant diffuser that she knew Hanna loved, fresh new linens on the bed, and brand new towels and accessories in the bathroom. She purchased two bouquets of mixed flowers; Maryanne picked up special bouquets of Stargazer and Oriental Lilies, Hanna's favorites. The stage was set. Maryanne would be ready to unfold the story to Hanna at some point during the visit.

A call came in from Mario. Another attempted abduction had taken place in the same vicinity as the last. It was only six blocks from the house on Mapleton Drive, where they had previously moved from. The target escaped unharmed but had a good description of the assailant. It concurred with past descriptions of sightings and attacks. The detectives were closing in on the perpetrator and had picked up more evidence to add to the mix. The assailant or assailants were getting more careless in their desperation, as their target pool had diminished with the extensive TV and Radio warnings. Fliers had been posted all over town and state-wide warnings were covering the media. The mystery would soon be solved and detectives were beginning to breathe a little sigh of relief. People had been doubling their own security and carrying weapons to protect themselves. The gun shops were selling weapons like candy. Classes teaching hand-gun safety were springing up all over town. Residents of Boulder were waging a war against the Slasher and it seemed to be working. The latest description seemed to fit right in with Maryanne and Joan's description of what they had seen when the ravens had taken up temporary residency in their yards. However, Maryanne had no recollection of the memory of the horrible encounter with the earlier incident where she had been drawn into some kind of seducing trance and attacked by an unknown assailant. There was no way for her to know if it was the same assailant. But if it was the same as had previously made its appearances accompanied with the birds, she might make the connection, unknowingly. Hopefully she would not remember the incident.

Mario would stay late from work, as he had most of the last few days. Detectives had been on extra duty since the attacks had become more frequent. Maryanne would be playing the single life, returning to her novel for extra company and diversion. Almost at the end of her book, after a riveting high point, she was on the edge filled with excitement when loud bang resounded from the floors above and below. Lying on the bed in her nightgown and robe when the loud noise echoed through the house, she jumped up, threw down the book and took the gun Mario had left in the closet. Relieved she had taken the classes, she carefully loaded the .38 special Smith & Wesson, making her way toward the stairs that led to the great-room, holding the revolver in front of her. She stayed close to the wall as she made her way down the hall and onto the staircase. Light was barely peeking in through the windows that lined the room. She stayed her pace and took chary steps one at a time down the long staircase. When she stood at the bottom, noises were more persistent, only now they were coming from the pantry or kitchen on the other side of the room. She sent calls out on her cell; first 911, and then Mario. The police were dispatched and told her to stay hidden, but she moved stealthily toward the sound, a bit more daring, with revolver in hand.

"Whoever is in there, I have a gun and I'm a good shot. I'll use it if I have to." A loud groan and then a shriek rang through the house. Outside, a storm was brewing and thunder rumbled off in the distance. She kept the lights off for her own protection and used the small flashlight to see her way across the room. Nearing the kitchen another loud crash arose as if someone had fallen into the cookware. Shivering and heart racing, Maryanne was not about to cave, and kept moving forward. Almost to the kitchen door, the groan became louder and more profound.

"I'm coming in with a gun. Please leave this house. I will use it if I am forced to. Don't make me do it!" She warned the phantom intruder. Leaning up against the wall next to the kitchen entry, she cocked the gun. Ready to fire, she moved forward holding tight to its cold steel, scanning the light around room. A bright light flashed into her eyes, blinding her as she entered. A figure came toward her and she pulled the trigger. A loud scream rang through the air and she pulled the trigger once again. The unknown visitor ran back into the pantry. Heart racing, she took the flashlight and searched through the space. A trail of blood drops dotted the floor of the kitchen, and to the pantry. She had hit her mark. Someone fell against the wall in the room ahead, and she moved toward it. Her hands holding the gun steady, despite the fear running through her and she continued toward the kitchen, edging along the wall. She took a deep breath and then another, trying to keep herself calm. Fear had done terrible things to her in the past. She was not about to let it happen again. Trained now for self-protection, she was more able to deal with the situation at hand. Her experience had shown her the paranormal side of the house, but she was not sure whether this was the case. Maryanne moved toward the pantry, gun steady, she moved through the entry.

"Come out! I will shoot to kill. I don't want to hurt you, so please don't force me to. Who are you? The police are outside and you have no way out. Give your-self up," she pleaded with the intruder. A thud came from the supply closet. She moved closer and opened the door. A pile of clothes covered in blood lay on the floor. There was no sign of anyone in the room. The only way out was through the window, which was not open. The police had arrived and she called out. By the time the EMTs arrived, Mario was busy at the scene scouring for any kind of clue. Forensics gathered the clothes and took blood samples. When they had finished, Mario stayed home with Maryanne. The team was baffled at the disappearance of the intruder. Maryanne and Mario finally gave into sleep at four a.m. He awakened her to let her know he was leaving for work, at eleven.

Maryanne climbed into the shower, perplexed and disconcerted. When she finished dressing, she called the station. Mario updated her. Nothing of any significance had been discovered. They were calling it a burglary at this point, knowing full well there was much more to this incident than met the eye. The team was keeping this under wraps, so they could work the case, without the perps knowing how much they knew. Maryanne was positive there had to be a more sinister explanation, but understood how the department worked. Her gut told her that this illusive intruder had something to do with the last abduction, being able to appear and disappear at random. The department was on full alert, trying to connect the various crimes, still to no avail. DNA and other tests were being done to assist in solving the very unusual events.

31

anna was prepared for the visit on Saturday, anxious to see the Manor almost completed. The back yard was near perfect. Fountains had been restored and the pool was in pristine condition again. Statues of majestic lions had been restored and placed on each side of the incredible fountain and looked as if they had just been created. The landscape was a work of art, and Hanna would be pleased at the spectacular results.

The contractor had worked non-stop to finish the project and only a few minor items were unfinished. Maryanne could not be more satisfied with the results. He would spend the day going over a few minor touch-ups that would top off the renovation. He was proud of the end results and knew that it had been his best work ever. Maryanne was in awe and complimented Don on his unprecedented work. Her appreciation was well accepted and he was glad that she had been so impressed at the results.

"Except for a few surprising ghosts and bones here and there," he said jokingly, "all in all it went rather well." His face expressed gratitude and pride as he joined Maryanne at the table for a cup of coffee, while they exchanged small talk.

"If you have any problems with the power, plumbing,

or anything in between, please call me immediately. I doubt you will have any serious problems but once in a blue moon there could be something that needs attention. I will be at your service." Don drank his last sip of coffee and grinned, satisfaction written all over his face.

"Thank you Don, I will call if anything needs your special touch, to be sure. I will definitely recommend you to all of my friends and associates. You are truly the best!" she took his hand and at that moment she knew he would be missed, not only as a great contractor, but his delightful presence that seemed to light up the place when he was around. He was definitely second to none, except, of course, for Mario.

Maryanne walked him to the door and waited while he gathered up a few tools that he had used to finish up. He filled up the tool-belt and walked toward the door. She reached over and gave him a warm hug and again felt that familiar urge run through her, that she quickly dismissed. She watched as he walked down the stairway toward the gate. His blonde hair reflected the sun as he turned and looked back, a wide grin covering his striking face. He locked the gate and was off in the truck for one last time. She would miss him indeed.

Tomorrow was another day and Maryanne counted the hours until Hanna would arrive. She spent the rest of the day at the store, all the time thinking about how to explain to Hanna, that she was the Mother that Hanna could not remember. She had never seen her Mother since the moment of her birth. Maryanne had never seen her until she had been captive at the Valencia Manor for two weeks, over a year ago, and just found out recently that it was her own Daughter. How could something like this happen? Maryanne's thoughts swirled, trying to make sense of it all.

Saturday and Maryanne touched up the house one last time before Hanna arrived. Mario had gone to the station, still working diligently on the complex case of the disappearing intruder. Everything was in place and perfect for Hanna, who would be driving in shortly. She had called before leaving Denver to let her know that she was on her way.

Maryanne had prepared a lunch that she knew Hanna would enjoy. A crispy mixed salad and turkey salad wraps would fit the bill. She had put together a tasty fruit plate for appetizers. Maryanne looked out the front window, anxious to see Hanna again. Her thoughts wandered back to the hospital when Hanna had been so distant and confused. Things had come a long way since those days and Hanna was now an intelligent, beautiful and almost graduated student of a superior design school in Denver. Hanna's car pulled up, and Maryanne's heart raced. Today would be the day Hanna knew for the first time, that Maryanne was her Mother. She ran to the door and opened it, walking toward the stairs in anticipation. Hanna stepped through the gate smiling and walked to Maryanne where they met and held each other like long-lost friends. In this case, the outcome was not clear, but Maryanne hoped Hanna would take the news without causing any emotional upset. Maryanne was prepared to tell her, but would wait until after lunch when they were relaxed in the grand-room. There, she would unfold the story that would unlock the mystery to Hanna's past.

The day seemed to go very well. Hanna was excited at the completion of the Valencia and at times, stood just staring into its vast beauty, thinking. Thinking that she had lived her for many years as a prisoner, and now she was part of its mystery and beauty. She smiled and giggled as she went from room to room, admiring and remembering at the same time, without serious consequence.

"It's amazing, Maryanne! I am so glad I had a part in helping to design it. It gives me pleasure to realize its beautiful state of completion to such excellence!"

They sat at the kitchen table for lunch, and spent an hour talking, laughing and enjoying the delicious food that Maryanne had prepared. When they were finished they retired to the grand-room, where they sat back on the elegant sofas and chatted. Maryanne was trying to find the right time to open the subject that she had waited so long to tell her. Finally, she realized it had to be done now, or she may never get the nerve to tell her. The subject seemed to jump right out of Maryanne's mouth as she started to speak.

"Hanna, there is something I have been waiting to tell you that will be of some surprise or shock, to say the least. The doctors told me to wait until you were totally ready to handle such important news before I revealed it. I am now ready to divulge the information and hope that you are not upset that I waited so long. I only found out about this recently, myself, so here goes. You know that we had not been able to find your birth parents and I had tried very hard to find out through many resources. Up until a few weeks ago, I did not have a clue, until I was at the Manor and had an apparition of my own Mother. She came to tell me something that I had been longing to know for many years." Maryanne continued to reveal the story about her as a young girl, being pregnant and forced to give up her child in an adoption that her mother forced upon her. She explained that she did not want to give up the child and how it had bothered her for many years. She told her that she had done many searches, which came up empty-handed as to the location of the adoptive parents.

"My own Mother, who died many years ago, came to me to tell me how sorry she was that she had forced me to give up my own child and then she proceeded to tell me where my child was and who she had adopted her to. At that time, I didn't know whether she was a boy or girl. When she told me who it was, I was as shocked as you are about to be." Maryanne took several deep breaths as she looked into the face of a bewildered young woman who had no idea what she was about to reveal.

"The child that I had given birth to is none other than you,

Hanna Michele," she finally made the words come out, waiting unknowingly how Hanna would respond to such news.

Hanna's face changed to that of confusion and astonishment. She sat quietly, as if she hadn't heard the complete story, mulling it over in her mind. Maryanne was worried that she might have told her too soon and praying it did not ruin the relationship that they had built since Hanna was taken to the Hospital after the terrifying ordeal at the Valencia. Suddenly Hanna's face broke out into a smile and then she began to cry. Maryanne moved to her side and sat, holding her as she wept, profusely. They sat, holding each other for a time, until Hanna had regained her composure.

"Mother? Oh my God! I am so happy and so relieved. This is the best thing that could have ever happened to me. Nothing I could ever imagine would be as great a gift as having you for a Mother." She held onto Maryanne again, not wanting to ever let her go. Indeed, this was the best moment in either of their lives and now they both felt a satisfied completion to a part of their lives that had tormented them for years. The rest of the day was nothing but happiness and laughter. Memories, stories and more stories, Maryanne and Hanna were at last together as Mother and Daughter. They would share this moment for years to come. Their lives would be changed forever.

When Mario returned, Maryanne informed him that she had finally let Hanna know the truth. They spent the evening catching up and sharing for the rest of the visit. Hanna had to leave by six a.m. for work. She had been employed at the school on her days off, in the research and development office since school had started. Hanna would graduate soon and a job had already been offered to her in the spring with a large company in Denver for excellent pay and benefits. Hanna returned to school and work, keeping in close contact with Maryanne at all times. After all…Maryanne was her Mother.

The case had tightened. The blood analysis had concluded

again, that the strange DNA string had shown the same inconclusive results as the earlier sample. An odd and non-identifiable make up that was not able to be determined, connected to the earlier sample from the victim who had lived through her attack. The recent information on the living victim was a new surprise that no one had been ready for. She had been physically and mentally metamorphosing into someone who she didn't even recognize at times. She had been seeing a doctor, and they were testing to find that her DNA was almost identical to that of the two unresolved samples taken from another attacks. Somehow, they had to find out why and whom this DNA was linked to. They were in a deadlock, until one night another attack had taken place at a city park.

Two unwary college students were jogging through the park not long after dusk, when the moon had just embarked its usual journey over the city. It was a cold night and a bright ring had begun to take form around the late October moon. A group of three who were walking had discovered their bodies, apparently not long after the attack. By the time the ER, Police, and Detectives had arrived, the bodies were still warm. As in other cases, gashes on both necks were apparent and blood was profuse and still oozing, as if the predator had been scared off by the three unsuspecting visitors.

After yellow tape had been wrapped around the crime scene, not unlike a college prank with toilet tissue, a huge team was organized and began its intense investigation. Forensic and other vehicles were on the scene going full bore trying to find the perpetrators and clues to yet, another horrific assault. One big break, the two victims were both alive. After being stabilized the victims were immediately transferred to Boulder Hospital, where the ER team worked diligently to keep them alive until the specialists arrived.

Mario had arrived shortly after the discovery had been called in. He worked hastily to make sure every possible lead was followed up and double checked. They were closer now, than ever to unraveling and putting an end to the murders. The MO was quite similar, and because the attack had been interrupted, the victims were still alive and luck was turning in their favor. The scene was fresh and Mario had a feeling this was going to be the straw that broke the camel's back. Careless and desperate criminals were making far too many mistakes. With a chance to push forward and solve these gruesome murders, Mario ordered specific blood samples and fingerprints, as well as other clues, carelessly left behind that had finally given them a fighting chance to put this behind them.

The City of Boulder was pulsating with squad cars, sirens, and teams of Detectives who were combing the area, taking in every possible witness, clue and video that they were able to obtain. Mario was finally making his case. Foot prints and a piece of torn clothing found hanging on a bush, left behind by a desperate fiend helped close in on someone who Mario would never imagine in his wildest dreams could be involved.

A call came in and Mario quickly answered, not looking at the ID. A strange voice that he did not recognize spoke, "Detective Ramos, I have something to tell you and I do not want to speak about it on the phone. Can you meet me where we can discuss it? I have important information that may help you solve the crimes that are happening there in Boulder." A heavy breathing accompanied the voice, and he felt the person was trying hard to disguise himself.

"Who am I speaking to," Mario queried.

"Never mind, just meet me at the old school at the end of Mapleton Drive." I'll be there in twenty minutes. Be there, if you are curious enough." Click.

Mario was about twenty minutes away from there, and he jumped in his truck, hooked up his seat-belt and took off straight away, not even thinking to call anyone and tell them where he was going. Mario was determined to solve this case and nothing else was on his mind. He sped along until he was at Mapleton and turned a hard fast left, thinking he'd better slow down, or get a ticket. That would screw things up and he couldn't afford any chance of being late. He was primed and ready, gun loaded; holster unsnapped. He drove down the dark street and past Maryanne's recently sold house where lights were on and the black Mercedes sat in the drive. He passed by, looking closely at the house, wondering why the call was coming from a place so near their last abode. He closed in to the end of the deserted street where the road turned in toward the run-down school and he slowly drove toward the building. He could not see any vehicles present. It was dark and eerie with no street lights or light poles lit in the old school yard. Moving in, he parked near the side of the dilapidated brick structure and sat inside the truck, lights on, wondering if the caller would show. He had another small revolver fixed to his leg just in case things got testy. He had no idea what he was in for, but ready for anything at this point. He climbed out of the truck, leaving the lights on and scanned his flashlight around the building. Mario jerked back when he heard a rustling sound coming from the back. He drew his gun and took off in the direction of the sound. Another rustling and he put himself on auto pilot as he advanced closer. A screech rang out and he swaggered as he stopped, heart beating in full mode, and then moved closer. Another loud screech, and then he jumped back as a black cat ran out of the bushes in front of him. He sucked in a deep breath and moved on, slightly relieved, but disappointed at the same time.

Dark and quiet around the school-house, his quest was unnerving. He spoke loudly,

"Where the hell are you? You called me, remember? What's your game? Hope you're not playing one, because if you are, you picked the wrong man for an opponent. I'll splatter you all over the ground before you know what hit you, and it won't be pretty."

Finally, Mario must have hit a nerve and he heard footsteps up ahead. He spoke again, "Where are you? Come out you cowardly son-of-a bitch." I've got a job to do and I don't have time for this bullshit!"

There ahead of him, near the corner of the building, he could see a figure peek around the corner. Then a voice shot through the darkness.

"Yeah, I heard you! Just keep it cool. I'm not your perp. I'm gonna give you some information, and that's it. Put the gun away, or I'm not comin' out."

"You come out, hands showing and I'll put the gun away. Don't worry I'm not trigger happy, so don't get yourself in an uproar, okay? You're a lot more important to me alive than dead." Mario held the flashlight and gun, walking toward the corner.

"Okay. Don't shoot. I promise it's all good." The unidentified man spoke as he moved around the corner, hands held high. Mario didn't recognize him. He continued walking toward Mario and then stopped about twenty feet away. He was an older man about fifty or so, Mario could see as he moved in, holstered his gun and slowly came within six feet of the alleged suspect, not knowing for sure what the purpose of this meeting was. Mario had sent a text to the station with the address, and told them to stand-by, but don't come unless he sent a 911. Mario was eye to eye with the stranger.

"Why do you want to help?" Mario questioned.

"These two freaks chased me down and they couldn't catch me, but I hid and followed them after they gave up the chase. I followed them to this school, and watched as the two strange people; one was a woman, stopped their car and got out. The man was like something from a movie. Dark, slightly white hair and wore a cape. The woman with him was young and beautiful. They stood talking for some time and then got back in their car. They drove back down the street. I ran to see where they were but no tail-lights were in view. They either hid or were pretty damn fast. Like I said, they were a very strange pair. I heard about all the attacks and figured someone needs to check it out. They may be here in this neighborhood, 'cause like I said, they disappeared in that car damn fast. I called as soon as I could."

"Where did you get my number? Why not call the station down town?" Mario was a little skeptical.

"Because I been readin' the paper and watchin' the news. You're always the main guy on the scene other than the Chief of Police. I think you probably know more than most. My cousin was busted last year for an assault and you were the guy that told the truth in court so he got a fair shake. He got into a fight with a doorman at a club downtown and hurt the guy. He said you're a good cop. So he gave me your number and I called, after I called him. I'm a little scared those freaks are going to find me, so I want to stay incognito. I'm sure they know I'll give a description and want me out'a the way." I got'ta lay low until they're caught."

"Sounds a little far-fetched but I guess it makes sense. Who is your cousin?"

"Rex Roberts. Remember him?"

"Yeah, I remember him. The club owner had a lot a cash and a high-rollin' attorney, so I figured it was gonna be a hard one to prove, but I knew what happened and found a witness to testify and got him off. Plus, the door-man had been involved in two other altercations that I had knowledge of. I hope he's keepin' his nose clean now."

"Yeah, he got married and has a kid now. Working for the City and doing well."

"Well, I wanna know more about the description of the two that tried to attack you. Can you come downtown?"

"Yeah, but I don't want anyone to see me. Keep it cool. All right? I don't' need some freaks following me around tryin' to shut me up. Can you keep me safe? Those two are really strange. When they attacked me, the freak tried to hypnotize me and I started feeling really weird until I took off like a bat out of hell, knocking her down and running. Their car was parked right there and they jumped in and started following me, until I lost them. I know this neighborhood like the back of my hand. Didn't take me long to shake 'em. Born and raised here. I live a few blocks away in an apartment house near Sycamore."

"What's your name?"

"Dennis Browning. I work for the Museum of Natural History. Maintenance. Married and have two kids. Don't want those weirdoes to have any knowledge of where I live. Understand?"

"Yeah, gotcha. I'll keep it under the radar." They walked toward Mario's truck and he drove to the station. After an hour of interrogation, he took Dennis back to his car, which was still parked along Sycamore, near where the perps had accosted him. He would definitely be a great witness. He got a good look at the car as well. Mario gave the information to the Chief. A search had been ordered for the car. He didn't have a plate but a pretty good description. A sketch-artist had been called in to meet with the witness, as soon as possible. The artist had already sketched one with the help from Julia White. If the two matched there could be some headway. Mario would meet him and take him back for the sketch in the morning. Meanwhile, Mario posted guards at his apartment.

A team was dispatched for the immediate area around the school and a mile radius. Officer Jackson called in a car description to the station. They checked it out and it belonged to Borislav Vasiliev. Jackson called Mario immediately and they headed to Mapleton Avenue to check it out. When Mario got the call, he knew right where it was. The address was Maryanne's old house on Mapleton Avenue. Jackson and Mario arrived at the house within minutes and pulled up in front of the house. Officers in the area were on alert and they walked up to the door, search warrant in hand. The Chief had done some fast work obtaining the warrant. Mario noticed the car was not in the drive and he felt a cold chill as they approached the door. The lights were off and Mario beat against the door and hit the door-bell. Again, he knocked hard against the door, to no avail.

"C'mon, let's go around back." Mario led the way guns ready and flashlights beaming, scanning every inch of the area. When they got to the back, Mario jumped a fence to enter the yard. Jackson followed. They inched their way to the deck up the stairs and to the door. Mario beat on the door once more, and nothing. He shined his light into the house but nothing was visible. He was sure no one was there. Mario took out a tool and opened the screen and then the back door.

"Are you sure this is okay?" Jackson was worried they might break protocol.

"Right now, I don't really give a damn about protocol. Too many dead bodies out there and I am willing to take the risk."

"You're right, let's just go in." Jackson stood close, gun out and ready.

The door opened and they quickly went inside, scoping everything with their flashlights as they combed through the house. Mario knew every nick and cranny and Jackson followed suit. Everything looked in order, nothing odd or suspicious was apparent.

"Follow me," Mario ordered.

Jackson stayed behind Mario and kept watch as Mario unlocked the basement. Last time he was down there had been a while but he knew every inch of it. Down the narrow stairway they went, cobwebs still hanging in low areas that clung to their hair. Mario reached the bottom.

"I'll take the right and you go left." Mario ordered again. They split up and began a search in the small, concrete cellar. Mario reached the door that used to be a coal room years ago, long before the heat was converted. The door was locked. Maryanne had used it to store boxes of what he called useless memorabilia that they had since moved out and to the Manor,

what hadn't been donated to Salvation Army. It had a large
padlock fixed to it, which had been added since they moved
out. It was a tough lock, but Mario wasn't about to quit now.
He picked up a hammer on the bench near the door and began
pounding the lock, but it wouldn't budge. "I'll shoot the damn
thing off, let me at it," Jackson bellowed.

"I hate being that obvious but I have a feeling we are about
to find out what is going on here. Go for it."

Jackson pulled the trigger as they stepped back. Once
more, and the lock gave way. Mario pulled the door open and
they stood wide eyed at what they saw. Meanwhile, there was
noise coming from upstairs

Someone was in the house, and they had a problem.

"Shit!" Jackson was white as a sheet. Mario and Jackson
stood in, not sure what to do next.

"Get ready. From what I see here, we're in the battle of
our lives, Jackson." Mario cocked the gun and they stepped
away and headed toward the bottom of the stairs. Mario wasn't
sure what to expect, but he had come prepared. The Psychic
had given him certain articles that could just be of help in
this situation. After looking inside the room, the two coffins
were enough to let them know who these people really were.
Mario handed Jackson two silver bullets and he loaded two
into his gun. He took a silver cross and handed Jackson the
vial of holy water.

"Don't ask any questions right now, I don't have time to
explain. Just shoot to kill and aim for the heart when I give
the word. If you have to, use the holy water and be ready for
anything. You've been warned."

Up the stairs they made their way. The door slammed at
the top and the perps locked them in the basement.

"Shit, I guess I should have waited, huh?" Mario retorted.

"You're tellin' me!" Jackson agreed.

"Down the stairs they rambled, and headed for the window.
It was small, but he had already alerted the team, so Mario

figured they could wait it out. Jackson was surprised when the dark stranger appeared out of nowhere, eyes staring him down and a half-smile on his pale face. Jackson's gun was loaded and he pulled the trigger. Borislav moved so fast he didn't even come close. Mario held up the cross and Borislav was blinded as he held his hand over his eyes. Mario moved toward him, touching him with the cross. It sizzled as it burnt the skin on his face. Borislav became more violent but weakened. Jackson sprinkled the holy water and it backed Borislav into the corner. Mario made aim and shot, missing his heart, but hitting him in the shoulder. He still had one bullet left. Adriana appeared in the doorway of the stairwell and Jackson shook the holy water toward her as she backed away. Mario made another attempt to shoot the Vampire and it got him square in the chest. Borislav began to choke and fall. By the time he hit the floor, he had begun to change. Mario stood dumbfounded at what was happening. Adriana ran full force toward Mario. He held the cross up and she moved quickly aside, her eyes red with blood, evil all over her face. Jackson took the holy water and emptied the vial onto her throwing her into frightful, seething spasms. Mario knew Jackson had one more bullet.

"Shoot the bitch, Jackson. Make it count! One bullet left, use it! Now!"

Jackson pointed the gun at Adriana and she lunged toward him. The gun went off as she came in contact with him and they went down. She landed on top of him when they hit the concrete floor. Mario thought Jackson was done for. He heard him cough twice, and Adriana rolled over as Jackson pushed her off. She had been hit right through the heart, where it counted. She was history. And so was Borislav. When Mario looked over at Borislav, he was nothing more than a pile of bones, turning to dust. Adriana was fast changing as well. The two novice vampire hunters had made their kill, and could not even fathom what had just taken place.

Upstairs, the team had arrived, but the work was done.

Officer Jackson and Detective Ramos had finally solved the case, or so they thought. The team was beginning a complete evidence check and Maryanne's old house was now the subject of the most horrific crime story that Boulder had ever experienced. It was over, and the two wearied officers left the premises, exhausted and overwhelmed at the recent scenario that played out like a scene right out of a horror movie, they thought. As far as they were concerned, it felt surreal; like they had been characters in a bad dream. Chief Olson ordered them to take the rest of the night and get some rest so they could piece this complex story together and hopefully tie up the loose ends.

Loose-ends were many, but the worst was over. Mario arrived at Valencia Manor, where Maryanne worried, and waited for his return. Coffee was brewing and aromas from food she had prepared filled the Manor. After a scrumptious feast, Mario hit the shower and dragged Maryanne with him, which she hardly objected. They had been somewhat strangers for the past week or more.

The pair lay in bed as they reflected on the events that had just played out. They were not able to fully comprehend the impact of what had been accomplished in the long and complex journey. It began with the Valencia Manor, and ended in what one would believe as a fantasy and not reality, at the Valencia Manor.

The long process had introduced Maryanne not only to terror and paranormal mystery, but returned many blessings that she may had never realized had she not taken this path. Her friend Vivian Gilbreth, had said it best,

"Sometimes you have to endure pain and suffering, but in the long-run, the good usually outweighs the bad. In your case all is not lost. You tipped the scales when you found your Daughter, Hanna Michelle. You met a wonderful man, and now you have a chance to be happy, with a good and productive life for all of you."

Epiliogue

Maryanne and Hanna Michelle enjoy a close Mother-Daughter relationship. Hanna graduated from her school of design and is realizing a successful career in the field, opening an office in Boulder, where she is enjoying her new life.

Joan Bishop is further advancing in her real-estate career. Joan has completely separated from Steve and since he continued therapy, his life has been improving. He started back to work at the department.

Vivian Gilbreth and Maryanne remain close, as if they were Mother and Daughter. From time to time they get together for new and intriguing paranormal excursions, sometimes including Marshall Dunne and Jonathon Livingston and their new ghost-hunting enterprise.

Mario and Maryanne enjoy their life together. Chief Olson retired after a long career and Mario now holds the position of Chief of Police in Boulder. They all remain good friends.

Though the journey was long and difficult, good things rose from the rubble. Mystery, murder, mayhem and terror will not be forgotten, but deeply buried in the subconscious, put away in the library upstairs for safekeeping…until a later time, perhaps.

Until then…